Home Sweet Holiday

Home Sweet Holiday

Michele Paige HOLMES

Copyright © 2020 Michele Paige Holmes

Print edition

All rights reserved

No part of this book may be reproduced in any form whatsoever without prior written permission of the publisher, except in the case of brief passages embodied in critical reviews and articles. This novel is a work of fiction. The characters, names, incidents, places, and dialog are products of the author's imagination and are not to be construed as real.

Interior Design by Cora Johnson

Edited by Cassidy Wadsworth and Lisa Shepherd

Cover design by Rachael Anderson

Cover Image Credit: Shutterstock #158641856 by Albert Pego

Published by Mirror Press, LLC

ISBN: 978-1-952611-04-9

HOLIDAY HARBOR SERIES

A Holiday Affair
Home Sweet Holiday
The Heart of Holiday

To Jack,

who willingly put up with and was an extraordinary stepfather to a sometimes grumpy and emotional teenaged girl.
May you fight the strong fight and conquer, so you can get back to the business of being a father and a grandfather to so many who love you.

Home Sweet Holiday

Nearly four years have passed since Anna Lawrence fled her hometown the same day her best friends broke her heart and she was left at the altar. She's hardly looked back since, while forging a new and solitary life in Seattle. When duty calls her home, she reluctantly returns to take care of the family store while her parents are away.

Eli Steiner is visiting his late great-grandfather's estate in Holiday, Alabama, for the first and last time—to see the place he's inherited and meet the other benefactor of his great-grandfather's will before turning everything over to her. When the woman he meets is both the same, and very different, from the one in his grandfather's letters, Eli's intrigue leads him to stay longer, to uncover the mystery of Anna Lawrence and possibly heal her heart.

Chapter 1

September

"Have you ever considered just getting a cat—or three?" Kerry frowned as she turned a slow circle, taking in the greenery in Anna's apartment. "Cat ladies are legit. People get that. But plant ladies . . ." Her voice trailed off as she stared up at a seven-foot Norfolk Island Pine. "This is insane. You don't need someone to look after your plants; you need a horticulturist."

"Plants don't require litter boxes, and they don't shed." Anna handed Kerry a clipboard with several papers on it. "Are you up for this or not?"

Kerry took the clipboard and began leafing through the pages. "How long did you say you'll be gone?"

"Twelve. Weeks." Just saying that out loud required Anna to take several deep breaths. *Twelve weeks in Holiday.* She had no idea how she was going to manage twelve hours, let alone three full months. But what choice did she have? "My parents have to go to the Mayo Clinic for my dad's treatments. They need someone to take care of their store while they're away."

Kerry folded her arms. "And your siblings can't help out with that because . . ."

"My brother just got a promotion at work, *and* his wife gave birth to their second child last month. My sister has three children and can't be gone from them that long, and she can't just pull them out of school to live in Holiday."

"You don't have a job too?" Kerry asked. "You don't have a life?"

Her questions rubbed an already sore spot, rehashing the same arguments Anna had given her mother, albeit half-heartedly. Of course she would come home to help. Hearing that her dad was seriously ill and the reminder that she'd seen him only twice in the last four years, both times when he and Mom had flown out to see her in Seattle, had felt like an ice-cold bucket of guilt and regret dumped over her head. She shouldn't have stayed away so long. She should have visited her parents, at least, if not her whole family and everyone else she loved.

Not everyone. Not Carson. Not Bree. Two of the people she'd loved the most. And the two who'd hurt her so much she'd fled Holiday and never returned.

"I don't know." Kerry was still flipping through the plant-care log. "Twelve weeks is a long time. A lot could happen. What if I kill them all?"

Twelve weeks is a very *long time.* At least Anna wasn't worried about killing anyone now. For a while, when she'd hit the anger stage of grief during that first year, she'd fantasized about terrible things happening to Carson and Bree. But that was long past. And she'd known she could not really do anything hurtful herself. No matter how bad their betrayal had been.

"You won't kill them." *Too many of them, anyway.* Anna fully expected there would be casualties in her absence, but that couldn't be helped. "Fifty dollars a week is six hundred bucks," Anna reminded Kerry. "Well on your way to that Alaskan cruise you've been dreaming of."

"What's this one?" Kerry asked, fingering a glossy leaf of one of Anna's favorites.

"A miniature magnolia tree. They have them all over the South—large ones, that is."

"Ah." Kerry nodded. "You didn't say, 'Can you take care of my *trees* while I'm gone?' You asked if I could water your plants."

Anna rolled her eyes. "If you can't do it, I'll ask Beth two doors down. She could probably use the extra money with that car repair she had last month."

"All right. I'll do it." Kerry sighed dramatically, then tucked her fuchsia hair behind her ears and rolled up her sleeves. "Let's get to it. You'd better explain each one. Oh, and I think I'll film while you do." She pulled her phone from her back pocket.

"Great. We'll start on the first page, with the ones that need to be watered the most frequently. These roses . . ."

It took forty minutes for Anna to go over instructions for all the living things in her apartment. By the time she'd finished, she was starting to see Kerry's point. "I guess this is a little much. I'm so used to it, and I got them all a little at a time, so I didn't realize."

"A little weird is more like it." Kerry snorted.

"Says the woman with purple dreadlocks and more holes in her jeans than—"

"Than what?" Kerry frowned, looking down at her threadbare pants. "These are breathable. I like them."

"And I like my plants," Anna countered. "They help *me* breathe."

"It does smell pretty good in here," Kerry admitted. "A bit like a florist shop."

Anna smiled. "It smells like home."

Home. Or close enough—closer than she'd been or wanted to be for a long time. Anna peered out the window as the plane descended over the waterways and buildings of downtown Mobile. Four years ago she'd been on the brink of accepting a job offer here. *This might have been home.* At the time it was appealing, though not quite as appealing as the idea of living on the West Coast had been. She'd been wavering between the two options, undecided and unwilling to decide until after her wedding.

Our wedding. That had become *theirs* instead—Carson's and Bree's. Her two *former* best friends.

It had turned out that California wasn't far enough away. Anna had left Holiday the same day Carson jilted her at the altar. With hardly a stop for food or sleep, she'd crossed the country to the opposite coast and had kept right on driving, past LA and San Francisco, north through the Redwoods and into Oregon. She'd driven through Portland and on to Seattle, stopping there only because she realized she was almost out of highway in the United States and had left her passport at home—in the suitcase she'd packed for her Caribbean honeymoon.

Seattle was home now. She had a good job, a healthy bank account, and an apartment overflowing with greenery to show for her past four years. What more could a person want?

Anna gripped the arm rests, bracing for impact as the plane touched down. *No going back now.* Her fantasy about being rerouted due to weather, followed by all Alabama airports being closed for weeks, hadn't come to pass. Her parents would already be here, waiting.

They'd probably made a day of it, visiting some of their suppliers before coming to pick her up. Another fifteen minutes and she'd be in the Excursion with them, sandwiched between crates full of pickled beets and jars of preserves, heading south to Holiday and a past she didn't feel ready to face.

All around her the other passengers began gathering

belongings and preparing to depart as the plane taxied toward the terminal. Anna remained immobile, staring out the window at scenery not vastly different from what she was used to. Was that why she had chosen to search out a job in Seattle instead of taking the one already offered in Monterey? Had she, subconsciously, searched for a place like home?

She didn't want to think so, didn't want to think that she'd missed anything about Alabama—except her family. *I didn't try to find a replacement for home,* she told herself firmly. Seattle was a big city; Holiday was about as small as towns came. In Holiday everyone knew everyone else and their business—including the reason her former fiancé and best friend had eloped and left her alone, in her wedding dress in front of a church full of people. In Seattle, Anna made sure no one knew her business. No one knew her thoughts, her mind, her heart. No one knew her at all.

Outside a marshaller waved the plane toward the jetway. Her time was almost up. She closed her eyes and gripped the armrests harder, feeling a tension headache mounting.

"We've landed now. It's okay," the guy next to her said.

"I wish," Anna mumbled without looking at him. "Flying was the easy part."

"I'm sorry to hear that."

She glanced at him for the first time since he'd boarded on the connecting flight in Dallas. She'd been in the middle of a movie then, with her headphones on, and had hardly noticed who was sitting beside her. She was like that these days. Keeping her head down, keeping to herself, was safer.

He was busy stuffing a book in the bag beneath the seat in front of him. When he looked up again, his clear, grey eyes widened briefly, as if he somehow recognized her. "Let me guess, going home?"

"Yes." Anna felt certain she'd never seen him before

today. Handsome as he was, she thought she would have remembered. And he didn't have a Southern accent at all. *Definitely not someone from home.* She turned away, staring out the window as the "Fasten Seatbelt" sign went off.

The man rose from his seat. From the corner of her eye she watched as he shouldered a laptop case. "Well, I hope your visit turns out better than you expect."

"Thanks," Anna mumbled. *Doubtful.* Hope was one of the emotions she'd all but forgotten.

Chapter 2

"Oh, Annabelle, my baby girl. Let me look at you."

After a suffocating hug Anna felt herself abruptly released and held at arm's length.

Her mother smiled and touched Anna's cheeks. "Beautiful as ever. You could still wear the crown for Miss Holiday."

Miss being the key word. "*Mama.*" Anna rolled her eyes, grateful for the distraction from sentiment. Her eyes had been watering since she'd first caught sight of her parents. When they both gathered her close for another long hug she didn't protest, but held on tightly, an arm around each, and lingered in their embrace.

This she had missed, being held, feeling safe and loved. Her parents were huggers. Showing affection wasn't just daily, but more like an hourly thing in their house. Passing someone in the hallway or unloading a dishwasher together was cause for her mom to enfold a family member in her arms. And after being married for nearly forty years, Dad was almost as touchy-feely too.

At last Anna released them and stepped back, wiping her eyes, in spite of her best efforts.

"You look good, Dad."

"So good you're crying?" A corner of his mouth lifted. "Don't worry about old Pops. I'll have my running shoes on and be out tearing up the pavement again soon enough. A little prostate cancer's not gonna stop me. Besides," he nudged Anna with his elbow, "if that's all it took to get you to come home, I would have asked for this illness long ago."

"*Daddy.*" Anna linked her arm through her father's, feeling like she was nine years old again instead of twenty-nine.

Her mother took Anna's free hand, and the three of them walked toward the luggage carousel, Anna mentally reviewing the clothes she'd brought and realizing she hadn't accounted for the perpetual Indian summer or humidity of southern Alabama. Seattle weather was decidedly cooler this time of year—pretty much all of the year, compared to the South. Her cozy fall sweaters might remain cozy in her suitcase the entire twelve weeks while she raided her old closet for T-shirts. Good thing there wasn't a dress code for working at the store.

She'd been right about the Excursion and the boxes and overflowing baskets and crates crammed inside. There was barely room for her suitcase, and her backpack had to sit on her lap the whole ride home, while her feet rested on a case of fresh-canned apple pie filling.

"Looks like you had a busy day," Anna said, peeking into the various boxes surrounding her, more curious than she thought she'd be. "I see it's business as usual at the Mulberry."

"Always," her mother said. "Grow local, bake local, make local, shop local, sell local, buy local. Better for you and the world and your neighbors."

"How about your bottom line?" Anna asked, still wondering how her parents managed to make a living, let alone a good one, off of their generations-old, family-owned-and-operated market.

"There are lots of bottom lines," Dad said. "The one that matters—people—is doing pretty well."

Anna sighed internally and let the subject go—for now. With her parents away for twelve weeks, maybe she'd have a chance to poke around and discover what was up with the store's finances once and for all. If nothing else, she could call her brother and sister and see what they knew about it. With her parents getting older and her dad sick, it seemed like it was time for their children to know a little more about the family business—especially if her parents expected it to stay in the family.

And who will run it when they are no longer able? Not her brother or her sister. They were too established elsewhere. *Which leaves...* Anna pushed the thought aside, unwilling to think about anything long term right now. *Twelve weeks. Just. Twelve.* That's all she'd signed up for.

She settled against the seat and tried to enjoy the ride. The last week of September in Alabama meant colors were just starting to turn, with many of the trees still green and full. After the rain and damp of Seattle the warm weather was a welcome change and not as stifling as it would have felt a month earlier.

They crossed the bay and headed south on the ninety-eight toward Fairhope. It was tempting to ask if they could stop at one of their favorite seafood restaurants for an early dinner. Anna wasn't particularly hungry, but anything to delay her return to Holiday a bit longer. Originally she'd booked a later flight, wanting to arrive well after dark, to sneak into town under cover of night, but her mother had asked her to change to an earlier arrival, citing her dad's need to get a lot of rest and be as healthy as possible going into his treatments.

Remembering that conversation, Anna swallowed her request and instead stared out the window in silence as the miles slipped by.

Dad pointed out the right side of the car. "If you look over there you can see some of the changes they've made since the hurricane. The original sea wall did very little. The new one is considerably more substantial."

"Was there much damage in Holiday?" Anna remembered hearing about the hurricane three years earlier, watching reports online. But once she'd been able to talk to her parents and learned they were safe, she'd mostly forgotten about it and the storms that threatened the South every summer and fall.

"Some damage. Some houses—and people—missing for a day or two." Her mother and father exchanged a mysterious glance.

Probably Bree's dad and brothers out searching for road kill. Anna kept the thought to herself, not wanting to bring up Breanna or anyone in the Wagner family.

"Most has been repaired now," Mom continued. "Dauphin Island had it the worst. I was grateful you'd finished your program and weren't there anymore."

"Me too," Anna said, only half meaning it. Her months spent doing graduate work at the Dauphin Island Sea Lab remained some of the happiest of her life. Unfortunately her job in the marine biology lab at the University of Washington wasn't quite as thrilling or hands on as she'd envisioned her career would be. The program there was new and still taking off. Too late she'd realized she would have been better suited to the position in Monterey.

This isn't the way I imagined my life. Lately the thought seemed to creep into her mind more and more, catching her in frequent moments of dissatisfaction at work or times of reflection on the past when she was at her apartment.

Carson had wanted to get married as soon as they'd finished their bachelor's degrees, and she had put him off another two years, citing the labs and internships she needed for her master's. Had she been wrong to ask that of him? To put her studies first?

After the fiasco of her wedding day she'd been too hurt and then angry to even consider such a possibility—that any of what happened was even remotely related to her choices. It was Carson's fault. All of it. His and Bree's. But now, nearly four years after the fact, Anna had started to have the uncomfortable feeling that maybe she was a little to blame too.

If I had agreed to marry him sooner . . . If I hadn't been so focused on my career. A career that felt increasingly unfulfilling lately . . .

The late-afternoon sun sank lower as they turned inland toward Magnolia Springs and Holiday. All too soon they were driving across the bridge that separated the two towns.

Welcome to Holiday, Alabama
Population 767
Come Sit a Spell—You'll Never Want To Leave

Unless you're me. Anna noted the changed numbers on the sign as they entered town. Two new residents since she'd left. Was one of them Carson and Bree's baby? Or did they live in Birmingham or elsewhere? She'd never asked her parents, and if anyone ever even mentioned Bree or Carson, Anna immediately shut them down. She didn't want to know what they were doing with their lives. She didn't care.

"The sign isn't quite accurate at present," her mom said, as if she'd been privy to Anna's thoughts.

"Oh?" They made eye contact in the rearview mirror. "Was someone born—or did someone die?" Anna asked.

"Two people passed," Dad said. "Sonny finally left us last month. He was ninety-nine."

"Wow." Anna barely remembered the town hermit—"the old coot," as Breanna's brothers used to call him, because they felt he was constantly poaching the best fishing spots. "I guess there's some truth to all those statements about eating fish being good for your health. Ninety-nine is a pretty ripe old age."

"He wasn't our oldest resident," Mom said. "We also lost Gabriel Steiner last month. He was one hundred two."

"Mr. Steiner. . ." Anna smiled wistfully and held a hand to her chest as a pang of sorrow touched her heart. He'd seemed old when she was a kid—because he had been. "I would have liked to see him again. Were you still bringing flowers to his house every Wednesday?"

"Until the very end," Dad said. "Delivered them myself that last week."

"I'm glad." Anna allowed a wave of nostalgia to wash over her. From the time she was ten until she graduated high school and went away to college, delivering Mrs. Steiner's, and then later Mr. Steiner's—after his wife had passed away—weekly flower arrangement had been her job. His place by the river was only a mile or so from the harbor at the center of town, but to her it had seemed like another world. Behind the wrought-iron fence and tall pines lining his property lay a proper Southern mansion, a remnant from the old plantation era. The grounds and house were kept meticulously, from the perfectly manicured drive to the lavish, circular foyer, with its mahogany table placed directly in the center. It was there, on top of a hand-crocheted lace doily—made long ago by Mrs. Steiner's great, great grandmother—that Anna placed the weekly flower deliveries.

Her mother always took extra care with the arrangements, taking a picture of what she'd done each week and keeping the photos in a binder, to check that she didn't duplicate the arrangements too often, or veer too far from the traditional flowers Mrs. Steiner preferred.

The delivery was always made after school on a Wednesday. If it was summer, Anna could never deliver in the morning, but still had to wait until after three o'clock. The vase full of flowers would be waiting for her on the counter in the tiny shop attached to the Mulberry Market, along with a personal note from her mother, wishing Mr. and Mrs. Steiner a pleasant week.

Anna remembered carrying the box with great care, at first awed with such an enormous responsibility. Mrs. Steiner was her mother's most loyal customer—her only customer some weeks. When she was young, Anna had asked her mother a time or two why she even bothered with a florist's shop. Unless there was a formal dance, or it was Mother's Day, or someone died, hardly anyone ever came in to buy flowers. Aside from being small in numbers, Holiday wasn't a particularly well-to-do community. Flowers were a luxury not many could afford, unless they came by the ones that nature grew so well here.

"I keep my shop for two reasons, Anna." Mother had been working as she spoke, carefully evaluating each stem before placing it in an antique pale pink vase—one of many recycled back and forth between Mrs. Steiner and Mother. "First, I love it. Flowers bring me joy. I need to be surrounded by them, almost as much as I need to be surrounded by my family. Sometimes I need their calming influence more—when you kids are acting out." She glanced up from her work to give Anna—who had been complaining about the extra work the flower shop required— a slightly exasperated look.

"The second reason I keep the shop open is that it *is* needed by others. Not always and not often, except for Mrs. Steiner. But for her alone, it is worth the work each week."

"But Mama," ten-year-old Anna had protested. "She can't even see what you make. Why doesn't she just get some fake flowers? She could save so much money."

"I don't think the Steiners need to worry about money." Mama placed the last gladiola and stood back to admire her work. "And there are more ways than just using your eyes to see. Mrs. Steiner sees in her memory now. She wasn't always blind, and in her mind she can still remember what different flowers look like—but only if she is reminded of them often. What does she do each week when you bring her arrangement?"

Anna shrugged. "She thanks me."

"What else?" Mother coaxed.

Anna thought for a second. Most of the time after placing the vase on the round table, she got busy munching the cookie always offered to her, and then taking a minute to peek at the grand house while Mrs. Steiner . . .

"She smells them," Anna said, a light bulb going off in her young mind. "And touches them and names them all. I always thought she did that to make sure we hadn't forgotten anything she'd ordered."

Mother shook her head. "She does it to remember."

"But why every Wednesday?" Anna had been grumbling about missing out on an afternoon spent down at the river with Bree and Carson. "Why does it matter when they're delivered?"

"Tradition," Mother said. "Mrs. Steiner grew up in that great big house, as did her mother and grandmother before her, back when women wore only dresses, and there were balls and dinner parties and all sorts of social customs and expectations we can't even imagine. Flowers delivered on Wednesday afternoon had sufficient time to open fully and be at their best bloom— but not yet wilting—by Friday evening, just in time for company. I suppose that Mrs. Steiner likes to run her house as it was when she grew up, and to keep with that tradition."

"Maybe she's remembering those dinner parties and dances." Anna put her elbows on the counter and leaned in close, eyes squeezed shut as she sniffed the flowers. "I understand, Mama."

She understood now that she'd come home too late to say goodbye to a once-dear friend. "I wish I'd known Mr. Steiner was ill."

"He wasn't," Dad said. "One morning he simply didn't wake up—that's the way I want to go. I'm telling you both right now. When I reach a hundred two, or even a hundred, I'm going to call it one night and just slip away in my sleep."

"Good plan, dear." Mom took one hand from the wheel and reached over, squeezing Dad's. The gesture made Anna's eyes moist again.

"You'd better be around that long, Dad."

He turned toward her in the back seat. "I intend to be. Don't you worry. Maybe after I'm done with chemo I'll start spending less time at the store and more time catching those fish that kept old Sonny so healthy."

What kept Mr. Steiner so healthy? Anna wondered. His wife had been gone more than a dozen years now. She'd passed away when Anna was in high school, but that hadn't meant the deliveries stopped. Not at all, though Mr. Steiner hadn't been a stickler for regular floral arrangements each week and probably wouldn't have thought of it after his wife's death.

But Mom did . . .

"Oh my—come in, Anna. What do I owe you?" Mr. Steiner stepped back, and looked around awkwardly, as if he wasn't at all certain what to do with the flower arrangement she held.

"No charge." Anna felt a little burst of joy as she said the words, then came inside to place the spectacular floral arrangement on the center table. Her mother had outdone herself this time. Mrs. Steiner would have loved this.

"I wasn't expecting—didn't realize Delores had ordered in advance—"

"She didn't." Anna reached for Mr. Steiner's speckled hand and clasped it in her own. "But my mom and I think your wife would like you to have these, that she'd want you to still have pretty flowers in the house each week and enjoy them and think of her when you do."

"I don't know what to say—you have to let me pay you."

Anna shook her head. "Please, let us do this. Your wife

was our most faithful customer for years. We want to be faithful to her memory." When she said *us,* she meant it. For the past two years she'd been helping in her mom's shop and arranging flowers too.

"There must be something?" He looked around, as if searching for what to give her in return.

"Actually—" Anna said, another burst of happiness surfacing "—I usually have a cookie when I come. So maybe you'll share these with me?" She held up a paper bag, full of a half-dozen chocolate chip cookies she and Bree had baked that afternoon.

Anna and Mr. Steiner had shared them together, out in the rockers on the sprawling front porch, while he talked out his grief and Anna—having one of those rare teenage experiences where life wasn't all about herself—discovered what it was to truly listen and care and love.

It had been the beginning of a new tradition—cookies with Mr. Steiner on Wednesdays. Sometimes she supplied the cookies; sometimes he did. Sometimes Carson joined her, if he didn't have football or work. Breanna came occasionally, though she was usually too busy taking care of things at her house. Once in a while all three of them spent an enjoyable hour or two in the old man's company, as he regaled them with stories of the way things used to be.

Anna stared out the side window of the Excursion. *It used to be I cared about people. I took the time to get to know them, to love them.* Those days seemed long ago, like another lifetime in which she had been naïve and trusting. She hadn't been afraid to give her heart away then, hadn't known anything other than the currency of kindness and love.

That really was the way of things in Holiday. Or it had been when she was growing up. It started at the beginning of each week, Sunday mornings, with Reverend Armstrong—

aka Mister Rogers' twin—giving heartfelt and moving sermons to his congregation. And it continued throughout the week, with small acts of kindness. Everything from taking the time to wave at Mabel Higgins or maybe bring her paper up to her as she sat rocking on her front porch, to neighbors exchanging plates of pecan bars or secretly raking each other's leaves.

Sit a spell... You'll never want to leave. For a brief second Anna remained so lost in the past that she couldn't remember why she *had* left. She'd been happy here. And in leaving she'd abandoned those she cared about most, from her parents to Mr. Steiner—she'd never even said goodbye to him—to her best friends.

Carson. Bree.
Heartbreak. Humiliation.
I had to leave.

Instead of the sorrow Anna had grappled with so long, she reached for the anger and blame more easily accessible these days. *It's Carson's fault—Breanna's too—that I wasn't here to see Mr. Steiner.* Because of them she'd missed his last years and even his funeral. What else had she missed? What other things had she been cheated out of because her two best friends had, together, cheated on her?

Her emotions in turmoil, Anna felt torn between wanting to press her face to the window and take everything in, to wishing she could shrink down in the seat and remain unseen.

As they reached Main Street her mother slowed the car to twenty-five, a good five miles below the speed limit. Those few people who were out and about waved at her parents' familiar SUV, and her father waved back while her mother honked in response.

"*Mom*," Anna said. It was bad enough they were arriving when it was still light out. It would be all she could do to slip into the house without one of the neighbors coming over to greet her. Holiday was friendly like that—*too* friendly sometimes.

"Just being polite." Mom smiled at her in the rearview mirror. "Have you forgotten how folks are here?"

"Not entirely," Anna mumbled. Holiday, Alabama, was probably the only place in the nation where honking was considered a sociable gesture. It wasn't uncommon to see signs posted in people's yards or outside any of the few businesses, inviting people to use their horns.

Honk, it's my seventy-fifth birthday—in front of Clara Wilson's farmhouse. *Honk if you voted today*—outside the community center on election day. *Honk if you believe in the Savior and Santa*—all during the long month of December. Most people said carols or sleigh bells were the sounds of the season, but forever she would associate the Christmas holiday with blaring horns.

They drove past the Mulberry Market, and Anna breathed a sigh of relief when they didn't stop. Tomorrow, Saturday, was soon enough to step out and face the employees and customers there. Maybe she could arrange to spend the day organizing and stocking the backroom shelves with the products from the suppliers they'd picked up today. She glanced around the packed SUV.

I could make that task last all day, couldn't I?

Right. A five-year-old could get it done in a couple of hours. Anna brought a hand to her head, the tension she'd experienced on the plane mounting again.

"Not feeling well, dear?" her mother asked.

"I'm not," Anna said. "It's been a long day." She'd locked her apartment at five o'clock that morning and headed to the airport. Not quite twelve hours later, she felt herself already questioning that recent past, her other existence. The pull of

Holiday was that strong, and she hadn't even stepped out of the car yet.

Mom turned onto their street, then hit the remote for the garage as they drove closer to the house.

Almost there. Anna breathed a sigh of relief. *Almost home.* The intruding thought unsettled her. Holiday *wasn't* home anymore and couldn't ever be again. Not after what had happened. But being here, just the simple act of driving through town and the memories that evoked, threw into stark reality just how much Seattle wasn't her home either.

I don't have a home. Maybe she never would again.

She thought of Sonny, transient until he'd stopped in Holiday years ago. Even here, he'd spent his days wandering. *Searching for—what?*

Was she really any different, keeping to herself, living alone with her apartment full of plant knock-offs from the South? At least Sonny had been searching for something.

She had given up long ago.

Chapter 3

Sunlight filtered through the partially closed shutters, sending streaks of warmth and light across the wood floor and the plush rug atop it. Anna flung a hand over her eyes, unused to the brightness so early in the morning. Unused to it at all, anymore. The bedroom in her Seattle apartment faced west—no morning sunshine there, even on those rare days it wasn't overcast.

With a sigh she rolled over, toward her bedroom door and the heavenly aroma wafting from the kitchen below.

Her stomach rumbled, reminding Anna that she'd eaten practically nothing yesterday. Though she didn't yet feel ready to face the day, she threw the covers back and sat up in bed. Her mom's cooking had a tendency to do that to people—summon them as a siren's call might. Mom's culinary creations never failed to deliver.

Anna stood, grazing the side of her head on the low canopy in the process. She stepped away, looking at her girlhood bed with an odd mixture of disdain and nostalgia. Nothing in this room had changed since the morning she'd left it—three years and seven and a half months ago. She'd left her parents first, at the church busy explaining to all the guests what had happened and figuring out what to do about the brunch that had already been set up.

"I'll be home soon, dear," her mother had said, after holding her tight in the vestibule while Anna sobbed her heart out.

But she hadn't waited for her mother to return. Heedless of the expensive buttons and hand-sewn lace, Anna had practically ripped the elegant dress from her body and thrown it across the bed. Fifteen minutes later she'd shoved enough of her other clothes in a suitcase and was dressed in jeans and a sweatshirt, ready to leave. Without a backwards glance she'd run from the house, gotten in her car and driven away from home, Holiday, her family, and all else she'd held dear—including her cheating fiancé and her former best friend.

To be here again now, with nothing unchanged from the last time, felt like stepping back into the past, one she had no desire to revisit.

With another weary sigh, Anna forced herself to cross the room to the closet, hoping she'd left behind something appropriate for early fall in Alabama. The closet, too, proved unchanged and sparse, just as she'd left it. Her formal gowns, including the one she'd lent to Bree for the junior prom she'd attended with Carson, clustered in the back corner. A few of her more summery and teenage-looking dresses hung beside those. There were no pants or shirts. Her wedding gown was nowhere to be seen.

Maybe Bree borrowed that too. Anna closed her eyes and breathed deeply, trying to force the bitterness away. That wasn't who she was or wanted to be. It was part of the reason she hadn't returned to Holiday. Staying here was a constant reminder or all she'd lost and the wrong done to her. In Seattle, no one might know her well enough to be considered a good friend, but at least she hadn't turned into an angry, bitter woman. In her case, running away had seemed the best option for keeping intact the pieces of her she had left.

Her dresser drawer yielded nothing but her old Miss Holiday, Alabama, pageant shirts. No way she was touching those. Out of options, Anna pulled a three-quarter-sleeve sweater from her suitcase and paired it with her favorite jeans. Not exactly cool enough for today's projected eighty-seven degrees, but it would have to do.

She pulled a brush through her hair, wound it in a knot on top of her head, then followed her nose down to breakfast. At the landing she paused, taking in the comfortable great room of her parents' home. The wood floors gleamed beneath furniture that offered both fashion and comfort. Throw pillows—pillows she and her siblings used to frequently throw at one another—were scattered along the sofas. Magazines about flowers and plants covered the coffee table, beside which a basket of children's books overflowed.

Her nieces and nephews wouldn't even know her anymore. Two had been born in her absence. Yet one more thing she'd been robbed of. *I'm a terrible aunt.*

Fall leaves twined along the mantel of the seldom-used fireplace, and a pumpkin-scented candle burned on the sofa table. But it was more than this aroma beckoning her.

Anna hurried down the last four steps, crossed the great room and dining room into her mother's kitchen.

Dad sat at the table already, a pile of papers spread out before him. Mom stood at the island, just lifting a waffle from the iron.

"Pumpkin pecan waffles." Anna inhaled appreciatively. "You're the best, Mom."

Just the scent of the anticipated treat and being here with her parents in this kitchen lifted her spirits. If only she could hide out here—with them—for the next twelve weeks. But today and tomorrow was all she'd have. After that they'd be in Jacksonville, Florida, for her father's treatments at the Mayo clinic. Because his kind of prostate cancer was rare, they'd elected to go to a facility with doctors who specialized in his type of tumor.

That her dad had cancer at all, that he was seriously ill, was still a lot to wrap her mind around.

"Speaking of pumpkins, come over here." Dad patted the chair beside him.

Anna obliged, leaning in to give him a quick hug first. "Good morning, Dad. What do you have there?"

"Schedules for the next two weeks, and payroll. This is all on the computer as well, but I thought I'd show you a hard copy first." He started to slide the stack of papers toward her, but Anna's mom set a plate down in front of Anna, blocking his way.

"Breakfast before work." She set a second plate down in front of Dad, as soon as he'd moved the papers aside, then returned to the counter to retrieve a third plate, this one for herself. She slid into the seat on the other side of Anna.

"Anna, will you say grace, please?" Mother looked at her expectantly.

"Of course." Anna clasped her hands together and bowed her head, suddenly cognizant of how long it had been since she'd uttered a prayer out loud. *Or at all.*

A childhood of prayers served her well, and the words, asking the Lord's blessing and thanking him for their bounty—or was it supposed to have been the other way around—fell from her lips. Amens were said, then Anna cut a piece of her waffle and took a bite of crisp, sweet pumpkin, topped with her mother's homemade syrup, fresh-whipped cream, and crumbled, candied pecans. Her mouth closed around the fork in bliss.

"This is the best thing I've tasted—"

"—Since you left home," her mother finished.

Anna nodded. No point in arguing that one. For all the fabulous Southern cooking she'd been raised on, she wasn't much of a cook herself. Not yet, but maybe there was still time to learn. If she could eat like this in Seattle, it might feel a little more like home. *The good parts.*

She took another bite, thinking about this possibility and wondering how difficult it would be to learn to make at least some of the things her mother did. She'd never really cared or seen the need for the skill before. Unlike Bree, who'd had to learn quickly—if she wanted to eat at all— after her mother had died when she was thirteen.

Lucky for Carson he married her instead of me. The resentful thought soured Anna's next bite. Where did these keep coming from? Why was she doing this to herself? In Seattle she rarely had these kinds of thoughts anymore. If time hadn't completely healed, it had at least sealed over her wounds—or so she'd thought. But already, being in Holiday felt like ripping the bandage off a deep cut that apparently hadn't scabbed over.

"So, tell me about the schedule." Anna took a drink of juice and pulled her eyes from the waffle enough to focus on her dad.

His hair was almost completely grey now, but he still had a lot of it. Anna wondered if he would after his treatments. When she looked at him closely, she detected a weariness that hadn't been there before—or at least, she didn't think it had. There were dark circles beneath his eyes, and he seemed worried about something as he shuffled the stack of schedules her direction.

"We have a dozen employees currently."

"A dozen—that's a lot." He really must be slowing down. "I'm assuming you have the same people as when I left? Is Mettie Fillmore still bossing people around? And the Fredericks? They still rounding up eggs, milk, and cheese each week? What about Robert?" He'd been kind of old when she'd left, but Dad hadn't mentioned any other deaths. "Is he still running the soda fountain?"

Dad nodded. "We got him some help, but yes. He comes in the afternoons. Mostly Bob just entertains the few customers who actually order something and stay to enjoy it."

Yet another example of her parents' generosity—which made Anna question again how they made any money at all.

Most of the people who worked in the store didn't actually *do* that much work. That was her recollection, anyway. "Who have you hired since I left?"

"A few people. Another waffle?" Mom pushed a plateful toward Anna.

She shook her head. "No thanks. I'm stuffed already." She wasn't used to eating a big breakfast, or even a little one these days.

"You've lost more weight." Mom shook her head. "You're five feet, eight inches tall, Anna. You need to consume some calories."

So much for how beautiful I looked yesterday. "I do. I will." Anna had no doubt that she'd gain plenty of weight— were Mom to be the chef for her entire visit.

"I've seen your apartment and your refrigerator," her mother continued. "Sometimes I wonder how you're even still alive."

Me too. Or, more specifically, Anna wondered what she was alive for. What her purpose was. Once, she'd thought it was her passion for helping sea creatures and her love for Carson that were her purposes in life. The latter was no longer an option, and with the former it was difficult to see that her research was making any difference. Mom wasn't finished with her lecture yet. "What did you eat yesterday?"

Anna remembered staring at the inside of her refrigerator the previous morning, before her flight. Aside from a half-full bottle of ranch dressing and some take-out leftovers of unknown date, the only option for breakfast had been an apple—a not-too-crisp one, at that. But she'd eaten it on her way to the airport and then had pretzels on one flight and nuts on another. "I had fruit and protein and grains yesterday." True—sort of.

Mom frowned. "I can imagine. Finish your waffle." She pointed her fork at Anna's plate.

"Yes, ma'am." There she was, nine years old again. Was that how this visit was going to go? Maybe it was good her parents were leaving.

Anna turned to her father. "You were about to tell me who you'd hired."

"Ye-es." He and Mom exchanged a long look. "Ella Mikkes works for us now."

"Little Ella?" She wasn't even ten, was she?

"She's fourteen," Mom said. "She helps in the florist shop, especially when I have a large order. She also makes the small grocery deliveries now, and she's good at sweeping up or stocking—really anything, though we haven't trained her on the register yet."

Without saying much, her mother had just told an entire story. The Mikkes family lived way out of town, in the backwoods, where folks were even poorer than many of those in town. Likely her parents had hired Ella after she'd come to the store yet another time, asking for credit for her family. It was like a bad episode of *Little House on the Prairie*, only Anna's parents weren't like mean Mrs. Olsen. They'd sooner give away the store than not help someone.

That Ella made the small deliveries meant she was taking groceries to those elderly on the "no charge" list. Anna could just imagine her mother's thought process on that one—have the poor give to someone even poorer. Some of Holiday's oldest residents did have it very bad. At least Ella's father had a job, even if it didn't pay enough.

"Okay. Ella." Anna made a note to teach the girl everything she could in the next twelve weeks, so she could be of some real help if her parents needed it when they returned. "Who else?"

"Evan Wagner. He does some of the stocking and heavy lifting."

"Why not all of it?" Anna asked, her eyes narrowing.

Evan, really? She'd never met anyone lazier than Bree's brothers. "Does he lift one box while you carry five?"

"Nope." Dad shook his head. "I haven't lifted much of anything for a long time, excepting yesterday, when we picked a few things up on the way home."

A few things. Anna thought of the loaded car waiting to be unpacked. "Does that mean you're not stocking shelves either?" Some of them were high, the ceilings in the old building being ten feet. She couldn't imagine that lifting and reaching were good for her dad's back or anything else.

"Carson takes care of the stocking. The rest of the heavy lifting too. He manages all of that now." Dad reached for her hand, but Anna pulled away.

"*Carson* works for you?" Her father might as well have slapped her. She wouldn't have felt more stunned.

Dad nodded. "He's been a godsend too. I'm not sure what we would have done without him."

"Or Breanna," Mom added quietly.

Anna's gaze flew to hers. "*Both* of them work for you?" This meant they must live in Holiday or nearby. Sooner or later she was going to have to see them. And it would be sooner, if they really did work at the store. "How could you—after what they did? Why is Carson even working for you, anyway? He has a master's degree and a good job." Or he had when they were dating. Had something happened? *Serves him right if he got laid off.*

"They had some big medical bills between their baby and—"

"Just twist a knife in my heart, Dad. Geez! I can't believe you two." Anna pushed her chair back from the table and stood. "I'm not even home twenty-four hours, and you're reminding me of all they took from me. And now you casually tell me they *work* for you. Do they come over for dinner too? Are you all chummy with them and their *baby*?"

"You don't know the whole story," Mom said calmly.

"They both cheated on me, Bree got pregnant, and they eloped on what was supposed to have been mine and Carson's wedding day. That's plenty! I don't want to know anything else about them—and you knew my feelings on this, so why would you hire them?" Anna felt like pulling her hair out in frustration. "Why did I even come if they've got the market so well in hand?"

"They don't," Mom said. "They each work a few hours a week and are very good at what they do. But they have no idea the ins and outs of running the Mulberry—not like you do."

Anna folded her arms across her chest and stared at the opposite wall. She felt like she'd been betrayed all over again. This time by her parents.

"When their daughter was born a month early, there were an awful lot of medical bills," Dad explained. "She was in the hospital up in Mobile, in the newborn intensive care for quite a while."

A baby girl. Anna felt like putting her fingers in her ears and humming loudly, the way she used to when she was a kid and her brother was teasing her. *I don't want to hear this.*

"They would have lost their house if we hadn't given them a loan. Helping at the store is part of the way they're paying that back."

They have a house too. Probably here. Probably one of those big ones just down the street, with the beautiful yard and trees that Carson dreamed of owning.

Anna felt the waffle she'd just eaten shift in her stomach. She felt ill. "I'm not sure I can stay." She turned and walked from the kitchen, wishing she'd never come.

Chapter 4

ANNA ENTERED THE Mulberry through the back door—just to be safe, though it was after six on Saturday and they'd closed until Monday morning. She'd stayed at home, in her room, pouting, the first half of the day, letting her parents know how much they'd hurt her and giving them the excuse that she had some online work to do. As a marine biologist. She doubted they'd bought that, but they'd left her alone.

Really, she'd been searching for flights back to Seattle until her guilt—she really had to stay—and then curiosity—where did Carson and Bree live, anyway—got the best of her. She'd switched from airline websites to trolling Baldwin county records, trying to find out their address so she could avoid that street at all costs. When she couldn't find any records for them in town, she felt the slightest bit better. No chance of running into them when she was out running. *If* she decided to take that up again while she was here.

It had been a thing she and her dad had done. All during junior high and high school, their special time together. He couldn't run now. She hadn't for a long time. But like everything else that was returning to haunt her in Holiday, she felt a sudden need to lace up her running shoes and hit the harbor trail before the sun was up.

Maybe Monday.

As far as working at the market went, she'd just have to be sure *not* to be there when Carson or Bree were. And since she would soon be the one making the schedule, she ought to be able to manage that. Maybe she'd even write them right *off* the schedule while her parents were gone. No one could blame her for that, could they?

Anna reached overhead, pulling the chain for the light, and after a second the bulb flared to life. Instead of seeing the normal chaos that was the market's back room, Anna found herself facing newly built—or new to her, at least—floor-to-ceiling shelving, all neatly organized and labeled. Alphabetically, she realized, as she strolled around the room, examining everything from jars of home-canned applesauce, sacks of dry beans, baggies that contained hand-crocheted doilies, hammers, stacks of paper, antique silverware, and cans of wheat. She couldn't remember ever seeing quite so much inventory in the long, narrow room and had to offer silent kudos to whoever had built the new shelves and so efficiently organized and stocked everything. *Unless it was Carson. Of course it was.* She mentally cringed, hating to think that with a few shelves he'd somehow wormed his way back into her parents' hearts.

How could they allow it? How had they seemingly forgiven him for ruining her life?

Her frustration fueled her energy level for the next two and a half hours as she worked to unload the Excursion and stock the shelves, careful to place everything in the right spot and to rotate older food items to the front.

Who is going to buy all of this? Anna worried that much of the merchandise—the perishables, at least—would sit too long. And who actually bought doilies these days? *Now that Mrs. Steiner is gone.*

Anna decided she would buy one, maybe even a few of them, before she returned to Seattle. They could sit beneath some of her plants and remind her of home.

With the car unloaded, Anna left the back room and moved to the front of the store, checking to make sure the blinds were drawn before she turned on a light. She hit the switch for the string of bulbs that dangled over the soda fountain. Their warm glow lit the back half of the store, and Anna took a minute to look around and let it all soak in.

The building was more than a century old. The store itself was like something out of *Little House on the Prairie*, from the red brick walls and old-fashioned cash register—for looks only these days—to the long candy counter with its glass jars full of delights, the barrels scattered around the store, and the working wood stove in the middle.

Anna lifted her hand and traced the faint scar that ran along her left index finger. Once, when she and Carson and Bree had been playing hide and seek among the barrels—and Carson had just spotted her and was coming to get her—Anna had run too close to the wood stove, brushing her finger along the hot metal. She remembered howling as her mother had sat her on a stool at the soda fountain and put an ice cube on her finger. Bree's and Carson's mothers had fussed over her too. Carson had been scolded for chasing—which wasn't really fair, since they'd all done it.

Served him right, Anna thought. Everything unpleasant that had ever happened to him now seemed just and fair in her mind. And never enough to make up for the pain he'd caused her.

I loved you. I trusted you both.

She forced her mind to happier memories—the three of them eating ice cream sundaes at the counter while their mothers poured over the latest McCalls pattern book and discussed which costumes to sew for Halloween.

Back then there had been six of them. Three mothers who were best friends, three children following suit—no matter that Carson was a boy. He'd endured tea parties fairly well, so long as there were actual cakes involved, and Anna and Bree hadn't minded playing at the river, catching frogs or fish or just digging in the mud.

I had a carefree, wonderful childhood. Anna sank onto the same stool her mother had placed her on all those years ago.

She'd had no reason to believe her adult years would be any less wonderful. She'd pursued her educational dreams, and Carson had pursued her. Theirs would have been the wedding of the decade for Holiday. *Star football hero marries valedictorian and Miss Holiday.* Of course, those things had been long in the past by the time they were to marry. She and Carson had each gone away to college. They'd graduated. He'd already landed a great job. She believed she might have found hers in California.

All of that, taken away in less than a minute—with first the phone call to Carson's father and then, later when she'd finally opened Carson's note and read the words, "I'm so sorry."

Was he sorry? It didn't seem like it—marrying Bree, buying a house… *Being all buddy-buddy with my parents.* It was like he—they—didn't miss her at all. Carson and Bree had just carried on with their lives, forgetting that Anna was the one who'd first suggested their club, that she was the one who'd found the old Jackson Five album in the room of odds and ends above her parents' store and played it for them.

ABC was just BC these days. Breanna and Carson. *Before creeping around. Before cruel.*

Rapping on the front window jerked Anna from her thoughts and nearly knocked her to the floor.

She regained her balance on the swivel stool, then sat silent and unmoving, waiting for whoever was out there to go away.

The closed sign was out; she could tell from here. So who could it be? An employee? Bree or Carson? Panicking, Anna jumped up and ran to the back room to check that she'd locked the door.

Finding it secure, she heaved a sigh of relief—short-lived, as the knocking came again, more persistent this time, and accompanied by a plea for her to open.

More irritated than frightened now, Anna marched to the front, pushed the shade aside and came face-to-face—through the glass—with a man. He was tall and dressed far too warmly for the weather and too formally for Holiday in his three-piece suit.

The cornstalks from the autumnal scene her mother had painted across the window blocked much of his face, but what she could see of the man, she didn't recognize. "We're closed." She pointed to the sign.

"I know." He nodded. "I'm really sorry. I just got into town. Are there any other grocers nearby? I just need a few staples to get me by until Monday."

"There's a Piggly Wiggly about twenty-five minutes from here," Anna said loudly through the glass.

The man brought a hand to the back of his neck, apparently frustrated. "How about a gas station?" he asked. "The one down the street is already closed too."

"Yeah, Santa—I mean Ernie—Mr. Jensen—closes early on Saturday. Everything does."

"So I see." The man didn't sound angry but looked at her again, a plea in his eyes. "I don't have enough gas to make it another twenty-five minutes. My rental wasn't full when I picked it up, and I didn't realize that until I got out here. Is there any way you can help—just send a couple cans of chili through the mail slot or something? I've got some cash. I can pay you."

Cans of chili—as if. He really wasn't from around here.

"Our store doesn't exactly work like that," she attempted to explain. "It's sort of—old fashioned. I could give you some beans, but they'd be dry. And you'd need onions and seasoning to go with them, a pot to cook them in. . ." At his perplexed look she gave up. "Just a minute."

She left the window, letting the shade fall into place, then pulled her phone from her back pocket. She turned on her flashlight and moved among the barrels and shelves, trying to figure out what to give the man and how to give it to him. Small town or not, she had no intention of letting him inside the store.

After a few minutes she came back to the window with a small sack of rolled oats, a jar of applesauce, another of peaches, several pieces of beef jerky, and a bottle of soda. Not exactly a great meal, but the best she could come up with. She'd considered peanut butter—one of the few packaged items carried in the Mulberry—but there wasn't any bread in the store, or milk or butter or eggs, and wouldn't be until the Monday-morning deliveries arrived. Whatever perishables hadn't sold today Ella would have delivered shortly before closing. And somehow this guy—in his fancy suit—didn't seem the type to know what to do with dry beans. She wondered how he'd even come to be here and what his business was. Maybe he didn't have any at all and the empty gas gauge was what had landed him here.

Anna returned to the window, tapping to get his attention, since he stood facing away from her. She held up the paper sack. "Stay where you are, and I'll bring this to you."

"Thanks." He nodded, looking relieved.

She wondered if he'd be as appreciative once he saw what was inside.

Anna switched off the lights over the soda fountain, then hurried to the back room. She grabbed an odd spoon from the recycled silverware and a bowl with a chipped rim. She supposed that wherever he was staying had water.

If he's staying somewhere.

Anna let herself out the back door and climbed into her

parents' SUV, careful to lock the doors. She drove around to Main Street, all but deserted after eight in the evening, and slowed as she came to the man standing at the front of the store. She didn't see the rental car he'd referred to parked anywhere. There was only a small delivery-type truck down the street.

She put her foot on the brake, instead of putting the Excursion in park. Then, as an afterthought, she grabbed a pen from the console and sprawled her parents' address across the front of the bag, telling herself that was exactly what they would have done, if they were here instead of her.

The man came forward as she rolled down the car window partway and held the bag out. He paused, staring at her a second before a smile lifted the corners of his mouth.

"So, is your visit home better than you thought it would be yet?"

His handsome face jarred her memory. "You! You sat next to me on the plane."

"Or you sat next to me." His grin widened.

"I was there first," she reminded him, returning his smile and feeling slightly smug about— *what?*

He reached for the bag and took it from her. "Thanks. I really appreciate this." He glanced up the street, then bent his head, studying the writing on the bag. Beneath the Mulberry's string of outdoor lights, always left on, Anna studied his profile, wondering that she hadn't really noticed him on the plane. He was more than handsome. *Striking.* With a face that could star in movies, her mother would say.

Maybe that was why he was here. Maybe they were filming something nearby.

He looked up at her, a question in his gaze. "This your address?"

She shook her head, horrified he might have the wrong impression. "My parents'." *The town do-gooders.* Even for the town do-badders, she'd learned. This guy didn't seem bad, at least. Just a little lost.

"I don't know where you're staying, but—" *Please be staying* somewhere. The last thing she needed was to show up with a stray man her first day home. "*Are* you staying somewhere?"

"Other than in my gasless rental truck?" He followed her gaze down the street to the truck parked there. "Yeah. I'll be at my great-grandfather's place. I even have a key." He dug in his pocket and pulled out an old-fashioned skeleton key.

Good luck with that. Anna could imagine the kind of dilapidated house that went with a key that ancient. There were more than a few old, crumbling residences in and around Holiday. Absently, she wondered which one he was headed to and who his great-grandfather was. Or had been. A key like that could belong to one of the abandoned houses around here.

"Well—" Anna cleared her throat. "Since you don't have any way to get gas or groceries until Monday morning, you're welcome to come to dinner tomorrow evening. We eat at four."

Hopefully that hadn't changed in her absence. Sunday had always meant family dinners, "family" including any strays she or her parents or siblings happened to bring along. After Bree's mother had died, Bree had eaten at least one Sunday dinner with them a month—for years. Occasionally her dad and brothers had come, though they were often away hunting.

Carson's dad, too, had been a frequent visitor after his wife passed away. For such a small town, Holiday had its share of sad stories and situations, which meant it was a rare Sunday when there was only Lawrence family at her parents' table.

The man glanced at the bag again then back at Anna.

"Thanks. I might take you up on that, depending upon what I do or don't find at my grandfather's."

"You know where you're going, then? Do you need directions? I might be able to help."

"I'm sure you could." He smiled again, as if he found this amusing. "But I'll be okay. Shouldn't be too difficult to find, and I've got a little gas left."

"Oh, well in that case—good night." She pushed the button to roll up the window and took her foot off the brake.

He raised a hand in farewell. "Good night, Miss Lawrence."

Chapter Five

ANNA STOOD IN front of the full-length mirror in her room, debating what to wear. Her mother was right. She had lost weight, and her clothes didn't fit like they'd used to, like they should. She hadn't really noticed or cared before. She'd never bothered to find a church in Seattle, and she didn't date, so she hadn't put on a dress in years. The clothes she wore to work were plain, drab, comfortable. Meant to be covered up by her lab coat each day. The best days, the days she actually cared what she was wearing and doing, were days out on the water. Her wetsuit was her favorite piece of clothing.

"Not exactly suitable for church." She smiled at the thought, and the reflection in the mirror didn't look quite so discouraging. Hoping to improve it more, Anna blow dried her hair until it was smooth and soft, hanging straight down her back. She'd had it cut about a week before she came home and was glad that at least that part of her looked decent.

A touch of mascara, a hint of lip gloss, and a safety pin at the waistband of her skirt, and she was ready to go. Or so she told herself.

The last time she'd set foot in Holiday's church—in any church—was the day she was supposed to have been married. *February fourteenth. The worst day of my life.* She hated Valentine's Day with a passion that surpassed the love she'd once felt for Carson. It was the one day of the year she took a vacation day, and the one day of the year she took a sleeping pill, spending most of the twenty-four hours buried beneath her comforter while the rest of the world celebrated love.

Anna sank onto her bed, holding onto one of the posts that held the canopy in place. How was she supposed to walk in there and not feel like it was that day all over again? And what if Carson and Bree were there? What then?

"Anna, you ready?" Her mother's voice was followed by a knock and the door opening slowly. "Oh, good. You are. Let's go."

"I'm not sure I can do this, Mom." Anna felt an odd panic in her chest, as if the oxygen around her was being slowly sucked away.

Mom walked over to the bed and sat beside her. "Is it being in the church or seeing Bree and Carson?"

So they will be there. Great. "Both. It's everything. Being in Holiday is just . . ."

"Hard?" her mother said.

Anna nodded. "Unimaginably so."

"Is being in Seattle any easier?" Mom took Anna's hand in her own. "Are you happy there—truly?"

Leave it to Mom to ask the difficult questions. She'd always been good at that, had somehow always known how to pry the truth from her kids, even when they hadn't wanted to give it. There was no point in even attempting to lie to her mother.

"Easier, yes. Am I happy, no. I haven't been for a long time."

"I know." Mom squeezed her hand. "It shows in your countenance. You've lost the light that used to live there."

"I think that's just the Seattle weather you're seeing." Anna attempted to joke. "I'm pale because the Northwest doesn't get sun like the South."

"Maybe, but your soul is pale, too."

"And what do you suggest for a remedy?" Anna asked, knowing advice was coming whether she wanted it or not.

"Just what you're doing." Mom stood, tugging Anna

along with her. "You're facing the past so you can leave it behind, and you've come home. Maybe everything won't get fixed this visit. I can't promise all will be right with your world, but it's a start, and I guarantee you're going to feel better for it. And the next time it will be easier."

"First time is always the hardest." That was her dad's saying, not her mom's. The first algebra test, the first event at her first track meet, her first college application, first night away from home.

First time returning to the church where my heart was broken.

Her mother nodded. "It will get easier. Trust me."

Anna didn't say anything as she slipped on her sandals. She wanted to trust, wanted to believe this hurt would eventually go away. It would be so wonderful if she could someday tell her mother that she'd been right.

He was there—the very first person Anna saw as she walked through the blue double doors. He sat on the far edge of the back pew, closest to the doors—as if he might need to make a quick escape—looking every bit as polished and out of place in the same charcoal-grey suit he'd had on last night. His brown, nearly black hair was neater this morning, styled precisely, full of some expensive product, no doubt. Perhaps accommodations at his mysterious grandfather's house had been more adequate than she'd assumed. Last night's curiosity renewed.

He looked up as Anna walked in behind her parents. "Good morning, Miss Lawrence."

"Is it?" she retorted, then immediately wished she'd not been short. Her tumultuous emotions weren't his fault. "I'm sorry. That was rude of me." She tried to smile. "I'm not feeling very well this morning."

"Apology accepted." His warm smile conveyed the sincerity of his words.

Anna attempted one in return and started up the aisle once more, aware of the widening gap between her and her parents, but then paused, turning back to the stranger she'd met three times now. "How do you know my name?" She thought she'd only imagined him saying it last night.

"I know all about you, Miss Lawrence—Annabelle." His smile widened to maddening proportions.

Unsettled, she considered demanding to know why, but people were coming in behind her—people she didn't want to have to talk to—and her parents were already almost at their bench. She settled on one question for the time being. "What is *your* name?"

"Elijah Steiner."

"Oh." *Mr. Steiner's grandson?* She hurried to catch up with her parents. Something about him rang a bell, but she couldn't remember what. Maybe it was just that they'd met on the plane. She was certain she'd never heard his name before. An unusual name like Elijah wasn't one easily forgotten. Mr. Steiner had gone by Gabriel. Though now that she thought about it . . . Wasn't Elijah his middle name?

Too late she realized she should have acknowledged Elijah Steiner's loss, should have said she was sorry to have not visited his grandfather at all the last few years. Maybe *that* was what he knew about her—that she'd once been a caring friend but had abandoned his grandfather and their friendship without so much as a note or a letter explaining why.

At least Carson and Bree left a note.

As if that excuses anything.

Anna slipped into the pew beside her parents, wishing her siblings had come for church. The more family she could have had surrounding her today, the better. But they'd been here just a month ago, at the end of August, for Founder's

Day, when anyone and everyone who'd ever lived in Holiday returned for a homecoming sermon and picnic at the church.

Except me. She'd missed three years in a row.

Her siblings *would* be here for dinner tonight, for which Anna was grateful. In addition to being a lousy daughter, she'd been a lousy sister and aunt these past few years. It was time she started making up for that too.

Her mother leaned close. "Who was that young man you were talking to?"

Young? He was youngish, maybe—like her—but not what Anna used to consider young. Her twenties had all but fled. Middle age loomed before her, but somehow it felt like she'd missed several years of being young along the way.

"I think he's Mr. Steiner's grandson," Anna whispered. "I met him on the plane, and he came by the store last night for a few things. He must be staying out at Mr. Steiner's house." She felt silly, remembering how she'd worried for him, thinking he was headed to some old shack in the woods. The key he'd had must have been to the old kitchen door at the back of the house. Mr. Steiner had redone the front, double doors with a keyless entry several years ago. She still remembered the code, after so many Wednesdays letting herself inside to deliver his flowers and check on him.

Mom patted Anna's knee. "You should invite him to dinner tonight."

Uh oh. "I already did." She'd done it out of charity, not interest, but Mom wouldn't see it that way.

Anna jumped as Betty Oxford hit a loud first note on the organ and proceeded to pound out a prelude that was anything but reverent. She'd long had a problem with volume—the choir could seldom be heard over the organ—but since she was the only one in town who played, no one could complain—much.

As it was, Anna knew Carson's dad worried about what

would happen when Betty was no longer with them. She'd been in her seventies forever, it seemed. *In her eighties now?* Whatever age she was, it didn't seem to have affected her ability to rattle the glass in the windows and jar the congregation to silence.

Today Anna welcomed the noise. Another few minutes and the service would start, and no one had come up to talk to her—a huge relief. Thanks to Elijah Steiner she'd survived what she had most dreaded—simply walking into the church and facing the memories and people. He'd been enough of a distraction that for a welcome minute or two she'd forgotten to be stressed and worried.

Betty's fingers ran up the keys in what could only be described as some gothic melody. If the setting had been different it would have been positively creepy—great haunted-house music. It really was a wonder that no one had ever talked to her about more appropriate prelude music—she'd always treated the five minutes before services started as her own, personal concert, never mind that the captive audience hadn't come to see her.

Mister Rogers—Reverend Armstrong—certainly wouldn't say anything. Anna had never met a gentler, kinder soul than Carson's father. It had always seemed a bit odd that he'd raised two rough-and-tumble, sports-minded, good-at-tackling-and-throwing—*and cheating*—boys. She would have thought his kids would be more the academic, bookworm types, soft-spoken as he was and wearing sweater vests all the time.

One would have thought a lot of things. Like that she and Carson, who had dated all through high school, would be the ones married and with a child—instead of him and Breanna, who had just walked past as they made their way to a side bench. Anna sat stiffly, though her heart was anything but still.

Her gaze slid to their entwined fingers. *Carson used to*

hold my *hand that way.* Anna tried to swallow and couldn't. Mom reached over and took her hand instead.

Anna forced her lips to curl in a fake smile. After nearly four years, this wasn't supposed to hurt so much.

Bree and Carson reached their seats. They didn't have a child with them, and Anna's heart gave a queer little leap as she wondered why. Her parents had said the baby had to be hospitalized and that there were a lot of medical bills. Had they said anything else? Had the baby even lived?

From the corner of her eye Anna watched as Carson looped his arm behind Bree. He'd always been one to display affection. One of the many reasons he'd fit into Anna's family so well. But what about fitting into Bree's family? Her dad and brothers were about as far away from affectionate, church-going folk as a person could be. In the years since her mother's death, Bree had endured a life of neglect and loneliness.

No longer. Seated beside Carson, she looked happier and healthier than Anna had ever seen her. There was a peace and a tranquility about her, a contentment, but also an underlying worry evident in the way Bree's teeth rested on her bottom lip. It was a habit from childhood that Anna had long tried to help her break.

Where is their baby? It wouldn't be a baby now, but a child. Anna couldn't stop thinking about that, wondering—worrying, herself.

Because I wished them ill so many times.

She shifted uncomfortably, forcing her gaze to the front, telling herself that she had nothing to do with whatever might have happened. That much was absolutely true. If it was something terrible, they'd brought it upon themselves by getting pregnant in the first place. Even knowing that, and still hurting from it, she couldn't seem to feel any better, any less concerned.

Once, she and Bree had told each other everything. If

there had been a crisis, Bree wouldn't have had a mother—or Anna—to turn to. *What happened? How did you get through it, Bree?* Anna had anticipated many uncomfortable feelings today, but empathy and even a yearning for her former best friend hadn't been among them.

Reverend Armstrong came down the aisle, greeting his flock, and a look of joy spread across his face when he made eye contact with Anna.

"Anna. It's so good to see you. Your parents told me you were coming home. We're so happy you're here."

We? She doubted he meant to include the rest of his family in that statement. She couldn't think Carson would be glad to see her. She planned to do her best to avoid him the next twelve weeks. If they never said so much as hello to each other again, that was fine by her.

"Thank you." Anna shook his Reverend Armstrong's outstretched hand. He clasped it affectionately, as one who was not only her clergyman but who had almost been her father-in-law.

"I'm sorry for the unfortunate circumstances that brought you back to us, but sometimes the Lord works in mysterious ways. I pray these next weeks will bring the peace you've been searching for."

Peace? Was that what was missing from her life? It seemed a bit more than that. But who said she was searching for it, for anything?

Anna withdrew her hand, and Reverend Armstrong leaned across her to greet her parents. She wanted to feel annoyed with him, to remind him that if she lacked peace in her life it was because his son had gotten her best friend pregnant and they'd run off together. *A few hours before he was supposed to marry me.* But it was impossible to be angry with such a gentle soul. Reverend Armstrong really was Mister Rogers, wearing a hand-knit sweater, barely visible beneath his robe, and genuinely caring about and assuming the best about every single person in Holiday.

If only he had a neighborhood of make believe where Anna could ride the trolley and talk with puppets who could explain her jumbled feelings and help her sort them all out.

Chapter Six

ANNA PULLED ONE of her mother's aprons from the hook in the pantry and lowered it over her head. She reached behind her to tie it and found her mother already in command of the strings—as with everything else in her kitchen.

"Look at this." With one hand Mom nudged Anna to turn around, then finished tying the apron strings in a bow in front, over the wide pocket. "These have to go around you twice—just like you were a little girl again." She looked up at Anna. "Except you're not." Shaking her head, she backed out of the pantry. "You're the one who looks sick, not your father."

Take me to Florida for treatment then, was on the tip of Anna's tongue, but her father's cancer was nothing to joke about. Nor would being snippy with her mother help anything.

"I'm sure I'll gain some weight during my visit." Anna went to the sink and started washing the potatoes piled on the drainboard.

"Only if you cook for yourself. I'm not going to be here, remember?"

Only too well. Sometimes—in moments like these—Anna could almost feel grateful that, starting tomorrow, she'd have the house to herself. Mostly, though, the thought made her sad. And worried about her father's health, as well as how she'd handle being here without her parents. Next Sunday she'd be sitting on that bench at church alone.

"I'll cook," she promised. "Your kitchen is well stocked, and all your recipes are here." She glanced at the old tin box on the counter. A literal treasure trove of knowledge and deliciousness lay beneath its worn façade. This really was the perfect place and time to improve her minimal skills. If she mastered at least a few of her favorites while here, she could start doing a better job feeding herself once she returned to Seattle. The thought of accomplishing something while she was here brightened Anna's mood. She'd felt dreary since the sermon ended and old friends and neighbors had swarmed her, welcoming her home, asking about the Northwest, her job, and her personal life. No one seemed to believe her when she'd told them she didn't have much to share.

Nor had her eyes obeyed her and avoided staring at Carson and Bree as they exited the church. Instead, she'd felt her gaze glued to them, the magnetic pull of her former fiancé and her best friend too much to resist.

He's still so handsome.
I miss Bree so much.
I miss them both.

Why should she miss them? It seemed some cruel trick of fate that it felt like no time had passed since her wedding day that wasn't. She'd seen both Bree and Carson the night before, never dreaming it would be the last time she spoke to them.

Anna peeled and then diced the potatoes with extra vigor, slamming the knife through the vegetables and onto the cutting board as if she were chopping wood. Sometimes it seemed the pain of losing the two people she was closest to rivaled the pain of what they'd done to her. And that made her so angry. She didn't want to feel that way, to wish they were a part of her life again.

Anna dumped the massacred potatoes into the pot on the stove and ignored her mother, pretending not to notice her raised eyebrow and pursed lips.

"I think I'd better roll out the pie crust," Mom said,

snatching the rolling pin out of Anna's reach. "Who knows what you're liable to do with this right now."

"Fine." Anna cleaned up the mess she'd made while her mom finished the crust and turned the roast. It had been cooking since early this morning, and the house smelled heavenly. Anna breathed in deeply as she stood at the sink, allowing the aromas and familiarity of home to soothe her frazzled nerves. Together she and Mom rolled and cut the biscuits, then made and tossed the salad.

"That was kind of you to invite Mr. Steiner's grandson to dinner," Mom ventured when they were nearly done and after Anna had managed to delicately slice both tomatoes and an avocado without any intent to harm.

"*Kindness* was my only motivation." Anna dropped a handful of thin-sliced radishes in the salad. "I was just doing what you and Dad would have—offering to feed someone in need."

"He didn't look too needy to me." Mom gave a low whistle and fanned a hand in front of her face. "Quite handsome, isn't he."

Anna pointed the paring knife in her hand in her mother's direction. "If you act like that tonight, or even insinuate that I have any interest at all in him, you will be short one dinner guest—me."

"No reason you shouldn't be interested." Mom crossed the kitchen to slide the pan of biscuits into the top oven. "You're single. He's single . . ."

Anna let out a frustrated breath and counted to ten. "You don't know whether he's single or not. We don't know anything about him."

"He wasn't wearing a wedding ring."

Anna stepped back from the island and held up her hands. "I'm done." *With a lot more than the salad.* She reached down to untie her apron.

"There are beans to be snapped." Mom handed Anna a bowl of fresh-picked green beans before she could sneak off to her room for a nap or a tranquilizer. She might need one to get through dinner tonight.

"I'll take them out on the porch." Anna grabbed a second bowl and set off toward the front of the house, away from her mother's meddling.

With the screen door closed behind her, Anna started for the porch swing, then thought the better of it and headed for one of the rockers instead. The last time she'd sat in the swing had been the night before she was to be married. She and Carson had sat there, holding hands and talking about their future.

She remembered feeling guilty that she hadn't given him an answer about her job yet. In true Carson fashion, he hadn't pressured her but had merely asked and then patiently waited until she was ready to give him an answer—much the same as when he'd asked her to marry him shortly before they'd both graduated with their bachelor's degrees.

Anna wondered now if his patience had anything to do with his own guilt. Just a few hours after he'd kissed her goodnight, Carson had eloped with Bree. He might not have planned that, but he'd clearly made a serious mistake months before. *And then a second, not telling me.*

And if Carson had told me . . . Anna wasn't sure what would have changed, except that she wouldn't have been humiliated in front of the entire town. She and Carson could have discreetly broken their engagement. She could have accepted the job in California, and all would have been well—or if not well, at least better than it was now.

She sat down hard on the nearest rocker and settled the bowl of beans in her lap. Absentmindedly she began snapping them, discarding the ends into the bowl near her feet.

How quickly her perfectly planned life had snapped in

two. And worse, the ends had come off as well. She couldn't go back to the beginning—home—and expect anything here to be the same for her. But going forward it felt like she'd come to a dead end.

Maybe it was time to look for a new job—something more challenging and rewarding. Possibly something in the Gulf. That would be closer to home, at least. Maybe after this trip she would be able to handle visiting a couple times a year. Maybe.

Snap. Snap. Snap.

The trouble was, she wasn't motivated. For all her passion for the ocean and its creatures, her work with both felt empty. Unfulfilling. It was, as if the day her heart had been broken, other pieces of her had broken too. She felt like she was in pieces. She'd been limping along numb at first, then half-functioning, but that wasn't going to work forever. What energy and enthusiasm she'd had left for life had waned.

Her sister and brother-in-law's minivan pulled into the driveway just as she finished the beans. *Just like Chelsea. Show up after the work is done.*

A pang of regret immediately followed the uncharitable thought. *What is* wrong *with me?* She hadn't seen her sister in nearly four years, and she felt grumpy with her already. *I really am turning into an old shrew.*

Anna set the bowl aside and ran down the front porch steps, pretending more enthusiasm than she felt. "Chels." She hugged her sister and received a hug in return.

"Hey, little sis." Chelsea stepped back and looked up at Anna. "So unfair that you're taller than me. And now it's not even fun to say that I'm older." She made a face.

The van doors slid open, and her four children piled out. The youngest clung to Chelsea's leg and peeked shyly at Anna. The middle one walked right past her, heading toward the house along with Chelsea's husband.

"Good to see you, Anna." He paused long enough to give her a sideways hug.

"You too, James." Anna smiled. She really did like her brother-in-law. He and Carson had always gotten along well. *Not that it matters now.*

Chelsea's oldest two, the twins, stopped long enough to give Anna awkward greetings as well. Anna could hardly believe the changes in them, from scrawny eight-year-olds when she'd left to gangly twelve-year-olds in the throes of puberty.

She pressed her lips together, trying not to smile as Tristan's voice cracked when he said hello.

With an arm still around her sister, Anna turned to follow the entourage into the house.

"You look good, sis." Chelsea's compliments had been few and far between growing up, so this one surprised Anna.

"Tell that to Mom. She's been on me about needing to gain weight since I got here."

"You can have some of mine," Chelsea offered. "Mom will probably ask me tonight how my diet is going, or how many times I made it to Jazzercise last week. She keeps telling me I need to take better care of myself. Honestly, most days I'm lucky to shower and brush my teeth. The kids are all so busy. Between football practices and games, dance lessons, piano and band, I feel like I live in the car."

"It sounds like you do," Anna said. "I'm sorry I can't relate." She went ahead of Chelsea and opened the door. The happy sounds of family wafted from inside.

"I'm sorry you can't relate too." Chelsea placed a hand on Anna's arm. "Thank you for coming home. Not just to watch the store, but for Mom and Dad. They've missed you and worried about you."

"I've missed them too. I wish this visit was truly that. I'll hardly get any time with them."

"Won't they be home the week before Christmas? We can all visit then."

Anna frowned. Her flight was scheduled for the twentieth, two days after her parents were supposed to return home. She couldn't stay for Christmas even if she wanted to. Twelve weeks was the max she'd been able to swing for family medical leave, and Kerry was going out of town a few days before Anna's return. There would be no one around to take care of her plants.

She would have to make sure her mother understood all of this before she and Dad left tomorrow.

Inside the house Mom took the bowl of snapped beans from Anna and returned to the kitchen. Dad had just awoken from his nap—little wonder, given the escalated noise level in the house.

"Girls, set the table please," Mom called from the kitchen.

"Just like old times." Chelsea grinned at Anna as they took their places at opposite ends of the table and pulled it open to add the leaf.

"Seriously," Anna said. "Where is that lazy brother of ours, anyway?"

"Right here." Someone banged on the front door. "Give me a hand, will you," Justin called.

Anna left Chelsea to fit the leaf into place and went to open the screen. Justin had a baby carrier in one hand and their three-year-old in the other.

"Where's Mia?" Anna asked, propping the door open for him.

"At home." Justin stepped inside. "Our newest munchkin doesn't believe in sleeping more than an hour at a time yet, and Mia's wiped out, so I suggested she stay home to nap."

"You look a little wiped out yourself," Anna noted. The dark circles beneath his eyes didn't look too dissimilar from their father's.

"Good to see you too." Justin held out the baby carrier, and Anna took it from him, then lifted the covering to peek inside.

An adorable cherub of a baby gave her a wide-eyed look from the bluest eyes Anna had ever seen. "She's gorgeous. Just like Cami." Anna waggled two fingers at her three-year-old niece and received a bashful grin in return before Cami buried her head in her dad's shoulder.

"She doesn't know you," Justin said, as if that wasn't obvious. "Give her some time to warm up."

"Of course." Feeling like an outsider amongst her own family, Anna lugged the baby carrier into the living room and put it down by her father. She wanted nothing more than to sit and hold her new little niece but felt somehow inadequate, since she'd been away for so long. With a yearning glance at the baby, she returned to the dining room to help Chelsea.

Together they spread her mother's favorite fall tablecloth across the long expanse of farm table. Chelsea removed plates from the buffet, while Anna took silverware from the drawer.

"Mom said you invited someone for dinner."

Here we go again. Thanks, Mom. Anna cast an irritated glance toward the kitchen. "Yes, but with Mia not here tonight, we're still only twelve."

"Where did you meet him? How long have you—"

"It's not like that," Anna interrupted, wanting to end this conversation before it went any farther. "He's Mr. Steiner's grandson. You remember the Steiners we used to deliver flowers to?"

"Mmhmm." Chelsea moved around the table, setting plates out.

"His grandson is in town. I invited him over because I was afraid he'd starve between last night and Monday when the market opens again. I think he expected more services in Holiday and wasn't very prepared when he arrived."

"So this is a pity invitation," Chelsea said, sounding skeptical.

"Not pity. Charity. There's a difference." Pity was the way people who knew what had happened on her wedding day looked at her now. "I don't feel sorry for him, nor did I ask him to come for any other reason—no matter what Mom said. I would have invited him if he was seventy years old, bald, and overweight. I was simply trying to be kind."

"Mmmhmm," Chelsea said again. "But he's not seventy years old, bald, and overweight. According to Mom, he's quite a dish."

"A *dish*? Seriously?" Anna rolled her eyes. "When did she even have time to talk to you about this? She saw him for two seconds at church."

"She sent me a text on the way home."

Anna shook her head, disgusted with her mother and dreading the coming meal. No pot roast, no pie, no biscuits could make up for the kind of harassment she feared was coming Elijah Steiner's way. He would have been better off fasting until Monday rather than facing her family.

"But is he?" Chelsea continued to pry, her voice rising above the sound of the mixer in the kitchen. "Good looking, I mean? Handsome? *A dish*?"

"I'm not sure. What do you think?"

Both girls whipped their heads around, staring at the very man in question. Elijah Steiner had removed the suit coat he'd been wearing at church, and his shirtsleeves were rolled up to the elbows, but he'd kept the tie. He held a bunch of wildflowers that looked like they'd just been picked, and a hint of amusement flickered in his eyes. Who had let him in? Anna hadn't heard a knock.

He turned sideways. "Here's my profile, so you can better decide."

"Mom's right. A definite dish." Chelsea stepped forward to greet him, but it was Anna whose horrified gaze he caught.

"I'm sorry," he apologized. "Eavesdropping wasn't very mannerly of me. The front screen was open, and I thought maybe that meant I was to just come on in. You know—Southern hospitality and all. Which, extends, apparently, to all—even the geriatric, balding, and obese." He smiled at her, clearly hoping for a laugh he didn't get—from Anna, at least.

Chelsea, however, turned on the charm, not only laughing at his joke but shaking his hand and introducing herself to Mr. Steiner—Eli, he preferred—and welcoming him to their home while Anna withdrew into herself, moving around the table in the opposite direction, placing silverware and glasses in their proper positions.

"I brought these for your mother. She likes flowers, doesn't she?"

"That's an understatement. She has her own florist shop." Chelsea took the flowers from him and set them in a vase on the sideboard that looked like it had been waiting specifically for his offering.

"Annabelle, aren't you going to greet *your* guest?" Chelsea's emphasis on the word your was almost enough to make Anna throw down the napkins and storm upstairs. Instead she mustered a smile and a few polite words without moving any closer to Elijah Steiner. "We're glad you could join us, Mr. Steiner. Holiday may not offer much in the way of amenities, but hopefully we can offer you a decent meal and an entertaining evening." *More entertainment than you bargained for.*

"It smells far better than decent." He sniffed the air appreciatively. "And I welcome the company. It's pretty quiet out at Gabriel's place."

It seemed odd that he referred to his great-grandfather

by his first name, but Anna wasn't about to question Eli about it.

"Come help me, girls," Mama called from the kitchen. "Everyone up to the table. Dinner's ready."

Chelsea's twins raced in, reached the same chair at once, and began fighting over it.

"Boys," Chelsea snapped. "Act your age."

"We are." They continued punching each other until James separated them.

Dad carried baby Sarah in, crying and flailing her hands. The other kids and Justin took their places. Chairs scraped against the wood floor. Benches filled. Anna set the mashed potatoes and salad on the table while her mother and sister made room for the other dishes.

In a matter of a few minutes everything and everyone was assembled, the remaining introductions were made, and the noise in the dining room had risen to a level where Anna could barely think. She took her seat across from Eli and looked up to find him watching the chaos with an expression of odd fascination. He caught her looking at him and smiled.

Anna shrugged. "Welcome to dinner at the Lawrence home."

Chapter 7

Eli took exactly three bites before the questions began, though they weren't directed at him as he'd half-expected, especially after overhearing the interesting conversation upon his arrival.

"Tell us about Seattle, Sis," Anna's brother Justin said as he added salt to a roast that Eli thought was the closest thing to perfection he'd ever tasted. Introductions had been hasty, but he'd paid attention as requests were made to pass things those first few, almost frantic minutes when everyone was trying to load up their plates. He thought he had most of the Lawrence family names down now.

"It's damp and very cold compared to Alabama. The ocean isn't like the gulf where everyone swims."

"And *you* live there? Miss Can-we-go-to-the-beach-today? What else does it have, then? Must be something great to make up for that." Justin broke a biscuit in half and began slathering it with butter.

"It's a big city. There are a lot of interesting museums and places to shop and things to see." Anna's voice wasn't quite convincing.

"A lot of good places to go on dates, you mean," her sister said and caught a warning look from Anna in return.

"Any prospects?" Justin asked. "No pun intended, though that was pretty good—prospectors, the gold rush, you know?"

"I'm aware of the area's history." Anna stabbed her salad in a way that made Eli wonder if she was wishing the tomato was her brother. "And no, no prospects. I don't date."

"Anyone? At all?" Her mother sounded appalled.

Anna set down her fork and took a deep breath. "I haven't had a date the entire time I've lived there, Mom. Are you satisfied now?"

"Of course not! What is satisfactory about hearing that my baby girl has no social life? Especially at this time, as you're approaching—"

"Enough, Mom." Anna sounded weary and looked like she was wishing she was back in dateless Seattle. Eli couldn't fathom why she didn't have a boyfriend or at least frequent dates. She was a beautiful woman, and from his grandfather's letters he knew there was a lot more to her than that. Bringing him some food from the store last night, after it was closed, and then inviting him to dinner seemed to prove his grandfather had been right about Anna's kindness.

"I just don't understand, Anna." Mrs. Lawrence had stopped eating as well and was staring at her daughter. "Don't you *want* to meet someone?"

"Not particularly, Mom."

Eli noticed Anna seemed to be doing her best to avoid looking across the table at him.

"I just want to be left alone. And it's really okay."

"Well, I'll be," her dad said, finally contributing to the conversation that had thus far been dominated by his wife and children. "Who'd have thought Miss Holiday, Alabama, three years running would go near four years without a single date?"

"Who'd have thought she'd be left at the altar?" Justin said around a bite of mashed potatoes.

Anna shot him a well-deserved, scathing look at the same time he jerked upright, as it appeared that Chelsea had kicked him under the table. Eli felt like kicking him too. If this was what having siblings was like, maybe he hadn't missed out on too much.

"That's quite enough," Anna's mother said.

Eli wished there was some way to draw everyone's attention away from Anna. He'd been worried about questions being directed at him—questions he didn't want to answer yet. But now he'd gladly take them if it meant Anna's family giving her a break. But it seemed they'd forgotten he was here at all, in their haste to interrogate their daughter and sister.

With a dignity that impressed him, Anna set her fork down once more and looked at each of her parents and her siblings in turn. "I haven't had any dates because of something I said my very first week at work and the misunderstanding that ensued."

At their curious expressions, she continued. "A coworker did ask me out, but I declined and told him I wasn't interested in dating men. I meant to say *then*, but somehow it came out *men*—probably a reflection of my mental state at the time. Sorry, Dad." She flashed him an apologetic smile.

"Next thing I knew, it had gone around the lab that I wasn't interested in members of the opposite sex. Which hasn't actually been all that terrible. I mostly work with men, and they all leave me alone now."

"Well, I'll be," her dad said again.

Beside him Justin turned red and started choking. He reached for his glass and gulped a long drink of water, coughing and spluttering when he'd finished, then finally looking up and bursting into laughter.

This seemed to be the signal for all others to follow suit and let loose, and pretty soon everyone at the table was busting up—even Anna, Eli was relieved to see.

He managed to catch her eye, and she shrugged again, as if to say, *This is the price of dinner—sorry.*

He wasn't sorry at all and, now that she seemed to be okay, decided this was the most delightful meal he'd had in a long time—and it was about more than the amazing food.

When the laughter died down Anna turned the tables on her brother. "What's with all the questions? Since when were you ever interested in my love life—or lack thereof? Did Mom put you up to this?"

"Yep," Justin freely admitted. "You know me, uncouth older brother, willing to do anything to get even with his little sister for all those times she spied on me when I was out on the front porch with a date."

James whistled. "Good thing Mia's not here to ask about those dates."

"No kidding," Chelsea said. "That porch swing has seen more action than make out point at the harbor."

"Not from me." Justin shook his head, doing a poor job of feigning innocence. "It was you girls who always kissed your dates on that swing. I was smarter than that and took my girlfriends elsewhere. Anna was the worst. I swear she and Carson—" He stopped abruptly, as if just realizing what he'd said. "I'm sorry, Sis. Prying into your life now is one thing, but bringing up the past wasn't my intention."

Eli waited one heartbeat, then two, along with everyone else in the total silence of the room. Even the baby had stopped crying.

"Can we please talk about something else now?" Anna asked quietly.

"If we must." Chelsea's shoulders sagged, and she sighed as if disappointed. "I had a list of follow-up questions. Mom said I'd get an extra piece of pie if I got you to answer at least half."

"Very funny," their mother said.

"You're not helping our cause to get your sister home more often," their father added.

Anna brought a hand to her forehead, as if it pained her. Now Eli understood why she'd had that exact same expression on her face as the plane landed. She'd probably been imagining this night.

"Here's the thing," Justin said. "So you were jilted. It was a big deal—three and a half, almost four years ago. There's been a lot of other news since. Even that year, once the hurricane hit, what happened to you at the church was all but forgotten."

"That's true," Mr. Lawrence said, jumping into the conversation again. "There was so much damage here, and with Breanna missing nearly three days, everyone focused on finding her, and then the massive cleanup aft—"

"Wait." Elbow on the table, Anna held a hand up. "What do you mean, Bree was missing?"

Anna's parents exchanged a quick glance before her mother spoke.

"She'd been alone when the storm hit. Carson was in Birmingham for work. It just about wiped out the home they were building, and it carried the boat Bree was staying on quite a distance upstream—before it sank."

"You never wanted us to talk about Breanna or Carson, or we would have told you," Chelsea said.

"But how was she missing—for *three* days?" Anna looked around the table expectantly until one of her sister's twins spoke up. "She got knocked in the head and nearly drowned or something. Then some creepy guy found her."

"Being old and poor is not synonymous with creepy," James said, shooting his son a look.

"It was Sonny who heard her calling for help and got her off the boat before it sank," Mr. Lawrence finished the story. "He had Bree at his place until her brothers found her."

"For *three* days?" Anna said, still sounding incredulous. "Doesn't he live in an old corn crib or something?"

"He did," Mrs. Lawrence said. "After Bree's rescue he came to live with Reverend Armstrong and then Breanna and

Carson after their house was finished. He was there until he died."

"A day into the search Carson came and asked for our help." Mr. Lawrence continued the story. "When they found the boat at the bottom of the river and then Breanna's phone with it, Carson was a mess. It seemed only a matter of time before they brought up her body."

Eli suppressed a shudder, imagining what that would have felt like, standing over the river, waiting for his wife's body to be recovered. He'd never been married, never had a wife to love and lose, but the thought alone was enough to convince him—not that he needed convincing—of both the merits of remaining single and the need to complete his business and get out of Holiday. Hurricane season had nearly passed, but it would come again, as it did every year for this part of the country. Chicago wasn't perfect and definitely had its problems, but he never had to worry about a tidal wave sweeping the city away.

Sorry, Gabriel. I just can't do it. I can't stay.

As he reached for another biscuit Eli stole a glance at Anna. She was the one looking upset at present, eyes squinted up, as if she was trying not to cry, face blotchy, fists curled around her silverware in a death grip.

"Bree was okay when they found her though?" Anna sounded genuinely upset.

Odd. If what Gabriel had written to him was true, then this Bree they were talking about was the one who'd eloped with Anna's fiancé. So why should Anna care what happened to her?

"Mostly okay," Justin said.

"Her arm was busted," one of the twins added. "I saw a picture later. The bone was all the way through the skin. It was wicked."

Anna's face turned the shade of her white napkin.

"Breanna is all right now," Mrs. Lawrence added hurriedly, as if she'd noticed Anna's pale complexion as well. "Her arm is almost as good as new. Acts up when we get a cold spell, is all."

"Anna, are you all right?" Chelsea touched Anna' hand.

"I'm fine." Anna shrugged her sister off and studied her plate as she pushed her potatoes around.

No good at lying, Eli noted with satisfaction. His job just became easier. Anna's initial reaction to his news would tell him a lot. Everything he needed to know, probably.

"We've been ignoring our guest," Mr. Lawrence said loudly, from the other end of the table, as if putting everyone on notice that the subject was now officially changing. "What brings you to Holiday, Mr. Steiner? I don't recall meeting you at your great-grandfather's funeral."

"You didn't." Eli grimaced inwardly, aware that he was likely about to get the same grilling Anna had. "I never met Gabriel, but he appointed me as executor of his estate. I'm a real estate attorney, so I have some experience."

"And how long will you be in town?" Mrs. Lawrence asked, a little too cheerfully.

Eli could guess where Anna's poor lying skills came from. Her mother's ulterior motives practically danced across the table.

"I'm not sure," Eli answered truthfully. "Aside from locating the benefactors, there are some things to sort through."

"I'm sure Anna could help you with that." Mrs. Lawrence beamed. "She knows your grandfather's house inside and out."

"Mama, I'm here to run the store—remember?" Anna's hands had ceased their viselike grip on her utensils in favor of shredding her napkin into a pile of little strips on top of her half-eaten dinner. She directed her attention to Eli. "My parents are leaving tomorrow, and I'm here to take care of the store while they are away."

Eli knew this already. It wasn't a coincidence he'd ended up here at the same time as Anna, or even that they'd been on the same flight. Though sitting next to her had been a surprise.

"You don't have to be at the store all day, *every* day," her mother said. "Helping Gabriel's great-grandson would be a kind thing to do."

Anna opened her mouth, as if about to argue, then paused and began again. "Of course," she said, agreeing far too easily to be convincing. She glanced at him once more. "I'll give you my number before you leave, and if you need anything, you're welcome to call."

Easier to agree than to argue. Eli held back a smile. "Thanks." He would definitely be calling Anna, and he had her number already. But he wouldn't be asking for help with the kind of sorting he had to do. Nor would he be asking her out on a date, as her mother was likely hinting at. It was too bad, really. Had he met Anna under other circumstances, he would have definitely been interested, but given what lay before them, pursuing her in any way was the last thing he should do.

"How unfortunate that you didn't know your great-grandfather," Chelsea said. "He was well-loved by everyone in Holiday—sort of the town's grandfather."

"It is regrettable," Eli said, truly wishing, as he had many times since receiving notice of his Gabriel's death, that he'd made the effort to get down here before the old man had died. "Gabriel's son, my grandfather, passed away several years ago. It was always my understanding that he and Gabriel had had a falling out. My grandfather left home in his late teens and never returned."

"The rift between them was never repaired." Mrs. Lawrence spoke as if she knew the story well.

"It wasn't," Eli confirmed. "Because of that, neither my father nor I ever met Gabriel. He and I did correspond through letters occasionally, though." It had been more than occasionally, and that correspondence had been mostly one-sided—from Gabriel to him—but Eli didn't see that mentioning any of that would help his cause.

"Will there be family inheriting the house, then?" Mrs. Lawrence asked. "It's such a lovely estate, and your great-grandparents always kept it up so well."

"I'm—not at liberty to say exactly what will become of it." Eli tried to look apologetic. How simple his task might be if he'd only say what the true purpose of his visit was, and say it here, now, with all of Anna's family around. *To bully her into accepting.* Tempting as the idea was, he dismissed it at once. Given the way they'd poked their noses into her other business tonight, he could only imagine how they would pounce on his news. She would be surrounded, ganged up on, he was certain. And while it might yield the outcome he desired, it wouldn't necessarily be to her benefit.

He was surprised to discover that he cared about her benefit. This woman had been through a lot already. He didn't want to make her life worse; yet presented wrong, he felt his news had the potential to do just that.

Timing is everything, his mother would say—usually when she was referencing approaching his father about something. Eli wasn't certain how waiting a few days or even a week might alter Anna's perception of the situation, but he felt the need to wait, all the same. She deserved a few days at least to get her feet under her again.

Chelsea fired another question at him, about his life in Chicago, and Eli gladly steered the topic away from Holiday and his late great-grandfather. Anna joined in, and soon they were comparing Seattle and Chicago, discussing the merits and inconveniences of each. For a big-city dweller, she hadn't gotten out much. But it did seem that Anna, and every member of her family, knew every square inch of Holiday. Soon the conversation turned local again, and Eli found himself bombarded with things he must attempt to see and do during his visit.

They weren't exciting things—he'd never tried bird watching, or tasted world-famous chili in a chili cook off, or entered a pumpkin in a carving contest. He wasn't much of a fisherman and didn't have any interest in floating the postal route with the local mail carrier. But there was a certain charm to their suggestions, all the same.

After the table had been cleared—a task with which he helped—and the dishwasher loaded, the pecan pie he'd been smelling all through dinner came out, along with a slew of board games from the cabinet in the family room. After a brief scuffle between siblings and their offspring, about which game would be played, he and Anna were directed to choose.

"Suggestions?" Eli asked, his hope of enjoying a slice of pie and making a quick exit fleeing as quickly as the setting sun.

Anna surveyed the beat-up boxes piled on the table, then reached for a pack of cards. "Spoons. We'll see how good your reflexes are, Mr. Steiner."

A challenge? It didn't escape him that she was keeping things between them formal. He guessed her "mistake" about not dating men wasn't a mistake at all—on some level, at least. His brows rose. "Fast, Miss Lawrence. At times my profession requires me to be quick on my feet."

"We'll see." Anna hummed as she shuffled the cards and dealt four to each space around the table. Justin put the other games away, and the adults and older kids each took a chair at the table. Mrs. Lawrence served the pie, topping each piece with a generous serving of fresh whipped cream.

One bite, and Eli was certain he'd discovered heaven. His

eyes closed in bliss as his mouth savored the cream and caramelized pecans. He knew the nuts had come from the Lawrences' tree out back, but did they have their own cow as well? The whipped cream was something else. He'd never tasted anything quite so delicious.

"Better eat quick," Anna admonished. "You get distracted like that and you'll lose for sure."

"This is worth losing for." Eli slid the fork into his mouth again as Anna gave the first command to pass.

It couldn't have been more than three seconds later that spoons were being grabbed and hands slapped as shouting ensued. Chelsea actually climbed up on the table, making a desperate grab to snatch one of the spoons from her son before he could tuck it safely away. Eli got to the one between him and Anna a second too late but managed to steal the one nearest her father.

"Who shuffled those cards?" James demanded once the laughter and accusations had died down. Justin was out—a good thing, he said, as his daughter's diaper needed to be changed, and he had to head home anyway so Mia could nurse the baby.

One of Chelsea's twins held up a hand with a mean scratch. "Thanks, Mom."

"Every man for himself," Chelsea said. "If you're gonna play with the big kids . . ."

They played another two rounds before Eli was out. He'd finished his pie by then and, while he wanted another slice, didn't think it polite to ask for one—if there was even any left. More than one member of the family had drifted into the kitchen and returned, munching on something.

It was the perfect time to excuse himself, yet he found he was loathe to go, now that it came down to it. Instead of leaving, he leaned back in his chair and watched a fiercely competitive Anna beat out everyone at the table, including her sister with the claws.

"Victory dance," Chelsea shouted, and Anna jumped up from her chair and began swinging her hips as she moved around the table to her family's chant of, "Winner. Winner. Guess who gets to clean up dinner?"

"*Not,* Anna," her father said, shutting the others down. "Not tonight. I have some things I need to talk to her about."

He beckoned Anna to join him on the back patio. Without so much as a backward glance at Eli, she headed outside with her father.

Well, then. He'd been considering talking to her tonight after all—in private, of course. But it seemed like that was off the table now. *Probably better.* His initial feeling that he needed to give her at least a few days in Holiday first was probably right. As was her having some time with her dad before he left.

Eli helped clear the table a second time and was handed a bag of leftovers as a reward.

"Thank you so much for coming. You remember to call Anna if you need anything," Mrs. Lawrence said as she walked him to the door. "Her number is on a sticky note inside the bag."

Covering her bases—or her daughter's, anyway. "I will," Eli said with a wave. He did need something from Anna. He really hoped it wasn't too much. A simple yes and a signature, and he'd be on his way.

Chapter 8

"It's been a long time since I had a Sunday stroll with you, Dad." With Anna's arm behind him, and his linked behind her back as well, they walked the path of brick pavers that followed the perimeter of the large yard and her mother's garden. "I remember you being a lot taller."

"And I remember you were prone to stepping on my foot frequently." Dad chuckled at the memory. "I can't remember what all those strolls were about anymore, what brand of mischief you'd caused to earn yourself a lecture."

"Playing at the river with Carson and Bree—before I even knew how to swim, then when I did know, going swimming alone without telling anyone. And the worst offense of all—"

"Driving yourself to Fairhope to go snorkeling alone." Dad nodded his head. "It's all coming back to me now. "My mermaid—I mean daughter—who thought life was better under the sea."

"It was." Anna sighed, remembering happier days when a dive made her feel like she was on top of the world instead of far below the surface.

"So how'd a girl like you end up in a town without a good beach?"

"Puget Sound is beautiful, Dad. You've seen it. And there *are* places to swim. It's just chilly. But there are plenty of species to study there."

"It is all those things," he agreed. "But is it the place for you, for my Annabelle? Is it fulfilling your dreams?"

She didn't answer, but guessed her dad would take that as answer enough. "I never intended to end up in Seattle. It just—happened. I needed to get far away from here, and it was about as far away as I could drive. It hasn't been an awful place to land."

"Nor does it seem to have been particularly great for you—*not dating men*." Dad snorted.

"I think it's kind of funny. Justin was right to laugh." *That's my life. A comedy of errors.* "You didn't bring me out here to talk about that. What's up? What's worrying you?" *Aside from your cancer and the treatment you're about to begin.*

Dad steered her toward one of the brightly painted benches nestled between flowerbeds. They sat side by side, and he placed his hand on his thigh, palm up. Anna placed hers in it, noting her father's hand wasn't as big as she remembered either. Though she knew it was a misperception—the size difference had to do with her growing up and nothing else—it still felt unsettling. Her giant of a father wasn't as giant as she remembered. And worse, he was sick.

"You think you can handle things here while Mom and I are away?"

"Of course," Anna said. "It's like riding a bike. Being at the Mulberry the other night felt as familiar as climbing into my old canopy bed. Not a lot has changed. I'll manage it well. I promise."

"It's not the store I'm concerned about. It's you I'm worried for."

"Me?" Anna turned her head to look at him. "Why? I'm fine."

"Are you?" Dad asked. "Truly? Is that why you almost cried tonight when we were talking about your best friend?"

"Bree's not my best friend. Not anymore." *I don't have one.* Anna hadn't exactly advertised for the position to be filled, either. Having had her best friends her entire life, she'd felt a bit baffled as to how one went about—as an adult in an unfamiliar city—making a new one. And even if she'd had that figured out, she wasn't certain she would have followed through with it anyway. Bigger than the issue of making a friend was the problem of *trusting* one. With two of the people she'd trusted the most having betrayed her, she wasn't sure how she could ever completely trust anyone—other than her family—again.

"You and Bree may have fallen out of contact," Dad said, giving Anna a pointed look of his own. "But you were upset when you heard about her misfortune."

With her free hand, Anna waved his accusation away. "I was surprised, that's all." Why *had* she been upset, anyway? She'd seen Bree at church today, so obviously she'd survived the ordeal. *But her baby...* "Did she—did the accident on the boat cause her to lose her baby?" Had Carson married her to do the right thing and then ended up not needing to do it after all? Not that it would have changed anything. *They still betrayed me.* If it ended poorly for them . . . *Why should I care?* Except she did. For some perverse reason Anna couldn't decipher.

"Breanna lost the baby before the accident." Dad gave Anna's hand a gentle squeeze. "She almost died from it. And then almost died again in the hurricane. If you can imagine..."

Anna didn't want to imagine either scenario, but she couldn't ignore the thud of her heart and the feeling of panic that swept over her at the thought of Bree almost dying— twice. What if she had died, and they'd never spoken again? *What if she died without knowing I forgave her?*

Wait. What? Anna slammed on the mental breaks, not at all liking the direction her thoughts were headed.

I haven't forgiven her. I don't want to forgive either of them.

Dad nodded his head, as if he were following Anna's brain waves. "Yep. There's your problem. Bree *is* still your friend—or you'd like her to be. But in order for that to happen, you have to forgive her first. And you're not certain how to do that when you're still hurting so much."

Anna opened her mouth to refute his ridiculous claims, but found she couldn't argue with the truth. She shook her head and looked away, staring dismally at the garden where she and Bree—and Carson—had spent so many delightful hours. "Maybe you ought to consider a second career to supplement your retirement. You could call it 'Dad's mind-reading therapy—spill your guts without saying a word.'"

"Nah." Dad grinned. "Therapists help people solve their problems. I just point the trouble out to my kids. None of you need therapy. You're all perfectly capable of figuring out the solutions on your own."

Anna leaned her head back, staring up at the cloudless sky. "Well, I'd sure appreciate any tips you have for this one. It seems pretty insurmountable right now."

"Step one," Dad said. "Come home and face your past. Step two—pray. Step three—listen to, and follow, your heart."

"Steps four through ten?" she asked, still waiting for something that sounded like it might actually help.

"This one's just a three-stepper," Dad said. "Cut and dried. And you're already a third done. You're here. You're facing your past, and it seems your heart is speaking to you. You just need to listen to what it's saying and pray to know what to do about it."

The simple faith of a child. Except her dad was sixty-four years old.

"Weren't *you* angry or hurt or embarrassed when Carson eloped with Bree and left me to face everyone alone at the church?" Didn't Dad love her enough to have been upset too? Had he ever wished them ill the way she had? Anna expected her dad to stick up for her, to protect her and take care of the people who hurt her—by hurting them. Or, at the least, by not allowing them anywhere near her or into their lives anymore. Instead, she'd come home to find that he'd hired Bree and Carson and expected her to work with them.

"I was all of those things, especially angry, for a good, long time." Dad let go of her hand and wrapped his arm around her shoulder, pulling Anna close. "They hurt my baby girl. Believe me, I wanted to wring Carson's neck. My only comfort, initially, was that I believed Reginald or his boys would take care of that before I could."

"And did they?" Anna sniffed. Her eyes and nose burned from the constant effort of trying to contain tears.

"No, actually. Reggie surprised us all. He got his act together and started behaving like the man he used to be. Instead of being angry at Breanna or Carson, Reggie felt a good deal of the blame was upon him, for not being the father Breanna needed."

"She was more of a parent than anyone in that house for a good, long time." Anna frowned, thinking of all that Bree had missed out on during their high school and college years—what should have been some of the happiest times of her life.

"That's neither here nor there now," Dad said. "Nothing that's in the past is. What matters is what you do with the time you have here, in the present. *Twelve weeks*, Anna." He turned toward her. "What a gift."

"What do you mean?" She'd seen this trip as anything but a gift. An obligation. A burden. A dread.

"For the next twelve weeks you have the unique opportunity to step away from your current life, examine your past one, and figure out what you want your future to look like. Not many people are able to do something like that, to leave their work and current surroundings so they can examine things from a different perspective."

Anna considered his words. She hadn't thought of this

trip like that at all, but rather as a painful confrontation with all that had gone wrong in her life and the people who had caused those wrongs. She'd been focused on survival. *Keep my head down. Keep to myself.* Her mantra for life in Seattle and now back in Holiday.

I didn't used to be that person. How many times had she sat on this bench with Dad before, hearing a lecture about how leaping before looking—both literally and figuratively—was a dangerous way to live. She'd been that fearless girl. Whether racing down a dock to jump off and plunge into the water below or applying for a two-month, sea-going internship without knowing the details—and finding out too late that they involved testing with sharks. She'd been outgoing and daring. She'd spoken up for others and been friends with everyone and anyone around her.

And now . . . She couldn't even speak up for herself because she didn't know what she was supposed to say, or what she wanted to say, or do. She was about as useful as plankton, floating on the surface of the water, waiting for some whale to come gobble her up.

"Can you do that for me?" Dad asked.

"Do what?" Had she missed something? What had he asked?

"Can you take a long, honest look at your current life and really think about your future?" His gaze was intense, serious. "I'm asking you to dust off your old dreams—or to create brand new ones. Either way, you've got to find some purpose in your life, Anna. All this drifting isn't good. You've been a floater long enough. It's time to be a swimmer again, and a strong one, at that."

He was right, of course. *Darn it.* Drifting, while not necessarily enjoyable, had proven safe these past few years. Nothing felt that way now. The bandage had come off, and she had to figure out how to stop the bleeding permanently and get her life working again.

"It's not any more than I'm asking myself," Dad added. Anna met his gaze.

"This stupid cancer—" He bent and picked up a fallen pecan from the ground beneath their tree "—has invaded a part of my body that is roughly the size of this nut."

"Actually, I think the prostate is about the size of a walnut," Anna said. "Still small, but—"

"—A nut's a nut," Dad grumbled. "Especially a bad one." He tossed the pecan over his shoulder. "The point is, there's this one little part of me that's threatening everything else—all the good in my body, in my life. But I'm going to beat it. I'm going to eradicate the cancer and take my life back. You need to do the same. This one thing that happened—which was larger than a nut, I'll give you that—is poisoning the rest of you. It's destroying all that was beautiful and happy and joyful in your life. It's taken my Annabelle away and turned her into someone I hardly know. I miss the girl who used to leap before she looked."

"When I did look, when I bet my future on what I thought was as sure and solid a guy as they come, I got soaked."

"Drenched," Dad agreed. "But you've had plenty of time to dry off now. So no more letting that experience dampen your spirit and everything else in your life. It's time to take some chances and start living again, to have friends and be a friend, to tell that injured heart of yours that you're done letting it rule your life."

"I'm done," Anna said, half-heartedly, not convincing anyone, especially herself.

Dad shook his head. "That won't do. What if I approach my cancer that way?"

"That's not fair," Anna said. "It's entirely different."

"Is it?" Dad's brows rose as he stood and pulled her up beside him. "There are all kinds of cancers. They all do the same thing—eat people up inside. What happened to you has become as toxic as a physical cancer. But unlike my disease, yours can be eradicated without months of painful treatments. You get to keep your hair," he added, joking.

"Oh, Dad." Anna wrapped her arms around his waist and held onto him. She loved him so much. Why had she stayed away so long? What if he didn't get well?

He returned her hug. "I love my girl, and I don't want her hurting anymore. You've gone through enough pain already."

"I know." The tears she'd been holding in all night wet the front of his shirt.

"I need you to get better for me—*with* me," Dad insisted. "I want that promise, or I'm not going tomorrow. I'll stay here and fight your fight with you if that's what it takes."

She shook her head and leaned back, looking up at him. "I've got this one, Dad. I'm still a strong swimmer. Just a bit out of practice."

He smiled. "That's my girl."

Chapter 9

October

"BE SAFE. GET better..." Anna kept her hand raised in farewell until her parents' car turned the corner at the end of the street and disappeared from sight. She lowered her hand and wrapped both arms around herself, to ward off a chill that wasn't present this morning but she felt nonetheless.

Alone at last. Given first her father's garden-stroll talk and then her mother's late-night chat, Anna supposed she ought to feel relieved they had gone. But the reason for their trip weighed heavily. The next time she saw her father he would be bald and likely a lot sicker than he seemed now.

If the treatment doesn't kill me . . . He'd joked about it, but deep down they all sensed this was no joking matter. He'd engaged in a life-or-death battle. *It's his to win.* "It's ours." She remembered the promise she'd given him and vowed that today would be good. If he could battle cancer, she could fight to find her happiness and purpose again.

Neither Carson nor Bree were on the schedule today, so she could look forward to a day free from that stress, at least. But Mondays at the Mulberry were always crazy, with all the deliveries first thing in the morning. Anna returned to the house, grabbed a piece of toast for the road, then headed out to the Excursion. If nothing else, today promised to be full.

Sunshine poured through the south-facing front windows as Anna lifted the blinds. She readied the till with the small amount of bills and coins she'd gathered from the safe in the back of the store.

She turned on the sound system and found it tuned to her mother's favorite bluegrass. Instead of changing the station, as she had often when she was younger, Anna smiled at the familiar sounds of banjo and mandolin. "I must be getting old."

The music soothed her, as did all else about the Mulberry, and for a few seconds she felt almost giddy at the thought that it was hers to run for the next twelve weeks, the best twelve weeks of the year in many ways, as Mom had reminded her last night.

The last of the autumn harvest would be coming in, and it would be up to Anna to sell what she could and deliver or preserve the rest, so none went to waste. Corn, apples, peaches, pears, beans, pumpkins, squash, cucumbers. She might not be a great cook with everyday things, but she'd grown up canning produce and—in an odd sort of way—relished tackling such a task again.

Then there was the pumpkin-carving contest to organize, along with soliciting pies for the pie-eating and chili for the cook off. Her parents weren't in charge of all of it, but a great deal depended upon them and the Mulberry's generosity.

After Halloween there would be turkeys to order and deliver, yams and sweet potatoes to find. In December her mother's flower shop would be full of fir branches to be made into fresh wreaths, and poinsettias to deliver.

So many things to order. So many balls not *to drop.* Anna pulled out an apron with the deep red mulberry logo on it and slipped it over her head. She went to the candy counter, opened the jar of lemon drops, took one out, and popped it in her mouth, savoring the sweet-and-sour combination, but determined that sweet would win the day.

The egg delivery arrived first, just a few minutes after

seven. Anna hauled last week's empty cartons out to the truck, while the delivery boy from Keplar Farms dropped off the full ones.

Anna felt a moment of dismay as she stared at the cartons stacked carefully on a low shelf on the left side of the store. "No cooler. Right." How had she forgotten that? She remembered thinking it so strange, once she'd left Holiday, that eggs elsewhere in the U.S. were kept in refrigerated sections of the grocery stores. But then, a lot of things about other grocery stores were unusual to her. Produce was rarely fresh. Bread was often stale. Most food was processed and packaged. "Not so at the Mulberry." She smiled, feeling a new pride in her parents' store. Their business was unique and useful and served the citizens of Holiday and beyond.

How sad for most of the United States, that it would never have the opportunity to shop here.

The milk, cream, and butter arrived next, and *was* stored in a cooler. Bread and other baked goods sold trickled in over the next hour, from various suppliers, as did the produce. Anna filled out order forms for each vendor and made sure to send those, so there would be no delay in the supply.

By eight o'clock the shelves were stocked she'd unlocked the doors and flipped the sign to open, and business was brisk, with more than twenty people milling about the crowded space. Anna couldn't remember if that was usual or not. Nearly everyone who'd come in had come to the counter to visit with her first, and several of their purchases didn't seem like particularly pressing items—not enough to draw a body to the market first thing Monday morning. But she chatted with them all, remembering the old adage on her mother's kitchen towels: *Be pretty if you can, witty if you must, but be gracious if it kills you.*

To Anna's surprise it wasn't killing her at all. In fact, she found herself enjoying seeing familiar faces and hearing about the goings on in Holiday the past few years during her absence.

The first swivel stool protested loudly as Ernie Jensen settled on it. Anna left the register and hurried over to the soda fountain.

"Your usual, Ernie?" She smiled at him, glad to see that the town Santa was alive and well and still larger than life. She'd always had a soft spot for Ernie, and he for her—or so she imagined.

The Christmas she was eight years old, and really too old to still believe in Santa—or so Chelsea had told her—Anna had asked for something only he could bring. She'd done it as a sort of test. Ernie wasn't really Santa, after all. Why would Santa work at the gas station in town when he had the entire North Pole to run? Anna remembered going back and forth, up and down on the belief scale. Was there really a Santa or not? If so, could it possibly be Ernie?

The night of the Christmas party at the community center, Santa—aka Ernie—sat on the stage, in one of the old, ornate dining room chairs from the Steiners' house. A fresh coat of gold leaf had been applied to the arms, and a new, red velvet cushion adorned the seat. Anna had watched Carson's mother sew it the previous week.

The little kids were all lined up to see him, while the older ones, the kids her age, hung around the stairs, whispering amongst themselves and acting cool because they knew the real story, that there was no Santa. When five-year-old Miles Tucker climbed up onto Santa's lap, some of the bigger boys thought it would be fun to ruin things for him and all the rest of the little kids within earshot.

"There is no Santa! He's a fake," had echoed from the group around her. Anna couldn't remember who'd said it first, but she remembered wishing Carson was with her to beat them up. But he and his brother were missing the party that year because they'd gone to visit their grandmother.

"That's not true," Anna had shouted, then jumped up on the stage. "He's real, and he's right there." She pointed to Ernie.

"Prove it," one of kids had shouted.

"She can't," another yelled.

"Oh yes, I can," Anna said. "I just have to ask him for something only he can get for me."

Thinking of her bold statement now, as she filled a mug with hot cocoa and topped it with whipped cream, Anna wondered if Ernie hadn't blanched a little at her request.

She'd asked him for something she truly wanted more than anything—her dog Cooper returned to her alive and well. He'd been missing for over two weeks, and her parents had just told her the night before that she needed to get used to the idea that he probably wasn't going to be coming home. He'd dug out under the fence again, and this time he'd likely met with trouble.

Anna remembered kneeling by her bed, pouring her heart out and begging God to keep Cooper safe and bring him home. But this time her prayers weren't being answered. She didn't understand why. But if God couldn't help, maybe Santa could.

So with a child's hope and faith she'd asked Ernie, confident that at least she would know, one way or another, whether or not Santa was real. At most, she would have her beloved, and naughty, Cooper back.

Christmas morning she'd awoken early, to the sounds of knocking—and barking. Anna remembered racing down the stairs, her siblings and parents close behind. She'd pulled the front door open, and Cooper, fluffy and clean and wearing a bright red bow, had jumped into her arms. Justin and Chelsea had joined her, hugging him and exclaiming over the

Christmas miracle that it was. He'd been gone more than a month by then, and it seemed only a miracle could have returned him to them.

For months after that, Anna bragged about Cooper's return and Ernie to everyone, and she'd used any excuse she could think of to go over to the gas station and say hi to him.

Now it seemed he'd come to say hello to her—and to have his usual morning treats. The holidays were approaching, after all. And he had a figure to maintain.

Anna set the steaming cocoa on the counter, then went to the covered cake platter to retrieve an apricot Danish, one of Maryanne Metford's specialties. Her weekly sales of baked goods to the Mulberry kept Mary and her spinster sister afloat financially, at least as far as groceries went. The home they lived in had long been paid for, and Anna was pretty sure the Holiday benevolence fund covered their utility bill. What she wasn't quite sure of was where the town's benevolence fund got its money. Something else she intended to look into while she was here.

Ernie stood and leaned his large belly over the soda counter, reaching for the whipped cream Anna had intentionally left out. "Has everyone caught you up on all the news 'round here?"

"I think so," Anna said. "Nothing much exciting seems to have happened in my absence, not like the year Santa brought my dog home." Just thinking of it made her a little teary. Cooper had died when she was in high school, and Anna wished she could have another miracle again. A dog to hug and love might do her a lot of good.

Ernie flushed red but couldn't hide his pleased smile. "Still remember that, do you?"

Anna nodded. "Always." She moved closer to whisper, "It was the best Christmas I've ever had—thanks to you."

"Aw shucks." Ernie grinned. "I suppose I ought to try and top that this year. You got another impossible wish for me?"

"Nothing's impossible for Santa," Anna said, quoting her eight-year-old self. She propped her elbows on the counter and studied Ernie. "How *did* you ever come to find Cooper?"

"Santa never reveals his secrets." He winked. "Though let's just say that dog of yours wandered a lot farther than anyone could have imagined. I placed flyers in every town between here and Fairhope, and he'd almost gone that far."

Anna placed her hand over Ernie's and gave a gentle squeeze. "You really are Santa."

His cheeks reddened, but a pleased smile curved lips mostly hidden by his white beard—and whipped cream. "Maybe, but nothing exciting like that has happened around here for a long time. Just the usual shenanigans."

"Most of which are attributable to the current generation of teenagers milling about?" Anna straightened and began wiping crumbs from the counter. Holiday could be tough for teens looking for excitement. She'd been plenty restless herself, heading out of town to the beach whenever possible.

"That's about right," Ernie said. "I suppose you heard about the stunt Blane and Evan Wagner pulled while Reggie was on his honeymoon?"

"*Reggie Wagner* remarried?" Anna stopped wiping the counter to stare down Ernie, in case he was pulling her leg.

"Near two years ago. To a pretty little gal. She's been good for him."

"I hope he's been good to her," Anna said, recalling the years of neglect Bree had suffered after her mother's death.

"He don't have no choice but to be, smitten as he is. He'd do anything for that gal." Ernie launched into the story of how Blane and Evan captured a live raccoon and had it at the house, awaiting their new stepmother's arrival. There were so many other, dead, stuffed things in the house that the sleeping raccoon wasn't noticed at first.

"They'd fed it Nyquil," Ernie explained and bobbed his head along to Anna's horrified gasp.

"You can guess how things went down when it awoke. Those boys were lucky no one got rabies. But such a ruckus you've never seen or heard. That whole house was darn near destroyed. And the new Mrs., she was having none of it. She ordered a dumpster and had the whole place emptied within a week. Not a single head mounted on the wall in there now."

"That's—astonishing." Anna giggled a little, picturing the scene. She could imagine the mayhem, given the usual amount of clutter and chaos at the Wagners', including the deer heads from which boys' boxers were frequently found hanging. "That is some news. Best I've heard since I came home." It was about time those boys had someone to take them in hand.

Ernie blushed again, then bit into his Danish with gusto. "It's good to have you here, Miss Anna. We've all sure missed you."

"I've missed you too, Ernie," Anna said and found it true.

Chapter 10

AFTER THE GAS station opened and he filled up the obnoxious truck he'd rented from the extremely shady rental company, Eli drove down Main Street and parked in front of the Mulberry Market. It was eleven in the morning, and he hoped Anna was having a good day. He hoped what he needed to eventually tell her would make her visit better and not worse.

The diner down the street looked like it offered decent fare, so Eli decided he'd ask her out to lunch. That would both check the box on her mother's expectation that he take Anna out on a date—which, for some odd reason he now felt compelled to fulfill—and it would hopefully provide him a better glimpse into her mindset about Holiday. It definitely hadn't been good on the plane, but perhaps that was starting to shift in his favor a bit.

But first he had some grocery shopping to do. Last night's leftovers had been breakfast, and he'd eaten his way through Anna's simple offerings before he'd even gone to dinner at the Lawrences'.

What he really wanted was a large combo pizza and some sub sandwiches to stock his great-grandfather's fridge, but for now he'd settle for a few staples to get him through the rest of the week. If all went well, he should have no problem wrapping everything up by Friday and heading home.

The drive to Chicago would take a little more than fourteen hours in the truck, putting him home in plenty of time to return to work on Monday. *So far so good.*

Eli pulled open the door and stepped inside, beneath the tinkling bell overhead. In the few seconds it took for his eyes to adjust to the dimmer light, he experienced the phenomenon of having traveled back in time a good hundred years or so. He stopped just inside, staring, open-mouthed at the wood stove front and center, the tall barrels surrounding it, the long, wood candy counter and soda fountain, and the floor-to-ceiling shelves that held home-canned produce, similar to the jars Anna had given him Saturday night.

A half-dozen people milled about, dressed—thankfully—in jeans and shirts appropriate for this century, if not quite the right decade. Eli glanced around for a shopping cart but didn't see any, not that there would have been room to maneuver one in the crowded space. The only baskets he could find were those in a heap by the door, an odd assortment of actual wicker variety in every shape and size. A sign above the pile advised shoppers to take one or a bag—all canvas, of course—for convenience.

Eli grabbed one of the mid-sized baskets and instantly felt like a kid about to hunt Easter eggs.

Eggs. Definitely. He searched the store for a cooler section and found only one in the far corner. This yielded a fair selection of dairy products, but nothing more.

"Can I help you find something?"

"My way home," Eli suggested, turning to Anna, standing beside him, looking as quaint and adorable as the market in a Mulberry apron and with her hair in a bun. The only thing missing was a floor-length dress beneath. "I feel like I've been transported back in time."

"You have." Anna's smile was warm. It appeared she wasn't offended by his comment. "My parents refuse to embrace the twenty-first century in favor of the way things have been done forever."

"I have to say, my mind is kind of blown by this place." Eli brought a hand to his head and pulled it away, his palm open. "Where do you get all of—this?" He pointed to the jars of preserves, the baskets of fresh breads, the boxes of produce, the barrels of . . . whatever the barrels held.

"Nearly everything in the store is sourced locally. Seventy-five percent of our products are from Alabama, with another ten from neighboring states like Georgia. Fifteen percent come from elsewhere—things we just can't grow or produce here, like avocado and pineapple. My mother has a greenhouse, and she's really tried, but she couldn't grow enough to supply even our little population."

"Still, seventy-five percent local. That's really impressive." Eli studied the shelves, wondering how many products they were talking about. "You're onto something here, you know. The rest of the country has no idea where most of its food comes from, and everything else— things we don't eat—comes from China."

"We're fortunate to have a pretty tropical climate and a long growing season," Anna said. "But you'll also notice we don't have a lot of things regular grocery chains do. You won't find many canned or packaged foods. And sometimes we run out of things, if our suppliers have a problem or a poor crop."

"Sounds like a risky business and a hard way to make a living." Yet, having been to the Lawrences' house, he'd seen that they did at least fairly well for themselves.

"I know, right." Anna's hands went to her hips as she looked around the store. "Honestly, I don't know how my parents do it. Aside from a really slim margin of profit on most everything, they also give away a lot of food. It doesn't add up to any kind of sustainable business model I've ever seen."

"Hmm. A mystery then." Maybe the Lawrences weren't doing so well financially. Maybe they had other troubles in addition to her father's cancer. *Maybe my news will be a much-needed blessing.* And who could be more deserving than the family that fed the town?

"So, what's on your list today?" Anna rocked back on her

heels. "You chose a good time to come in. Most everything is delivered fresh Monday mornings."

"I don't actually have a list, but the basics would be good—milk and bread, eggs, cheese, stuff for a salad. Oh, and a steak, maybe. And some potatoes. Can you help with all that?"

"Easy." She snapped her fingers. "May I?" She reached for his basket.

"Sure." He handed it to her, glad to be relieved of it, not really being much of a basket-toting kind of guy.

Anna led him to one of the barrels first, where she directed him to choose the potatoes he wanted. Eli chose two large bakers. One probably would have been enough, but he'd have another for lunch later in the week.

Next she had him choose which bread he wanted.

"Hmm . . . All of them?" Eli asked, his mouth starting to water just looking at the beautiful artisan loaves. "How many people bake for you?"

"We have fifteen different suppliers for bread and other baked goods," Anna said. "And sometimes it doesn't seem that's enough."

"I can see why. They all look delicious." Eli settled for trying two different loaves and some muffins. He could always come back later in the week or on his way out of town.

"They'll be even better with this jam. Trust me." Anna pulled a jar off the shelf and placed it in the basket.

Dairy came next. She handed him a glass bottle of milk, then added tins of butter and cheese to the quickly-filling basket. "I forgot to mention that we recycle everything. If you'll promise to bring your jars and bottles and tins back, then I don't have to charge you extra for them."

"No problem," Eli said, feeling more and more confident that his news was going to be well received and that stopping by the store later in the week wouldn't be a problem. The cheerful woman assisting him right now seemed vastly different from the one he'd met on the plane or even the one he'd sat across the table from at dinner last night. Anna acted right at home in the Mulberry, and playing shopkeeper seemed to suit her.

She excused herself for a few minutes to ring up the other customers. It appeared that only one other person, a rather elderly lady, was working, and her extents of usefulness seemed pretty narrow. Currently she was rolling a skein of yarn into a ball, at a rate guaranteed to take the task a good week to accomplish.

A few other customers entered the store as Anna rang up the others, but Eli was pleased when she returned to him instead of offering to assist the newcomers milling about.

"Thanks for waiting," she said. "I don't remember it being this busy Monday mornings, but I suppose it's a good thing."

Of course it was busier today. It wasn't difficult to see that Anna was the main attraction here and likely throughout the town. He'd watched her similarly mobbed at church yesterday. *All good signs.* She had a history here, and people liked her.

"I'd better get some eggs before they're all gone." He turned a circle, looking for another cooler.

"Over here," Anna said, leading him to a set of shelves.

Eli stared at the racks of room-temperature eggs. "Is that safe?"

She laughed. "That was my question the first time I saw eggs refrigerated. I assure you, these are fine."

They moved onto produce next, and as Anna filled his basket she told him a bit about each thing she added—where it had come from and the family that grew it.

"Meat is over here," Anna said, looking back at him.

"Follow me, and we'll get you that steak." She turned away again, then stopped so abruptly that Eli bumped into her.

"Sorry." They both spoke at the same time, but it took only a second for Eli to realize she wasn't talking to him.

Anna knelt down. "Are you all right?" she asked a little girl directly in front of her.

The child nodded.

"I'm sorry I didn't see you," Anna said. "Would you like me to get you something from the candy counter?" She inclined her head toward the jars lining the counter just out of the girl's reach.

The little girl nodded. "May I have a sucker?" she asked with a politeness and eloquence surprising from someone so small.

"Of course." Anna handed Eli the basket. "Hold this, please."

"I can see who the more important customer is," he joked.

"Clearly." Anna flashed him a smile of gratitude. She removed the lid from a jar of suckers, lifted it from the counter, then crouched in front of the little girl. "Which flavor is your favorite?"

"Root beer." Little fingers dug through the jar, in search of the desired lollipop.

"Excellent choice."

"I said no candy today, Anna."

Anna fell back onto the wood floor as her head jerked upward. Still clutching the jar of suckers, she looked up at the man striding toward them. Eli felt affronted on her behalf. Who was this guy to be scolding her?

The little girl shoved the sucker in her mouth a second before the man reached her and placed a hand on her shoulder. Slurping quietly, the little girl stared at her wiggling toes.

Eli followed Anna's gaze as it went from the man to the child, then back to the man again. "You named your daughter *Anna*?" Accusation and disbelief laced her words.

"We did." He offered a tentative smile. "It was Bree's idea, and I agreed wholeheartedly."

Bree. The former best friend. Then this must be . . . Carson?

"Unbelievable," Anna muttered.

A pained expression flashed briefly in Carson's eyes before he turned his attention to his daughter. "Where is it?"

Eli set the basket down, then held a hand out to Anna and pulled her off the floor—the last place she should be when facing this jerk again for the first time.

With a frown and a dramatic sigh and slumping of her shoulders, the little girl turned to her father and surrendered the lollipop, placing the sticky candy in his palm.

"Go pick some nice apples for us instead." Carson patted her head with his non-sticky hand and watched a second as she trotted off toward the barrels of apples near the front.

"Thanks." Anna said without meeting Eli's eye. She turned away, set the jar of suckers on the counter and marched toward the back of the store.

"Anna, wait." Carson followed her. "Let me explain."

She whirled around to face him. "What is there to explain? You got my best friend pregnant, eloped with her on what was supposed to have been our wedding day, and *then—*" She paused, arms folded in front of her, as she looked up at the ceiling. "Then you gave your daughter *my* name." She turned away once more, resuming her march toward the doorway near the back of the store, even as the rest of the market appeared to have frozen, following the drama unfolding near the candy counter.

"Wait—please. You don't understand—" Carson stopped talking as Anna disappeared into the back room. Still holding the sucker in one hand, he ran the other through his hair.

"She doesn't understand," he said, glancing Eli's direction.

"You're right. She doesn't." Eli pulled a hundred-dollar bill from his wallet and slid it toward the register. "She doesn't know how *very* lucky she is that she didn't marry you."

"Exactly," Carson agreed, with absolute sincerity.

Didn't expect that. Instead of acknowledging the response, Eli picked up his basket of food and headed toward the door. He'd have to come back for the steak. He'd have to take Anna out to lunch another day too. He had a feeling her past was about all she could deal with right now. The future would have to wait a little longer.

Chapter 11

ANNA CLOSED AND locked the door separating her mother's flower shop from the Mulberry, then drew the front shade. She sank onto a crate behind the counter, buried her head in her hands, and—didn't cry. Instead she inhaled deeply. One slow breath after another, and allowed the floral aroma to soothe her frazzled nerves. *No tears,* she'd told herself this morning. Her well was dry, siphoned alone in her room the previous night, with worry about her Dad.

Something worth crying about. Carson wasn't. Even if he had done something stupid like naming his daughter after her. Deep breath in, deep breath out.

Bree's idea. "Ha." Did they think she'd be flattered? That naming their child after her—the one that had been conceived while she and Carson were engaged—would somehow make everything better?

The child conceived while . . . But Dad said. Anna frowned, trying to fit the pieces together. Last night Dad had told her Bree lost her baby. And yesterday at church she and Carson hadn't had a child with them. But today Carson had called that little girl Anna, and he hadn't denied that she was his. Something didn't add up. The little girl *looked* about the right age.

"Absurd." Anna gave up trying to figure it out. What did it matter? Intent on some floral therapy, she rose from the crate and went to the refrigerated glass case to see what her mother currently had stocked. Bunches of sunflowers, daisies, and tangerine roses, along with the usual fillers took up most of the shelves. Mom had obviously been thinking about autumn arrangements when she'd made her latest order.

Anna glanced at the locked door, knowing she ought to get back to the Mulberry. Running out on the job her very first day back probably wasn't the best idea. But as long as Carson was there, she had no intention of returning. Besides, he was an employee now, wasn't he? So what if he wasn't on the schedule today and didn't usually work the register? He'd upset her, so he could handle things.

A quick look at her mother's calendar, and Anna was surprised to see an actual order. Those were rare, excepting occasions like Valentine's Day, Mother's Day, weddings, or funerals. Not that the lack of business ever kept her mother out of here. Flowers were her escape, this shop her happy place.

It will be mine too. And if there was an order, she'd better fill it, hadn't she? Could she?

"That's odd." Anna flipped the page over to see if anything was written on the back of the order. The receipt didn't say what day or time it was to be delivered—only sometime this week. It didn't even list the recipient's name. There was only an address that Anna didn't recognize. No matter. The GPS on her phone would guide her.

After a minute of consideration, Anna pulled a rustic wood box from a shelf. She set this on the work table, pulled up a stool, and grabbed the tools she'd need for an arrangement. Foam went in first, cut to the shape of the container and moistened to receive the flowers.

She took a handful of each from the case and began placing them one at a time, starting with the larger sunflowers then adding the accent daisies and finally the roses. Poms, bells of Ireland, and green huckleberry filled out the design nicely. Anna hummed along with the familiar bluegrass tunes as she worked, snipping stems, moving them around in the box, until they were just the way she wanted. When she was done, she sat back to admire her work and realized she'd destroyed the room. Cut stems littered the table and floor. Bits of foam were scattered about amidst petals and leaves. Her mother was never this messy, was she?

She focused her gaze on the arrangement itself and felt herself smiling. It had turned out well, a stunning combination of autumn colors.

"Thanks, Mom." Anna glanced at the picture on the wall of the three of them—her, Mom, and Chelsea—taken after a long day spent together in the shop, completing the flower arrangements for Chelsea's wedding.

There was no similar picture on the wall from the day they'd all worked on *her* wedding flowers. Anna remembered taking one, but since the memory hadn't led to good things, she guessed her mom had never put it up.

The disquiet she'd felt earlier threatened to return, but she refused to let it. Instead, she put the arrangement in the cooler, cleaned up her mess, then returned to the market to find all quiet. Mettie still sat in her chair, balling yarn, but everyone else appeared to have left. Anna let out a sigh of relief.

"Money's in the till. Your boyfriend left a hundred for his groceries."

"Carson's *not* my boyfriend," Anna said, appalled that anyone—even Mettie—would think that now. "He married Bree, remember?"

"I remember." Mettie's gray head bobbed up and down. "I wasn't talking about him, but that other fellow who followed you around with puppy-dog eyes."

"What other—oh, you mean Mr. Steiner's great-grandson?" Eli, he'd asked her to call him last night.

"That's the one. Left a hundred-dollar bill for you. I put it in the drawer."

"Thanks," Anna said, relieved that Mettie was capable of handling more than she appeared to be. Poor Eli. Anna wondered if he'd gotten that steak he wanted. What must he think of her now, between last night's dinner and today's episode? She sighed, frustrated that she'd made such a poor impression. Somehow it felt as if she'd let Mr. Steiner down. "By chance did Eli grab a steak before he left?" she asked Mettie.

"Nope. He let your old beau know what he thought of him—not much." Mettie leaned forward in her chair, her brows doing the funny little jig they did whenever she felt that what she was telling was important. "Told him off, and then he up and left—basket and all."

"I'm sure he'll bring it back, and if not, his hundred more than covers it." The basket was the least of Anna's worries.

"After that Carson helped everyone check out and then left himself."

"Good." Served him right that he had to step in. What had he thought, that she'd be happy to see him and his— daughter?

"You should bring Mr. Steiner's great-grandson a steak," Mettie said. "After all, he stood up for you."

"That's a good idea," Anna said. "Tomorrow." Today her energy was just about spent. A trip out to Mr. Steiner's estate would likely make her feel sad, and she was fighting enough of that already.

One demon at a time.

Chapter 12

"I CAN DO hard things," Anna muttered as she stared at Carson's car parked in back of the store. She'd known he was on the schedule today but had hoped he wouldn't be here this early. "Darn his punctuality."

Summoning the outrage she'd felt yesterday upon learning his daughter's name, she entered through the storeroom and stopped short, shocked to find a double row of boxes lined up in the middle on the floor. Several were partially filled, with Carson up on the ladder apparently retrieving more items.

Anna peeked into the first box and found an assortment of homemade jams as well as a variety of biscuit and pancake mixes—items with plenty of shelf life left.

"What are you doing? Deliveries don't go out until the end of the week, and we don't give out staples that will keep—like this jam." She took a jar of peach preserves from the box. It was one thing, twice a week, to give away the fresh items that hadn't sold. But if they started giving out free food every day—and items that weren't in danger of going bad anytime soon—the Mulberry would be bankrupt in no time. Was that Carson's intention?

"These aren't giveaways." Carson descended the ladder with a box of seasoning packets in his hand. "These are the online orders that came in over the weekend and on Monday. We ship every Tuesday and Friday."

"Since when does the Mulberry do business online?" How had her father failed to mention this?

"Since I created a website for the market a couple of years

ago." Carson set the box of seasonings on the table and began shuffling through it. "It's been a huge boost to sales. A lot of people elsewhere in the country want to purchase homegrown and handmade items but don't have a local store where they can do that. This time of year business really picks up, with a lot of people ordering not just food, but some of the other, more unique items we stock for Christmas gifts."

Like rag dolls and doilies. She noted both in one of the boxes. "I see." Anna put the preserves back from where she'd taken them, then walked down the row, looking inside each box, mentally adding up the profit. "Is this a typical weekend's orders?"

Carson shook his head. "This is just the first batch I'm processing. We usually have forty to fifty total, but there isn't enough room back here to fill that many at once." He reached for a jar of pickles. "Bree prints the orders out when they come in and organizes them, grouping similar requests together so they're easier to fill. I take care of the packaging and shipping—and then restocking. That takes the longest. We have a lot more supplier deliveries than we used to, so we can keep up with demand. Of course it would be easier if we had a big warehouse, but then we wouldn't be the kind of company customers are looking for. We've found that people really like the idea that they are supporting a little mom-and-pop operation."

"May I see the orders for today?" Anna folded her arms across her middle, a lame attempt to disquiet her inner turmoil. Her initial reaction was that this was brilliant. She couldn't deny the relief she felt at seeing proof of an actual, viable income stream for her parents. On the other hand, that Carson was the one who had orchestrated it—and probably suggested it in the first place, too—rubbed her in all the wrong places. He was supposed to be the bad guy. He *was* the bad guy. Helping her parents didn't fit that description.

"Over there." Carson inclined his head toward a stack of papers in a basket on the shelf near the door. He dropped Cajun seasoning packets into a couple of the boxes, made a check mark on the papers taped to the front of each, and headed back up the ladder.

Anna picked up the basket and leafed through the stack. There were a good forty orders inside, most for multiple items. She glanced at the addresses next and found they were from one coast to the other, north to south. It seemed Mulberry Market was no longer Holiday, Alabama's secret.

Of course Carson would have built a great website and known how to position it to reach consumers. As a web designer, this sort of thing was his area of expertise. So why *was* he climbing ladders and packing boxes?

"How much profit are my parents making—after expenses and payroll?"

"Boxes and tape cost a little," Carson said, "but we've got a bulk deal now, so it's not too bad. Consumers pay postage, though I think we'd do better if we start offering free shipping after a certain dollar amount spent. Bree and I don't get a paycheck. We're repaying a loan from your parents."

"Must have been some loan," Anna muttered.

Carson turned to her, his expression serious. "It was. We owe them a lot. Bree and I are both extremely grateful to them."

He was sounding more and more like his father. Gracious, kind, a genuinely good guy. *The same good guy Carson has always been.*

Anna turned away, eyes brimming. Being in the same room with him was so hard. While she didn't feel the desire to rush into Carson's arms—as she'd feared she might before coming home—there was a definite longing within her all the same. She didn't want to be at odds with him. She was happy to realize that she didn't *want* him the way she used to, yet she still wanted something all the same.

Resolution, perhaps? *That would mean forgiving him.* How was she supposed to do that when she couldn't forget the hurt and humiliation he'd caused? And when, because of him, her life had derailed so completely?

"The online thing seems like a good idea," she finally managed, telling herself that acknowledging something good he'd done didn't mean she was absolving him of former wrongs.

"Thanks." Carson sounded a bit surprised. Anna was too, that they'd managed a civil conversation for ten minutes. Screaming at him as she had the other day—in front of Eli and the entire store—was more how she'd envisioned their interactions would be from now on. Except that encounter hadn't left her feeling better about anything. Instead, she'd felt worse about *everything*.

She set the basket of orders back on the shelf. "I have a floral delivery to make this morning. You okay here by yourself?"

"Of course. And Mettie should be in soon," Carson added, a hint of amusement in his voice.

"Never missed a day of work in thirty years," Anna said, barely containing a smile. *Not that she ever does much work.* She kept the uncharitable thought to herself.

"About yesterday," Carson began as he hurried down the ladder.

Anna held up a hand. "I don't want to talk about it." *I can't talk about it.* Curious as she was about the truth regarding his daughter, she didn't feel strong enough to learn the details, especially from Carson. "I should be back within the hour." She practically ran to the front of the store, more eager than ever to deliver flowers.

Her GPS took her to the outskirts of town, just before the bridge separating Holiday from Magnolia Springs. She turned off the main road, onto a dirt one, with a vague sense of familiarity about it. There used to be a haunted house out here—or one that looked like it could be haunted.

The Baker place. She remembered a story about the family who'd lived there decades ago. Their son had been reported as missing in action somewhere on the European front during WWII. It was said the grief had killed his father, who still haunted the place, searching for his missing boy.

Creepy. She wondered who lived there now and how they could afford to order flowers if they lived in such a rundown house.

A long drive angled off the dirt road, and Anna followed it, expecting to see the old house any second. Instead, a newly constructed home beckoned at the end of the driveway, its porch steps lined with an assortment of potted mums and pumpkins.

Anna parked the car and got out, balancing the flower arrangement carefully. She climbed the steps and knocked, noting the clean, almost bare porch. Paper blinds—the cheap, temporary kind—hung at all the windows. The one closest to her was partially open, revealing a front room as bare as the porch, with only one chair in it.

Maybe they just moved in.

Footsteps sounded on the other side of the door as it swung open.

"*Anna.*" Bree stood there, looking as surprised as Anna felt.

Bree.

Hope blossomed on Bree's face. "Come in." She stepped

back at the same time Anna did, putting more distance between them.

"No." Anna shook her head, as much to clear it as in denial. *Bree. Right here. How—why?* Remembering the delivery, Anna set the flower arrangement on the porch, instead of moving closer to hand it to her former friend. "I suppose those are from Carson." He'd have known, of course, where she was going. Anna's fury with them both resurfaced.

Bree glanced at the flowers and frowned. "He doesn't send me flowers. We can't afford it."

Does she expect me to feel sorry for her? Anna took another step back, noting that, oddly, Bree hadn't sounded hurt or sorry for herself.

"Won't you come in?" Bree asked again, the hope fading from her expression with Anna's retreat. "Please."

"I can't."

"Can't or won't?" Bree challenged.

Anna felt her eyes widen at this new, bold side of Bree that she hadn't seen... *In years. Since before her mother died.*

"Shouldn't," Anna said. "I have to get back to the store." A lame excuse, since Bree obviously knew Carson was there this very minute. *Does she worry about that? About Carson and me being alone together?* Anna had never worried about the two of them together. *My mistake.*

Instead of going back inside Bree came out onto the porch in her socks, stepping around the flower arrangement to move nearer to Anna again. "Carson told me what happened yesterday."

Anna turned away and hurried down the steps.

"Our daughter isn't the child I was pregnant with when Carson and I eloped," Bree called after her. "I miscarried that baby."

"And had another awfully fast." Anna winced, hating the bite in her voice. It was a terrible thing to have said. She could only imagine that miscarrying a baby—under any circumstances—would be traumatic and heartbreaking. Instead of apologizing, she stopped on the driver's side of the car and dug in her pocket to find the keys. She had to get out of here before she said anything worse.

"We adopted Anna." Bree came down the stairs to the driveway. "I can't have any more children. I hemorrhaged and had to have an emergency hysterectomy when I lost the baby. It was a miracle I didn't die as well."

A miracle—but no more children? None? Anna grabbed the Excursion's handle. *Oh, Bree.* She looked up, meeting Bree's eyes through the car windows. *How did you bear it? How can you now?*

"I don't know if we'll ever be able to adopt another child," Bree said quietly. "We're in so much debt now. And if I was only going to have one child, one precious daughter, I wanted to name her after my best friend—who has always been the kindest, most beautiful person I know—inside and out. Everything I'd ever want my daughter to be."

Anna's fingers trembled on the handle. Once, she might have been those things, but not now. She no longer lived up to praise like that. She wasn't kind or beautiful, inside or out. She'd become a hermit, like old Sonny. Coming out only when necessary, and not letting anyone get too close to her, never putting forth the effort herself to be close to anyone.

Safer that way. But nothing here in Holiday was safe. It felt like her heart was breaking over and over again—for different reasons—every day. Just now it had startled painfully at Bree's disclosure and ached—for Bree, for her loss. *And because she went through it all without a mother—or me—at her side.*

"Anna, I'm so sorry." The hope in Bree's eyes had been fully replaced now, tears of regret taking its place. "We never meant for it to happen. We never wanted to hurt you."

The reminder of why she hadn't been by Bree's side was like a splash of cold water in the face. *Why should I feel sorry for her when—*

"I know you probably think what happened is no more than I deserve."

No. Anna hadn't thought that. She wouldn't. She hadn't become such a horrible person that she'd think someone—especially someone like Bree—deserved such heartbreak. Bree had experienced more than her share already.

But still . . . She and Carson had done an awful thing. Their betrayal cut so deep, Anna feared the wound would never heal. She grasped the driver's side door and opened it, half expecting Bree to follow suit, on the other side. But instead she stepped away from the car, almost as if she feared being run over.

Anna jammed the key in the ignition and turned it. The car roared to life, but she backed up carefully, aware that a little girl was likely lurking about somewhere.

Anna. Named after me. My best friends have a little girl. Not my best friends. My enemies?

She pulled out onto the dirt road and drove a little ways before pulling over. Grabbing the steering wheel, she banged her head against it once and stayed there, eyes squeezed shut. *Let me wake up in Seattle.*

Maybe Santa could do something for her and grant that request early this year. Except that it would mean letting her parents down. Her dad had his first treatment this morning—surely a far worse day than she was having. He was working to eradicate his cancer. She had to get rid of hers as well.

Turn around. Go back. Talk to Bree.

"I can't." Anna rubbed her chest as panic bubbled up. *I can't.* It hurt too much already. Allowing Bree in again would only make it worse. As it was, Anna was barely treading water.

Being near Bree or Carson would only make her drown that much faster.

Chapter 13

IT WAS FRIDAY afternoon before Anna made it out to Mr. Steiner's house to bring a steak to his grandson. Tuesday she'd been too frazzled from her unexpected encounter with Bree to do anything more than wait on customers and avoid Carson working in the back room. Wednesday she'd heard from her mom and learned that Dad was pretty sick from his first treatment. To cope with that news and feel like she was doing something useful, something that might potentially make a small difference, Anna went home and spent the afternoon and evening destroying her mother's kitchen as she taught herself how to make some of her dad's favorite foods. When she had successfully frozen a quiche and a batch of his favorite cookies she felt slightly better, though too exhausted to clean up.

Thursday had been a pretty low-key day at the Mulberry, so she'd used the time to pry through the computer files, trying to make sense of her parents' accounting system and figure out where they stood financially. They owned the store outright—she'd known that for years—but beyond that it was a difficult mess to piece together. Individually Mom had kept an accurate record for all of the vendors, both goods received and payments made. From there things became dicey, as Anna could find no indication of what percentage of goods sold versus what had been given to charity or still stood on the shelves. Boxes and boxes of register receipts seemed to be the only evidence at all that anything had ever been sold. It was almost as if her mother didn't care about record keeping, beyond making sure vendors were paid.

It had been with a weary sigh, papers scattered all over the worktable in her mother's flower shop, and a headache that Anna had gone home yesterday evening—to a sink full of dishes she hadn't washed from the previous night. Her parents hadn't even been gone a week, and already she was leaving a trail of messes.

It had taken her an hour to clean the kitchen, after which she went to bed without eating anything of substance for dinner. So much for gaining weight while she was here.

This morning she again found Carson working in the storeroom when she arrived. Since her plans to take him off the schedule were no longer feasible—unless she wanted to take over packing and shipping all those orders—Anna decided the next best thing was avoidance.

After ringing up customers all morning and then cleaning the paper mess she'd left in the florist shop, she spent an hour teaching Ella how to use the register. With Mettie and Carson around to keep an eye on her new trainee, Anna chose a package of steak out of the cooler and headed out to deliver it to Eli.

She'd expected to see him at the Mulberry again before now—he'd purchased some staples, but not enough to get a grown man through a week. But when he hadn't returned by this afternoon, Anna guessed that he'd driven to the Piggly Wiggly for a more traditional grocery shopping experience, and likely to avoid more drama like that he'd witnessed from her on Monday. Who could blame him?

Recalling her behavior, Anna winced. She owed Eli an explanation and an apology, at the least—along with some change. The hundred he'd left had more than covered his groceries. She hoped the peace-offering steak would leave things between them better.

Though why that mattered, she didn't know. It had been a long time since she'd cared what people thought about her.

She supposed his opinion was important because of who he was and what the Steiners had meant to her.

I've let them down, and now him too. She was too late to make amends for deserting Mr. Steiner, but she still had a chance to leave things better with his great-grandson.

A wave of nostalgia washed over her as she passed through the tall iron gates and started up the long drive. How many hundreds of times had she been here over the years—most often on Wednesday afternoons.

Instead of parking out front she drove past the manor, between it and the separate carriage house, now turned garage. She swung into one of the stalls near the back kitchen, reserved for deliveries, and was glad to see the truck Eli had rented was parked there too, backed up to the kitchen, as if he'd been loading things into it. It appeared that he was here, and she could make her apologies and hopefully check one item of guilt off of her growing list.

She grabbed the steak, got out of the car, and walked up to the back door. She rang the bell instead of knocking, knowing he wasn't likely to hear a simple knock in the nether parts of the mansion. With more than twenty rooms, it was ridiculously enormous—the perfect place for hide and seek. Anna smiled, remembering the few times she and Bree and Carson had been lucky enough to play here.

The door swung open, revealing Eli, wearing a T-shirt and jeans with holes in the knees, and looking a bit dusty and disheveled—like he'd been hiding under beds or in closets. "Anna. This is a nice surprise." Rock music blared from an unseen speaker behind him.

"About to get better, I hope." Speaking loudly, she held out her offering. "Special delivery from the Mulberry. I believe you forgot this on your recent trip."

Eli took the paper-wrapped bundle and held it up. "Is this what I think it is?"

She smiled. "Filet mignon. Grass-fed beef, from the great state of Alabama."

"Sweet." Eli grinned at her. "Thank you. I've about starved this week." He glanced behind him. "Alexa, pause the music."

It stopped at once, to Anna's relief. She didn't want to have to shout their entire conversation, nor did it seem right to have music like that blaring through the halls of Mr. Steiner's home. Maybe if she told Eli about the old console record player and records he would consider using those instead.

"You haven't been getting groceries at the Piggly Wiggly?" Anna asked.

He shook his head. "Why would I do that with your market right in town?"

Not mine. She shrugged. "Maybe because the current manager went off the deep end in front of you a few days ago. I'd understand if that was enough to make you reconsider where you purchase your groceries."

"Nah." He waved her suggestion away, then changed to motioning her inside. "Do you have a minute to come in?"

"I don't, actually." She racked her brain for an excuse. "My mom is going to be calling shortly with an update on my dad. I'd like to be home when I talk to her."

"Oh. Sure." He seemed disappointed but then brightened almost at once. "How about later? You could come over for dinner. I'll throw this on the barbeque and bake those potatoes I bought earlier in the week. I haven't gotten around to that yet."

"What have you been living on?" Anna asked.

"All that bread was really great. And you were right about the jam—wow. I've got to buy some more of that before I go home. Other than that, I've mostly eaten at the diner all week."

"Ah," Anna said, feeling oddly hurt that he'd been in

town, right across the street, and not come by. *To visit psycho woman? Right.* "Southern comfort food at its best."

"I don't know about that." Eli rubbed the back of his neck. "I'd say your mother has it beat. I've never tasted a roast or biscuits that topped hers."

"I'll be sure to tell her." Anna turned to go, hopeful he'd forget about sharing his steak, though she had included a couple in the package.

"So, will around seven work for you?"

No such luck. "You don't need to feed me," Anna said. "I really came to apologize—for Monday. I never helped you finish shopping, and my behavior was very unprofess—"

"—Understandable," Eli finished. "Personally, I would have thrown something at him."

Anna laughed. "Too bad I didn't think of that."

"There's always next time."

She shook her head. "No. There can't be. I mean, Carson actually works at the Mulberry—for my parents. They made him a loan or something. They've got an arrangement. I don't really understand it, but whatever. And since I have to work with him, I have to keep my cool. You'll be happy to know I haven't screamed at anyone since Monday."

Eli gave a low whistle. "The dude who broke your heart works for your parents?" He sounded as disbelieving as she'd felt when she'd first heard the news. It made her feel better, like maybe her reaction hadn't been out of line.

"Kudos for dealing with that civilly," Eli said. "I don't think I'd be nearly as gracious."

I'm not. Every minute is killing me. "I'm trying—for my dad." Anna stepped back off the stoop and turned to go to the car. "See you later."

"At seven." He followed her to the Excursion. "It will be nice to have someone out here for a couple of hours. It's too quiet.

"Didn't sound particularly quiet when I got here." Was she really going to have to come back? *Would that be so terrible?*

"The music masks the quiet. Otherwise . . . it's a little weird staying in a place that's more than one hundred fifty years old. I mean, think of all the people who've lived here before."

"Like your great-grandfather," Anna said, sadly. "Eli, I appreciate the invitation, but I'd rather not go inside his house just yet." Aside from not knowing Eli well enough to want to be alone with him, she didn't want to go inside a place that had been so dear to her—without the old gentleman who had made it so. "It's been a hard week, and this house holds a lot of memories for me. I'm afraid you'd be in for another Anna meltdown if I came in."

"Ah—right." He glanced at the wrapped steak, still in his hand. "What if we eat outside? The barbeque is out here, anyway. And if it's me you're uncomfortable with, bring someone along. You can even bring your ex, so I can tell him off properly for you."

Anna rolled her eyes. "No thanks. I'd rather just pretend he doesn't exist." She opened the driver side door.

"Seven then. Outside—on the front porch," Eli added, upping his game. "So people can see us from the street."

Because we get so many people driving out this way.

"I know you don't date men," Eli added. "But this isn't technically a date, so you won't have broken your three-and-a-half-year record."

His lopsided grin melted the last of her resistance. "Fine. I'll be here. I'll even bring dessert."

"Yes!" Eli pumped his fist in the air. "I have a non-date tonight. Someone to talk to besides the ghosts. Plus dessert from the daughter of the best cook in town."

"Don't get those hopes up too high," Anna said, only

half-teasing. "Sometimes talent genes skip a generation." She climbed in the SUV, started the engine, and drove away, watching Eli from her rearview mirror as he waved. *He really must be lonely.* She supposed Holiday was a little too quiet for a big-city guy like him.

Chapter 14

Eli added a cucumber, a little basket of colorful grape tomatoes, and a baggie of fresh-made croutons to the other items already in his basket. After Anna had gone, he'd realized he didn't have everything he needed for a decent meal. Man could not entertain on steak and potatoes alone, so he'd made a quick trip to the Mulberry to grab ingredients for a salad and some more of that delicious bread. He tried two different loaves and two bags of rolls this time, plus more fresh-churned butter and homemade jam to go with them.

He made his way to the register, not surprised to see Anna's ex nearby, on a high ladder, stocking shelves.

"Excuse me," Eli called up to him. "Do you carry wine?"

Carson turned around. "She doesn't drink."

Eli frowned. "Who doesn't?"

"The woman you're hoping to impress tonight."

Had Anna told him? *Doubtful.* Besides, she'd said she was going home to wait for a phone call from her parents, so how could she have said anything? "I don't see any woman." Eli stretched his neck and made a point of looking around the store. His eyes landed on Mettie, rolling yet another ball of yarn. "Except you, of course, Ma'am."

"I drink." Mettie grinned at him, her dentures flopping in her mouth. "You can take me home with you and fix me dinner."

I doubt you could eat the steak. Eli gave her what he hoped was a friendly smile, without responding. Where he was from, it was generally easy to tell when someone was joking. Here, he wasn't so certain. He glanced up at Carson again. "So do you carry wine here, or not?"

"Behind the counter. But I'm telling you, Anna doesn't drink. It was part of her platform as Miss Holiday. She saw what alcohol did to her best friend's father, and she made a vow never to touch the stuff—any of it."

Her former best friend? "Good to know." For a guy who'd left her at the altar almost four years ago, Carson still seemed way too invested in Anna's business.

"Maybe you drove her to drink," Eli muttered under his breath as he held his basket aloft and maneuvered around barrels of dried beans and wheat to the cash register.

"I can help you if you're ready." A girl who looked too young to be working started toward him.

"I'm ready." He set his basket down. *Ready to be out of this town.* Some things about Holiday were very pleasant and wouldn't take much to get used to. Other things—like everyone somehow knowing everyone else's business—were liable to drive him mad. No wonder Anna had left.

"I'll help him," Carson said. He stepped behind the counter and began pulling things out of the basket. "Looks like it will be a good dinner."

Eli considered a second before responding. "Just a guy trying to make a nice meal—for the prettiest woman in town." He added the last, deciding it would be good for Carson to hear that he found Anna attractive. It would also be good for Carson to think she had moved on. Even if she hadn't and still wasn't over him—Eli's assessment, based on her not having dated anyone for almost four years, plus the mini breakdown he'd witnessed Monday. He hadn't been able to forget the hurt in her voice when she'd realized Carson's daughter bore her name.

"Anna is more than just a pretty face." Carson put the last

of the produce in a cloth bag with the Mulberry logo stamped on the front.

"I'm well aware of that." Far more aware than Anna or anyone else in Holiday realized. Anna was the real deal, a woman of substance. Eli leveled his gaze on Carson. "I have no intention of doing anything to hurt her." Absolutely true, though he had a nagging feeling that, in spite of his best intentions, she might be upset with him in the end. This afternoon, when she'd told him she didn't want to go into his great-grandfather's house, had been a serious red flag that trouble was on the horizon. *If she can't even go inside . . .*

Eli gave Carson some cash to cover the groceries. It was a good thing he'd brought plenty on this trip—no credit cards or apple pay here.

Carson handed him his change.

"Thanks." Eli picked up the bags from the counter. "I'll bring these back before I leave town."

"When will that be?" Carson shut the register drawer.

"When my business here is done." Eli turned away before Carson could fire any more questions at him. Man, that guy rubbed him wrong.

Eli was halfway home before he realized he'd forgotten the wine.

Chapter 15

ELI STEPPED BACK to view the table setting. Long white cloth, real silver, crystal goblets, china plates. *No* candles. Elegant, but hopefully not romantic. He'd found everything in the buffet in the formal dining room, and the stately, columned porch lent itself to sophistication all on its own. The picnic table from around back wouldn't have done at all.

At 6:55 Anna pulled into the driveway. She parked in front this time, just past the curve at the front of the house, so her SUV was pointing toward the street.

For a quick getaway, if needed. Eli guessed there had been other reasons she didn't want to be alone in the house with him. He didn't blame her. A woman couldn't be too careful these days.

He stayed at the barbeque he'd hauled to the front porch, flipping the steak and acting casual. This was nothing more than a business dinner, after all. True, Anna was a remarkable woman, and one he'd dreamed of meeting for years. To be here in Holiday, about to spend an evening alone with her, was a fulfillment of his teenage fantasy. Still, nothing could or would come of any time they spent together. Chicago was calling him—literally. He'd fielded a dozen calls for work today and twice as many emails. He loathed doing business that way, instead of in person.

A few years ago he'd recognized this pet peeve as a weird quirk of his upbringing. After being mostly ignored by his parents, as a child and teenager and even an adult now, he wanted to be very certain not to do the same thing to other people. Being impersonal and aloof were two traits he didn't want to pass onto the next generation—if there ever was one. Unlikely, at this point. Regardless, he didn't want to perpetuate those habits. When he was talking to someone or working with a client, Eli gave that individual his undivided attention. For a couple of hours tonight, he was looking forward to giving it to Anna.

"It smells wonderful." She walked toward him, looking stunning in a navy sundress that showed off her blonde hair and clear, baby-blue eyes. He was glad he'd changed to a button-down shirt and some jeans without holes.

"I am a bit of a grill master back home." Eli speared the steaks and swiveled to face her so she could inspect them, if she wanted. "How do you like yours cooked? These are about medium rare right now."

"I'll take mine a little less rare, if that's okay." Anna climbed the wide steps to the porch.

"Not a problem." Eli hefted the fork in the air, caught it in his other hand as he turned, then tipped it toward the grill, sliding one steak neatly over the fire. The second . . . was nowhere to be seen. He glanced at the grill again, double checking that they weren't stacked on top of each other.

"Back here," Anna said in a voice that sounded choked.

Dread filled him as he whirled around and spotted the steak lying on the porch floor. "That wasn't supposed to happen." Eli felt his face reddening.

"That's good," Anna said in that same choked voice. "I was hoping that wasn't some sort of grill master secret seasoning."

Eli glanced at her and realized she was trying not to laugh.

"Ten-second rule," she suggested.

"Are you kidding? Gross. You know how old this house is. Think of the hundreds, if not thousands, of feet that have crossed this porch over the years."

Anna folded her arms and stared at him. "I wouldn't have taken Big City Boy for a germaphobe."

"I'm not, but—would you eat that now?" He stared at the steak, lamenting its loss, the aroma still wafting in the air around them. They'd have to share the one still left, and he was hungry enough to eat both.

"Not now I wouldn't," Anna said. "*But*, if you were to take it inside and run it under scalding water for a few minutes and then put it back on the grill for a while, I'm sure it won't kill us."

"I was hoping it would transport us to heaven or something, being grass fed, Alabama beef and all." Eli bent and speared the steak again, still disbelieving that he had actually dropped it. So much for the suave guy act.

Anna waved his comment away. "That's the only kind of beef you'll find in the Mulberry."

"Back in a few," Eli said, heading toward the front door. "Unless you'd like to wait inside."

"No thanks. I'm good out here. Too many memories—you know." Her shoulders lifted in an apologetic shrug.

Strike one. If she couldn't face the past here, how was he ever supposed to get her to take a chance on a future in Holiday?

Anna braced her arms on the porch rail and leaned back, managing to look both like a magazine model and as if she was completely at home—as if this were exactly where she belonged.

Because it is. Eli hurried to the kitchen, one hand held beneath the steak so it wouldn't drip on the wood floor or antique rugs.

He ran the steak beneath the scalding water Anna had recommended and used a knife to scrape off all the seasoning. He'd just have to start again with this one—his now. Anna could have the one still on the barbeque.

Not wanting to top his performance with a burnt offering, Eli ran from the kitchen through the formal dining room with seating for forty, through the grand foyer. He paused just before going outside. Anna still leaned against the rail, a tranquil, almost wistful expression in her eyes, her lips slightly curved. He'd have bet a hundred bucks she was remembering some other time she'd been here. Maybe his quest to get her to stay wasn't as hopeless as he'd feared this afternoon.

He returned to the porch, set the steak carefully on the grill, turned Anna's steak, then walked around the table to hold her chair out for her.

"Thank you." She slid into it, bumping his hand, still resting on the chair back.

A different kind of warmth lit inside him. *Not good.* Definitely not. She was beautiful, and he was more than a little attracted to her, but that didn't mean anything. There were plenty of women in Chicago he could pursue if he was interested in a relationship. The one he could absolutely *not* pursue was seated before him, taking a sip of her water.

"Aren't you going to join me?" Anna looked over her shoulder at him, and Eli realized he was still standing behind her chair, staring off into space like a buffoon.

"Yeah. I thought I saw something in the yard." He inclined his head across the lawn to the towering pines that bordered the property. He'd seen something, all right. His perfectly laid plans messed up, thwarted, as they had been all week by people and circumstances.

Not tonight. Not by me.

Reminding himself that he wanted to break all ties with Holiday and return home *more* than he wanted to get to know Anna, Eli finished bringing the food to the table, concluding with the cooked steaks, and sat opposite her. Had he been striving for romance, he would have seated himself beside her, where they could have fed each other from their own plates and all that other gushy nonsense he'd seen friends of his in love do.

No thanks. Not for me.

"I hope water is okay." Eli poured more into the glass she'd just drunk half of. "At the Mulberry I was *advised* that you don't drink any sort of alcoholic beverage—even wine."

"True." Anna placed her napkin in her lap. "I've seen too many of the effects firsthand. Bree's father—" Anna broke off abruptly, as if just saying the name of her former friend pained her. "Anyway, I know a glass of wine doesn't equal a drinking problem, but it was easier to campaign for Miss Holiday on a platform of abstaining from alcohol rather than trying to draw a line between recreational drinking that was all right and that which wasn't."

"And you won, so your campaign obviously worked."

"How did you know I won?" Anna angled her head and gave him a look filled with suspicion.

"The other night—at dinner. Your father mentioned it." Good thing he had, too, or that comment could have caused trouble. Though Eli had been dropping hints every time he saw her, he didn't want to play his whole hand at once or drop his news like a bomb.

"Right." She gave him a quick smile, appeased—hopefully.

Her look turned thoughtful. "I heard Bree's dad remarried and is doing a lot better, so that's good news."

"Speaking of hearing things—" Eli speared a potato and put it on his plate. "How does word get around in Holiday so quickly? Specifically, how did your co-workers know you were coming over for dinner tonight?"

"That's easy," Anna said as she served herself salad. "I called Mettie and told her I wouldn't be back in the rest of the day and asked her to have Carson close up. Perks of being the manager." Anna smirked. "Mettie, of course, asked if everything was okay, which was her polite way of snooping. I told her I had a hot date with the new guy in town, and that if I didn't show up for work tomorrow, to call the county sheriff."

Hot. Date. Was she serious? He'd practically had to beg her to come.

"Actually, I told Mettie it was a mercy visit—that you had no idea how to cook a steak or anything else you'd bought at the Mulberry. I told her you were likely to starve if I didn't come over to help."

"Ah." Eli nodded. "That sounds more like it. Keeping my ego down. Either way, I have, what—maybe twelve hours or so to either burn the house down with my cooking or kidnap you for nefarious purposes before anyone will come searching?"

"Less than that, I'd guess." Anna inclined her head toward the street. "Haven't you noticed how many cars have gone by in the last fifteen minutes?"

"Uh, no." Eli stared at the road. It wasn't exactly close to the house, given the gate and long drive that separated them.

"No doubt Mettie told everyone at work what I said, along with anyone else who happened to come by. A new guy in town is big news—surely you've noticed."

"Sort of." He'd been welcomed heartily by no fewer than a dozen souls at church, and everywhere he went in town people had stopped him to ask who he was and where he was from and what he was doing in Holiday. He'd even had a few neighborly deliveries from some of the town's finest bakers. But he'd chalked all that up to friendliness, not curiosity, and felt a little deflated now at the realization that he was likely an oddity more than anything else.

"Folks with nothing better to do have decided to go for a drive this evening—right past your great-grandfather's house." Anna smiled as she buttered her roll, apparently not at all bothered that they were the local Friday-night entertainment.

"Seriously? They're driving by the house just to look at us?" Eli had a hard time believing people cared about each other's business that much. Then again, what else was there to do around here? The one movie playing in town was over a month old, and the diner on Main didn't exactly make for a culinary experience.

"So this is small town life, eh?" He waited until Anna had finished with the dressing before serving himself. "Would it be this way with everyone, or is it just because I'm an outsider?" The truth hit him before Anna could finish chewing the bite she'd taken to answer. "Or does it have nothing to do with me, and everything to do—with *you.*" Eli glanced at the road as another car drove by at what had to be ten miles per hour. "It is you," he guessed, then had it confirmed when she blushed. "This whole town adores you, so they're all looking out for you, making sure you're safe with me."

Anna shrugged. "Maybe. More likely people are just bored."

He seriously doubted it. He had a stack of letters at home, all filled with Anna stories—the kind things she'd done for people, the many lives she'd touched. Including his great-grandfather's. She really was the town sweetheart—or she had been. *Come home at last, after having her heart broken and running away.* Of course all those people who loved her weren't about to let that happen again.

Eli took a bite of steak and tried to figure out how Carson fit into this scenario. He'd seemed as concerned about Anna as everyone else—maybe more—and didn't act the part of a total jerk. Though he had to be one, given what he'd done. What business did Carson have even thinking about Anna now? And how had he wormed his way back into her parents' hearts and lives? Something didn't add up, and it was really starting to annoy Eli. He wasn't one to leave a mystery unsolved. But he had bigger fish to fry—as they probably said often here in the South.

A job to get back to. A life waiting in Chicago—filled with appointments, lunch meetings, and good take-out for dinner almost every night. Home was a high rise-condo that was a reasonable size—two thousand square feet versus twelve thousand—a group of associates, if not friends, to hang out with on weekends. A good paycheck and a respectable position. By today's standards, he'd made it. He was thirty-one years old, independent, free—content to be a bachelor. Not tied down to anyone or anything. He probably had his parents to thank for that mindset. If they'd taught him anything it was to think of himself first. And so he had, and he did.

But the woman seated across from him did not and had not. Was it the enigma of her, of that phenomenon of giving, that he found so very alluring?

Aside from being interested in better knowing Anna, there *was* something about this place, a gentle pull he was starting to feel. *All the more reason to talk to her soon and get the heck out of here.*

"For a guy who wanted company, you're awfully quiet tonight," Anna said, her voice uncertain and perhaps slightly hurt, as if she was the reason for his silence.

She was. Just not in the way she probably thought.

"Sorry," Eli said, feeling his face warm again, and furious with himself for acting like he was a spellbound twelve-year-old in the throes of his first crush. He glanced toward the street and another car cruising by at a turtle's pace. "We should give them something good to talk about. You know, since they're investing their Friday night into keeping an eye on you."

She looked at him over the rim of her glass as she drank. "What did you have in mind?"

"You'll see." He raised and lowered his eyebrows several times and attempted a mysterious look that made Anna laugh.

The sound reminded him of the delightful dinner he'd had at her parents' house on Sunday—all the candid conversation and laughter. Especially the laughter. He couldn't ever remember anyone laughing at the dinner table at his house.

Doing his best to ignore the cars—some of which he was pretty sure had gone by more than once—Eli steered the conversation to Anna, trying to get her to open up a little more. He'd thought he understood her and knew who she was before he came to Holiday, but he realized the girl his grandfather had written about had changed, and not into the person he would have guessed she'd be. Glimpses of the spunky girl from the letters peeked out occasionally, but overall she seemed far more reserved than he would have guessed. Having her heart broken by her two best friends had obviously affected her. She was guarded with her words and careful not to say too much about herself.

The closest they came to discussing her personal life was when Anna started talking about marine biology. Then her entire countenance changed. She became more and more animated as she talked, sharing stories of her internship studying sharks, and describing the thrill of diving near Bermuda. She'd had some incredible adventures during her college years, and he was as astonished as her brother had been that she'd landed somewhere those experiences couldn't continue. Anna needed an ocean nearby—one fit for swimming, snorkeling, and diving.

Yet another reason for her to stay in Holiday.

He cleared their plates and turned on the outside lights while Anna retrieved the dessert she'd brought—a plate of homemade peanut butter cookies that all but melted in his mouth. When he'd eaten more than he should have, he beckoned her from the porch out to the large side lawn, where he'd set up a target he'd found in the detached garage.

"Check these out." Eli opened a trunk he'd also found. Inside lay an assortment of old firearms.

"Those look like they ought to be in a museum." Anna leaned closer.

"That was my first thought," Eli said. "My second was to get the Antiques Roadshow people out here to tell us what we're looking at. Some of these date back to the Civil War."

"I'm sure." Anna started to reach for one, then hesitated. "May I?"

Eli nodded. "I was counting on it—on you not being so much of a Southern belle that you're averse to shooting a gun or two."

"You're planning to *shoot* these?" Her widened eyes and slightly parted lips showed her disbelief—or perhaps her belief that he'd lost his mind.

Eli pulled a revolver from the top of the stack. "How else will I know if they work or not? Plus, I found ammo in the garage as well." He nudged a second, smaller box with his toe. "You game?"

"Sure . . . I guess."

"It's legal out here. I checked," Eli added, in case that concern caused her hesitation. "And think what a rise we'll get out of people driving by when they hear gunshots. By tomorrow morning there will be more stories circulating through town than you can imagine."

"I *can* imagine," she said glumly.

Eli silently kicked himself for reminding her of the past and the gossip that had likely ensued after her failed wedding.

"These stories will be good. We'll make sure they are. 'Former Miss Holiday and town newcomer chase off gang of outlaws.'"

"Sounds like you've watched too many westerns. Besides,

any outlaws would have to be mad to pick Holiday as their target. What are they going to steal—potatoes and beans from the market or folding chairs from the community center?"

"Maybe they're just here hiding out until their next job. I don't know." Eli tossed up a hand. "I'm sure we can come up with something good."

"Not too good," Anna warned. "You know we don't have any hospitals nearby. So if you shoot your foot off or something, it's likely to be permanent."

"I'll be sure to remember that. Are there any doctors in Holiday? A clinic or anything?"

"Nope." Anna shook her head. "You can imagine how that worked when we were growing up. It had to be pretty serious to drive all the way to a doctor. Most of the time a mom—mine or Bree's or Carson's—simply patched us up."

When she'd said "we" he'd thought she was referring to her siblings, not her friends. It was telling that she still referenced them so frequently. At dinner the other night, she'd been visibly shaken by the news of her friend's near escape from death. *Anna doesn't want to care about them, but she still does.*

Eli wondered if she realized that herself yet. Perhaps the bigger question was, did her friend Bree still care about Anna? On the surface it would seem she didn't—not with what she'd done. But so far the people at Holiday had surprised him.

"No accidents today. We'll be careful." Eli handed her the revolver while he opened the box of ammunition.

Anna held the gun close, studying it. "Did you see this engraving?"

"Saw it. Looked it up online. It's a scene of the victory at the Battle of Campeche in May of 1843."

"Wow." She held the revolver a bit more gently, cradling it in both hands. "Are you sure we should shoot it? It's obviously an antique."

"Gabriel's entire house is. Besides, anyone examining this gun for its value would do the same." Eli looked up from the ground where he'd laid out not only the balls, but the measure of powder. "I watched a video on how to load these," he confessed as he took the revolver from Anna and proceeded to load it.

"Are you planning to sell the guns?" Anna glanced toward the house. "And other things that were your great-grandfather's? Is that what you brought the truck for?"

Eli wasn't sure how to take the accusation in her words. *If she cares about this place . . .* That could only work to his benefit, right?

"I'm not planning to sell anything right now." *For a good five years, at least.* "I don't have a thing in the truck, either. I rented it, thinking I'd come across some furniture or boxes of pictures or china or something that I'd feel I should take home with me, but so far—nothing. It's not that the house isn't full of treasures. I guess I'm just not much of a collector."

"Oh. Well, that's good. I mean, if you wanted to take something to keep for yourself, that would be fine. You're a relative, after all. And Mr. Steiner would want things to stay in the family."

Not necessarily. Eli lifted the pouch of gunpowder carefully.

"But it would be sad if you—or whichever relative takes over this place—sold everything off. That wouldn't seem right. This house and everything in it is kind of like a piece of Holiday's history."

"Including your own?" Eli asked quietly.

"Yeah," Anna admitted, her expression sad as she stared at the house.

Bingo. This was better than he could have orchestrated if he'd written the script himself. After they shot the guns, he'd see if he could convince her to at least stand in the open doorway and peek inside the house. Then, while sentiment was high, he'd tell her it could all be hers—with a few strings attached, of course.

"Do you shoot much?" Anna asked as he finished loading the revolver.

"Not too much," Eli said. "Scout activities mostly when I was growing up."

"You were a Boy Scout?"

"You sound surprised." He glanced at her. "Kids from the city can't be Scouts too?"

"It's not that." Anna clasped her hands in front of her and shrugged. "You don't seem the type, is all."

"Not rugged enough, huh?" Eli tried to pretend her comment hadn't stung a bit.

"I didn't mean—"

"No offense taken." *Not too much, anyway.* He stood again. "I was a Boy Scout, a member of the chess club, swam on the swim team, attended summer camp—all summer—each year from the time I was eight to eighteen, took computer programming after school at the library, was in a community theater group, and earned my black belt in karate."

"That's some diversity." Anna whistled. "And I thought I was a busy kid. How'd you ever have any time at home, or to hang out with friends?"

"I didn't. That was the main reason for all those activities—kept me busy." *And out of my parents' way.* He turned toward the target before she could say more.

Behind him Anna cleared her throat. Eli turned and saw that she had a pair of goggles and ear muffs dangling from her hand. "You forgot these, Mr. Boy Scout. You wouldn't want to go deaf or take out an eye."

"Right." He'd grabbed two pairs of muffs and plastic eye wear protection before leaving the garage. Anna put hers on, and he did the same, then turned toward the target again.

"I'll shoot six. Then you can try. Loser washes the dishes."

"Guess I'd better win then," Anna said. "Or plan to drive the plates home in my car."

Strike two. If she was really that averse to even going in the house, how was he supposed to get her to consider his proposal?

Anna moved farther away from him, and Eli took aim. The trigger was stubborn, sending his first shot high and right. After that he got the hang of it and didn't do a half-bad job of hitting near the center of the target.

Outside the gate a car slowed, then actually stopped.

"Your turn." Eli prepped the revolver, and Anna took it from him. She held it out at an odd angle, displaying obvious discomfort.

"When's the last time you shot a gun?"

"Hmm." She considered. "Might have been when my best friend's—Bree's—dad and brothers took us hunting with them. When we were close to a deer, I shot my rifle in the air to scare it away because I couldn't bear the thought of it being killed."

Eli laughed. "I bet that went over well."

"Oh, yeah. In retrospect, I'm kind of surprised they didn't shoot *me*."

"Go ahead and try now," he urged. "No deer will be harmed in the process."

She faced the target, used both hands to hold the revolver away from her body and—after some effort—pulled off a shot. It missed the target completely and veered off into the bushes behind.

"That was pitiful." She turned back to him with a wry look. "Let's hope no one is ever threatening me and my life depends upon firing a gun accurately."

The thought of Anna being threatened unsettled his

stomach. "Want some help?" he asked before fully thinking the offer through.

"Sure. Give me your best tips."

"You had the right idea." He came up beside her, an arm on either side, and placed his hands over hers on the gun. Her skin was soft and cool. She had goosebumps, though it didn't feel at all chilly out to him. Her slender arms trembled, as if the revolver was taking her strength.

"Good thing we started with this one." Eli tightened his grip, steadying hers. "The others in the trunk are a lot heavier."

Anna didn't say anything—didn't move at all or acknowledge him.

"Hold it a bit higher, and look down the barrel." He tried to focus on the task at hand, but her hair brushing up against his face and her body so close to his was distracting. "Ready." His voice sounded strained.

Together they squeezed the trigger. This shot hit the target.

"Better," Eli said. "Try another."

"I can't." She jerked her hands from his grasp. Eli fumbled with the revolver as she ducked beneath his arm and started running toward her car.

"Anna, wait! I'm sorry. I didn't mean—" *To frighten you?* He sounded like Carson calling after her at the store the other day.

"I know." She turned and ran backward for a few steps, facing him. "My fault. I'm sorry." She held a hand out, palm facing him, as if to warn Eli to stay where he was. He did.

"I still owe you change from Monday," she called. "I forgot to give it to you earlier. I'll—leave it in an envelope at the market. You can pick it up anytime." She turned around and continued running.

Was she too rattled to give it to him now? Not that he

cared about the money. He hadn't expected any change. He did care that he'd done something to scare her off like this.

The Excursion door slammed, and the engine roared to life.

Eli rubbed the back of his neck, exasperated as Anna made the quick escape he'd envisioned earlier, never imagining she would actually feel the need for one.

Strike three. He still hadn't talked to her, and his good intentions tonight were backfiring all over the place. She was scared—of men in general, perhaps. And now, of him. He hadn't been trying to make a move on her, though he could see how she'd read it that way.

His own reaction to being so close to her hadn't been stellar, either. Having his arms around Anna had felt great. It wouldn't have taken much to go from an honest attempt at helping her shoot better to turning her toward him to enjoy other activities, particularly those involving her lips.

This was Anna Lawrence, after all. The girl he'd been hearing about and dreaming of since high school. His fantasy literally right before him, at his fingertips. *It would have been so easy . . .*

Who was he kidding? Nothing about this situation had been easy thus far. What had Gabriel been thinking to do this to him? *Payback for never visiting.* Eli imagined he could hear the old man's voice in his head, though he'd never actually heard it in real life.

He returned to the lawn and put the revolver back in the trunk. He toted it into the house, then started on the mess on the front porch, alternately cursing and thanking Gabriel for the predicament he was in.

Because of him, Eli was out here in the middle of nowhere USA, where everything closed down by eight o'clock, the local market didn't sell anything requiring a can opener, and people drove their cars slowly by his house for Friday-night entertainment.

On the other hand, because of Gabriel, he'd finally met Anna Lawrence and had even been able to have dinner with her on a Friday night. *Until I frightened her off.*

Eli gathered up the last of the dishes, then carried them toward the front doors. He nudged one open and paused on the threshold, staring inside the vast, empty foyer. "What do you want to happen here, Gabriel?" Eli whispered aloud the thought that had haunted him since he arrived. No answer or vision came to him. Instead the empty halls, grand staircase, and covered furniture seemed almost to mock his efforts thus far.

Eli stepped inside, and the door shut behind him. He was alone again, as he had been for much of his life. Only in this place did it seem to bother him. *I can't stay.* For some reason he couldn't say that out loud here. Not yet. Maybe he did believe in ghosts. If they were real, he wished one would give him a straight answer.

"What did you hope for, Gabriel?" Eli spoke louder. "What did you expect us to do with all this?"

Chapter 16

ANNA'S PHONE BEGAN ringing as she pulled into the driveway. *Mama. At last.* Anna's mind switched gears quickly from the distressing end of her evening to the earlier, distressing news about her father. She reached into her purse and hit accept. "Hello."

"Hi, Anna. I've called to apologize."

Not Mom. Eli. Anna punched the button for the garage door harder than necessary. She was going to have to give him an explanation for what had just happened back there, but she couldn't right now. Not when she didn't understand it herself.

"No apology necessary. I'm sorry I freaked out." *Again.* She edged the Excursion into the garage.

"I'd say that was a pretty normal reaction for someone who hasn't been on a date in almost four years."

"That wasn't a date." Anna put the car in park. Her eyes narrowed as she picked up her phone and glared at it—as if he could see her expression on the other end.

"It wasn't," Eli repeated, sounding as adamant as she felt on that point. Which, for some absurd reason, made her feel even worse.

"So I can see how my actions at the end were way out of line. I wasn't thinking. I'm really, really sorry. Honestly, I was only trying to show you how to shoot straight."

He was certainly shooting straight right now, essentially telling her that the moment she'd felt between them hadn't been a moment at all.

"The last thing I wanted to do was make you angry."

"I'm not angry." Not at him, anyway. At everyone else in Holiday—possibly.

"Well, frightened then. Or shocked, frustrated, uncomfortable, blindsided—any of those cover it?"

"Yeah." Blindsided came closest. It wasn't Eli who'd frightened her, but her own reaction to his nearness. She hadn't felt anything like that for a *long* time. That it had come out of nowhere and happened so suddenly had been alarming. It still was, as was the fact that the scent of Eli's cologne still lingered, and she couldn't stop thinking about his arms around her. Anna leaned her head back against the headrest, annoyed with herself for what had clearly been an overreaction on her part.

She covered the phone and blew out an exasperated breath. "It's all right, Eli. All is forgiven. I'm sorry I was so jittery and quick to rush off. Thank you for the lovely dinner." It really had been lovely. All of it, even the awkward moment at the end, if she were being honest with herself.

"Thanks," he said, sounding vastly relieved.

Anna pulled the keys from the ignition and dropped them in her purse. "You're welcome. Though I think that was your line, after I thanked you."

"Yeah, probably. Guess you're not the only one out of practice with social stuff."

"Goodnight, Eli." Probably another faux pas, cutting him off just as the conversation was getting good. But it was better this way. He'd be out of here shortly. There was no reason to pursue any—anything. Anna opened the car door and stepped out.

"It was a good night, Anna. Thank you. See you around sometime." It seemed he'd caught the message and ended the call just as another came in, the one she'd been expecting.

She'd hoped for a few minutes to think about the

conversation that had just ended, but no reprieve. Her mind switched gears again.

Anna swiped her finger across the screen. "Hi, Mom. I've been waiting for you to call." She had been—mostly. Though for a while there, during dinner with Eli, she'd forgotten about the phone call, the Mulberry, Seattle, and most everything else in her life. For an hour or so, she'd behaved like any normal woman spending time with a man who intrigued her and to whom she was attracted. And then—

"Sorry I couldn't talk earlier." Mom sounded tired.

"That's okay. I saw your text. Is Dad feeling better now?" Anxiety for her father returned, hitting Anna squarely in the chest as she entered the kitchen and flipped on the light. She stared through to the family room and Dad's favorite recliner, empty.

"A little better," Mom said. "It's been a really rough week. Much harder than either of us anticipated. They tell you to expect and prepare for the worst, but I think it's in our nature to always hope for the best."

"That needs to keep being in your natures," Anna said firmly. She slipped off her sandals and walked barefoot into the family room, making a beeline for the recliner. "A positive attitude can do a lot."

"You sound like your mother," Mom said with a slight laugh.

Anna felt better, just hearing it. "My mom's a pretty smart lady. Smart enough to know that she ought to tell her daughter everything that happened this week, and especially today."

"I intend to, but first how was *your* week?"

Anna dropped her purse on the floor and collapsed into the rocker, throwing her legs over the side like she used to. She didn't want to rehash the last five days, but she'd have to tell her mom something. "Mostly good. Busy."

"Has Gabriel's great-grandson asked you out yet? Have you been over to help him?"

Right to the point, Mom. "Yes, and yes," Anna said. She had been over to Mr. Steiner's, and technically tonight could have been classified as a date. "I had dinner with him this evening and just returned a few minutes ago."

"That's wonderful, Anna." Mom's buoyed spirits were nearly tangible, all the way from Florida.

"He's very nice," Anna continued. "He's also only in town for a short time, so don't get any ideas."

"Of course not. But you went on a date—that's a great first step."

Anna frowned. "I thought the first step was coming home and facing my past."

Mom paused—a rarity unless she was caught off guard. "It is. I just meant—"

"I know what you meant, Mom, and I know what you're up to, and it's not going to work. In a perfect world I would come home and fall madly in love with someone and live happily ever after in the house next door to you—but life isn't like that. I'm not going to have some Holiday romance while you're away."

"Not this time, maybe, but—"

"Enough about me," Anna interrupted, realizing the circular nature of their conversation could cause it go on for hours. "How is Dad?"

Mom paused again, making Anna suspect she was choosing her words carefully.

"Sick. Worse than I've ever seen him. They told us to expect a reaction about a day after his treatment. They said it would gradually lessen in the days that followed, but it hasn't. He's become sicker and sicker. He couldn't keep anything down and just kept vomiting. I finally took him back to the hospital this afternoon. He was so dehydrated. They've given him an IV, and they're going to keep him overnight."

Oh, Dad. Anna clenched a fist close to her heart. "Is he going to be okay now?"

"I think so."

Mom's answer wasn't the reassurance Anna wanted.

"They're going to have to adjust his meds to something not as strong."

"He won't be happy about that," Anna predicted. "He wanted the big guns." *I'm going to torch this thing,* he'd said. He'd intended to leave it smoking, a figurative pile of ash on the road of his life.

"He's too sick to protest much right now," Mom said, sounding worried again.

"Should I drive over and give him a pep talk?" As she spoke, Anna realized the offer was as much for herself as for any benefit to her father. She wanted to see for herself that he was all right.

"Not yet. Not now," Mom said. "Let him recover from this treatment and try the new regimen. Then maybe you can visit."

"Okay." Anna clenched a second fist alongside the first, her anxiety escalating even as she felt slight relief. Dad hadn't acted all that sick last weekend. The evidence of cancer had been there, if she looked closely, but mostly he'd seemed like her same old dad. Strong, solid, sure. She wanted to keep picturing him like that, not weak and suffering in a hospital bed. But if it came to it, she *would* go. For both of her parents. In the meantime, she felt a sudden and renewed sense of purpose about the Mulberry and keeping things at home running as smoothly as possible for their return.

"Things at the store are good," she said, forcing a chipper note to her voice. "Lots of customers this week. We won't have a lot for the boxes tomorrow afternoon."

"Make sure there's plenty in them," Mom said. "Pull things from the storeroom if you need to. I've even had Carson stop at the Piggly Wiggly for produce if we're out. It's important those deliveries have some fresh items too."

From the Piggly Wiggly? Was she serious? "You've been buying things from another grocery store to give away for free?"

Mom laughed. "Put that way, it does sound a little ridiculous. We don't have to do it often. Don't worry."

"I do worry, Mom. This is your retirement. How can you expect to keep a business running with all that you give away and donate? What is the ratio of your paying customers to the charity cases?"

"The ratio doesn't matter."

Anna imagined Mom's dismissive flutter of fingers.

"And don't worry about us. Dad and I have a good retirement planned. We're going to be just fine."

"If you say so."

"Besides, we've done more business the last two years than ever before," Mom said. "Thanks mostly to the website and online orders."

Thanks to Carson, she might have said. "You might have told me about that," Anna said, trying but not entirely able to keep the edge from her voice. "And that floral order to Bree was sneaky too."

"Can't blame a mom for trying to help."

Anna imagined Mom's carefree shrug.

"And we intended to tell you. We tried," Mom said. "We wanted to talk to you about Carson's role at the store, but you went to your room and pouted, remember?"

"Hmm." Anna couldn't argue. She had done that. But it had been better than the alternative, lashing out at her parents.

Thinking of that, of *them*, softened whatever harsh words she might have said. All that mattered was that Dad got well and they came home again. She might not belong in Holiday anymore, but they did.

"How are *you* holding up?" Anna asked, imagining how difficult it would be to see either of them suffering.

"It's hard—" Mother's voice cut off abruptly, followed by a hiccup that preceded a sob. "It's really, really hard."

"Oh, Mom." Anna grabbed the phone, took it off speaker and pressed it to her ear, as if that might somehow make them closer. "What can I do for you? Are you sure you don't want me to come?"

"No. Not yet. Not at all—hopefully. I just keep thinking about—remembering when Darlene . . ."

Carson's mom. Cancer. Of course Mom would be thinking about that now. *I should have been thinking about that too.* Mom and Darlene had been best friends. Losing Darlene had been like losing a family member. Anna had adored the woman she'd believed would one day be her mother-in-law, and Mom and Darlene had been practically inseparable from the time they were young girls—fifty years of friendship by the time Darlene succumbed to breast cancer four years ago.

Anna clutched the phone, wishing she knew what to say to bring comfort to her mother. How frightened she must be, remembering Darlene's losing battle with cancer. She couldn't lose her other best friend too.

Please, God, not Dad. Not now. Not yet.

Prayers didn't work like that. Anna knew better. She could ask, but she couldn't demand. She couldn't dictate the outcome. Mom, of course, knew that too.

"Dad isn't Darlene," Anna finally said at last, forcing determination and strength to her voice. "Dad's cancer is small. It's isolated. They're going to get it all, and he's going to be just fine. I mean, this is *Dad* we're talking about. How many times have you said he's the most stubborn man on the planet?"

"Perhaps too many." Mom sniffled, but sounded a bit better.

"Perhaps, not," Anna said. "Stubborn can be good when it comes to fighting cancer. He's going to make it. He's going to be well again."

"So are you," Mom said, her voice filled with emotion. "You are your father's daughter, after all."

"Yours too," Anna said. "I love you, Mom. I love you both so much. I'm sorry I waited so long to come home."

"You're there now," Mom said. "That's what matters."

Anna stared at the phone for long minutes after they finally ended the call, each teary. She curled her legs up beneath her on the recliner and pulled the blanket draped over the back over her. If Eli had been here right now and offered his arms around her, she would have accepted gladly. He could have held her close while she figured out a lot of things far more important than how to shoot.

Chapter 17

ANNA POURED HER worry into work at the Mulberry from early Saturday morning until well after closing, doing everything from cleaning out coolers to polishing the 1950's-era soda fountain that still stood sentinel behind the counter. Long after the others had gone home, and when she was finally too exhausted to work any longer, Anna turned off the bulb lights over the counter and headed toward the back room, pausing a second to glance toward the blinds drawn over the front window.

Had it only been a week ago that Eli had tapped on that window, looking a little lost and forlorn and very hungry? A day before that she'd sat beside him on the plane. And now... She'd had dinner with him twice. Part of her wished it had only been once, that she hadn't seen him after he'd had dinner with her family. The other part of her wanted to see him again and wished he'd appear at the window as he had before.

Dangerous thoughts. She crossed the back room, let herself out, and locked up. *Dangerous, but better than thinking about Carson and Bree.* As she drove away from the store, Anna realized she'd made it through the first week. *One down, eleven to go.* But the first one had to be the hardest, and—aside from unexpectedly meeting Carson and Bree's daughter on Monday—it hadn't been as bad as she'd imagined it would be.

The first hurdles were crossed, and there was hope she might make it through the next several weeks to return to Seattle no worse than when she'd left—maybe even better. If she could just make it through church services alone tomorrow . . . Her parents would expect her to go. And now that she was home, Anna somehow expected it of herself too.

Anna walked through the open doors of the church, eyes straight ahead, intent on reaching her family's usual bench without having to talk to anyone. Seeing people in the store this week—when she was wearing her "temporary manager of the Mulberry" hat—had been one thing. Fielding questions and sympathetic looks at church was another, one she didn't care to deal with.

Her plan was simple—no eye contact, walk to the bench quickly, open her Bible, and pray for Betty to start one of her especially fervent, window-rattling preludes as soon as possible. Anna accomplished the first two steps and turned toward the pew—only to discover it wasn't vacant.

Eli stood as she began making her way toward him.

No turning back now. And if she had to talk to someone, he was safer than were the rest.

"I wasn't sure if you'd sit here again—if it was an every-week thing," he said. "But I thought, if you did you might like company. I thought maybe it would be better than sitting alone. But I can move elsewhere if you'd prefer."

"You can stay." Anna hadn't seen this side of him before—uncertain and almost nervous. Who could blame him, after the way she'd run off Friday night? That was twice now that he'd seen her flip out. She was surprised he wanted to sit within twenty feet of her. "It was a nice thought. It will be better than sitting alone."

She didn't offer him more than that and didn't sit too close. Already tongues would be wagging. And she felt unsettled, being even this close to him and remembering his arms around her Friday night. Would there come a day when going to church would just feel *normal* again? When her greatest worry would be keeping a straight face while the frequently off-key choir battled Betty for volume?

Anna set her purse on the floor and smoothed her skirt. At least she was here, and it did feel the tiniest bit easier.

"Mind if we join you?" Clarence Ward and his daughter, seven-year-old Julia, moved sideways toward Anna, a third of the way down the pew already, so that she couldn't very well tell them that, yes, she did mind. *Very much.*

That they'd asked at all was considerate—it wasn't as if her family owned the bench. They'd just sat here for the past couple of decades. But they often shared it, and there was definitely plenty of room today.

Clarence sat—far too close to Anna for her comfort. As soon as he was distracted for a second, helping Julia get settled, Anna took the opportunity to scoot farther down the bench. Better close to Eli than to Clarence, who had graduated high school the class before hers and whose wife had left him when Julia was just a toddler. It had been well known for years that he was in search of a replacement.

He'd said a brief hello to Anna at church last week, and in the space of the few seconds that he'd held onto her hand longer than necessary, she had seen clearly that he was interested in pursuing more than a casual reacquaintance. She, of course, was not. But that didn't mean she could be unkind to him. What Clarence had been through made her pain look minimal. So without trying to be encouraging, she'd taken the time to talk with him when he'd visited the market last week, and now she smiled, shook his hand again when he extended it, and listened to him talk, yet again, about his peanut farm.

"We got ourselves a bumper crop this year, don't we, Julia?" He elbowed his daughter. The little girl nodded and leaned forward, facing Anna, making her uneven braids appear even more lopsided than they already were.

"That is great news," Anna said, noting that Julia's dress was in need of repair, or at least of better laundry detergent.

"We're going to get a dishwasher." Clarence pushed his chest out proudly. "And we got a new dryer last year. No more hanging clothes out on the line during bad weather."

"What a luxury." Anna's smile faltered when Clarence scooted closer again.

"Maybe you'd like to come out and see the place. It's real pretty this time of year with all the leaves turning golden."

"This seat taken?" Donald Andersen's arrival saved her from having to answer. Without waiting for an invitation, he squeezed himself into the space between Julia and the end of the pew. With an expression of terror, likely due to the very real fear of being crushed, Julia hurriedly scooted closer to her father, who in turn moved so close he was practically on top of Anna.

With a quick glance at Eli, to assure him she wouldn't do the same to him, Anna scooted farther down the bench as well, placing as much distance between herself and Clarence as possible, still keeping a hand's width between her and Eli.

"Popular today, aren't you," he whispered, followed by an amused grin and a hint of mischief in his expression.

Anna rolled her eyes, then forced her attention to Donald, who'd just said her name for the second time.

"I say, Miss Annabelle, how are you faring all alone, with your parents gone—in that big ol' house, with its fine kitchen and dining room? I expect it's kind of lonesome with just one for dinner." Donald shifted to better see her, and the bench groaned beneath his extraordinary weight—topping 375 pounds, if Anna remembered correctly. That's what it had been several years ago when, at the Founder's Day picnic, he'd taken guesses for a dollar—all proceeds going back to the church, of course.

Anna forced her lips into a smile. Being kind to Clarence

was one thing. Donald was harder to have sympathy for, given it was common knowledge that he chased anything in an apron. He didn't want a girlfriend or a wife so much as he wanted his next meal.

"I'm hardly alone at all," Anna said. "There's so much to do at the Mulberry. And the little free time I do have—"

"—she spends with me."

Anna turned to Eli, leaning forward on the bench beside her. He winked, then continued. "After that fabulous dinner with her family last week, Anna's been showing me around Holiday, helping a city boy figure out the ropes and adjust to country life."

"You're here to stay, then?" Clarence asked, the frown that had appeared with Donald's presence deepening.

"It's a possibility, yes." Eli sounded so convincing that Anna wondered if there was some truth to his answer. At any rate, it seemed to subdue her two would-be pursuers. She took the welcome lull in the conversation to move her purse closer to where she sat now. She retrieved her phone and scrolled through her mother's latest text, hoping that was enough of a sign that she was done conversing. *With all of them.* Eli included. Though he hadn't really tried talking to her since she'd sat down.

Because he hasn't been given the chance?

"You're not off the hook yet," Eli whispered—too close to her ear for comfort when she was still reeling from the other night, the few minutes of physical contact with him that had cost her two nights of sleep.

"This bench is sure popular today." He looked past her.

Hardly daring to move her head to see who might be thinking of joining them now, Anna glanced toward the aisle and saw tall, lanky Marcus Peterman being prodded up the center beside his mother, Gladys, her eyes fixed directly on Anna, or more particularly, the approximately ten inches between her and Clarence. There was still room on the other side of Eli as well.

Oh no. Not the Petermans. This was too much. "Help me," Anna whispered, sending a frantic glance to Eli.

"You sure?"

She hesitated. He wouldn't tell anyone off, or kiss her in church or anything like that—would he? She only wanted him to somehow prevent Marcus and his mother from sitting here. If they did, then after the service Gladys would, no doubt, block Anna in, forcing her to agree to a date with Marcus—on which Gladys would be sure to accompany them.

Donald, parked on the end of the pew, ought to have been deterrent enough, but somehow Anna knew he wouldn't be. No one in town was as strong-willed—or intimidating—as Gladys Peterman.

Anna gave a slight bob of her head. "Please," she whispered under her breath. "Desperate times . . ."

"They must be." Eli chuckled softly. "All right. Don't freak out." He raised his right arm in a fake stretch, then placed it on the back of the bench behind her. Anna stiffened, the contact affecting her every bit as much as it had Friday night. But Eli didn't move his arm. Instead his hand grazed her shoulder, then stayed there a few seconds before his fingers began a soft stroke at the edge of her butterfly sleeve and onto her skin.

Anna suppressed a shiver and worried her escalated heartbeat could be heard by all, especially by Eli. But his ploy appeared to be working. From the corner of her eye, Anna watched as Gladys reached their bench, stopped, and stared.

"Lean into me," Eli whispered.

Anna complied, or did her best to. She hadn't *leaned into* anyone—other than her parents, briefly, a week ago—in years. Eli's hand slid lower, wrapped securely around her arm in what Gladys would surely see as a possessive maneuver.

At the end of the row, Gladys lowered her spectacles, staring down her nose at Anna. She wasn't the only one who was staring. Clarence was looking at her like he might cry, and Donald's mouth twisted in a look of grim disappointment. After several long seconds, Gladys let out a huff, grabbed Marcus's arm, and dragged him to another bench.

Anna sagged against Eli's shoulder with relief.

"That's better." He angled his head closer to whisper in her ear. "Much more convincing."

Anna wondered how long he would keep up the charade. Her heartbeat was just starting to slow to normal speed again, but the goosebumps persisted. She'd had the same reaction when he'd wrapped his arms around her in the yard Friday night.

Eli's hands had been warm on top of hers. His muscular arms felt strong and protective, wrapped around her. The stubble on his chin had caught her hair and tickled. His cologne had smelled so good. It still did. Until that moment, she'd all but forgotten what it felt like to be held by a man—to feel safe, secure . . . aroused. It was the last sensation that had sent her fleeing, running for her life before something could happen to hurt her again.

The whole notion was ridiculous, of course. Eli had been entirely focused on teaching her how to shoot the weapon. She was the one who'd focused on him. He wasn't about to break her heart, because he had no interest in capturing it to begin with. So why was she so afraid?

Because he makes me feel something. Like so much else about being back in Holiday, Eli was awakening emotions she'd worked hard to bury since leaving. After being numb for so long, the feeling returning to her stung as much as fingers and toes did when thawing after being out in the cold.

It's better to stay frozen.

Too late. With every stroke of Eli's thumb against her

shoulder, Anna melted a little more. It felt good to be touched. *Nothing good will come of it.* It was nice having someone care enough to look out for her. *He doesn't really care. He's just pretending.* It felt good to be close to him with his arm around her. *He'll be gone soon. Don't even think about getting used to this.*

Carson, Bree, and their daughter sat in the front pew, directly in Anna's line of vision. The familiar ache echoed through her. Eli gave her shoulder a little squeeze. "You're going to be okay."

Anna nodded as grateful tears surfaced. Just hearing those words from him meant so much. There would be consequences later for enjoying this comfort now, but she needed it. And she'd survived worse. "I know I will be." For the first time she began to think that, maybe, it was true.

Chapter 18

ELI FOLLOWED ANNA across the church lawn. She stopped before they reached the street where her car was parked. "Thanks for . . . you know." She clasped her hands in front of her and shrugged. "You saved me from at least one awful date."

"Seems like I owed you that much after the way Friday ended." Eli stood a respectable distance from her, now that the need to fend off potential suitors had passed. "So . . . do you have dinner plans tonight?" It was risky asking Anna to come over again so soon, and he didn't want to seem like all the other guys hounding her, but he'd put off talking to her long enough.

"I do," she said, surprising him. "A grilled cheese sandwich and a bowl of tomato soup, followed by a couple of the Hallmark Channel's Christmas shows from last year. Comfort food and movies at their best, though possibly a bit warm—and fuzzy—for eighty-five degrees in Holiday."

"Ah." Eli gave a slow nod, acknowledging her skillful decline. *She doesn't date men—then or now.* He was about to suggest lunch tomorrow, and hint that this was more than a date—that he had something to talk to her about with regard to Gabriel's estate—when he glimpsed trouble approaching.

"Don't turn around now, Eli said, instinctively moving nearer to Anna. "But that lady and man who stopped at our bench earlier are coming up behind you."

Anna's eyes widened with a look of panic. "Gladys and Marcus Peterman?"

"If they're the same ones who stopped earlier, then yes. She's got some wicked-looking spectacles."

"Everything about that woman is wicked." Anna shuddered. "And now she's between me and my car."

"Trust me again?" Eli didn't wait for an answer or her permission this time but closed the distance between them. "Put your hand on my arm, like I'm about to escort you somewhere."

After only the slightest hesitation, Anna complied, and none too soon.

"Miss Lawrence."

"Yes?" Anna feigned surprise as Eli turned them around, so together they faced the older woman and her son.

"Hello, Mrs. Peterman. Marcus." Anna smiled and dipped her head to the side as she gave what Eli could only describe as a miniature curtsy. *A perfect Southern belle.* She really was—from the curls gathered in a large barrette at the back of her head, to her elegant blouse and charming manners. The only thing missing was a long dress with a hoop skirt beneath.

"Good day to you," Mrs. Peterman said, addressing Anna and completely ignoring Eli, as if he wasn't there at all. Marcus said nothing, though the way his beady eyes stared at Anna rather reminded Eli of a vulture honing in on its prey.

He guessed Marcus to be in his mid-to-late thirties, somewhat of a nerd—from the cluster of pens protruding from his pocket—and easily domineered by his mother. His pants were a good couple of inches too short, and he wore white athletic socks—a mistake not usually seen on a grown man, but with teenage boys who didn't care about fashion. His hair was dark and oily, slicked over to one side, in a likely attempt to conceal premature balding.

Poor guy. Eli almost felt sorry for him. But not sorry

enough that he'd let Anna be bullied into a date she didn't want.

"We'd like you to come to dinner this evening," Mrs. Peterman said, speaking again to Anna, this time with an air of expectancy. There had been no question to her words, no invitation, but more a statement of fact. "You may bring a salad and rolls or a dessert."

"That's . . . very kind of you," Anna said. "But I'm afraid I must decline." Her fingers pressed into Eli's arm.

"We have plans already," he said, taking her cue.

Mrs. Peterman narrowed her eyes, lowered her spectacles, and pinched her lips.

A human prune.

She looked first at Anna, then at Eli, then back to Anna again. "Have you not been back in town for precisely one week and one day?"

"Ye—s," Anna said, uncertainty in her voice.

Eli could guess where this was going, and he didn't care for the tone of accusation from this busybody.

"Your parents have been gone less than a week, and already you have taken up with this man you've just met. At least three people saw you *alone* with him last Friday night, under very suspect circumstances. You should be grateful I'm willing to overlook such scandalous behavior and have not retracted my invitation. *Having his arm around you in church.*" Mrs. Peterman clucked her tongue angrily. "What would your mother say?"

"My mother would be thrilled," Anna said.

No lie there. Mrs. Lawrence had practically offered Anna to Eli on a platter.

"Mrs. Peterman, you misunderstand the situation," Eli said, nearly biting his tongue to stay civil. It would only hurt Anna if he wasn't. "It's true that Anna and I just met for the first time last week, but thanks to my great-grandfather, through correspondence, we've known each other for years. We caught the same connecting flight in Dallas and flew in together."

"So you see, Gladys—" Anna began

No more Mrs. Peterman, your royal highness. Eli suppressed a smile.

"There is nothing untoward in our friendship." Anna leaned into Eli a little more as she spoke. "My parents met Eli last week before they left, and they wholeheartedly encouraged us to date."

"I suppose they are just that desperate for you to marry after the fiasco of your last wedding."

"Not as desperate as you obviously are to marry off your son," Eli muttered.

Anna's fingers dug into his arm, and she shot him a warning look, cutting off the rest of the intended, Chicago-style dressing-down he wanted to give old prune-faced Gladys.

Anna's voice was surprisingly even. "Good day, Gladys. Marcus." She nodded to each, then tugged on Eli's arm, steering him in the opposite direction of their cars. Maybe they were walking home instead. He'd probably need a mile or two to cool his temper.

"You don't want to get on Gladys's bad side," Anna said when they were out of earshot.

"You think she *has* a good side?" Eli asked, with a glance over his shoulder. Gladys was already huffing away in the opposite direction, her handbag banging along at her hip. Marcus, however, still stood where he'd been, a forlorn expression on his face as he watched Anna's retreat.

Eli felt even sorrier for him.

"You were great," Eli said. "If it hadn't been for you I would have—"

"Thrown something at her?" Anna smirked as she looked at him.

"No. Never at a woman." Eli feigned hurt at her accusation. "I reserve violence for men. But I would have told her how it is."

"I'm pretty sure you did." Anna dropped her hand from his arm and put a little distance between them—much to his disappointment. He liked having her close.

"Mrs. Peterman has been trying to get her son married off for years."

"Is there something wrong with him?" *Aside from the obvious lack of fashion and grooming skills.*

"Not that I'm aware of," Anna said. "Other than having a bully for a mother, that is. I don't even really know why she wants him to marry. She never lets him out of her sight, so he's not going to be allowed to move out of her house if he does marry. Really, I think it's about Gladys finding someone else to do the chores." Anna shuddered. "Thank you for saving me—again."

"No problem," Eli said. "What's the story with the other two guys who sat with us today?"

"Sad," Anna said. "For Clarence, at least. He was the guy with the little girl."

"The ragamuffin," Eli clarified. "Poor kid." She was the epitome of what he imagined the Deep South looked like—nearly a century ago, during the Great Depression.

"Yes," Anna said, then paused. "I wonder if there isn't a way to get some new clothes for Julia. Maybe a couple of our vendors could sew some items for her for Christmas."

"I take it she has no mother," Eli said as they reached the edge of the grass. Anna began walking the perimeter of the lawn, and he followed, assuming they'd circle back around to their cars.

"Julia's mother left when she was about two years old. It

broke Clarence's heart. If he hadn't had Julia to live for, I'm not sure he would have made it. But he seems to be doing better now."

"He's getting a dishwasher, after all," Eli said.

"Stop." Anna nudged him with her shoulder, then stepped quickly away as if surprised at her own action. "Be nice," she said, more quietly. "Clarence had his heart broken—worse than mine. I can only imagine the hurt he's gone through."

"You're right," Eli said. Anna had a kindness streak a mile wide. Instead of rebuffing the awkward and obvious guy, she'd talked to him, and listened. *I could take a page from her book.* Eli wasn't used to such selfless behavior, to thinking of others—especially others he had no interest in or use for. Life in the windy city was more harsh and unforgiving. And an every-man-for-himself attitude seemed to permeate his profession.

"What about the big guy?" Really big guy, as in Eli had worried the dude would break the bench, or at least tip it his direction.

"Donald—" Anna sighed dramatically— "is always looking for his next meal. True love for him is a 32-oz. porterhouse. He's also particular to sweets. And he wastes no time between meals, scoping out his next culinary conquest. Look." She pointed across the street, where Donald stood talking to a woman.

Eli squinted. "Isn't that the organist?"

Anna nodded. "Betty Oxford. She makes a mean—"

"—Key lime pie."

"How did you know?" Anna turned her head, a suspicious look in her eyes.

"She brought me one last Wednesday," Eli confessed. At the time he'd thought she was being neighborly, but now . . . He wasn't so sure. Given the attention Anna had received today, it didn't seem so farfetched that a woman over twice his age might have been hitting on him. *Only in Holiday.* He decided to start a list with that title, chronicling all the oddball things he'd observed the past week. He needed to get out of here soon, before he starting adopting weird habits as well.

But before he could leave, he had to talk to Anna. Really talk to her. "So," he said casually. "We're dating now?"

"You and Betty?" Anna's brows wrinkled with a look of incredulity.

"No!" Eli leaned his head back and laughed. "You and I are dating—or so the town believes."

"Um—sure." Anna looked away, but not before he caught the frown of worry marring her pretty face.

"If you really want to have grilled cheese at my place sometime before you return to Chicago, I suppose I owe you at least that." She wagged a finger at him. "But don't even think about cuddling on the couch during a Hallmark movie."

Still gun-shy. Eli smiled, loving how serious she was. "No cuddling," he agreed. He didn't need to complicate his life either. Having his arm around her in church had been difficult enough. Difficult, because it would be easy to get used to. "No need for a sandwich either. I can make my own. I was thinking of some place more public." *Safer for both of us.* "Isn't there a path down by the river? Maybe we could go for a walk this evening when it's a little cooler."

"The harbor trail." Anna's smile returned. "Surely someone will see us, and that will only corroborate our charade in church."

"Exactly," Eli said.

And tonight, no matter what, he'd also tell her about Gabriel's will.

Chapter 19

Having declined Eli's offer for a ride in his rental truck, at exactly 5:30 p.m. Anna pulled into the drive of the Steiner plantation. The same wave of nostalgia she'd experienced a few days earlier overcame her again, but this time—as had been the case with going to church—it felt a little easier to bear. A little less sad. Mr. Steiner was gone, but his great-grandson was here, and he was growing on her.

Eli stood on the veranda waiting, looking incongruent with the stately surroundings in his jeans and untucked shirt. Anna drove past the fountain, at present filled with nothing but leaves, and pulled up in front of the wide steps.

Eli jogged down them and opened the passenger door. "Evening', Ma'am," he said in a poor attempt at a Southern drawl.

Anna made a face as he climbed in. "That was awful. You'd best be careful who you speak to like that around here. You're liable to offend someone."

"So long as it isn't the lovely manager of the Mulberry Market."

It was the first time he'd complimented her—even backhand and casual as it was—and Anna took notice. Was he flirting? Should she be worried?

Eli pulled the door shut and fastened his seatbelt as she drove up the opposite end of the drive. She noticed the target was still out in the side yard, but there was no sign of the trunk full of antique guns. Hopefully they were stowed safely back where they'd come from.

"It takes more than a mocking accent to offend me,"

Anna said, reliving Gladys's harsh words this morning. Somehow she'd managed to let those roll off her—largely because she'd had Eli with her. Now she had this walk to look forward to. The harbor trail was one of her favorite, and one of the most beautiful parts, of Holiday, and she hadn't been down there yet in the week she'd been home. She was excited to show it off to Eli, and to see what more she could find out about his plans. He'd hinted at the possibility of staying in Holiday, and she was curious to know if there was any truth to that.

Careful. She told herself there was no harm in knowing whether he'd be here or not, because in eleven weeks *she* would be back in Seattle. Right now, amidst all this sun and warmth and color, that seemed a dreary prospect.

Not wanting to think about the future, Anna glanced at Eli, determined to learn more about him on their walk. "As terrible as your drawl was, at least you don't have a Chicago accent."

"What would that even sound like?" he asked. "Chicago has people from all over the place."

"Gangster, of course," Anna said without hesitation. "You know. Al Capone. The Godfather."

"Now who's being offensive?" Eli flipped down the arm rest and leaned back, not looking the least offended. "Seriously, that's what comes to your mind when you think of Chicago?"

"You can't tell me you didn't have any preconceived notions about the South before you came down here." Anna stopped at the end of the drive and looked in either direction down the lonely street. Today, of course, there was no traffic.

"I did," Eli admitted. "And more than a few have been spot on."

"Maybe mine are too." Anna turned left and headed toward the harbor. "Maybe you didn't really rent that truck.

Maybe you drove it down from Chicago full of the bodies your gang recently knocked off. This whole harbor walk could be a cover for you to scope out the river for a good place to dump them."

Eli whistled, then grinned, letting Anna know she hadn't gone too far. "If marine biology doesn't pan out, maybe consider writing novels—or being an attorney."

"Attorneys don't make up stories a lot—do they?" *Do you?* She didn't want to believe that of him. She wanted him to be as honest, noble, gentle, and generous as his great-grandfather had been.

"Some lawyers are good at bending the truth to their purposes," Eli said, frowning. "Fortunately that doesn't come into play much with real estate law. Titles and deeds of ownership are usually pretty straightforward."

"Good," Anna said. "Though you were showing some mad storytelling skills yourself this afternoon—about how we'd known each other for years."

"I *implied* that. What I said was at least partly true—thanks to Gabriel I do feel like I've known you for years."

Anna narrowed her eyes as she looked over at him. "How so? When the two of you never even met?"

"Letters," Eli said simply, not offering more, a knowing, mysterious gleam in his eye. "I wasn't lying about that."

"Hmm," Anna said. That explained a lot, actually. Though she wasn't sure how she felt about it and wondered what, exactly, Mr. Steiner had written about her. Certainly not much the last few years, since she hadn't been around.

"Well then, it seems only fair I learn your life story. Let's start with the easy stuff. Do you like being an attorney? Is it interesting?" Friday night he'd asked her all about her job, but somehow they'd never gotten around to discussing his.

"Mostly I like it, and it can be interesting. Do you mind if I roll the window down? It's so nice out."

"Go ahead," Anna said. "We're only a few minutes away, and this really is great weather." Seattle summers might be much more pleasant, but it was hard to beat the other three seasons of the year in the South. "You want to elaborate on *mostly* and *interesting*?"

Eli hit the button for the window. "I like the people I work with, though the work itself isn't always the most exciting or fulfilling. It's certainly not *Law and Order* or anything like that—not that I ever envisioned that for my career. A lot of paperwork, tracking things down, documentation . . ."

"Maybe there is no such thing as a dream job," Anna mused as she turned into the harbor parking lot. "There's too much paperwork at my job, too. Though I get the need to keep a record of everything when doing research." She headed toward the few stalls reserved for those not towing boats.

"I think any job can be a dream job—if we decide that's what we want it to be." Eli craned his neck, looking back at the harbor as they drove past. "Wow. That's like a postcard."

"Especially at this time of day," Anna said. "A lot of artists come to Holiday just to paint our harbor." She pulled around and parked her parents' SUV facing the harbor. She turned off the engine and took a moment to appreciate the view while Eli's window rolled up again.

Late-afternoon sunlight slanted across the river, adding a shimmer and glow to the surface. Tall pines and giant oaks lined the far bank, with an archway of enormous magnolias fanning out over the path on their side. A few fishing boats dotted the harbor, bobbing up and down lazily, as if their owners were in no particular hurry to go anywhere. They probably weren't. Anna had known some of the fishermen around these parts to spend all day in their boats, drifting along lazily, or not at all, depending on the current.

She and Eli got out of the car and walked toward the trail.

"How would one go about making any job a *dream* job, as you suggested?"

"It's a matter of finding something to love about it." Eli's eyes were darting back and forth as they walked, as if he was trying to take it all in. "Holiday is a pretty little town, but this—is the crown jewel. How is this not a major tourist destination?" He turned suddenly. "Was that a deer?"

"Probably." Anna smiled, pleased that he appreciated the harbor's beauty. "Is there something you love about your job?"

"Not yet," Eli said. "Nothing I hate, either. But it's not the place I want to stay forever. Kind of like your situation." His gaze slid sideways toward her.

"True enough." Anna admitted out loud what she'd been thinking more and more lately. Maybe she wasn't going to be in Seattle forever.

"I also think our dreams change over time," Eli continued. "It's not all that uncommon for what people study in college to end up being different from their careers."

"What does someone do in that instance—if he finds himself not loving the career he trained for? What would you do, if you decided you didn't want to be an attorney anymore?"

"Have my head examined." Eli laughed. "From a financial viewpoint, I've got a pretty sweet gig."

They reached the trailhead at the end of the parking lot. "Which way would you like to go?" Anna looked down the trail in either direction. "Left or right?"

"What would you recommend?" Eli asked. "Is one better than the other?"

"Not really," Anna said. "They're both beautiful. But let's go right—downstream—we might see an animal or two that way. There's a little less activity on the river that direction."

"Sounds good."

They started off, Anna making sure to keep a safe

distance between them. She'd come home from church feeling all out of sorts again, though Eli's actions had been purely directed at helping her. With no one else on the trail right now that she could see, there was no reason for them to pretend they were dating. No reason for them to be close, physically or otherwise.

No matter that it was nice. Especially *because it was nice.* She'd never really dated anyone other than Carson, but she'd seen plenty of short-term romances during her college years and at her job at the university. Maybe it was her upbringing working in a market and living in a small town that harkened back to simpler times, but if she ever became brave enough to venture into romance again, she wanted what she'd had before—or thought she'd had. She wanted something long-term, someone committed. Eli could obviously be neither.

Not that there is anything between us.

But she did feel a connection—friendship—with him. Since being home, she'd begun to realize how little she'd connected with anyone these past few years. It wasn't in her nature to be so withdrawn, but somehow that was exactly how she'd become and who she was—the quiet loner. At work, in her apartment complex. Not even a cat to talk to, just plants. Kerry was right. *There really is something wrong with me.*

So fix it, already. Be the girl you used to be.

"So are *you* thinking about changing career tracks?" Eli asked, bringing her back to their previous conversation. "Is it time to reinvent yourself? Return to school? Jump ship? Try something new?"

Was she? *A new job, possibly away from Seattle?* It would mean leaving the safe zone she'd carved out for herself.

It seemed a terrifying prospect, no less frightening than jumping off a high cliff. But if she stayed where she was . . . "I don't know," Anna answered truthfully. "I'm not *un*happy with my job, but I'm also not really excited to go to work each day."

"But are you excited about your paycheck?" Eli grinned. "I'm not too thrilled Monday mornings, but Friday paydays are a different story."

"So, for you, job satisfaction is all about money?"

"No." He shook his head. "But it goes a long way. I'm willing to put up with quite a bit for the salary I take home."

"Maybe I should have gone to law school," Anna joked. Being a marine biologist was keeping her well above the poverty level, but she wasn't exactly wealthy.

"Nah." Eli shook his head. "Money isn't what makes you tick. People are. Especially your family."

She stopped walking and faced him. "And you know this because . . ."

"Letters."

"Those must have been some letters." She got the feeling he was taunting her with them, that there was something he was trying to get her to ask, or something he wanted to say. What *had* Mr. Steiner said about her? Not ready to rise to Eli's bait, Anna started down the trail again, grateful for the shade of the magnolias. The breeze flowing through the open car windows had felt good, but standing outside was still a tad uncomfortable—warm for what she'd become accustomed to.

"I see where the Magnolia River gets its name." Eli reached to touch a low-hanging branch. "This is really beautiful. And I'm surprised the path is paved. That's pretty fancy for a little town. How did they afford it?"

"You really don't know?" Now who had the secrets? He might think he had something on her, but she'd bet she knew plenty about his great-grandparents that he didn't. "Over here. Read this." She jogged ahead to the first of several benches on the trail that ran a couple of miles in either direction from the harbor. "Read the plaque."

Eli placed one hand on the back of the bench and leaned close to read out loud.

Holiday Harbor Trail
Made possible by the generosity of
Delores and Gabriel Steiner
"Come sit a spell—you'll never want to leave."

"My great-grandparents paid for the bench, or the trail as well?"

"Both," Anna said. "There are about a dozen benches, and they paid for the trail to be paved. It was a long time ago, before I was born. Every five years or so, on Holiday Helpers Day, the community gets together and repaints the benches. If you look closely you can see where some volunteers were less careful than others, and there are smudges on the plaques or paint splatters beneath the bench. The 4H boys and girls always get assigned the same one now. It's pretty recognizable."

"Holiday Helpers Day." A slow grin formed on Eli's face. "This really is Mayberry." He lowered himself onto the bench.

"Because of people like your great-grandparents," Anna said. "People who saw a need and stepped up to fill it. Mr. Steiner told me that once Delores lost her sight she became fearful of going places—even places she'd once enjoyed. She loved the harbor and the river, but the path back then was uneven, with rocks and roots that protruded. Mr. Steiner had the idea of getting it paved so she and others with disabilities—anyone, really—could enjoy it."

"So his generosity was more about helping his wife than the town." Eli pushed off the bench and stood facing her.

"No." Anna shook her head, starting to feel frustrated that Eli wasn't getting it—wasn't understanding what an incredible heritage was his. "It may have started that way for this project, but there were plenty of causes your great-grandparents gave to that they didn't personally benefit from." Except, of course, the happiness that came from doing good.

"They paid for the community center," Anna added. "And I don't remember them attending many events there. It's kind of run down now, but back in the sixties it was state of the art, with microphones and everything. And it's still a big deal for a town this size to have the space."

Eli chuckled. "'Microphones and everything.' Never thought I'd hear the day when microphones and dishwashers were both given such praise."

"Why shouldn't they be? We appreciate the little things down here, city boy." It occurred to Anna that it had been a long times since she had done that herself.

"What else did my *great*-grandparents do?"

He started walking again, and Anna followed.

"Every year they were in charge of Holiday's Sub for Santa program. And when I say in charge, I mean that they were pretty much the ones who did it all. Pre-Amazon, they'd spend a couple of weekends in early December going to Atlanta or Nashville or some other big city to buy everything." It made Anna happy to think of Mrs. Steiner hanging onto her husband's arm as he guided her through the toy department, describing each and every doll or Lego set to her, so she could tell him exactly what to get.

"My family and Carson's and Bree and a couple other families in town would get together at Mr. Steiner's house on a Sunday. We kids would spend the whole day wrapping and organizing the presents while our mothers baked cookies and our dads helped Mr. Steiner hang his lights and set up his tree. He had this big old console stereo system and all these great records he'd play."

"Those sound like good memories."

"The best." Anna's smile faltered. "Who is going to do all

that this year? Now that Mr. Steiner is gone? What will happen to all those families who need a Sub for Santa?"

"I'm not sure," Eli said. "There are several charities mentioned in his will, but I don't remember reading anything about a Sub for Santa program."

Anna folded one arm across her middle and propped her elbow on it, hand to her chin. "I'll have to ask my mom. Maybe she knows. But we can't let that program die. There are a lot of families who live around here—out in the backwoods country—who won't have anything at Christmas if someone doesn't help them."

Eli pursed his lips a moment before turning with a smile meant to charm her. "Sounds like the perfect job for the temporary manager of the Mulberry Market."

Chapter 20

ANNA CONTINUED WALKING a step or two ahead of, to the side of, or even behind Eli on the trail, bouncing around out of his reach, making it clear that she had no intention or desire to continue the charade they'd started in church.

Not a problem. He wasn't offended by her skittishness. With a little luck, he'd be on his way home in the next day or two. Anna's reminiscing about Christmas at Gabriel's house couldn't have been any better timed. She was recalling happy memories in Holiday, while he was busy planting ideas for her happy future here.

"My dad and I used to run on this trail almost every day." Anna bent to pick up a particularly colorful leaf. "The last time was my wedding day. I wasn't planning on running that morning, but Dad saw the light under my door at five thirty in the morning and invited me to go. 'A run calms nerves,' he said. So I went." She stood and stared down the trail, as if remembering.

"What were you nervous about?" Eli asked, genuinely intrigued. The idea of marriage would have had *him* in full-blown panic, but Anna didn't seem that type, and from the letters he knew that she and Carson had been dating for years, prior to their almost-wedding.

"I don't know, really." Anna twirled the leaf by its stem. "Maybe just that everything was about to change. I was excited, but also a bit uncertain. I hadn't committed to either of the job offers I had yet, and I think I was worried that if I accepted the one in California Carson would be unhappy."

She gave a false laugh. "Funny that I was worried about *him* being unhappy."

Funny that she was thinking about which job to take instead of her wedding and marriage. But Eli didn't share that thought out loud. Just filed it away under interesting facts about Anna.

"So this trail is special to you." He attempted to redirect the conversation. He didn't need her thinking about negative things when he was about to pitch Holiday, Alabama, as her future—at least for the next five years.

"Mmmhmm. It's special. I can't wait to run here again with Dad. When he's better." Her words were wistful, slightly worried.

"Sounds like you'll need to be back here within the year." *Or, you could save yourself the trouble and never leave.*

"I will." Instead of sounding dismayed by this prospect, as the woman he'd met on the plane surely would have, she sounded resolute. "Just as soon as Dad is better, I'll be back to run with him."

"Not before?" Eli asked. "Won't your mom need help when they return home? He won't be able to work yet and will likely require some care, but the store will still need to be run. You won't be around to do it."

Anna sighed. "I know. I've thought about that—a little. But I can't take any more time off. The only reason I was able to get a twelve-week leave of absence is because I've literally never taken a vacation since I started working there, and because it was family medical leave."

"Will it be difficult to return?" Eli asked, interested in her answer as much or more than he was in planting the idea of a change of plans in her mind.

"Yes and no," Anna said. "I'd pretty much wrapped up the project I was working on when I left—handed off what little needed to be tied up. So I'll be assigned something new when I return. But it probably will feel a little weird. A little cold, for certain." She hugged her arms, as if anticipating the Seattle weather.

Or something more?

"Cooler temps and cooler relationships?" Eli dared guess.

Anna didn't answer immediately, but her pace slowed. He hurried a bit, and soon they were side by side, shoulders nearly touching. She didn't seem to notice.

"I don't have any relationships there," she said at last. "Not at work or elsewhere. I pretty much just keep to myself."

"I find that hard to believe," Eli said, remembering her at church and the store this week. "Everywhere you go here people seem drawn to you. And you never let them down—even when you probably don't really want to talk to them. You have a way of making others feel important and valued."

"Thank you." Anna glanced at him, a shy smile lighting her face. "That was a very kind thing to say."

"You're a very kind person," Eli said.

"I used to be—I want to be again. It's both easier and more difficult here."

"You were kind to me my first night in town," Eli reminded her. "Saved me from certain starvation. Was that so hard?"

"Not at all. I was happy to help." Anna's smile reached her eyes.

Directed at Eli as they walked, side by side, it felt a little intoxicating. What would it be like to have a woman look at him like that every day? To talk to one every day, as he and Anna had talked several times this week? He wasn't used to interaction like this. At work it was all business; outside of work it was usually sports. What else was there to talk about in his world? Not his family. He and present-day Anna, or Seattle Anna, had a lot in common. They kept to themselves and were loners.

"Dad is the reason I ran in high school." Anna continued her musings. "He was there at every one of my events, cheering loud, embarrassing me a lot of times." She grimaced. "Secretly I loved it, of course."

"Of course," Eli said, as if he understood the concept of having a parent attend something he was involved in to cheer him on. He'd had plenty of events over the course of growing up, with all of the things his mom had enrolled him in, but it was rare that either one of his parents had bothered to attend. By the time he was in high school he'd stopped asking.

"Tell me about your family," Anna said suddenly, catching him off guard.

"There isn't much to tell, being an only child." *Only and lonely,* he'd thought while growing up. But maybe it wasn't so bad. He didn't have any family obligations, no nieces or nephews to buy presents for or to babysit, no brothers or sisters who expected him to call or come over. Those very things used to bother him, but at this point in his life he'd begun to see the merits. "My parents retired a few years ago and entered the world-travelers stage of life. They were in Belgium last I checked."

"Do you ever go with them?" Anna asked. "I'd love a trip with my parents."

"I've never considered it," he admitted. "And they've never invited me. We're not particularly close."

"Why?" Anna stopped walking and faced him, her expression a mixture of genuine curiosity and concern. "Did something happen when you were growing up?"

"No." He paused. "They're not really the family type. They were never really into being parents—kind of the opposite of yours. My parents never said as much, but I'm pretty sure I was an accident. They both had careers, and it always felt like they were never quite sure what to do with me. Now that I'm older our relationship is fine, but nothing like what you have with your family."

"I'm sorry," Anna said, fixing him with another look of sympathy as she had the night she'd given him the food outside the Mulberry. "That must be hard."

Was it? He didn't think about it that way much anymore. It was just the way life was, and he'd managed to turn out fine. Though if he'd had the chance—would he have chosen to grow up in a close and loving family like Anna's? *Probably. Definitely. Yeah.*

"Of course my family isn't perfect either." She frowned. "You saw that well enough yourself at dinner last Sunday."

"They were giving you a pretty hard time," Eli agreed.

"Because they care about me." Anna sighed. "They mean well. I didn't go all the way to Seattle to get away from them, and I really regret that I've missed the past few years. My nieces and nephews don't even know me."

Jackpot. Having Anna reach all these conclusions on her own was all he could have hoped for and more. And now he was about to give her a house and inheritance that would make it possible for her to live much, much closer to her family. Eli started walking again, searching for the nearest bench. She should probably be sitting down when he gave her the news.

Anna strolled beside him. "But I don't think I can ever live in Holiday again. This town is so small. It would be impossible to avoid Bree and Carson."

Eli felt like a punctured balloon. The wind whooshed from his sails much faster than it had entered. "So don't avoid them," he suggested and earned a hurt look from her.

"Never mind." He held up his hands. "What do I know? I've never been in love."

"You haven't?" Anna sounded as astonished as she had at his admission that his family wasn't close. "Never?"

"Never," he said, feeling irritated.

"I find that terribly hard to believe. I'm sure there's a woman or two out there who has fancied herself in love with you."

"I don't think I'm particularly loveable." Eli shoved his hands in his pockets and shrugged, not overly concerned about it. "A flaw of my genetics or something. Look at my relationship with my parents. And my dad wasn't super close to his father, and of course my grandfather left home at a young age and never spoke to his father again."

Anna shook her head. "That is seriously messed up. Mr. Steiner was one of the most loveable people I've ever known."

"In his old age," Carson said. "But what about when he was younger? My grandpa used to say that his dad was really hard on him—too hard. He expected the impossible."

"I can see that he could have been like that," Anna admitted. "But he had a lot of other good qualities. And I imagine you're right—that he mellowed a lot in his old age."

"Maybe losing his son taught him a lesson," Eli said.

"Did losing your great-grandfather—without having met him—teach you one?" Anna asked.

"No," Eli said, perplexed as to how their conversation kept coming back to him when he was diligently trying to make it about her. "Should it have?"

Anna shot him a disappointed frown. "Yes. But I suppose it's precisely because you didn't meet him that you don't understand what you missed. If you'd met him, if you'd known your great-grandparents—both of them—you would have realized what having a close family means. You would have learned to value that, to want it yourself."

"Is that what you value?" Eli asked. "What you want? If so, you're doing a poor job of chasing those goals, out there in friendless Seattle where you don't date men."

"We're not talking about me right now," Anna said, a

mild tone of exasperation in her voice. "I'm trying to find out who Eli Steiner is and what he's all about—which is only fair, since apparently you already know all about me from your great-grandfather's *letters*."

"I do know about you—or I thought I did before this trip." Eli grabbed her hand as it swung back, stopping her forward motion. As expected, Anna jerked away and hopped back like she'd been stung by something.

"The girl Gabriel wrote about wasn't skittish," Eli said. "She was bold, fearless, and loved adventure. She was kind to a fault, always thinking of others and doing things for them. She made time for people. She was everyone's favorite, everyone's darling—a ray of sunshine in an otherwise ordinary town."

"Holiday isn't ordinary," Anna said defensively. "And you make it sound like I was some kind of saint. I wasn't, and I'm not. And I don't want to talk about my life, so whatever Mr. Steiner wrote in those letters—just keep it to yourself, okay? Chalk it up to an old man's delusions, if you must."

"He may have been many things, but he wasn't delusional," Eli said quietly. "And I can't keep those things to myself, Anna. Those letters are why I'm here. *You* are why I'm here."

Her brow furrowed, and she took another step back, as if she feared he might be dangerous. "What are you talking about?"

He sighed heavily. "Gabriel's will. You're in it." Eli motioned to a bench a dozen feet down the path. "Can we sit for a few minutes—please?" he added when she didn't respond. "I promise my truck isn't full of people I knocked off, and I'm not scoping out the river for a place to dump bodies." He smiled, hoping to restore her earlier humor. That he'd put her on alert simply by complimenting her was beyond odd. *What woman doesn't want to talk about herself?*

One who's had her heart broken and doesn't trust men.

Eli dug in his pocket for the partial copy of the will he'd stuck there before she picked him up this evening. He pulled it out. "Or you can just read it if you'd like, and I'll go away and leave you alone."

"No." Anna shook her head. "I'm sorry. I just—"

"Freaked out on me?" He was still smiling to let her know he wasn't upset. He got it, actually, or at least he thought he did. She was cautious now and hyper aware of anything a man might do that could signify interest. He didn't blame her. He'd just have to remember and tread carefully.

He held his hand out, indicating the bench. Without another word Anna turned away from him and walked toward it. She sat at the far end, perched on the edge.

Ready for flight.

Eli sat at the opposite end but turned toward her. "I'd like to tell you a few things—about the letters—before I read the part of his will that's pertinent to you. Is that okay?"

Anna nodded. Her lips pressed together, not like she was angry, but like she was trying not to cry. Her watering eyes confirmed his suspicion. *Great.* He hadn't even read anything yet.

"What's wrong?" he asked.

She brought a hand to her mouth, partially covering it, as if to hold back a sob or perhaps the truth. "I don't want anything. I don't *deserve* anything," she clarified. "I wasn't as good a friend to Mr. Steiner in his last years. I never even said goodbye to him when I left Holiday. That he would think of me at all makes me feel terrible."

"I'm positive that wasn't his intent." Eli felt the mountain before him growing instead of diminishing. Not only did he have Anna's feelings about staying in Holiday to contend with but her guilt as well. "Gabriel knew why you left, and he, maybe more than anyone else, understood what it felt like to have someone you love run away or betray you, like Carson and Bree did. In a sense his son did the same."

"I hadn't ever thought about it that way," Anna said. "I suppose maybe he did understand."

"It's before you left that I want to talk about for a minute," Eli said. "Not to embarrass you or to flatter you into going on a date with me or anything like that. I want you to understand where Gabriel was coming from when he made his will."

Anna drew in a deep breath. "All right. I'm listening."

Eli took a breath of his own, then launched into what he hoped would be enough to prepare her. "When I was in tenth grade a letter arrived one day. It was from a man named Gabriel who claimed he was my great-grandfather. At that point I hadn't even known I had one—that he was alive. My father had told me, in the vaguest terms, the story of his father leaving home and never returning. He didn't really care one way or another that Gabriel had written to me, and it was up to me to do what I would with the letter. I read it and stuck it in a book somewhere and forgot about it—until exactly a month later when the next one came."

"After Mrs. Steiner died I suggested he write to someone in his family. Apparently he chose you." Anna smiled wistfully, as if remembering that conversation.

"I'm glad he did," Eli said. "If for no other reason than to be here right now talking with you." When Anna didn't bolt at that compliment he continued. "Gabriel's letters brought Holiday to life. He was great at describing things, from the rushing river each spring to the exuberant organist, to an ill-fated Easter egg hunt where the person in charge forgot to hard boil all the eggs."

"I remember that!" Anna laughed, then groaned. "It was *such* a mess to clean up. Because the egg hunt had been held outside the church, Carson and his brother had to collect all the broken shells and yolks. I helped." She frowned, as if the memory had turned suddenly sour.

"I sat in my room and laughed until I was nearly crying when I read the description of that day. Sobbing little girls with egg all over their pretty dresses from the boys who'd realized what had happened and capitalized on it. Eggs flying everywhere—hitting the church and cars, the back of women's heads... I could see the whole thing the way Gabriel described it."

Anna nodded. "It was just like that. For so many years Mr. Steiner had to be his wife's eyes. He had a lot of practice noting and relaying details for her. I'm sure translating that into your letters helped him."

"I don't know if it helped him, but his letters helped me. They got me through some rough patches in high school. The world would seem a bleak place, then this little spark of humanity would arrive in the mail. In particular, hearing stories about this girl named *Annabelle* really helped me."

Anna looked down at her lap, but not before Eli caught her blush.

"No need to be embarrassed," he said. "And definitely not ashamed of who you were and what you did. I was in awe of it—still am, actually. Gabriel wrote these stories about you—incredible, almost unbelievable tales, like how you challenged some big-shot fisherman to a contest as to who could catch the biggest fish from the river." Eli glanced at the water, imagining teenaged Anna standing at the edge, hands planted on her hips as she faced off with the fisherman. "The winner had to donate money to the church or something."

"That's right." Anna's smile returned. "The old organ was broken—little wonder, the way Betty pounds on it—and the church needed money for a new one. Phil Ebern had money. He only came to Holiday a few times a year to fish. He had the fanciest boat this harbor has ever seen. But I thought

I could beat him. If I lost I had to clean out all the fish he caught." Anna made a disgusted face. "Given that, no way I was going to lose."

"How did you do it?" Eli asked, though he knew from the letters already that she had won the bet.

"It was simple." Anna's eyes sparkled with mischief. "Phil fished from his boat on top of the river. *I* could fish below. I'd just completed my Junior Open Water Diver certification, so I could dive alone. It took me three different tries—about twenty-five minutes each—to hook a good-sized trout. Carson was in a rowboat up top and had to help me haul it in, it was so big. There's a picture of it in the case at the community center—or there used to be, anyway. It may be they've taken it down now."

Eli added stopping by the community center to his mental list of things to do before he went back to Chicago. "Phil didn't call you out for cheating?" he asked, even more fascinated hearing the story in person than when he'd first read it.

Anna shook her head. "I hadn't broken any rules. I had a hook and line just like he did. I caught a few smaller fish and released them before I caught the big one. Bree's brothers had told me where to go, and they were right. There are some seriously huge fish in this river."

"No alligators though?" Eli had wondered about that—about the wisdom of swimming in a river known to host the occasional gator.

"No." Anna shook her head. "Carson and Bree were both playing lookout for me. I had a rope tied to my suit that they could tug on if there was a problem, and Bree had one of her dad's guns loaded and ready to use if needed."

"What if she had accidentally shot you instead?" Carson asked, his concern growing, though Anna had obviously survived.

Anna shrugged. "Bree's a good shot. I wasn't worried. Of course, our parents didn't know what we were up to."

"Free-range parenting at its best," Eli muttered, feeling a stab of jealousy at her adventures, while every minute of his life had been scheduled right up through his high-school graduation.

Anna tilted her head and pressed her lips together with a look of slight chagrin. "They found out. I got in trouble—probably would have been more, but they couldn't be too mad, since I walked away with a check to cover the cost of the new organ for the church. Phil was only a little irritated—a lot astonished though. He ponied up the money without too much fuss."

Eli slapped his knee and laughed out loud. "That is a great story."

"One-hundred-percent true." Anna's smile remained.

A good memory, then.

He treaded carefully into the next. "Gabriel also wrote about the time you got the flu right before prom. He said you lent your dress to your best friend and encouraged her to go with your boyfriend instead."

"Maybe not the wisest choice, in retrospect," Anna said sarcastically. Eli was glad for that reaction instead of a more volatile or tearful one.

"I remember reading that and rereading it, certain I'd misunderstood. Because no kid I knew would ever dream of doing anything like that. It was kind and generous—selfless. The girls I knew would sooner claw their friends' eyes out for just looking at their boyfriend."

"Bree had never been to prom," Anna said. "Or any formal dance in high school. She didn't date a lot. She was always at home taking care of her dad and brothers, and she didn't have money for a nice dress or time to really date or do much outside of regular school hours. I'm still glad I told her to go," Anna said decisively, as if she'd just come to that conclusion. "She was really happy that night, and I was happy for her."

"See what I mean," Eli said. "Not a selfish bone in you. It's pretty amazing—like the summer you dedicated every single Saturday night to the senior social club."

"Oh my. Mr. Steiner would write about that." Anna leaned her head back but continued to smile. "Carson, Bree, and I had a unit on social dance in PE. Your grandpa had all these old records—and somehow the two meshed into this idea to get the town dancing. And since a lot of Holiday's residents are older . . ." She shrugged. "It became the summer of the seniors—who are pretty darn hilarious, actually. I honestly had so much fun with them."

Eli nodded, though he honestly had no idea what she was talking about. The most he'd ever been around old people was this past week in Holiday. And he hadn't found any of them overly entertaining. He supposed growing up in a tiny town meant a lower standard for entertainment. "Gabriel said you'd drive around and pick them all up. He said you made cookies and served punch, and that it was one of the best summers of his life."

"He did?" Anna sounded surprised. "I didn't know . . . He didn't do a lot of dancing but preferred being in charge of the music. I worried he was missing his wife a lot."

"He was," Eli said. "He wrote about that too, but you and your friends did so much to fill that void. He enjoyed watching the dancing and living a bit through you."

"My life was better because of him," Anna mused, her smile turning sad. "I wish—I wish I'd come back to see him."

"He understood why you didn't," Eli reiterated. "And he had a lot of good memories with you to recall. He'd always include the songs you were working on together. At one point in your visits you started bringing your guitar. So he got out his banjo, and the two of you would jam on the porch."

"Jamming might be a bit of a stretch," Anna said. "My skills were never more than passable. Mr. Steiner was something else with that banjo, though—" She stopped abruptly, a look of revelation lighting her face. She looked at Eli. "That's what he's left me, isn't it? His banjo." She clasped a hand to her heart. "I think I would like that—unless there's someone in your family who would play it."

Eli shook his head. "No one would cherish it like you. It's yours."

"Thank you." Anna sagged against the bench, relief evident in her suddenly relaxed features. She turned to Eli again. "I feel better. About your Mr. Steiner, I mean. Thank you for talking to me. I'm glad to know that I maybe helped him a little. He was one of my dearest friends."

"You were his—you were like family to him, Anna." Eli unfolded the document, almost dreading reading it, dreading that he was likely going to pull her from the place of contentment she'd just reached. "He left you a bit more than the banjo."

Anna's expression at once turned wary—opposite of how most of the world would feel upon discovering that they'd been named in an extremely wealthy individual's will.

"Aren't you the least bit curious?" Eli smoothed the papers on his lap.

"No," she said decisively. "I told you already. I don't feel like I deserve anything. I don't want anything of your grandfather's. His banjo is already more than enough."

We'll see. "I didn't bring the entire will with me today, but I have a copy at the house for you. I marked the paragraphs that are pertinent. I'll skip details about his burial, and the list of charities he's long supported and the funding directives for those. These pages here—" Eli held them up—

"are those that concern you." *Us.* He held the papers out to her. "Would you like to read them?"

Anna shrank back on the bench and shook her head. "You can."

"Okay." Eli wiped his palms on his jeans, wondering at his sudden case of nerves. He couldn't predict her reaction, and it worried him. He didn't want to upset her. He liked the happy Anna he'd been privileged to enjoy off and on this past week. Particularly tonight, watching her remember events from her youth. It had been a revelation into her past, a glimpse of the girl from the letters. The one he'd spent half a lifetime fantasizing about.

That she was a real, tangible person, as delightful and spunky as the stories—beneath her reserved shell—lured him to her, much like the giant trout she'd caught. But that fish hadn't had a happy ending, and he wouldn't either if he allowed himself to be caught here, trapped in Holiday—even if it was with the woman he'd been fascinated by for over a decade.

"All right. Here goes." Eli glanced at her once more before looking at the pages. "If you have a question, it's all right to stop me."

"Okay."

He cleared his throat. "'Last will and testament of Elijah Gabriel Steiner II. I, Elijah Gabriel Steiner, resident in the City of Holiday, County of Baldwin, State of Alabama, being of sound mind, not acting under duress or undue influence, and fully understanding the nature and extent of all my property and of this disposition thereof, do hereby make, publish, and declare this document to be my Last Will and Testament, and hereby revoke any and all other wills and codicils heretofore made by me.'"

Eli paused and glanced up at Anna. Her expression remained calm, unreadable—completely the opposite of how he felt. Maybe he hadn't put this off for a week to give her time to adjust to being home. Maybe he'd put it off for personal reasons, like the very real possibility that he'd never be able to take a walk like this with her again, or have her over for dinner, or pretend with her at church the way he had today, once she knew the real reason he'd come. Not that he planned to be doing any of those things again. He was determined to leave, and to leave everything behind for Anna.

To have. To deal with. Somehow he guessed she'd feel the latter far more than the first. "Item one," he continued, somewhat reluctantly. "'I do hereby appoint Elijah Gabriel Steiner, V, as personal representative and executor of this will and ask that he be permitted to serve without court supervision.'"

"Would you usually have to have supervision?" Anna asked. "Or is this a special case since you're related?"

"It's legal jargon mostly, and it's not unusual for an executor to also be a beneficiary. The probate court system actually favors that."

"Execute away, then," Anna said with a flourish of her hand.

"Items two and three detail the various charities and organizations my grandparents supported while they were alive and left money to—legacy gifts, if you will. Item four is the one that pertains—to us." Eli didn't look up as he spoke, didn't check to see if Anna had caught the one word that really mattered. This wasn't just about her. It was about them and the way Gabriel had tied their futures irrevocably together, for the next five years at least.

"I'll start here," Eli said after a second passed and she hadn't said anything. He bent his head to the document once more. "'All the rest and residue of my property, both real and personal of every kind and description which I may own or have right to dispose of at the time of my death I give, devise and bequeath in equal shares to Elijah Gabriel Steiner and

Annabelle Elizabeth Lawrence.'" Eli paused, glanced up, and caught Anna staring at him with a curious expression.

"We're supposed to divide up what he left us, or share it?" she asked. "That's why you brought the truck—to take back your half."

"Not exactly," Eli said. "This is about more than who gets the china." He felt like he was describing a divorce. "Let me finish reading, and I'll explain. 'Should one of the preceding die before me, then I give, devise and bequeath the entirety of the estate and properties, both real and personal of every kind and description, to the remaining, above-listed party.'"

"Estate?" Anna said weakly.

Eli nodded. *Yeah.* "'In the event one of the above listed does not wish to accept his or her portion of said estate and properties and responsibilities attached therewith, after a period of five years, he/she may withdraw his/her claim, resulting in the entirety of the estate going to the remaining party.'"

"Wait." Anna held a hand up, then brought it quickly to her head. "When you said property, you meant—land? Like Mr. Steiner's *estate*? His *house*?"

"That's exactly what I meant—he meant." Eli understood her mind-boggled expression. He'd likely had the same when he'd read this the first time. "The entire document is twenty-seven pages—most devoted to a lengthy and very thorough list of everything left to us and how to care for it. Gabriel didn't leave anything out—from the roses out front to the forks in the silverware drawer."

"I don't want roses or forks," Anna said. "I'm not even sure I should take the banjo."

"You should," Eli assured her. "There's a bit more you need to hear. Then I'll do my best to answer any questions." So far so good. She hadn't shot the messenger yet. But then, he hadn't read the conditions of their inheritance. Nothing came free in this world, and this *gift* from Gabriel certainly didn't.

"'For a period of five years, beginning ninety days from the reading of this will, at least one of the above-named, Elijah Gabriel Steiner, V, and Anna Elizabeth Lawrence, are to reside at and care for, per enclosed instructions, the property at 10016 Oakdale Drive, Holiday, Alabama, 36555. At the conclusion of the five-year period, parties may continue to reside at and care for said estate per their own desires, or—if neither wishes the continued responsibility—the estate in its entirety shall revert to the town of Holiday, Alabama, 36555, to be maintained by members of the town council.'"

Anna laughed. "You're kidding, right? This whole thing is a joke. I mean, for one thing, have you ever seen our town council in action? They're all volunteers—half over seventy years old. I had to attend some of their meetings as part of my Miss Holiday responsibilities. It takes them three hours to decide which kind of light bulbs to put in the lamps on Main Street. There's no way they could maintain Mr. Steiner's estate."

His thoughts exactly, but Eli didn't say that. If Anna felt obligated to stay to keep the town council out of the picture, so much the better.

"This isn't a joke." He leaned forward, handing the document to her. Anna took it and scanned the page he'd just read, then flipped to the next, the ones that detailed caring for the house and grounds, including the continued delivery of fresh flowers every Wednesday afternoon.

"Gabriel gave us a little time—ninety days—to figure things out. Who is going to live there and all that," he said casually.

"You are." There was revelation, not question in Anna's voice. She looked up from the papers and gave him an understanding smile. "That's why you have the truck. It has your belongings in it, but you didn't want me to know until you'd explained all this. That's why, at church, you told Clarence you might be staying—because you are." Her smile widened. "It's okay, Eli. Really. In fact, it's great." She reached out and covered his hand with hers. "You're his family. You *should* live there. Your Mr. Steiner would be so happy. And I'll be super happy with the banjo. I'm touched that he thought of me at all."

Eli shook his head slowly, though he was panicked enough to feel the need for some quick, urgent action. Something to back up their conversation and allow them to take the other fork in the road before Anna had so definitively closed the gate. "You misunderstand, Anna." Boy, did she misunderstand. "I didn't bring anything other than my suitcase with me. I'm not staying."

Her face fell, and she withdrew her hand. "What do you mean? How can you live in Mr. Steiner's house if you don't?"

"This isn't my place." Eli leaned forward, elbows on his knees as he tried to explain. "I didn't grow up here, didn't know Gabriel. I strongly suspect that the only reason I'm even listed as a beneficiary is because there is often an investigation and wills get disputed when someone other than family is named as the sole benefactor. Gabriel knew enough about me—and that I knew enough about you—to name us both so the transition would go smoothly. He knew I wouldn't move here—if I didn't bother to come down to meet him when he was alive, some old house wasn't going to get me down here after he passed away."

Anna had, though. The whole reason he'd come was to meet her. He could have arranged for someone else to read her the will, but he'd wanted to tell her himself and to meet the woman he'd heard so much about. He'd told himself that he had wanted to see the estate before he decided once and for all that he didn't want it, but really, the property hadn't mattered all that much to him at all. Anna did, and he felt terrible that he'd let her down.

"It's not just some old house." She stood suddenly, looking down on him, anger flashing in her eyes. "It is a home that has been in your family since before the Civil War. It's full of history and memories and—"

"—Not my memories," Eli said. "Not my history. But yours—yes."

Anna opened her mouth as if to protest again, but no words came out. She turned away from him, arms folded across her middle, head down.

Crying? He hoped not. "Anna, I'm sorry. I didn't mean to jump down your throat or sound harsh. A conversation like this between us is the last thing Gabriel would have wanted. I'm sure he meant the gift of his house to bless your life."

"How?" Sniffle. "I don't live here anymore." She still wouldn't look at him.

Eli stood slowly, considering his next words, wishing he'd considered his last a little more carefully. "If you come back to Holiday you'll be near your family again. Near an ocean far more temperate for the activities you enjoy. You could find another job—one better suited to you—within commuting distance. You wouldn't even have to live at the house all the time. Maybe just on weekends."

"You're forgetting one thing." She turned toward him. "I don't *want* to live here anymore. Yes, there are good memories, but really bad ones too. And this town is too small to avoid the people who caused them."

"So what do we do?" Eli held up his hands.

Anna shrugged. "You're the executor, and you're his family. I will happily give up my portion of the estate to you at the end of the five years. In the meantime, I don't want anything. Consider it all yours."

"Oh no." Eli shook his head. "You're not getting off the

hook that easy. I can't just quit my job and move down here to take care of things."

"Yet you expected me to?" Anna's folded arms were back, her eyes watery, like she was as hurt as she was angry.

Eli could see now that he was a certified idiot for having believed she'd not only accept the inheritance but be gushing with gratitude as well. Most women would have been excited to learn they'd just inherited an estate worth millions. But Anna wasn't most women. He sighed wearily. "Chalk it up to my dysfunctional family. I obviously don't read people well—don't communicate or understand or—"

"—On the other hand, *I* understand perfectly now." Anger flashed in her eyes once more. "The whole reason you're here—the reason for inviting me over, being nice to me at church, flirting with me, even—it was all to win me over before you dumped this on me."

"Dumped—I hardly think a historic mansion, acres of property, and an extensive portfolio worth millions is dumping anything. And I didn't say I wouldn't help you. I'm just asking you to live in the house—the house *you* know, the one *you've* made memories in."

"You could have too, if you'd taken the time to come down here." The toe of Anna's sneaker began tapping agitatedly on the pavement. "So what you're saying is, I take care of the estate, and you'll happily manage the money?" She shook her head as a scowl grew on her lips. "Lawyers really do twist the truth to their purposes. I suppose that scenario looks just fine to you."

"It did," he admitted sheepishly. It had, until presented from her point of view. Eli rubbed the back of his neck, troubled by how this was playing out. It wasn't like he was going to be taking any of her share of the money. If anything, he'd be growing what she had. There would be work on his end too, managing investments, keeping track of charitable donations, and the like. All he was asking was for Anna to live in the house. She didn't even need to take care of it. There was plenty of money for her to hire gardeners and housekeepers—anything she needed.

He tried again to express this without ticking her off any more than she already was. "I truly think Gabriel meant for you to have the house. I don't think he wanted a repeat of what happened with his son to happen to you and your parents. He wanted to provide a way for you to be close to them still. They love you—everyone here does. Do you know I tried coming into the store to talk to you three times this week, but every time you were already talking with someone else—with usually three or four people surrounding you—so I gave up and left without you even noticing I was there. Everyone in this town cares about you—even your ex, who has been on my case all week."

This stopped her. Eli watched as whatever argument Anna had been about to throw at him died on her lips. "What do you mean Carson has been on your case?" The words came out soft—and hopeful.

Uh oh. "He—warned me not to hurt you."

"Because he hadn't enough already?" Angry Anna returned. "You heeded him well, I see." She threw her hands up. "I was starting to trust you, Eli, and I enjoyed being around you. I thought you felt the same about me. Now I feel like I've been betrayed—again." She took a step onto the path as if to leave, but he grabbed her arm.

"That's hardly fair, Anna. Yes, I came here specifically to meet you and tell you about the will. I'm sorry if you thought otherwise. I tried to make it clear, from the beginning, that I was here temporarily as Gabriel's executor. I'm sorry if I've hurt you, but I don't see how telling you about an inheritance comes anywhere close to running off with your best friend the night before your wedding."

"It doesn't. It's just—" Anna jerked from his grasp and stood stiffly, facing away from him.

Eli waited, unsure what to do. For the life of him he couldn't understand why she was so upset. He decided on an apology, since he had been wrong to assume she would quit her job and move back here.

"I'm really sorry I've upset you." They weren't even close to hammering this out, but dropping it for now seemed best. *So much for heading home tomorrow.* "I'd hoped that you would be happy. That the house and everything would be a good thing in your life."

"It might have . . . at one time." Her voice sounded soft and fragile.

It still could be. If only . . . "Can I give you some advice?" he dared ask.

She turned to him with a look that said she'd likely slug him if he tried. Figuring he didn't have much left to lose at this point, he dared anyway.

"A terrible wrong was done to you."

Anna nodded.

"But I'm with your brother on this one. It's been a long time. You shouldn't be allowing it to hurt you anymore. You shouldn't let it keep you from being near your family or the beaches you love, or the chance to own an amazing house. You need to get over it, Anna."

"Says the man who's never been in love," she huffed.

"If love messes a person up the way it's messed you up, I hope I never am," Eli said, not willing to back down now that he'd started. Someone needed to say this to her, and since she likely hated him already— "Let the past go. You need to start living again, to be the woman you used to be. Stop being bitter and get better."

"Leave me alone, Eli." Tears glistened in her eyes. "Go back to Chicago. I'll take care of the house until December.

After that it's your turn." Anna took off down the path, running away again. This time he let her go.

Chapter 21

IT WAS NEARLY dark by the time Eli reached the harbor and the parking lot. No surprise, neither Anna nor the Excursion were anywhere to be seen. He'd secretly hoped that she'd waited for him, that the several minutes' head start he'd given her had allowed time for her to cool off. He should have known better. Everything he'd learned about Anna indicated she was a headstrong, passionate person—and not the type to cool off quickly.

Eli looked around, considering his options, doubting there was much in the way of an Uber or Lyft or even a taxi around Holiday.

"Lost your moving truck?"

Eli turned to find Carson a few feet behind him, holding hands with and walking beside a petite, attractive brunette.

"Not my truck, just my ride." There was no point in trying to keep what had happened a secret. By ten o'clock tomorrow morning, no doubt half the town would know Anna had run off and left him to figure out his own way back. *So much for pretending to date.* Next Sunday at church she'd be on her own facing the vultures. Instead of being satisfying, this thought troubled him.

"We can take you home," the woman offered.

"That's a little far—Chicago's about fourteen hours from here," Eli said, attempting a joke that no one laughed at. "I'd appreciate a ride to Gabriel's place, though." He glanced at Carson, trying to gauge his reaction to his wife's offer.

"Sure thing. Not a problem," he said, as if it really wasn't.

No hard feelings, then. Their interactions this week at the store hadn't exactly been great. "Thanks." He waited for them to catch up then walked beside them through the parking lot.

"This is quite the harbor you have here." He looked over his shoulder for a last glimpse. "I'm surprised it hasn't been discovered by some travel magazine and touted as the prettiest little place in America."

"It has—a few times," the woman said. "But the Deep South isn't on a lot of people's travel bucket lists."

"Right." Eli nodded.

"I'm Bree, by the way." She leaned forward, in front of Carson, to smile at Eli.

"Eli." He returned her smile. "Gabriel Steiner's great-grandson."

"I know." Bree's hand swung back and forth in Carson's, carefree, as if they hadn't a trouble in the world. Yet, if what Eli had heard at the Lawrences' house last Sunday was true, they'd had quite a few. *Well deserved? For what they did?* Eli wasn't sure. If there was one thing being a lawyer had taught him, it was that there are two sides to every story. He wondered what Carson and Bree's was.

"I guess everyone knows who I am by now."

"It's a small town," Carson added, as if that wasn't already obvious. "So was Anna showing you her favorite place to run tonight?"

"Yep." *Was* and *run* being the key words. For a night that had started off so promising, things had ended very badly. Eli wondered if Carson knew this already. Or was he just guessing? "She's still running," Eli said somberly, then instantly regretted his words. The last thing he wanted to do was talk about Anna with the two people who had hurt her so badly.

"We know she is," Bree said quietly. "And we know it's our fault."

Whoa. Bree's response surprised Eli as much as Carson's had earlier in the week. So they *both* freely admitted guilt, and that their actions had hurt others. *Interesting.* And uncommon. At least in his line of work.

They stopped beside an older Camry.

"It's unlocked," Carson said. "No one worries about someone stealing a car in these parts."

Foolish. But then, Holiday's residents didn't seem the type to know how to wire a car, and Carson hadn't left the keys in the ignition, so maybe it was okay. Kind of nice, actually. Back home Eli not only locked his vehicle but had an extra alarm system installed on it as well. Car theft was simply a part of life in Chicago. Small-town living definitely offered less to do, and less to worry about, it seemed. He climbed in the back, watching while Carson opened the door for his wife. He came around to the driver's side and got in, then started the engine.

"We have a quick stop, and then we'll drop you off. Our daughter is at Bree's dad's house, visiting her biological mother tonight. We need to pick her up by seven."

Biological—they adopted . . . So *their* Anna wasn't the baby Bree had conceived while Carson was engaged to Anna. "I'm not in any hurry," Eli said. "Just grateful for the ride. I'd have been gone a lot longer if I'd had to walk back."

"If you're ever stuck again, call Ernie," Carson suggested as they left the parking lot and the picturesque harbor behind. "He runs the gas station in town, and he's got a tow truck out back. But even if you don't need a tow, he's happy to give anyone a lift. No charge, usually."

"Before nine at night, you mean?" Eli asked, recalling his first night in town. "I needed gas a week ago Saturday, but it was after nine and the station was closed."

"Ernie would have come over and opened for you," Bree said. "He lives close, and he doesn't mind calls at night. His wife has been gone for several years, so I think the occasional interruption is a nice break for him."

"Why doesn't he stay open later then?"

"No business," Carson said simply. "Hardly anyone goes out at night around here. It doesn't make sense to stay open for an occasional—and I mean very occasional—traveler who might be passing through."

"I can text you Ernie's number if you'd like," Bree offered.

Eli was about to tell her no thanks, that he'd be leaving tomorrow and hopefully never coming back, but before the words could leave his mouth he knew they weren't true. He was going to have to come back. If Anna really wouldn't stay, and it sure seemed that way right now, then he was likely going to be spending a lot more time in Holiday—coming down on weekends or something. Who knew when a late-night ride or tow truck might come in handy? "His number would be great. Thanks." Eli gave his own number to Bree, then glanced at his phone when the contact for Ernie Jensen came through. He opened it and made a note so he'd remember who Ernie was.

Old guy who runs Holiday's only gas station.

"Ernie is also the town Santa," Bree said, as if she had eyes in the back of her head and had somehow seen what Eli typed. "He's a bit of a legend and has pulled off some pretty spectacular Christmas miracles."

"Cool." Eli deleted the previous description and added a new one.

Holiday's gas station Santa, worker of miracles, owner of a tow truck.

"Would you like to come over for dinner tomorrow?" Bree asked, turning in her seat to face Eli.

"Uh—" He looked up from his phone, meeting Carson's gaze in the rearview mirror. His eyes were friendly, encouraging even.

"Sure," Eli said. *Why not?* An hour ago he'd been hoping to leave first thing in the morning. But he supposed staying one more day wouldn't hurt. Not that he expected Anna to change her view on anything or to stop being mad at him in the next twenty-four hours. But he couldn't deny the heavy dose of curiosity he felt about her former best friends. The chance to talk to the two people who had so completely derailed Anna's life seemed too good to pass up. It seemed almost opportune.

Rosie stopped in front of Eli's booth. "The usual?" she asked, notepad in one hand, constantly clicking pen in the other.

Eli pulled his gaze from the diner's large front window and the activity across the street to look up at the owner of Holiday's only eating establishment. Trained resistance—after a week of eating here frequently—kept his hand from rising to shield his eyes against the glare of her blazing, bright pink dress. *Rosie* was aptly named, her love for all things pink apparent just about everywhere one looked in the diner, from the pink checkered booths to the linoleum, to the rose wallpaper. "Yes, please. Thanks." He slid the plastic menu to the edge of the table, careful not to send the manila envelope beside it the same direction.

Rosie reached for the menu.

"Do you happen to know what time the library opens?" he asked, uncertain if Rosie was really the type to frequent such a place. Based on the chatter he'd overheard between her and other customers the past week, she seemed more prone to watching sitcoms than reading. "And if there happens to be a copy machine there?" he added. It was a lot to ask, but people in Holiday had to make copies sometimes didn't they? And surely the library had *some* hours today—or possibly not, based on Rosie's perplexed expression. Eli held back a sigh. A week here had taught him not to expect businesses or offices to be open when common sense deemed they ought to be.

"If you mean the bookmobile, it comes every other Thursday." Rosie stuck the pen behind her ear and crinkled her forehead in thought. "Let's see . . . I don't think it was here this past week, cause Thursday was the day Jed Cooper's tractor conked out in the middle of Main and was stuck there for six hours while he and his dad fixed it. The bookmobile wouldn't have been able to squeeze past. As it was, some of the other traffic had to come up on our curb to get by. You can still see the scuffs on the sidewalk out front. Like I have time to go clean those up." Menu in hand, she turned from the table.

"What about the library hours, though?" Eli persisted. "That old building at the very end of Main—the one with the Rockefeller plaque on it."

"That building hasn't been used since before I was born." Rosie didn't bother turning around as she walked. "Long before that. I think it closed during The Great Depression. A lot of people left the area then."

"Wait," Eli called, half-rising from his seat. "Are you saying there's no library here? None at all?"

Rosie shook her head, her platinum bun bobbing with the action. "Try the bookmobile. Sometimes they can get something for you if you have a request."

"Thanks." Eli sank down in the seat, feeling his heart sink with him. *Get something for you . . .* What he needed was to get out of this town. *No library?* Seriously? Wasn't that illegal or something? Didn't every community in America have something—better than a twice-a-month bookmobile?

A half hour later he exited the diner, discouraged both about the breakfast he'd been served and the lack of a library. He'd been hoping for a place to photocopy his great-grandfather's will with his own, recently added acknowledgment and acceptance signature. He wanted to leave a copy for Anna, as an apology of sorts—to show her he wasn't dumping the house on her. He wasn't ready to call it quits in Chicago and surrender to the maddening conditions of their inheritance, but he hoped he could find a loophole somewhere that would get them out of having to physically be on the premises. In the meantime, if that didn't pan out it looked like he'd be back here in December to start his turn estate sitting—or something.

Last night, as he lay in bed in the dark, anything-but-silent house—it creaked and groaned more than the combined noise of his hundreds of neighbors in his high-rise at home—he'd thought about Holiday and the actual possibility of staying. He wouldn't be able to work remotely from his current job. He'd have to quit, and the thought pained him, and especially his wallet. Then again, Gabriel had more than made up for any difference there might be in his income if Eli found a job closer to Holiday that paid less. Truthfully, he probably didn't have to work at all—if he managed Gabriel's portfolio well.

The old man had been shrewd, that was for sure. Eli couldn't help but be impressed as he'd read through the records of his great-grandfather's investments. Gabriel Steiner had known when and how to take risks, and those had paid off handsomely. For the past decade, the interest alone that they generated was enough for a couple of people to live on comfortably, if not luxuriously.

But Eli wanted luxury—or that he'd become accustomed to, anyway. He didn't appreciate the house with its claw-footed bathtubs and archaic plumbing. He also needed to be in a place that had more going on, more night life, more culture and opportunities—and books.

In the spaces between the many scheduled activities he'd

endured throughout his childhood and youth, he'd discovered that reading filled the voids of his life—voids of time, friendship, and family. From the age of twelve, when left at home by himself on weekends while his parents were away, he'd found it difficult to feel too lonely while off having adventures with The Swiss Family Robinson or sailing for treasure alongside Long John Silver. Middle Earth, Narnia, and Hogwarts had offered escapes from his reality. He'd secretly wished for a band of hobbits or dwarves to keep him company, and he'd envied Peter, Susan, Edmund, and Lucy, who always had each other—even if they didn't always get along. Eli knew what it was to be the boy who lived alone. Fine by him, he'd gradually convinced himself over the years, so long as he had books to read and later music to listen to, concerts to attend, a team to cheer for, and a prestigious job to stimulate his mind. He'd continued what his parents had started, filling his life and time with activities. By today's standards, he was living the American dream. He enjoyed what he considered to be the finer things in life, and he had no intention of giving those up anytime soon.

If he stayed in Holiday, he feared he'd go mad within a month. How did one survive without Cubs tickets, concerts at Lincoln Hall, or a really great library? Amazon might be able to deliver whatever things couldn't be purchased down here, but it couldn't replicate the high of attending an amazing concert or the hopefulness of walking up and down rows of books, searching for one he hadn't yet discovered. The feel, the smell, the quiet of both libraries and bookstores always soothed his stress away. Getting lost in a good story was the ultimate escape. He'd finished the book he brought on the second day here and had read two more on his tablet, late at night when he couldn't sleep, but it wasn't the same. He'd only been gone a little over a week, and he missed his access to all things normal and fulfilling.

That it took a while for current movies to make it to the theater here was understandable. And he got that not every place had the population for its own baseball team and symphony. But books were different—a necessity. A town without a library, or at least a bookstore, wasn't really a town at all, was it?

It was moments like these that made him feel like shouting at Gabriel in frustration, demanding to know how in the world he'd believed a loner city kid would want to move—could survive—in simple, folksy Holiday. *I can't. I won't.*

I have to, if I want the inheritance.

Eli stepped off the curb and smacked a hand on the hood of Gabriel's Cadillac in frustration. He'd thought to ask Carson to give it a jump last night and had been pleasantly surprised when it started. Cadillac wasn't exactly Eli's style, but anything was better than driving that monstrosity of a truck he'd rented. By this time tomorrow he'd be done with it and back home in his condo. The thought calmed him. He just needed to hang in there a little longer.

He unlocked the car—probably the only one it town that had been locked—and reached inside and dropped the lunch he'd ordered for later on the seat. The fridge at the house was empty, but with this to-go box and then dinner tonight with the Armstrongs, he'd have enough to eat until he left tomorrow morning to catch his noon flight.

He shut the car door and glanced at the thick envelope in his hands. He'd have to give this original to Anna. He could print another for himself at home easy enough. After the way they'd left things last night, he wasn't necessarily looking forward to seeing her again, but he also hoped for a better conclusion. Dropping this off at her store meant other people around, so hopefully their interaction would be brief and non-volatile, if not cordial.

She appeared to be in a happy enough mood this

morning. Eli had spent the past half hour watching from his booth in the diner as Anna unloaded pumpkins from a flatbed parked out front. The truck had pulled up promptly at eight, about the same time Eli had, and a man who looked to be about his age or possibly a little younger had climbed down from the cab and gone directly to Anna, waiting outside the Mulberry.

They'd shared a quick hug and then gone straight to work—if one could call it that. Eli had never seen her quite so smiley and upbeat as she was with the truck driver. Their body language spoke volumes—they knew each other well and were very comfortable around one another. Eli had practically heard their banter and laughter all the way across the street, as his eyes zeroed in on the many times the two discreetly touched, while passing pumpkins to one another, or *accidentally* bumped into each other climbing up and down from the truck or setting the pumpkins on the bales of hay stacked in front of the store.

Eli convinced himself that Anna was oblivious to what was quickly obvious to him—the delivery guy was totally into her. His eyes hardly left Anna the entire time they were working, and it was often something he said that elicited a smile or laughter from her. He was clearly leading the way—though it seemed Anna was willingly following.

And why shouldn't she? Eli waited for the one, lone car going down Main to pass before crossing the street. He'd told her himself last night that she needed to move on, to let the past go. Maybe this guy would be the one to help her do that. From a distance he appeared normal enough, unlike those who had hit on her at church yesterday.

Eli's thoughts drifted back to twenty-four hours ago—when he'd been the one with Anna, seated beside her in church with his arm around her. The sermon, like the previous Sunday's, had been surprisingly good. *And the company* . . . He'd enjoyed that a lot too. What guy wouldn't enjoy spending an hour sitting close to a beautiful woman?

Anna's skin was so soft, and whatever perfume she wore made him a little crazy—enough so that he'd offered to play her boyfriend in order to scare her pursuers away. He'd never had an experience like that before—sitting with someone in church and feeling like he belonged. It had only been a charade for both of them, but he'd enjoyed it.

Pushing those thoughts aside in favor of anticipating a long, hot shower—with actual water pressure—in his condo tomorrow, Eli took sure steps across the street and up the sidewalk toward Anna.

The pumpkin delivery guy was still there, though the flatbed was basically empty now. He stood a foot or so from Anna, talking with her, making her laugh again.

Did I make her laugh that much? Maybe he should have focused on that instead of lecturing her on letting go of the past.

Eli caught the second Anna noticed him approaching. Her stance stiffened, and the smile on her face transposed from genuine to a strained fake.

"Good morning, Anna." Eli came up behind the truck driver and stepped to the side of him. "I don't believe we've met. I'm Eli Steiner." Eli offered a smile that felt just as forced as Anna's and stuck out his hand.

"Charlie." The driver took his hand and shook it firmly.

Strong grip, but soft skin. This guy didn't do manual labor too often. Eli sized him up quickly. Charlie didn't have the appearance of either a farmer or a truck driver. So why was he the one delivering pumpkins? *Anna.*

"It was good to see you again, Anna." Charlie's attention returned to her, all but confirming Eli's suspicions. "Be sure to save me a dance at the Holiday Harvest Hoedown."

"If I go," Anna promised. Her smile turned more genuine

as she bid him farewell. But once Charlie had climbed into his truck, all pretenses were off.

"*Holiday Harvest Hoedown*?" Though it probably wasn't wise, Eli couldn't resist teasing her. "Did the same person who came up with Holiday Helpers come up with that one too?"

"It's a small-town thing. I wouldn't expect you to understand." Anna's tone was cold, opposite of the warmth she'd directed at Charlie. "I didn't think I would see you again." As if she couldn't stand the sight of him, she turned away and began arranging pumpkins on the bales of hay.

"I came to give you this." Eli held out the envelope, but she continued her work and didn't take it.

"I figured it would be best to deliver it out in public, in broad daylight—less chance of you completely ruining your life with a murder charge."

"Hilarious." Anna snatched the envelope from him and threw it on the top bale, near the door. "Your delivery is complete. You may go now. Before I risk a lifetime sentence."

"You might want to put that in your office first. Or the car—if it's locked. Somewhere safe. It's pretty important."

"Did you sign the whole thing over to me then?" Anna asked.

"No." Eli couldn't entirely fault her for thinking the worst of him.

"Ah, that's right." Anna hefted an extra-large pumpkin and set it down hard on his toe. "You can't. You're stuck for the next five years."

"Sarcasm doesn't become you," Eli said, wondering why he'd even been worried about hurting her feelings. "I signed the agreement. I accepted the terms and agree to do my part. If you'll give me until December like you said you would, then I'll figure out something by then and be back here to take care of the estate."

Anna froze. Slowly she set down the pumpkin she'd been

holding then straightened and turned to face him. "You're going to move to Holiday and live in Mr. Steiner's house?"

"I'm hoping to find some loophole that gets us out of that requirement. But if I have to, then yes. I will." *Move down here and live there.* The thought was enough to make him ill.

"Why?" She didn't narrow her eyes at him, but neither did she sound entirely trusting either.

"So you don't have to." Eli hurried on before she could interrupt. "I won't take back what I said last night—even though it upset you and I'm sorry about that. I do think you need to move on and put the past behind you. But *you* were absolutely right that I shouldn't have assumed that you'd just quit your job and move here and be all happy about it. I *don't* know anything about love or relationships, and it was wrong of me to tell you to just live here with your former life and *what ifs* staring you in the face every day. I'm sorry I said that, sorry I hadn't thought about your side of this more." Eli paused, out of breath and wondering what exactly he'd just committed to.

"All the information on Gabriel's investments is in that envelope, as is the copy of his will. You're welcome to be as involved as you'd like maintaining his portfolio. All decisions should be joint. We'll have to decide how frequently we want payouts from the interest. And, of course, you're always welcome to stop by the house when you're in town visiting your family."

Anna stared at him, her mouth partially open. "You're serious? Or is this reverse psychology or something?"

Here came the narrowed eyes.

"Well I'm really hoping neither of us have to live there," Eli admitted. "But if it comes down to it, then I'll do it. We have the ninety days as stipulated in the will, though we shouldn't wait that long to get going on some yardwork and maintenance things." *Like an entire master bath remodel.* If he ended up having to live in the house, there were going to be some big changes.

"I can take care of the upkeep." Anna's voice shifted gears from sarcastic to meek. She clasped her hands in front of her, looking contrite. "I don't know what to say, Eli, except thank you. I know you've got a life in Chicago—probably more than what I've got in Seattle. I know it will be an enormous sacrifice."

He shrugged as if it didn't matter, though really it mattered a lot. He didn't want to move to Holiday and live in that creepy old house. So why was he doing this? *Stop!* His brain was trying to tell him to put on the brakes, to throw this in reverse quickly before it was too late, but his mouth wasn't getting the message.

"Well, I guess I'll see you in December." He took a step backward. "I'll be in touch before then and let you know what I can figure out. I have your number." He held up his phone.

"Thanks to my mom." Anna didn't quite smile, but a corner of her mouth lifted for a brief second.

"I'll transfer a couple thousand before I leave," Eli added, strangely reluctant to say goodbye. "Do you think that will be enough for a gardener and a housecleaner? I can arrange to have that automatically deposited in your account each month."

"Two thousand would be enough for a gardener, housekeeper, butler, and nanny." A genuine smile lit Anna's face. "I don't need that much. Besides, I can do a lot of the work myself."

"The yard is gigantic," Eli protested. "It would take all day just to mow."

"About four hours on the riding lawnmower," Anna said. "Carson and I used to—" She broke off abruptly and looked away. "It was how we earned money for college. Anyway, I don't need that much."

"We'll start with a thousand a month and go from there." Eli ached for her. Her entire past really was tied up with Carson and Bree. It was better that she'd be going back to Seattle. Better to be in a place where her past didn't follow her every step of the day. "But you have to let me know if you need more. It's there, Anna. Look through his portfolio and the will, and you'll see what I mean. Basically, we are both very well to do now." He took another, smaller step backwards.

"I'll read all of it," Anna promised. "Thank you, Eli. And I'm sorry for running off last night and Friday—and last Monday. Mostly I'm sorry I'm not the same person you read about in those letters. I feel like I've let you and Mr. Steiner down."

"Never. You're still the same, Anna. Maybe sidetracked a little, but the core of who you are hasn't changed. Gabriel would just want you to be happy, and so do I."

Chapter 22

"I hope you don't mind eating outside." Bree placed a steaming bowl of chili and a plate of cornbread on the makeshift table in front of Eli. "This time of year it's finally starting to be nice out in the evenings, so we try to enjoy it as much as we can."

"This is great," Eli said, meaning it. The river was only a stone's throw away, and the sprawling lawn between it and the house was dotted with mature Magnolias and other trees. His grandfather's place didn't have anything on this little slice of heaven. "You've got a sweet piece of property here, and your house looks practically new."

"That's because it is." Carson took the seat across from Eli and beside Bree. The folding chair beside Eli had a booster seat on it, presumably for the precocious child who'd been running in and out and around since he'd arrived fifteen minutes earlier. He'd met her briefly yesterday, on the way home from Bree's father's house. But little Anna had been worn out from her visit and had kept mostly quiet and snuggled up against Bree on the way home.

Eli had been more than curious about her adoption, but he didn't know how much Carson and Bree discussed in front of their daughter, so Eli had kept his mouth shut and saved his questions for later. Hopefully tonight he could hear the whole story.

"We tore down the existing home and built this one," Carson continued. "We salvaged some of the original materials like the floor and a stained-glass window, but most of the house is new—extra new, actually. A hurricane damaged it while we were building, so we had to start all over again. We finished a few years ago, about the time our daughter was born."

It was the perfect opening to ask about the circumstances of her birth, but little Anna slipped into the seat beside Eli at that exact moment.

"Did you get any flak from the locals about tearing down an old building?" Eli asked instead.

"It was in really bad shape." Bree pulled plastic wrap from the top of a bowl of applesauce. "Not like your great-grandfather's house that's been kept up. We looked into restoring the original, but it would have cost more than starting from scratch."

"No one objected," Carson said. "And we picked up the property for a steal."

"You stole our house?" little Anna asked, her eyes large.

"What do you think? Do we steal things?" Carson asked, giving his daughter a pointed look.

She shook her head.

From the solemn expression on her face Eli guessed this might be a lesson learned from experience—perhaps from taking a lollipop at the market.

"What Daddy meant—" Bree began gently— "was that where we live was on sale for a very good deal."

"But he said—"

"—It's an expression, Anna." Carson directed his attention from her to Eli. "Anna is an astute listener, and she takes everything literally." To Anna Carson said, "I promise I didn't *steal* our house. We paid for it and are still paying for it, every month."

This brought up another thing Eli was curious about. What was the deal with Carson working for Anna's parents? What money had they loaned him, and why? Eli doubted he'd be able to ask that question tonight, without seeming completely rude. But if he understood the situation better then maybe he could help Anna understand it as well, so she might not be as hurt by her parents' decision.

"Are you thinking of making some changes to Mr. Steiner's home?" Bree asked, bringing their conversation back around to the original topic.

"Possibly. There are still quite a few things to be decided."

Carson and Bree exchanged an almost knowing look a second before Eli's stomach growled loudly. His takeout lunch had long since been eaten, and he was hungry—again. He'd been hungry more times the past week than he had in his entire life. Holiday needed more food choices.

"We're starving our guest," Carson noted. "Let's pray so we can eat." He took Bree's hand in his and reached for their daughter's with his other. After a brief hesitation and a nod from her mother, Anna held her hand out to Eli. He stared at it a second, then took her tiny fingers in his own. Their heads bowed, and Carson began.

The minister's son. Eli hadn't thought about that connection recently. This made the situation with Carson and Bree—and what they'd done to their best friend—even more intriguing. It wasn't every day that the pillar of a town had a child embroiled in scandal.

"Amen," Bree and her daughter echoed after Carson.

"Amen," Eli added hastily, realizing he hadn't listened to the prayer at all.

Anna slid her hand from his and gave him a shy smile. Eli felt oddly warmed by it—not the same as when Anna—his Anna, his business partner he would think of her, now that they were both connected to the estate—smiled at him, but happy all the same. He'd never had much interaction with children, not since he was one himself. And even that had been limited. His parents hadn't believed in inviting friends over, and because he never did, he was hardly ever invited to others' homes as well.

Somewhere along the way, he'd been led to believe that children were sticky, obnoxious creatures—or maybe he'd read that in a Roald Dahl book. Little Anna contradicted that belief quite nicely, and Eli soon found himself enjoying a very pleasant conversation with her. For a not-quite-three-year-old—her own description—she seemed rather advanced and was knowledgeable and eager to talk about everything, from a step-by-step description of how she'd helped her mom make the applesauce to a science lesson about the apples that grew on trees nearby where she and her dad and mom had gone to pick them. From there the conversation launched into colors apples came in, and why some were called pink lady when they weren't pink.

Hiding a smile behind his napkin, Eli nodded, agreeing the name was silly.

"That's enough, Anna," Carson said, sounding more proud than scolding. "Eat your dinner and let Mr. Steiner finish his."

Anna dug into her applesauce and managed four bites before she turned to Eli again, this time asking if he had any pets. Far from disappointing her, his answer in the negative seemed to only encourage her to tell him the merits of cats versus dogs. Eli enjoyed her animation and half suspected that if he could talk to her alone she'd be able to answer a lot of his questions.

Carson and Bree seemed content to let their daughter steer the conversation, and Eli had no objections listening to her chatter away while he downed two helpings of homemade chili that Bree had made, practicing for the chili cookoff at the upcoming Holiday Harvest Hoedown. With Mrs. Lawrence not entering this year, Bree confessed to being hopeful she might win the blue ribbon.

"Half the town feels that way," Carson said around a bite of cornbread dripping with honey.

"I think you've got a shot at it." Eli held up his spoon. "This is good stuff." The homemade applesauce was great as well. Overall it was one of the simplest dinners he'd ever eaten in his entire life—outdoors, seated on a folding chair, with an old door as a table. *Simple fare, simple folk.* Except neither Bree nor Carson struck him that way. They seemed as aware and upcoming as any of his associates back home. The only difference that he could see was that they were more down to earth, more nice. *Genuine. Sincere.* The pursuit of worldly possessions or wealth didn't seem to enter into their lifestyle.

For Anna's sake, Eli had wanted to dislike them, to find some evidence that they were two selfish people, paying for the wrong they'd done her. Instead he saw a happy family, a couple in love with each other and a daughter they doted over.

After dinner, the pink sky began to darken, not only with nightfall, but with an impending storm. Together they cleared the dishes and leftovers and brought them inside. Then Carson and Eli returned to the yard to put away the door table and carry the chairs into the house.

They were needed in there, as the only other thing available to sit on was a lone, upholstered chair in the spacious front room. This was offered repeatedly to Eli until he accepted, feeling guilt that the others were seated on the hard metal chairs or—Bree and Anna—the floor.

"We'll be able to get some furniture eventually," Carson said, sounding neither embarrassed nor concerned by what they lacked.

"We have to wait because I was 'spensive," Anna chimed in, grinning widely, as if proud of her costliness.

"I can see that." Eli leaned forward, elbows on his knees as he bent closer. "Those pretty curls must have cost your parents a fortune."

Anna giggled.

"And those legs," Eli continued. "I saw how fast they can run. Those must have been at least a hundred dollars—each."

Anna threw herself back on the floor and laughed, kicking her legs high in the air.

"I'd say it was a wise choice your parents made," Eli continued. "Buying you instead of a sofa."

Anna sat up abruptly. She looked Eli in the eye, her expression most serious. "They didn't *buy* me. I wasn't in a store. They adopted me. From a hospital. And from Candace."

"Then you are all very lucky."

"And you're lucky to still be up, Missy." Carson beckoned to his daughter. "Get your pajamas on and your toothbrush ready, and I'll come help you get ready for bed."

"And a story?" Anna asked, turning eyes Eli would have found impossible to resist on her father.

"It depends on how fast you are," Carson said.

"So fast." Anna jumped up and bolted toward the stairs. "I want Mr. Steiner to read it to me." With enough noise for three children, she clambered up the stairs and out of sight.

"The lady has spoken," Carson said, looking at Eli. "I hope you're good at animal noises. She's really into cat and horse books right now."

"Uh, sure." Eli sat up in the chair, then wiped his palms on his jeans, feeling suddenly nervous.

"Anna's adoption is an open adoption." Bree gathered pieces of the unfinished puzzle Anna had left behind. "My father's wife's daughter is Anna's mother."

"Father's wife's daughter . . ." It took a second for Eli to put that together in his mind.

"My mother died when I was thirteen," Bree explained. "My father remarried a few years ago."

"Ah." Eli nodded. "That makes more sense. Can I—can I ask you something?" He glanced to Carson as well, letting him know he wasn't intending this to be a conversation with only his wife.

"If we can ask you some things," Bree said. She tucked her legs beneath her as if settling in for a long discussion.

"Uh—sure. What do you want to know?"

"You first," Carson said.

"All right." Eli felt his palms sweating again but refrained from wiping them across his jeans. Why should he feel nervous about what he wanted to ask? It wasn't like he was asking for himself. He wanted to understand to help Anna. Nothing more. Still, he wasn't used to conversations that were so—personal. He felt much more comfortable discussing the Cubs' schedule or who they were likely to trade before next season. But this might be his only chance to ask, to find out something that might help Anna. "How did you come to adopt a child, since when you married you were—"

"Expecting one?" Bree asked, a wistfulness softening her already kind expression.

"We lost that child." Carson picked up his chair and moved it closer to Bree, then grabbed another from the stack by the door. "Bree nearly died and had to have emergency surgery." Carson set the second chair beside his, then pulled Bree up so they were sitting side by side.

"So, no more children—biological, at least," she added.

"I'm sorry." Eli felt like a cad for asking. Did Anna know this already? Would it matter if she did?

"Adopting Anna was an unexpected miracle and a great blessing," Bree said. "She's healed a lot of wounds for both of us."

Carson put his arm around Bree. "There were complications with her birth as well, and because she wasn't officially ours yet, the insurance company balked at paying her medical bills. We fought it, and eventually they covered some, but we were still left with over half."

"She was in the NICU for almost two months," Bree added with a grimace that suggested it hadn't been a pleasant time.

"So between those bills and Bree's three hospital stays—" Carson gave her shoulder a squeeze "—in a little more than a year of marriage, we'd racked up a quarter million dollars in medical debt."

Eli gave a low whistle. "Ouch."

"It was." Carson nodded. "And it would have been worse if we'd lost the house we'd just completed. We nearly did and would have if not for the Lawrences."

The medical bills. They'd answered his other question without him even having to ask.

"And your great-grandfather," Bree added quietly.

"What?" Eli's attention snapped to her. "He loaned you—"

"I'm ready for my story." Anna, wearing a purple princess nightgown, appeared on the stairs.

"You've been summoned," Carson said. "It's best not to keep the princess waiting."

"Okay—sure." They really expected him to do this? Eli rose slowly, his brain still trying to make sense of what Bree had said. He'd read through all of Gabriel's papers—the will, the annuities and the investments, all of his assets—liquid or otherwise—bank accounts, and IRAs, recurring bills on the estate. Nowhere had he come across anything about a loan to anyone named Armstrong—or anyone at all.

To his relief, Carson and Bree stood as well.

"Follow us," Bree said, taking the lead. "And we'll explain after the story."

Chapter 23

THE NEXT HOUR and a half passed in a surreal haze, like Eli was living someone else's life.

The first ten minutes were spent sitting in a chair beside a not-quite-three-year-old's bed, doing his best horse impersonation—he'd opted for neighing over meowing like a cat.

"Wise choice," Carson said from the hall, where he and Bree stood, just outside Anna's open door.

It's a plot against me—the final piece to me losing my mind before I leave this place.

When Anna demanded that Eli get down on all fours and show her how the pony in the book walked, he was certain she and they—everyone in this town—was out to get him.

Nevertheless, he complied, dropping to the floor and crawling around while making a *clip-clop* sound with his tongue. He'd already been humiliated, reading about Peaches the pony with the high-pitched neigh. What was a little more embarrassment? From the corner of his eye, he noted Carson and Bree with grins on their faces as they watched.

Ouch. Eli lifted a hoof—hand—and stared at the doll-sized shoe stuck to his palm.

His colleagues back home would never believe this, though they'd probably pay big money to see him crawling around the floor of a little girl's room, a Barbie accessory embedded in his skin. He flicked the tiny shoe away and returned to the side of Anna's bed.

"Satisfied?" he asked as he stood.

"Shh. Horses don't talk."

Home Sweet Holiday

Eli nodded and crouched over, galloping out to the hall. He would have kept on going down the stairs and out the front door if he wasn't so curious about Bree's mention of Gabriel.

"You've got a friend for life," Carson said as they headed back downstairs.

"Yeah. Well, I hope she never expects a repeat performance. That was a *once*-in-lifetime." Eli sank into the lone armchair, feeling he'd earned it now. "About Gabriel's involvement . . ."

"This may take a few minutes to explain." Bree settled beside Carson again.

"I'm in no hurry," Eli said. His flight wasn't until two o'clock tomorrow afternoon. He could get up late and still have time to return the truck and make it to the airport in Mobile.

Bree and Carson exchanged a look before beginning.

"You first," Carson said to her. "You'll explain it better. You spent more time with Mr. Steiner."

Why is that? Why had Bree spent any time with him? Eli couldn't recall any mention of her in the letters. But he kept his thoughts to himself—for now.

Bree turned to him. "The summary is that your great-grandfather made a gift to the Mulberry, and as a consequence the Lawrences loaned money to us, to start paying down our medical bills—enough that we could get on top of them and not lose our home."

"In return we agreed to work for them for the next five years," Carson explained.

"Carson designed a website and started mobile orders." Bree gave her husband a proud smile.

"And Bree helps in the floral shop and teaches seasonal literacy classes in the room above the store Thursday evenings. They aren't in session now because of the harvest."

"How does the latter help repay your loan?" Eli asked,

though that part didn't really matter to him. But it might to Anna.

"There's no monetary gain to the Lawrences," Bree said. "At least not right now. The classes are free for anyone who wants to attend. Anna's parents hope that increasing literacy among our local population—particularly those living out in the county—will eventually increase job opportunities for those people who come. They'll be more employable and better able to support themselves."

"Which helps the Lawrences how . . ." Eli still didn't see their motivation, beyond the altruistic, that is. And maybe that was all. It could make sense. More than once Anna had mentioned being worried about her parents' business model.

"For the past decade or so—since the recession of '08 and '09—the Mulberry has been more of a charitable organization than a profitable business," Carson explained. "The Lawrences are as generous as Mr. Steiner was."

"But without the same kind of means," Bree added. "They never turn anyone away—even when it meant they were about to go under themselves."

"Bankruptcy?" Eli's brow furrowed. If so, Anna had absolutely no idea.

Carson shook his head. "No. Mr. Lawrence is smart. He didn't wait for things to get that bad but took out a mortgage against the store. They've owned it outright for a long time, but when the economy finally caught up with them and sapped the last of their resources about five years ago, they decided they had to take out a loan."

"Anna didn't know," Eli guessed.

"No one did," Bree said. "Except Mr. Steiner found out. He was a shareholder in the bank in Foley, where the Lawrences went for the loan."

"I've seen that in his documents," Eli said. Gabriel was a shareholder in a lot of things.

"Well, he happened to see them—Anna's parents—the day they came in. He was there on shareholder business and saw the Lawrences meeting with the loan officer. Not wanting to embarrass them, but wanting to know what was going on, he stopped and said hello—and had a chance to glance at the paperwork they were filling out."

Sly. "So, to summarize so far," Eli began, "the Lawrences' generosity went a little too far and reached a point where they had to take out a loan against their market to keep it going. Gabriel happened to see them doing just that—*at* the bank where he is a shareholder."

"Perfect." Bree beamed at him like he was one of her students.

"What happened next?" Eli asked.

"Nothing. For a while," Carson said. "A few years passed. Bree and I had moved back and bought this property. We'd lost our baby and almost lost Bree—twice." Carson took her hand in his and turned to her with a look of tenderness. "Then we learned of an opportunity to adopt—it was handed to us, really. Anna was born, and we found ourselves willing to do about anything to keep her—even selling the house we'd barely finished building."

"We were ready to list it," Bree continued. "We talked to a realtor who then, unbeknownst to us, mentioned our house—and our predicament—to your great-grandfather."

"Let me guess," Eli said. "Moiyes Realty?"

Carson nodded.

"I saw Gabriel's records on that too." Though he'd not been active in real-estate for many years, as the head of the local office, Gabriel had received a cut of all sales. "His wife's—my great-grandmother's—maiden name was Moiyes."

"Ah," Carson said.

"She was plenty wealthy before they even met," Eli said, wondering for a second what the two Southern socialites must have been like in their younger years. Bringing his mind and the conversation back to the topic at hand, he summarized again. "So Gabriel knew about the loan against the market and that you two were about to sell your dream home."

"That was when Mr. Steiner decided to step in." Carson picked up where Bree had left off. "He paid the bank your parents' loan in full, some $50,000 at that time."

Eli gave a low whistle. "That's significant."

"Mr. Steiner brought the note to Anna's parents and told them what he'd done—he said it was repayment for years of free floral deliveries. Then he told them what we were about to do to keep our little girl." Bree sounded a little choked up as she spoke. "Together they came up with a plan that they hoped would help everyone—Carson and me and our Anna, the Lawrences, their store—and their Anna. Even Mr. Steiner stood to gain something if his plan worked out."

Though he had the answers to his original questions, Eli felt more confused—and curious—than ever. "Why would either—" He broke off, realizing how rude the question he'd been about to ask would be.

But Bree seemed to know what he'd been about to say. "Why would either of them want to help us?" she said, as direct and matter-of-fact as Carson had been earlier.

"Well . . . yeah." Eli rubbed a hand along the back of his neck. He could almost feel it reddening with embarrassment. "If what I've heard is true, the two of you really hurt Anna, and it's obviously her parents' store, and she and Gabriel were very close, so why—"

"—The Lawrences didn't plan to help us at first," Carson said. "It might have crossed Anna's mother's mind, but her husband wasn't at a place where he and I were good again. At the time it didn't seem likely we would ever be."

"But when Mr. Steiner paid off their loan so generously, that pay-it-forward phenomenon just sort of took over," Bree said. "First there was forgiveness—a lot more than $50,000 worth. Then the Lawrences paid down a percentage of our medical bills, about half the amount of the debt your great-grandfather forgave them."

Interesting. Eli rested an elbow on the arm of the chair, a hand to his chin as he tried to wrap his mind around that kind of generosity. "Except you have to pay it back—sort of."

"Sort of." Bree smiled, and it seemed there was almost a twinkle in her eye. She leaned forward, as if eager to finish her explanation. Her face sobered. "What Carson and I did to Anna was terrible. We've never said that it wasn't. We've always been sorry that we hurt her, and we want so much to see her happy again."

"We're sorry, but Bree and me marrying each other *was* the right thing." Carson bestowed another look filled with tender affection upon his wife. "Even if there hadn't been a baby involved it would have been right. I should have realized much sooner that Bree and I are meant to be together, and Anna and I are meant to be friends. So while this marriage came about in the wrong way, it's absolutely right—for everyone."

"Anna doesn't necessarily see it that way." It was all well and good that Bree and Carson were living happily ever after. But from Eli's observations the past week, Anna was still a bit of a wreck from the whole thing.

"We know," Carson and Bree said in unison.

"We know she's still hurting," Bree said. "Mr. Steiner knew it too. It was why he paid off the Lawrences' loan."

"To protect Anna's parents?" Eli could see how that could help her—she wouldn't have to support them. Wouldn't have to return to Holiday to fix a mess they'd made. Though here she was, anyway.

Bree shook her head, the twinkle in her eyes back,

sparkling almost mischievously now. He was missing something—something that should have been obvious?

"Gabriel couldn't have seen that as a smart investment." Eli frowned. "It goes against everything I've read and seen of his business dealings. He took risks, but not on things like small-town markets that were failing."

"He wasn't expecting to make any money off of it," Carson said. "But you're right. He was taking a risk—one based on a hunch."

"About what?" Eli asked, starting to feel frustrated. He didn't like games. He wished they'd just get to the point and spell out whatever they were trying to tell him. He thought of Anna and wondered if she'd felt this confused when he was explaining the will.

"Mr. Steiner believed that paying off the Lawrences' loan might put him in a position to someday help his biggest cause." Bree caught Eli's gaze.

Eli mentally shuffled through Gabriel's charitable contributions but couldn't pinpoint one that stood out more than the others. His great-grandparents had been extremely generous with a number of charities.

"Mr. Steiner was all about forgiveness and reconciliation," Bree continued. "His own family story turned out so painful and wrong, and he always regretted that. Helping others to overcome their grievances and avoid that same kind of pain became the thing that healed him—as much as he could be healed. From the time he lost his son, he was never really whole again."

Eli held their gaze. "And you know all of this about him because—"

Bree took a deep breath, as if just now getting to the heart of the story. "I delivered Mr. Steiner's flowers every Wednesday for most of the past year. More than the flowers, he enjoyed the company. During those visits he talked a lot about Anna—and you."

"*You* were his calculated risk," Carson said evenly.

"Me?" Eli leaned back in the chair, hands raised. "There's no way any of this has anything to do with me."

"It has everything to do with you." Bree's smaller smile had blossomed into one that took over her face. "Do you recall how many letters you wrote to your great-grandfather over the course of years you corresponded?"

"A handful," Eli replied, his temper and patience short. So he'd been a lousy grandson. That sin wasn't any bigger than theirs.

"Exactly three," Bree said. "Mr. Steiner shared them with me."

"Awesome." Eli placed his hands on his knees, preparing to stand. He'd had enough. These people were nuts. This conversation was going nowhere.

Bree stood before he could, then moved between him and the front door. "Each letter was written several years apart from the other, but they all had one thing in common."

Eli was slow to rise. There would be no stopping her from making her point. Besides, he knew what she was about to say anyway.

Carson said it for her. "*Anna* is what those letters have in common. You asked about her in each of them."

Eli tried to shrug it off. "Gabriel talked about her a lot."

"Oh. Is that all?" Carson said in a knowing kind of way that made Eli want to punch the smirk right off his face.

"That's all," Eli said. "Now if you'll excuse me, I've got to pack. I have a plane to catch tomorrow." Maybe he'd even try for an earlier flight. Get the heck away from these crazies as soon as possible.

Carson pulled Bree aside, and Eli started toward the door.

"Mr. Steiner left the estate to both of you for a reason," Bree called after him. "He paid the loan for the Lawrences so they would help us, so we wouldn't have a rift between our families—and so Mr. Steiner could get to know us better, so he could talk to us about Anna. He wanted his affairs in order and wanted a promise from us that we'd help him, after he was gone."

Eli placed a hand on the doorknob. He shouldn't ask. He wouldn't. He couldn't seem to stop himself. "Help him with what?"

"You," Bree said bluntly. "And Anna as well. He loved you both and wanted you to be happy. Mr. Steiner thought—he hoped bringing Anna home and the two of you together might be the answer to mending her heart and giving you the love and family you never had."

"It isn't." Eli pulled the door open and stepped out into the warm October night. Even the weather was messed up down here. Fall air was supposed to be crisp, not humid. "And I've got all the family I need," he said to the chirping crickets, or whatever they were, as he stomped down the driveway toward Gabriel's Cadillac.

As for love . . . An overrated commodity. If that, even. *Liability is more like it.* Look what it had done to Anna. He reached the car and paused as he glanced back at Carson and Bree silhouetted beneath the porch light, standing together, arms around one another. A stab of yearning caught him unawares.

Look what it's done for them.

Chapter 24

"Why is it that everything has to ripen at the same time?" Anna huffed as she lugged another bushel of apples to the Excursion. Last week they'd been inundated with pumpkins. This week it was apples.

"Everything doesn't ripen at the same time," Carson said, following her with a bushel of his own. "The peaches and most of the pears came on last month. Only the Winter Nellis pears are still left, and those are on their way. We should be seeing them any time now."

"Wonderful," Anna muttered. She handed her basket to Ella, who'd climbed in the back to help load. With all but the front two seats down, there was quite a bit of storage inside. Ella dragged the basket as far forward as possible, with the half dozen others already wedged there.

"We're almost out of room," she said, shifting to make space for Carson's basket.

"Too bad we aren't almost out of apples." Anna lifted a hand to her sweaty forehead as she stared at the nearly full car. She'd be up all night and the next five as well, trying to get these "seconds" made into applesauce. The Mulberry was the only store she knew of that not only accepted the poorest of the crop but advertised for it as well. Farmers sold them good apples of course, and those were placed in the market. But for as long as Anna could remember her parents had purchased the normally *un*sellable apples as well—the ones that had fallen on the ground and had one side bruised, or some that had been previously sampled by a worm or some other pest. Unfortunately, over the years, word of her parents' willingness to buy these seconds had spread like wildfire. The result was that every fall the Lawrences were overrun with apple seconds from a great number of orchards, local and otherwise.

"Because no one else is foolish enough to take them." Anna continued her muttering as she returned to the store for another bushel. Her mother's applesauce *was* delicious—yet another thing she was famous for in these parts. But her mother wasn't here to make it this year, and it had been *years* since Anna had helped with the long, laborious process. Just bringing up all the jars from the basement and washing them was going to be a chore. Anna felt tired even thinking about it.

They crammed three more bushels into the back and then one more on the front passenger seat. Anna closed the door, then fished her keys from her pocket. "You guys will be all right here if I head home now?" She glanced from Carson to Ella and Mettie, who had ventured out to supervise. "Robert will be in this afternoon to run the soda fountain. You can ask him to help with anything else you need as well."

"We'll be fine." Mettie waved Anna away, as if she was a pesky insect. "Get them apples home and in the house before they rot any more. Mind the worms, too, when you're cutting them."

Anna grimaced. Her gaze flickered briefly to Carson, then back to the ground. In years past, her mother had recruited him to help with the applesauce. Carson had taken great delight in handing Anna apple segments with dismembered worms still attached. She had given as good as she got, putting a worm down the back of his shirt a time or two.

Sour memories. All of them were now. It was as if her entire childhood and youth had been ruined when he and Bree eloped. Memories that should have been sweet only made her feel bitter.

"Evan should be waiting at your house to help you

unload all these." Carson slapped the side of the Excursion, then turned away.

"Thanks," Anna said, surprised and grateful he'd thought of that. It would be nice to have someone assist with unloading, at least. It wasn't as if Carson could come over and help with even that anymore.

Since her initial blowup over his daughter's name, and his brief attempt to talk to her last Tuesday, they'd settled on being both cordial and aloof with one another. Anna noticed he'd been careful to keep his distance—something she was both grateful for and that made her want to cry at the same time. Carson hugs had always been the best. Facing all these apples and the gargantuan task before her, Anna could have used a little bolstering about now.

Never again. She hurried to the car before she did cry. Over apples, of all things. *Over friends. Over loss.*

Maybe it was a good thing she'd have all this work to keep her busy to the point of exhaustion for at least a week. When there was nothing left to dream about, being too tired to dream was a blessing.

Anna wound the crank of her mother's old, metal apple peeler and corer in time with the beat of *Hamilton*'s "My Shot," though the words pounding through her head didn't seem to match. *I am throwing away—my life.* She wasn't particularly young anymore and didn't feel at all scrappy these days—just tired. Right this moment, of apples.

A glance at the kitchen clock told her it was nearly eight—good, because she'd barely made a dent in the apple population taking up the kitchen and front hall, bad because she wanted to call it a night but couldn't justify doing so until at least midnight.

If Mom can do this every year . . . "I can too." Anna

sounded anything but resolute. Yet she needed to be. Some of this applesauce would be sold at the Mulberry. Much of it, however, would be given away, donated to families with young, malnourished children. A bowl of applesauce might not be a big deal to her, but to a child who otherwise had no fruits or vegetables in his life, it could make a difference.

She pulled the now-bare apple from the prongs and placed it in the bowl beside the sink. A few more apples, and she'd have enough to cut up and start cooking down for another batch of sauce. First, though, came the distasteful task of cutting the fruit, checking each individual piece for worms or bruising. These might be seconds, but by the time her mother was through with them, they'd always been made into first-rate, blue-ribbon applesauce.

A knock at the front door interrupted Anna's rhythm just as she'd attached another apple and started cranking again. She paused the music on her phone, wiped her sticky hands on a dishtowel, and made her way around baskets of apples toward the front door. If it was Evan bringing more apples she was going to cry. Worse, it might be Donald Andersen, having followed his nose toward the aromas coming from her kitchen. If it was, she'd invite him in and put *him* in an apron for once. Maybe if she made him cut up five hundred apples he'd leave her alone.

But neither Evan nor Donald stood on the other side of the door when Anna pulled it open. Instead Bree's smile greeted her.

"Hello, Anna. I've come to help." Already wearing an apron, Bree ducked beneath Anna's arm and made her way into the house before Anna could protest.

Left alone by the front door, Anna considered her options. She could leave and let Bree help all she wanted. Or she could tell Bree to leave because she didn't need help—pretty much an outright lie, considering that a moment ago

Anna had contemplated inviting Donald's assistance. *Or . . . I could let her stay.*

The lure of free help was too much to resist. Anna closed the front door and retraced her steps to the kitchen. She was drowning in apples, and Bree, a pro in the kitchen herself, might just be her lifeline. But that didn't mean they had to talk.

In the kitchen Bree had already taken over the worst task—cutting the apples and checking the segments. The timer went off, signaling the end of the water bath for the two batches Anna had on the stove. Without a word she crossed behind Bree, turned off the burners, and opened the lids on the enormous steamers. Using a pair of heavy-duty canning tongs, she lifted the baskets out of the water so the jars could start to cool.

The counter between the sink and stove held enough clean jars for the next batches, and the island was quickly filling with the finished product, so Anna refrained from temporary escape to the basement to collect more of the jars her mother stored there. Throughout the year jars would be returned, or simply donated. Others her mother picked up at flea markets or yard sales in neighboring towns. No one knew how to spot a mason jar like her mother.

Back at her work station, Anna started the *Hamilton* soundtrack over again, louder this time, and continued turning the crank.

An hour passed in quiet companionship. Bree hadn't said a word but efficiently took care of every apple handed to her, while Anna kept the process going on both ends, from the peeling and coring to cooking and blending.

The kitchen smelled heavenly, just like home and just like fall, and Anna found she wasn't as tired as she had been earlier. Another hour passed. She was caught up in the soundtrack, reliving the musical she'd been fortunate enough to see in Seattle. She hadn't taken advantage of many of the opportunities living in a big city offered, but when her parents had visited last she'd treated them to *Hamilton* at the Paramount Theatre. Remembering that night, while at the same time being here, in her mother's kitchen, doing the familiar work of her youth, had her feeling happier and more relaxed than she had for several days—maybe since before her visit had begun.

"Stay Alive" ended, and "It's Quiet Uptown"—one of Anna's favorites from the soundtrack—started. She hummed along, imagining Alexander Hamilton at his lowest, estranged from his wife and having just lost his son, his career in shambles.

Perhaps an odd choice of songs for her to favor, but then her own life seemed rather a mess as well. She could identify.

The timer sounded again, reminding Anna that the applesauce had cooked long enough and was ready to be put in jars and sealed. But first she needed to move the previous batch from the canners. Anna crossed the kitchen to the stove once more and pulled two jars from one of the pots.

Holding them by their now-cool lids, she turned toward the island as one slipped from its lid and crashed to the floor, shattering glass and flinging applesauce in every direction.

Bree whirled around. "Don't move. I'll get the broom and some paper towels."

Anna nodded mutely as she stared down at the sea of glass surrounding her flip-flop-clad feet. It had felt too warm to wear anything else, but she realized what a foolish decision having mostly bare feet had been, as a trickle of blood wound its way down the side of her foot.

"Stupid," she muttered, frustrated at also not having followed her mother's oft-repeated admonition to never hold a jar by its lid. Carefully Anna crouched and plucked the offending piece of glass from a cut near her big toe. Smaller shards glinted on the top of her skin and on the wood floor around her.

Bree returned with the broom and dustpan and began sweeping while Anna picked up the bigger pieces she could reach and put them in the dustpan Bree held out.

"Thanks," Anna said, her eyes meeting Bree's for the first time all night.

"You're welcome." Bree held her gaze, her own all soft—and sorry.

In the background the song continued, words about where they were and where they'd started. *So different from what I imagined.* Bree was supposed to have been her friend for life. They'd been practically sisters. Nothing was supposed to come between them.

"Let me help you to the sink so you can rinse that glass off your feet." Bree set the dustpan down and leaned the broom against the counter. She stepped closer to Anna and wrapped an arm around her back, helping her hobble over to the counter. "Can you jump up?"

Anna nodded, backed up to the counter, and pulled herself up so she was seated near the sink. Bree moved a few apples out of the way, then turned on the spray function of the faucet and held it over the side of the sink with the disposal. Anna let the flip flops fall to the floor, then turned so her feet were hanging over the sink. Bree carefully pulsed the water over both, then got a spatula and ran the side over the tops of Anna's feet to check for any lingering glass.

"Better?" she asked when she had finished.

"Yes." Anna nodded. "Thanks."

Bree grabbed a handful of paper towels and began drying Anna's feet.

"I can do that." Anna leaned forward to take the paper towels from her, their heads nearly colliding.

"Forgiveness," the song chimed in the background. Anna's eyes met Bree's again.

Forgiveness. Could she imagine? Could she . . . Tears threatened. "Oh, Bree."

Bree's eyes were watery too. "Anna, I'm so sorry. Please can't we be friends again?"

Anna swung her legs around and hopped down from the counter. She threw her arms around Bree and felt herself equally embraced.

"I'm so sorry," Bree sobbed again. "It wasn't on purpose. We never meant to—"

"I don't want to talk about that. I don't want to hear about it. What's done is done, and—" *It doesn't matter anymore.* At the last second Anna stopped herself from saying the words. How could it *not* matter?

It was a big deal—three and a half, almost four years ago. Justin's words.

It's been a long time. You shouldn't be allowing it to hurt you anymore. You need to get over it. Eli's observation.

And Dad . . . *This one thing that happened is poisoning the rest of you. It's destroying all that was beautiful and happy and joyful in your life. It's taken my Annabelle away and turned her into someone I hardly know.*

Anna felt herself drowning again, sinking in the sea of despair that had been her life for so long. Yet here was Bree, holding her—holding her up. *A lifeline?* Once the very best lifeline Anna had known. But now it didn't seem possible that grasping onto her, onto their friendship, could buoy her up the way it once had. It didn't make sense. She didn't understand it. Dad's voice rang in her mind again.

I miss the girl who used to leap before she looked.

I need you to get better for me—with *me.*

"What happened—doesn't matter." Anna forced the

words from her mouth, praying she could mean them—step two—and following her heart—step three.

Bree cried harder and hugged her tighter. "I've missed you so much."

"Me too," Anna echoed. "I've missed *you*, Bree." *What happened doesn't matter. You're still my best friend.* There *was* too much history between them, too many years of girlish dreams and pranks, sleepovers, study sessions, laughter and love and just being there for each other. Warmth made its way from Anna's core outward. Her heart lightened, as if a chunk of the cage surrounding it had broken away. She hiccupped suddenly, then frowned as the smell of burnt apples assaulted her.

Anna pulled away, and in unison she and Bree turned toward the stove and the still cooking applesauce.

"Uh oh." Anna giggled as she looked around at the applesauce-coated cupboards and floor, and the pile of rotten apple pieces piled on the drainboard.

"Your mother would be appalled at the state of her kitchen." Bree pressed her lips together, as if attempting to keep a straight face.

"Horrified," Anna agreed, not even bothering to hold back her laughter. She was exhausted, and she hated apples—and she felt happier than she had in ages. She had her best friend back.

Bree's higher-pitched giggle joined hers, followed by an indelicate snort.

Anna turned to her best friend and smiled. "It's going to take all night to clean up this mess."

"Sleepover!" she and Bree said in unison as they faced each other with hands raised for a high five.

Anna grinned. She'd leapt without entirely knowing how she'd land, but it looked like things might turn out all right.

I've got this one, Dad. I'm still a strong swimmer.

Chapter 25

THE STOVE CLOCK read 4:30 a.m. by the time they called it quits for the night. Tired hands at her aching back, Anna surveyed their work. Every surface of her mother's large kitchen was covered with jars of golden applesauce. There was no way one family—or even a dozen—could eat their way through this anytime soon. *And we're only halfway done.*

She suppressed a groan. "Come on," she called to Bree, who was still finishing up dishes at the sink. *Without her help . . .* Bree had been running her family's kitchen since she was thirteen. Her efficiency came from years of practice.

Anna flicked off the lights as she left the room.

"All right, I'm coming," Bree called, not sounding nearly as tired as Anna felt. "Dishes at night are always better than dishes waiting for you in the sink in the morning."

"You sound like my mom." Was that because Bree had spent a lot of time here the past few years? Maybe she'd even helped with the applesauce in Anna's absence. The thought made Anna uncomfortable, though she couldn't say why, exactly. It wasn't like she should be jealous of Bree if, in Octobers past, she had spent hours on her feet in the hot kitchen, slicing apples until her fingers were raw.

Anna started up the stairs. *But time with my mom . . .* The uncomfortable feeling multiplied. She had mostly herself to blame for missing out on being with her parents the past few years. *But Bree . . . doesn't have a mom—or much of a dad.* At least, she hadn't up until a few years ago. Now that her dad had remarried, maybe things were better. *But still—*

Bree probably didn't understand how Anna could have

stayed so far from home for so long. Anna would never forget the way she and Carson had held thirteen-year-old Bree close, literally supporting her as she sobbed her heart out the day her mother died. *And at her funeral. After her funeral.* And days, weeks, months—even years later. Had Bree ever truly gotten over losing her mother? Was that something a person *could* get over?

Could I get over losing Dad if . . . Anna slammed the brakes on that thought. She wasn't going to lose her father to anything but old age—and that was a long ways off. But Bree hadn't been given that option. She'd lost her mother at one of the most critical times of life for a girl. *So I shared Mom with her. And if Mom and Bree kept that relationship while I was gone . . .* It seemed petty and selfish of Anna to begrudge either of them that time. So she wouldn't.

Anna paused at the top of the stairs. "You can use the bathroom first. Mom still keeps extra toothbrushes in the bottom drawer of the vanity." Maybe Bree knew that already. Maybe she'd been here frequently the past few years. "I just opened one myself when I got here. Somehow I forgot my own toothbrush in Seattle." Anna's pointless rambling likely didn't camouflage the conflicted emotions churning through her. A few minutes ago she'd been so tired, she was certain her head would hit the pillow and she'd be asleep in two minutes. But now the past reared its head again, causing all sorts of inner turmoil.

"Thanks," Bree said, sounding a little unsteady herself. She went into the bathroom and closed the door while Anna crossed the hall to her room, grateful for a minute or two alone. She wondered what Carson thought about Bree sleeping over. It hadn't escaped Anna's attention when Bree had sent a text earlier in the evening, about an hour after the shattered-jar incident. Such a little thing, but knowing Bree was texting Carson had broken the temporary illusion that things between her and Bree were as they once had been. They weren't, and they never would be. Somewhere out there was a new normal, but Anna still wasn't sure what that was or how to reach it without getting hurt even more.

"Your room looks almost the same."

Anna turned to Bree, lingering in the doorway, as if uncertain whether or not she could enter.

"Come in." Anna beckoned her. "Feel free to grab any of my t-shirts or sweats to sleep with—*in*," she amended, her face already heating from the blunder. Bree's stricken gaze met hers.

Anna managed to shut her traitorous mouth, but her mind wouldn't stop its forward motion down a path she didn't want to walk. *Bree slept with Carson, who belonged to me, and no, I didn't give permission for* that. Tears burned behind Anna's tired eyes. She looked down at her lap.

"Anna." Bree's voice held a plea, as if she was afraid she was about to lose the friendship she'd thought was hers once more. Anna didn't want to lose that either, but she couldn't persuade her brain from the direction it seemed determined to go.

Bree sleeps with Carson. They make love—even if they can't make babies anymore. He probably holds her close all night. Anna squeezed her eyes shut against the image of the two of them together.

An arm wrapped around her, and the mattress squeaked as Bree sat beside Anna and pulled her close. "I'm sorry. I'm so sorry."

How strange that the person who had caused her broken heart was the one offering comfort. And the person Anna *wanted* comfort from. She turned into Bree's embrace, holding tight as she gave up on holding back tears. They came fast, pouring from her eyes along with a host of unladylike sobs. The ugly cry.

"Oh, Anna. I'm so, so sorry."

How many times had Bree apologized now? Too many to count, yet the words weren't providing any kind of balm to Anna's soul. Because, no matter how sincere, Bree's apology didn't change anything. She and Carson were married and living happily ever after with their little girl, in the house they'd built by the river. The river they'd played by and that she'd swum in.

My river—ours. Occasionally Bree and Carson swam too. *My Carson.* Hers since junior high, when he'd first asked her to be his girlfriend—or had it been the other way around? Either way, their feelings for one another had been mutual. As proof, they'd started holding hands while walking home from school together. Before that it had always been the three of them walking home together. But after her mom died, Bree was no longer free to hang out with friends after school. Instead, she had to make the long walk to the elementary school to pick up her brothers.

And we left her to go by herself. A pang of remorse stabbed Anna's already aching heart. *Some* of the time they had gone with Bree, but mostly Anna remembered being in a euphoric state of first love, eager to walk home with Carson, her hand nestled snuggly in his.

Instead of the three of them rotating houses for an after-school snack, cartoons, and homework—as had been their habit since kindergarten—Carson and Anna had mostly gone to each other's houses, while Bree went home to an empty house, where she was the one expected to prepare a snack and dinner for her brothers and look out for them until her father came home—if he did.

Anna had still considered Bree her best friend, and they had still hung out together—at school each day, and after on those rare occasions Bree could break away from her responsibilities at home. But the dynamic of their threesome had changed.

Not only because of Bree's circumstances but also because of my choices.

The revelatory thought was one Anna hadn't considered before. While she'd been happily dating Carson, enjoying her Miss Holiday status, and pursuing her love of the ocean, what had Bree been feeling? Anna knew what Bree had been doing all those years—being responsible when her father was not.

On those rare occasions that the three of them had hung out at Bree's house—or tried to—it had been uncomfortable at best, with Bree too busy trying to fill her mother's shoes to be able to act like a teenager and have fun with them. Her brothers were always interrupting or fighting, and if her father happened to be home the atmosphere was tense.

Anna and Bree and Carson still had fun together—just not as much as they'd had before life changed, before Bree was forced to grow up too soon. And—*I became too selfish to notice or do more to help her.*

That wasn't entirely true. Anna had noticed—some of the time. She'd sent Bree to prom with Carson, hadn't she? *And when I went away to the university . . . And Bree couldn't.* Anna had kept in touch, texting Bree often and inviting her to come up to visit anytime.

Not that she could . . .

Anna's tears subsided, though she felt worse instead of better. *She* felt guilty of being a poor friend. And that made her mad. At herself and everyone else.

Bree released her, then leaned to the side and reached for a box of tissues on Anna's nightstand—an item not normally kept in her room. Intuition must have led her mom to put some there.

"Thanks." Anna took a tissue in each hand, then flopped backward on the bed, her feet still dangling over the side.

Bree did the same, lying next to her, looking up at the canopy. "Your pictures are gone."

"Yeah." Anna shut her eyes and pressed a hand to each. "I'm guessing my mom came in here to dust at least a few times while I was away, and she probably took them down." *Wisely.* Her canopy had always acted like a bulletin board, with photos and notes tucked between frame and fabric, where she could see them as she lay in bed at night. Most of the pictures had been of the three of them, and then later, of her and Carson at school dances. "My wedding dress isn't here anymore either." Anna turned her head to Bree and pulled the tissues from her face. "Did you wear it?"

"No." Bree sat up quickly. "Why would you think—"

"You stole the groom, so why not the dress?" Anna asked, sitting up as well, though her head felt like it might explode. Bree's hurt expression didn't stop Anna from demanding what she felt was her due, and in truth what she'd wanted to know for a long time. "Tell me about your wedding."

"I thought you said you didn't want to hear—"

"I don't want to hear about the night you got pregnant, but I want to know what happened after."

Bree hesitated, her teeth worrying her bottom lip as she sat silent, her expression slightly mutinous, or more so than Anna could ever remember her mild-tempered friend looking.

"All right. I'll tell you," she said at last. "But you have to hear *all* of it and promise to hear me out—no cutting me off in the middle."

"Fine." Anna kicked off the sneakers she'd changed into earlier, then lay down once more, on her side this time, with her knees drawn up close to her chest. *Assuming the fetal position already.* She fully expected that what she heard was going to hurt.

Bree took her shoes off too and scooted to the other side

of the bed, where she sat cross legged, facing Anna. "The night Carson's mother died he was a mess. He came straight from the hospital to my house. His dad had left before him, off to another hospital to help another family. And his brother was already drowning his sorrows in a beer. Which left Carson all alone. You were away at school," Bree added quietly.

"He could have driven a little farther to see me," Anna said, remembering that Carson had called her that night—and she'd been at a lecture about Beluga whale reproduction and had her phone on silent. Later she'd tried returning his call, but he hadn't answered. Now she guessed why.

"He could have gone to see you." Bree drew in a breath. "But he didn't. He came to me for comfort instead. I didn't flatter myself that it was for any reason other than I'd lost my mom too. He thought I'd understand how he felt, and I did."

A common bond they have that I don't. Anna remembered that when she finally had spoken with Carson—a day or two after his mother's death—he'd told her he was doing a little better, that he'd talked to Bree, who understood what he was going through.

"We sat on the couch, and I let him talk and cry it out," Bree continued. "Then I just held him—the way the two of you held me when I lost my mom."

"Where were your brothers and your dad?" Anna asked quietly.

"Hunting." Bree paused. "What happened next wasn't planned—by either of us. But if you want to blame someone, it should be me. Carson wasn't himself but was vulnerable and hurting. We were hugging, just sitting there holding each other, and then gradually this awareness of each other—as more than comfort—stole over us. We kissed."

Anna winced. This was what she *hadn't* wanted to hear. "Who kissed who?"

Bree met her questioning gaze. "It was kind of mutual.

We were looking at each other, and then it happened. I should have stopped it. I could have, and I didn't. Because the truth is, I'd wanted Carson to kiss me for as long as I could remember."

"You did?" Anna didn't need to ask. She'd heard only honesty in Bree's confession. "You never told me. Did Carson know?"

Bree shook her head. "I tried so hard not to let either of you know—or anyone else. I stayed away as much as possible, and I was careful never to be alone with him, except the night we went to prom."

"Did something happen then?" Had they been dishonest with her for years?

"Nothing," Bree said. "Carson was a perfect gentleman. We danced, and that was it. No goodnight kiss or anything like that."

"But you wished for it," Anna said, relieved, but not, at the same time.

"Yes," Bree admitted. "I wished he'd kissed me. I wished he was my boyfriend instead of yours. But I wouldn't do that to you, Anna. I wouldn't steal my best friend's boyfriend."

"Just her fiancé," Anna muttered.

Bree ignored her comment. "If you remember, I started dating Robbie right after prom. And I *kept* dating him, just so no one would suspect I cared for Carson. I stayed even farther away from the two of you than I had before. I had no intentions of doing anything to interrupt your future together."

"Yet it happened," Anna said.

"Yes." Bree's soft voice didn't lessen the pain of her words. "That night in November Carson kissed me, and I kissed him back, and it was everything I'd dreamed it would be—wonderful, perfect, right."

"*Not* right." Anna sat up. "He and I were engaged."

It was Bree's turn to wince. "Poor choice of words. What

I mean is that Carson and I—connected."

"I'll say." Anna crossed her arms in front of her.

"Not just physically, but our *souls* connected. What happened began as me comforting Carson, but it turned into something far more emotionally powerful—for both of us. A few hours later when we came to our senses again, we were both filled with remorse, but even then there was no denying that what had happened between us—for me, anyway—was important. A big deal. The real thing," Bree added. "I loved him."

"Then why not tell me?" Anna demanded? "Why keep your affair a secret and wait to elope on what was supposed to have been my wedding day? Do you know how humiliating it was to be there at the church, in front of the entire town?"

"No." Bree leaned forward and reached for Anna's hand. She clasped it in her own before Anna could move away. "I don't know. But I'm sorry you went through that, and I'm sorry it was my fault."

"You should be." Anna wanted to snatch her hand away, turn her back on Bree, and pout, but at five o'clock in the morning, after hours spent on her feet, she didn't have the energy to be angry. It was all so draining, and she was so incredibly tired of it—of feeling lousy about everything and everyone.

"You're wrong about Carson and me having an ongoing affair." Bree squeezed Anna's hand, as if to get her full attention. "It happened *once*, and I just told you the circumstances. We agreed after that it could never happen again, that what we'd done to you was terrible. We both felt terrible. We avoided each other after that, making absolutely certain we were never alone with each other again."

Once. Did that make it better? Easier to bear or understand? Anna's tired mind didn't have an answer.

Bree continued. "When I started feeling sicker and sicker

as your wedding approached, I thought it was the guilt from what I'd done, plus the knowledge that I was losing Carson forever. But even then, I was not going to take him from you. When I found out I was pregnant—just ten days before your wedding—I made arrangements to go away, to Mississippi, to a home for unwed mothers. I could live and work there until the baby was born and adopted. I told my grandmother, because I needed someone to look in on the boys and my dad. She threatened to tell Carson about the baby at the church, *at* your wedding, if I didn't tell him before."

"And as soon as he learned there was a baby involved, he decided the two of you should get married." Anna knew this much from the letter Carson had left for her—the one she *hadn't* found *before* going to the church, as he had supposedly believed she would.

"He suggested marriage," Bree said. "I agreed—sort of. I was throwing up so much I could hardly answer him. We drove all night to Chattanooga and were married at the courthouse by a judge. There wasn't anything lovely about the ceremony, except for maybe the pink bridesmaid dress I wore, the one your mother made for me," Bree added, guilt heavy in her words. "It's still the fanciest dress I've ever owned." Her voice turned wistful.

Anna wondered how often Bree had pined for pretty things—or other things she couldn't have . . . The opportunity to attend college, nice clothes and a nice house, parents who were present in her life, the boy she'd secretly loved for years. Had she felt as Anna had the past few years?

No. Because I wasn't pining for anything or anyone. Once she'd read Carson's note, there hadn't been a lot of *might have been* moments. What was done was done, and while it hurt terribly, Anna hadn't spent a lot of time on wishing for what would never be hers. Instead, she'd focused on how to protect her heart so it would never be broken again.

She'd become withdrawn, wary, mistrusting, and extremely private—a loner. The very antithesis of the outgoing Miss Holiday. Her dad was right about not knowing her anymore. She hardly knew herself these days.

"So your wedding wasn't great. At least you had one," Anna said.

"Barely," Bree said. "All through the ceremony I felt so sick I worried I'd throw up all over myself and Carson."

"Did you?" Anna asked, both appalled at the idea and also thinking it might have been a bit of poetic justice.

"No." Bree frowned, as if remembering something equally unpleasant. "I passed out instead. An ambulance came and took me from the courthouse to the hospital."

"Seriously?" It was Anna gripping Bree's hand now.

Bree nodded, and a slight smile lifted the corners of her mouth. "I had to have an IV and a shot in my butt. How's that for a wedding day I'll never forget?"

"Oh, Bree." Anna returned her smile, though she felt like crying again—this time for Bree. "What an awful way to start a life together."

"It was rough," Bree said. "Everything was for a while. We weren't prepared to be husband and wife. Guilt was eating us both alive. Carson was mourning you. I'm not sure how we made it. When I lost the baby, I felt like I'd ruined all of our lives, and I wanted to die too."

"I'm grateful you didn't." Impulsively, Anna leaned forward, hugging Bree again. Living with what Carson and Bree had done tore her apart. Only now was she starting to have a slight hope of recovery. *But if either had died . . .* That possibility brought even more pain. She never would have had the chance for this conversation, to be sitting here with Bree. *Friends again?*

"I wasn't the only one who considered death."

"What do you mean?" Anna drew back, staring at Bree.

"Carson didn't wish you had died." *From carrying his child.* She would kill him if he had even hinted at such a thing.

"No—no." Bree shook her head. "Carson brought me back from the brink. He was wonderful." Her eyes brightened. "But earlier—the night we eloped—right after he left the letter on your porch, he considered driving off the bridge into the river. Drowning seemed less painful than dealing with what we'd done to you."

"I'm glad he didn't kill himself, or you." Anna lay back on the bed, her eyes closed.

"He was sad for quite a while," Bree said. "He missed you. I even heard him call out your name in his sleep."

Ouch. Anna could imagine how that must have hurt Bree. But it wasn't anything less than she deserved, right? "Do you think—" Anna paused, wondering if she dared voice another of the questions that had plagued her since all this had happened. "Do you think Carson and I would have done okay if we had married—I mean, if what happened between you two never had?" She peeked at Bree, trying to gauge her reaction to the question.

"I think you would have been fine," Bree said. "You both would have made it work."

"But you think it would have been *work*?" Anna asked.

Bree looked directly at her. "I do. You and Carson are very different people, Anna. And while opposites attract, it doesn't always make things easy."

"What are you suggesting?" Anna's ire rose again, and she wished she'd kept her mouth shut. But their conversation to this point had been so brutally honest that she'd figured another difficult question wouldn't make a difference one way or another.

"I'm suggesting that while you and Carson definitely loved each other, that he wasn't the love of your life. He's the only love you'd known," Bree added hastily, her hand held up as if to stop the protest forming on Anna's lips. "You were always the one who dove in the water to explore. Carson and I were the ones who stayed in the boat. You were the risk-taker, the adventurer, the spontaneous one. You yearned for adventure and to see the world. Carson wanted to settle down here. Those could have been serious issues for your marriage."

All of what Bree said was true, and instead of hurting, as Anna had feared, it seemed to lessen the pain in her chest. She had loved Carson—fiercely, dearly, and with commitment. But she'd also had worries about how their life together would unfold. If loving him would have still allowed her to follow her dreams.

Ironically, nearly four years later, she had neither. *No love. No dreams.*

"You're right," Anna said at last, her words easing at least a few of the lines furrowing Bree's brow. "But I'm none of those things anymore. The closest I get to adventure is ordering a new plant through the mail from a company I haven't ordered from before."

"Well, you have to start somewhere." Bree smiled. "But I think you're wrong. You're still the same. You just haven't had anything worth leaping for in a long time. Maybe this trip will help you let go of the things weighing you down so that when something does come along, you're ready to jump into the river again—figuratively speaking, that is."

"Maybe." Anna forced herself from the bed so she could go brush her teeth. "But only if I get some sleep first."

Chapter 26

Bright Southern sunshine pushed its way between the slats in Anna's blinds, waking her far earlier than she'd intended. "Not morning, not yet." Anna flung an arm across her eyes, shielding them from the light. She'd probably been asleep all of an hour.

"Feeling okay?" Bree asked, sounding as chipper as ever, as if she hadn't stayed up all night as well.

"Exhausted. And ravenous. I could eat just about anything—except applesauce." Anna's stomach growled, seconding her words. She'd skipped dinner last night, but had she forgotten lunch as well? Her muddled brain couldn't recall.

"Actually . . ." Bree said. "I wondered how you were feeling about last night. About the things we talked about."

Anna's groggy mind considered the question and quickly determined it too early to answer. "I'm not sure, but scrambled eggs, hash browns, and bacon might do a lot to help me decide." To wake up, at least. And face another day at the store. The thought was enough to make her want to cry.

"Don't worry about the store," Bree said, as if she'd read Anna's mind—something they each used to be fairly good at. "I sent Carson a text and asked him to cover for you."

"Thanks." Just a few, short days ago, this might have rubbed Anna wrong—for a lot of reasons. But this morning the news felt like a godsend. "What about your—daughter?" The word still felt strange on Anna's tongue. *Bree is married. She is a wife and a mother.*

"Anna's with him." Bree pushed back the covers and got out of bed. "She loves helping at the market. And Mettie adores her. They'll all be fine."

"Good," Anna murmured and snuggled farther below the blanket, the temptation of sleep starting to outweigh her hunger. If the store was covered, then she could stay in bed as long as she wanted.

"I'm going to go down and get started on the rest of the apples." Bree shuffled toward the bedroom door.

Or not. "Can't we just throw them away?"

Bree shrugged. "Sure . . . If you want to lie to your mom. Because you know she'll ask how many quarts we got."

"Stupid apples." Anna groaned and pulled a pillow over her head. "Why . . ." She languished a minute more, then flung the covers back and forced her body from the bed. "If we have to can more applesauce, I need sustenance. We are going to breakfast before we touch another apple or another jar."

"Want me to just make us something?" Bree asked.

Anna shook her head. "We'll eat at Rosie's. My treat," she added, feeling generous and immensely grateful for Bree's help. "Give me five minutes, and I'll be ready to go."

It took her only three and a half—an advantage of not having anyone around to impress. For a fleeting second she thought of Eli. Would she have cared if he was still in town? *Of course not.* How quickly he'd proven himself untrustworthy, leading her to believe he had interest in her as a person, when really he'd been all about getting her to take care of his grandfather's house.

Though Eli said he'd be back in December, she'd believe that when she saw it herself. Until then, there was no point thinking about him. *Or any other man.*

Wearing jeans and a clean t-shirt, her hair in a messy bun, her teeth brushed, and her arm linked through Bree's, Anna entered Rosie's diner for the first time since her return home. Once, years ago, she and Carson had come here nearly every Friday night for burgers and fries.

"Morning, girls." If Rosie seemed surprised to see them together, she didn't let on. "Take your pick of the booths. Most of the regulars haven't come in yet."

"Thanks," Bree said. In unison she and Anna walked toward the booth beside the front window. They seated themselves on opposite sides, and Anna inhaled deeply, savoring the diner's familiar, comforting scents, along with the warm sunshine pouring through the window. She'd missed this—being warm most of the time and hot frequently. *The eternal summer of the South.* Maybe it wasn't that, exactly, but compared to Seattle . . .

"What can I get you girls?" Rosie's pen was poised over her notebook.

"Everything?" Anna suggested, feeling a bit like a girl again, back in one of her old haunts.

"Everything but the apple fritter. We stayed up all night canning applesauce," Bree said.

"I've got a couple of cases in the car for you," Anna added, looking up at Rosie. "I'll bring them in when we're finished."

"Thanks." The lines on Rosie's face seemed to soften. "It's always nice to have something to give away when someone comes and we're plum out of food for the day. I don't mind sharing our leftovers, but some days we don't have any."

"Applesauce isn't much," Anna said, feeling guilty for all her grumbling about the chore. It was just one tiny part of a town-wide effort to keep some of the poorest folks in these parts fed. How had she forgotten the difference their combined efforts could make—or not, if she didn't do her part?

"Not much to you, but so much to others," Rosie said. "I remember a time, not too many years past, when it made all the difference to my niece. It had been a poor year for the crops, and my brother wasn't much for knowing how to provide a proper diet for his little gal back then."

"And now Julia's grown into a lovely young lady." An image of the seven-year-old's lopsided braids and too-short dress flashed through Anna's mind. Clarence was doing his best, but perhaps he still needed a bit of help. "Speaking of which, I found some dresses that I think might fit her. Would it be all right if I dropped those off here sometime?"

"Of course. That's downright thoughtful of you, Anna." Rose smiled, erasing the last of the creases from her forehead. "Or . . . you could bring them out to Clarence's place yourself."

Oh no. Anna searched for an excuse.

"I can bring them out to Julia," Bree said, jumping into the conversation. "Between making applesauce and tending the store and keeping up with her other work while her parents are gone, Anna hardly has a second to herself. This morning is the first time she's had to stop and sit down for a real breakfast, and that's only because Carson is covering the register for her."

"The best real breakfast to be had this side of the Mississippi, then." Rosie flipped her notebook shut. "You both want the works—eggs, hash browns, bacon, flapjacks?"

"Yes."

"Please." Anna shot Bree a grateful glance as the ever-talkative Rosie finally left them. Anna leaned over the table. "Thank you," she whispered. "That was close."

Bree arched her brow. "What? You don't want to end up with a peanut farmer?"

"Clarence is nice," Anna said, feeling an odd need to defend him. "Just not my type. But I hope he finds someone—someday."

"So where are these dresses you've—*found*?" Bree placed

her elbows on the table, threaded her fingers together, and stared pointedly at Anna.

"It wasn't a lie—exactly. I didn't say they were from me, and they will be found—very soon. Just as soon as I can do some shopping online."

Bree leaned back in her seat as a smile grew on her face. "Still the same Anna."

"How so?"

"You noticed Julia needs some clothes, and instead of waiting around for someone else to do something about it, you're doing it yourself."

Anna shrugged. "I don't see how that makes me the same. I don't recall buying clothes for any little girls before."

"Maybe not that, exactly, but you figured out how to get a new organ for the church, you headed up—and somehow got just about everyone in town involved in—revitalizing Main Street. You threw 80th birthday parties for every single octogenarian during the years you were Miss Holiday, and you singlehandedly cured Everett Jacobs of speeding through town."

"I'd forgotten about that. Everett and his truck . . ." Anna grimaced. "That was the one time your brothers were actually helpful. And I'm lucky I didn't end up in jail for it." Only Everett's backlog of unpaid tickets and his history of fender benders had probably weighed in her favor—that and the fact that neither Carson nor Bree nor her brothers had ratted Anna out as the perpetrator. Her methods *had* been unusual— wiring an old car horn to Everett's starter and placing a screeching chimpanzee whistle in the exhaust pipe so that when he started the car and accelerated, every citizen within a mile had come outside to see what the commotion was and then to glare at him. She'd also filled his hubcaps with rocks, which had resulted in a further racket painful to the ears. One trip down Main had all the shopkeepers and everyone else ready to *throw* rocks at Everett and his old truck and had been effective in ridding the town of the motorized nuisance.

"You were always pretty great at problem-solving and unique solutions."

Anna squirmed beneath Bree's gaze, nearly as uncomfortable with her observations as she'd been with Eli's.

"You're still kind, resourceful Anna, go-out-on-a-limb Anna. Climb-a-tree-to-rescue-a-kitten-and-break-your-arm Anna."

"Don't remind me of that one." Instinctively Anna's hand went to her left elbow, shattered years ago during a fall from a very tall cypress.

"Even as you fell you made sure the cat was okay."

"One of us needed to be."

Rosie returned with glasses of water and juice, both of which Anna gulped down fairly quickly. She'd woken with a slight headache and guessed it was from more than the lack of sleep. Along with forgetting to eat yesterday, she hadn't had much to drink either. When their food arrived a few minutes later she attacked it with equal gusto, while also savoring every bite of the crisp bacon and fluffy hot cakes.

"Heaven." She grinned at Bree.

"Is the food swaying you in my favor, then?" Bree asked cautiously.

"Possibly, but not as much as you did last night." Anna poured more syrup. "Anyone who would show up to help with a chore like applesauce is a true friend."

Bree made a choking sound, then covered her mouth.

"Are you all right?" Anna pushed Bree's water glass closer to her.

Bree nodded. "Fine." Her tear-filled eyes met Anna's. "I'm just so relieved—and happy. I've missed you so much, Anna."

The same restriction Bree had likely felt in her throat

lodged itself in Anna's. This was it. She was really putting what had happened—with Bree, at least—behind her. They were friends again—something infinitely better than breakfast. She returned Bree's smile with a wobbly one of her own and raised her glass of juice. "Here's to best friends—for life."

Chapter 27

ELI HELD THE paper-wrapped delicacy close to his face as he crossed the street. The aroma of his favorite meatball sub wafted toward him, bringing almost euphoric anticipation. *Lunch. Alone in my office.* An hour by himself, with his thoughts, while staring out at the city view, sounded almost as good as the sandwich. After being gone over a week, he'd had a hectic several days back, with lunch meetings every day and even a few client appointments in the evenings to catch up.

His first weekend back hadn't been great, either. Baseball season was over, so he hadn't had a Cubs game to look forward to—a good thing probably, as he'd brought work home. What little free time he'd had was spent rereading all of Gabriel's documents and searching for a loophole to the requirements—so far a frustrating waste of time. His great-grandfather had been no fool.

Excepting his absurd belief that some fairytale romance with Anna could come of all this. That seemed about as likely as the possibility that Eli would actually find a way around having to move to Holiday—temporarily, at least. That subject was what he planned to devote his lunchtime thoughts to today. He needed to come up with a plan, some sort of proposition for his employer, that would allow him to be in the office only three days a week, while doing the rest of his work remotely. Based on how packed his week had been after his recent absence, he was going to have to think hard to come up with something good to pull this off.

The light turned green the other direction before Eli had

made it to the opposite sidewalk. He hurried his stride, but the taxi closest to him blared its horn, the driver sharing his displeasure at having to wait an extra couple of seconds—as if he wasn't on the clock, getting paid.

"Yeah, yeah," Eli shouted, then slapped the hood as he passed.

The driver's arm shot from the open window, his hand, with fingers artfully arranged, waving at Eli.

Impatient jer— Eli pitched forward as the bumper clipped the back of his calf and foot as the taxi surged into the intersection. Eli caught himself from falling, but the sub flew from his hand, flying end over end through the air. Eli lunged for it, leaving the shoe the taxi had smashed the heel of behind. His fingertips caught the edge of the sandwich wrapper, grasping at the waxed paper for a few, hopeful seconds, before they lost contact and the sub nosedived into the storm drain at the edge of the gutter.

Eli shouted his displeasure and received a chastising look from a mother standing on the corner with her young son.

"Sorry," he mumbled, then turned back for his shoe, only to see it completely run over by an SUV making a right-hand turn.

Holding further expletives in, he stomped up to the sidewalk, then turned to face the street, waiting for a break in traffic so he could reclaim what was left of his Cole Haan Oxford. The sandwich was a total loss—the shoe as well, probably—and his stomach and head pounded in unison at the thought of another five hours without both.

It promised to be another long afternoon.

Eli grabbed the knob on his office door and started to turn it, only to have the door pulled open from the other side.

"You're back." Lacee stood there, beaming at him.

"I've been back." He was impressed. She'd waited a week before coming to see him, though Eli didn't doubt that she'd known the exact second he first stepped foot in the building again.

"I left the valuations for the Kirkland property on your desk." She reached for him, but he skirted outside her grasp, a difficult feat, considering the condition of his shoe.

"Thanks." Eli hurried past her and moved behind his desk, wanting as much separation from her as possible. He set his laptop case down—right in front of a picture of the two of them at a Cubs game last spring. "*Lacee.*"

"You hadn't thrown it away. It was in your drawer. You wouldn't have kept it if it didn't mean anything."

Here came the desperation he'd been expecting. "I'll do it right now." He plucked the picture off his desk and dropped it in the trash can.

Lacee ran around the back of the desk and snatched it out. "You don't mean it. You can't throw this away any more than you can throw us away."

Eli braced his hands on his desk and looked her in the eye. "What we had was great, Lace, but it's over now—a memory. Let's keep it a good one instead of turning it sour with a bad end. If you want the picture, keep it, but that's all you're getting of me. Discussion closed."

Her lips puckered, then turned downward in an Academy Award winning pout. Tears would soon follow if he didn't get her out of his office quickly.

"Norman's on his way over," he said, referencing their boss. "You wouldn't want him to find out that we'd dated, given office policy and all."

"Everyone knows about us," Lacee said, somehow managing to speak and maintain her pout at the same time.

"There is no *us.*" Eli sat and removed his laptop from its

case. Maybe if he started working and ignored her she'd get the hint and leave.

"There used to be." Lacee drew in a shuddering breath. "And it was wonderful."

Eli didn't acknowledge her words but opened his laptop and entered his password.

"What is *wrong* with you, Eli?" Lacee planted her hands on the desk this time and leaned toward him. "Victoria and Elle warned me about you. I guess I should have listened. They told me you had commitment issues—that just when things would seem to be perfect, you'd bail."

"If they'd been perfect I wouldn't have."

"Tell me one date when we didn't have a great time?" Lacee demanded. "Did we ever fight? Or even disagree?"

"We are right now," Eli said, though not with the smugness he could have. There was a ring of truth in Lacee's words, and it was sobering. They'd had a good time together. But he'd been content to leave it at that—a good time now and then, not much different than going out with the guys. The thought of anything more hadn't entered his mind, so when it had entered hers, he'd known it was time to move on.

Lacee placed the picture back on his desk, facedown this time. "You should keep this," she said. "So that someday when you're old and lonely you'll realize that it's your own fault."

Chapter 28

GALE-FORCE WINDS and sheeting rain met Eli as he exited the building later that evening, at five thirty—a half hour later than he'd wanted. But a new client had called at four and asked to meet today. Knowing this new client potentially represented a significant amount of money for the firm, Eli had agreed.

Unfortunately, he hadn't agreed with the clients—two of them, a brother and a sister who'd recently inherited a quarter million each from their deceased father. Their problem was that seventy-two year-old Mom got the house—worth considerably more than their inheritances—and they wanted it.

Eli had listened patiently to their reasons why she wasn't capable of caring for the home and shouldn't be allowed to keep it; all the while he was thinking of the members of the seventies-plus club he'd met in Holiday.

Betty, the organist, came to mind first, with her Phantom of the Opera-esque preludes. Her key lime pie had been something else too, and she'd been a hoot to talk to. It was the only time in his life a woman over twice his age had flirted with him.

Then there was the town Santa, Ernie, aka Anna's second father. Eli hadn't quite figured out what the history was between those two, but Ernie had been watching out for Anna like a hawk since she'd returned. He had no doubt that Ernie's car had been one of those driving slowly back and forth in front of the house the night Eli had Anna over for dinner. And Ernie's daily trips to the Mulberry for a hot cocoa were nothing but a way to keep an eye on Anna and see how she was doing. Maybe he could help her fend off the unwanted suitors during the remaining weeks of her trip.

And of course there had been Gabriel. At one hundred two, his mind had still been sharp as a tack. *The sly old fox.* Eli was about ready to call it quits on finding any loophole to the living-in-Holiday requirement. Gabriel had dotted his i's and crossed his t's—twice with everything.

As had Mrs. Parker's husband—Eli hoped—after listening to their grown children whine at him for over an hour. It had been with no regret that Eli told them he wasn't the right kind of attorney for the job. The title transfers he did most frequently were straightforward, when a property was being sold by one party and acquired by another. They didn't have a situation like that here, but would need an estate attorney to pursue medical records and the like if they wished to prove their mother's incompetence.

Eli found himself hoping they could not, as he politely ushered them out of his office at 5:25 p.m.

Out the door himself now, he became keenly aware of his disabled shoe, when his sock was soaked within five minutes of leaving the building. The walk to the parking garage was short, thankfully, and Eli was glad he'd chosen to drive instead of taking a cab in today. He'd hoped to do some grocery shopping after work, but that would have to wait. He had no desire to limp around the store in a wet sock.

Once home he stopped just inside the door, slipped off his shoes, and shot them, one by one, at his kitchen trashcan, basketball style, watching with little satisfaction as they sailed through the air and reached their destination with a loud *thunk*. He'd have to add replacing a pair of his favorite Oxfords to his to-do list for the coming weekend. No doubt that would be the highlight, up there above picking up his dry cleaning and groceries.

With no games to look forward to, no good bands in town, and the next symphony performance weeks away, it looked like it'd be him and paperwork again this weekend. Great-grandson vs. Great-grandpa. Real estate attorney vs. real estate mogul and financial genius. The more time Eli spent learning about Gabriel, the more he was impressed. It really was a shame they hadn't met.

My fault entirely. His conscience reminded him of that and dozens of other things since his return to Chicago. He didn't need a picture on his desk to make him feel bad. His time in Holiday had already messed with his mind.

Eli removed his jacket and hung it over the back of a chair to dry. As they had so often since his return home, his thoughts drifted to Anna. He finally had a face to the person he'd already known, and now it was easy to conjure one of her smiles, her laugh, her mostly good-natured ribbing. Even her frowns haunted him—especially those he'd been responsible for. He wondered what she'd be doing with her weekend. Was it time for that Holiday hayride or whatever their fall celebration was called?

Had she been by Gabriel's house? He didn't think so, as he hadn't had any notifications from the security company. Before leaving Holiday, he'd reset the system, syncing it with the app on his phone, so he'd be notified whenever someone entered the house.

He hoped her dad was doing okay and hoped she was too—and that Carson and every other guy in Holiday was leaving her alone. Though that wouldn't be great for her either. Whether she was ready to admit it or not, Anna was a people person. She blossomed around others and instinctively seemed to draw the best from everyone around her. He'd enjoyed watching her at the market, with her family, even with the pumpkin delivery guy, who'd obviously been smitten by her as well.

Eli opened his fridge and stared at the dismal contents, moving grocery shopping to the top of the priority list, right after work tomorrow. He pulled out a carton of orange juice and some eggs and prepared to have breakfast for dinner again tonight. Not the best, but it would do until he went shopping.

No doubt Anna was eating better than he. Probably having something fresh and homemade, either from the Mulberry or from her mother's well-stocked pantry.

He cracked a couple of eggs into a pan and chugged the juice straight from the carton while they cooked. What was it about Anna that drew people to her? Why had he been drawn in as well?

Their first interaction on the plane certainly hadn't been anything spectacular. She'd been watching a movie on her phone, while he'd preferred the paperback in his hands to conversation with a stranger.

But after that . . . She'd helped him when he came into town the next night, and gone so far as to invite him, a complete stranger, to her family's table. She'd helped him again, when he'd come to the market. She'd driven all the way out to the house to bring a steak. And during their dinner, and their walk on Sunday . . . Anna had tried her best to get to know him, both plying him with questions and showing genuine interest—and concern—in and for his life and family. At the time Eli had found it almost annoying. He'd had an agenda, and talking about himself wasn't part of it. But Anna, not realizing that, had simply been herself—caring about other people and their problems.

She might be the only woman he'd ever met who *wasn't* all about herself. The women at his office, while nice enough, were definitely focused on their own agendas and climbing the career ladder. And why shouldn't they be? He was too. But Anna . . .

Eli flipped the eggs, waited another couple of minutes,

then turned the burner off. He slid his pathetic dinner from the pan to a plate, grabbed a fork, and walked over to his sliding glass door to watch the storm raging outside while he ate.

There wasn't much to see from this high up and being this close to other buildings. The garbage and leaves all blustered about below. But dark clouds blocked the space between the rows of high-rise condos, obscuring what little sunset he might have enjoyed.

What did the harbor in Holiday look like right now? Another spectacular sunset, the sky painted in pink and orange? Boats on the harbor, bobbing up and down beneath the lazy current. Maybe one of those world-class trout had just jumped from the water. And the trees . . . the magnolias would be arching over the path his great-grandparents had paved. Those incredible trees would shade the benches but still allow the sunlight to filter in through the spaces between their leaves.

Lovely. Stunning. An odd feeling of what he could describe only as a sort of homesickness washed over him. Which was about as absurd as Gabriel's hope that he and Anna would end up together.

To get his mind off the feelings of nostalgia welling within, Eli called his parents. They hadn't spoken in a couple of months—not since he'd called to tell them that Gabriel had died. Maybe talking to his mom and dad would ease this strange ache emanating from his chest.

"Eli? What is it? What's wrong?" his mom asked, launching immediately into questions.

"Hello to you to." Eli set his empty plate down and glanced at his watch, wondering what time it was where they were—and where that even was. "You guys still in Belgium?"

"Left there weeks ago." His father sounded groggy.

Middle of the night or early morning. Oops.

"Well, where are you now?" Eli asked.

"Milan," his mother said. "Why have you called? Do you need something?"

"No." Did they think he was still twelve and forgot to bring his retainer to camp? "I just hadn't talked to you in a while and wanted to see how your trip is going."

Silence. Then his father spoke. "You know how expensive international calls are. Don't want to spend all our money on a phone bill."

"Of course not." Eli's head bobbed, though they couldn't see him. He caught his reflection in the sliding glass door and hated the disappointment he saw. "Well, good to talk to you. Glad everything is going well. Night."

He intended to hang up before they could, but the line was already dead by the time his finger reached end call. Eli tossed the phone on the couch, then flopped down beside it, hands behind his head as he looked up to the ceiling, imagining how he would have liked that call to go.

"I spent about a week down in Holiday, stayed at Gabriel's place."

"What was it like?" his mother would ask, ever the interior decorator, even now that she'd retired.

"Grand, yet in need of an update. A historical gem—with just a little TLC. I—uh—spent some time with a woman while I was there too. The one Gabriel used to write to me about."

"What woman?" his father would have asked, having never heard the contents of Gabriel's letters.

"A special one, I think," Eli would have said.

This would have been met by silence, as his parents processed what he might be trying to tell them.

"Well, don't go getting in trouble," his father would have said. "Your mother and I aren't eager to be grandparents."

Eli snorted and shook his head, clearing his mind of the imagined conversation. It hadn't been a whole lot better than the real one. Even if they'd stayed on the phone together longer, nothing of substance would have been said. It never was.

What was wrong with his parents? *Everything. Nothing.*

They never wanted to be *parents.* Never had that seemed truer, now that he was grown up. He was grateful they'd had him at all—that he hadn't been one of the millions of abortions performed in the country each year. But maybe they should have given him up for adoption or something. For all the serious lack of interest they'd taken when he was growing up, it was even worse now that he was an adult. It was like they'd checked the parenting box and were done.

He could feed himself, dress himself, read, write, and drive. He'd had a good education and had a good job, so—task complete. His dad saw no need to worry about his namesake any more. Not that he really ever had. Mom had always been the one who arranged all the summer camps and extracurricular activities that kept him away from home most of the time. She'd made sure his school lunch fees were paid but had never made him a lunch—even on field trip days when other kids brought all kinds of cool stuff from home. He'd always been stuck with the standard school sack lunch—juice box, sandwich, apple.

He'd hated those lunches then, and he hated this feeling now, that he'd missed out on something important and was still missing out. But the truth was—*Mom and Dad really don't care. At all.*

Until recently, Eli had convinced himself that he didn't either. And now... Now he was all kinds of messed up. Worse than his shoe had been today. Somehow one measly week in Holiday had pulled the plug on what he'd believed was the perfect life. His job was driving him nuts, his apartment was too silent, his life too lonely. He was questioning past relationships, though he hadn't thought much of them at the time. He even found himself missing Rosie's diner and all the folks who'd made it their habit, each time he ate there, of stopping at his booth and saying hello and asking what he was up to that day.

Maybe it wasn't nosiness after all, but a way of life that was simply different—better. One that involved thinking about others and caring about what they were doing and who they were.

With Anna the poster child for that lifestyle. Or she had been once—before . . .

Gabriel had wanted to help her get that part of her back. He'd believed living in Holiday was key. *And I've let her off the hook.* Had he doomed Anna to a life of loneliness by taking over house-sitting so she could return to Seattle?

Eli hoped not, but he wasn't sure—about a lot of things. He reached for the remote and turned on the television, eager for a mind-numbing show he could lose himself in.

Chapter 29

"Look at me, Aunt Rosie!" Arms flung wide, seven-year-old Julia twirled in a circle, one hand nearly hitting the handle to the walk-in freezer while the other narrowly missed a stack of dishes on a metal rack. "Isn't this one pretty?"

"Smashing." Rosie caught Julia mid-twirl and pressed her arms to her sides. "Which is exactly what is going to happen in this kitchen if you keep dancing around. I'm glad you're excited about the new clothes, but we'll have to sell them to buy new dishes if you aren't more careful."

"Sorry." Julia ducked her head.

Anna and Rosie exchanged looks—one amused, the other exasperated.

"It's okay. No harm done—yet." Rosie ruffled the top of Julia's messy hair. "Now go change before the dinner rush starts."

Julia dashed off toward the restroom, then stopped and ran the other direction, straight toward Anna, stopping only when she'd reached her and had flung her arms around her waist. "Thank you for the pretty dresses."

"You're welcome." Anna returned the child's embrace and felt a tug at her heart as she looked down on Julia's tangles. *She needs a mother.* "I'm so glad you like them. And I'm glad you were here when I dropped them off, so I could see you try them on."

"Me too." Julia beamed at her, then skipped off, and Anna turned to go, her emotions in turmoil. Growing up she'd always assumed she would marry and have children of her own. Now here she was, nearly thirty, with neither. And beginning to wish for both. If she couldn't have a family of her own, at least she could bring a little joy to other families in need.

A couple of feet from the counter Anna stopped short.

Hands on her hips, Rosie blocked the way to the front of the diner.

"I've got to get going—another delivery to make," Anna said, not wishing to be rude, but she'd already stayed longer than she'd intended.

"You *found* those dresses, huh? Where? They certainly weren't from the back of your closet." Rosie folded her arms, apparently expecting an answer.

"Um . . . online." Anna shrugged. "I find a lot of things there these days." She hadn't lied, not really. It was all a matter of perspective—as Eli would have said.

"Why?" Rosie's eyes narrowed. "Are you interested in my brother? Because if so, don't go thinking you can get to him through his daughter. You don't need to do that. Clarence would be happy to—"

"I'd be happy to take you out on a date." Behind Anna, Clarence cleared his throat. "I'd be honored."

Anna froze. *Clarence, here? Now?* He must have come in through the back door. Lips pressed together, she didn't immediately turn to face him. It was bad enough that Rosie was likely witnessing her dismay. So much for doing something nice.

Composing herself, Anna drew in a breath and turned around. "I would never think of using your daughter that way, Clarence." She offered a wan smile. "I simply noticed that Julia could use a new dress or two—so I got her some. I—I like to shop online, and I can only buy myself so many dresses." She tilted her head and shrugged. "Please don't take offense."

"You bought her dresses just because?" Clarence scratched his head, clearly baffled. Based on his current and usual attire—worn overalls—nice clothing held little appeal or importance.

"Yep." Anna's forced smile grew wider. *Because I can. Because I wanted to.* Not *because I want to go out with you.* That was possibly the last thing she wanted. Donald would have been a better choice. No worry of hurting his feelings unless she denied him a piece of cheesecake. But Clarence was a sweet man who had been terribly hurt. She'd never want to do anything to further injure him.

"Well, then." Rosie relaxed her stance and moved aside, freeing Anna to go. "It was kind of you to think of Julia—something just like your mama would do."

"Thank you," Anna said, grateful for both the compliment and her imminent escape. "Now I've really got to be going."

"We could still go on a date," Clarence called before she'd taken two steps.

"I fear you're too late, brother," Rosie said. "That fellow from out of town already stole Anna's heart—or she stole his. I'm not sure which happened first. You saw them together at church. And the way he looked at her, the way he watched her from my very front window here, made his feelings abundantly clear. Mark my words, Elijah Steiner will be back before the year's end to stake his claim."

In one way Rosie was correct. Eli would be back in Holiday by the year's end. But Anna wasn't his claim. This place was.

Anna set the overflowing vase carefully on the Steiners' porch, trying not to think of the last time she'd been here, the evening Eli had cooked dinner for her, complete with a steak flopped onto this same floor.

She stood, punched the code into the keypad, and felt

dread rather than relief when she heard the familiar click. *No excuses now.* She collected the vase and pushed open the door, pausing on the threshold before taking that first, brave step inside.

The house was quiet—too quiet. Both before and after his wife had died, Mr. Steiner had made sure to keep the old record player loaded, with albums continually dropping and music echoing through the grand rooms. Mrs. Steiner had loved music—even more so after losing her sight. After her death, her husband had loved it even more as well, as it reminded him of his dear wife.

Anna glanced toward the parlor, wondering what had become of Mr. Steiner's vast collection of records and the large console stereo. *A quest for another day.* This afternoon she wished only to leave the bouquet she had spent the previous evening crafting. With the last of the applesauce finally canned and distributed, and Eli having been gone two and a half weeks, it was high time she started fulfilling her end of the bargain, coming over to the house. Thankfully she didn't have to live here yet, but the house and grounds needed attention. And if Eli truly was to take over responsibilities with the estate at the end of the year, it seemed the least she could do was to honor Mr. Steiner's wishes until then and look after his home.

The music might no longer be playing, but she could at least fill the front hall with the fragrance of flowers once again. *For the ghosts to enjoy.*

The idea that Mr. and Mrs. Steiner might somehow still be here brought comfort instead of disturbance. After closing the front door behind her, Anna took resolute steps toward the round table. Except for its usual doily, it lay still and bare, bereft for so many weeks now of its usual display of color.

Anna held the vase out, ready to place it on the table, but stopped at the last second, appalled at the sheen of dust covering the surface. Had Eli done any cleaning at all during his stay? If so, had this much dust accumulated in the past couple of weeks? Either way, Mrs. Steiner would have been most displeased. Though her eyesight had failed, her sense of touch never had, and to her dying day she had made certain that every last surface in the mansion gleamed.

Anna set the bouquet carefully on the floor, then continued toward the back of the house, to the kitchen. There she located a cloth she could use for dusting and returned to clean the table. Starting on one side, she worked her way across, plucking the doily from the table when she reached the middle. The lace caught easily in her fingertips, elevated above the surface, revealing a lone envelope beneath.

One that bore her name.

Both cloth and doily fell from her hands as she reached for the envelope. Mr. Steiner's unmistakable, shaky handwriting sprawled across the front.

Annabelle

Anna stared at it as her finger traced the letters he had penned. Tears sprang to her eyes. *Can I not go a week in this town without crying?*

On legs that felt wooden, Anna moved to the stairs and sat heavily on the second to last. For a long moment she stared at the envelope, scared to open it, to reveal what it said—to her personally. But at last she turned it over, broke the seal, and withdrew the folded, lined papers within. If curiosity killed the cat, it might get her as well, if this letter spoke of the hurt she knew she'd caused Mr. Steiner, abandoning him as she had. It was the reason she hadn't wanted to return to his house, the reason she couldn't imagine accepting it or any part of his estate. She hadn't been a good friend to him at the end but—like his son—had abandoned him.

Anna closed her eyes briefly, wondering if she ought to go home before she read the letter. But Mr. Steiner had left it here for her. He obviously wanted her to find it here, so perhaps this was where she was meant to read it as well. Her own, tender feelings, along with a fresh infusion of guilt, would be no more than she deserved.

She unfolded the pages, pressing the seams flat against her knees.

Dearest Annabelle,

If you are reading this, then you have come home and I have at last gone to be with my sweetheart, both of which I am grateful for. It will be my ongoing prayer—if the dead are still permitted to pray while (hopefully) in Deity's presence—that you choose to stay in Holiday, near your family and so many who hold you dear. I hope you will forgive me my part in orchestrating your homecoming. I trusted the bonds of our friendship enough to know you would be compelled to come at my bequest. It may seem unfair that I have tied my gift to such stringent conditions, but I promise it is in your interest that I have done so.

Mr. Steiner hadn't lived to know about her father's cancer. *But came up with his own means to lure me back to Holiday.* Would it have worked? Anna looked up from the paper and stared across the vast, lonely room, remembering the many happy times she'd spent here. If she closed her eyes she could still hear the music and the laughter. She could see Carson's mom and hers busy baking in the kitchen, while she and Carson and Bree helped Mr. Steiner wrap presents, and her father and Carson's put up the tree. She could hear Mr. Steiner's banjo and see the curtains blowing at the open windows and smell the fresh spring breeze. She could hear his somewhat gravelly voice sharing stories with her and could feel the touch of his age-spotted hand on her young one.

Would I have come?

Yes. Holiday Anna would have come at once—but she

wasn't so certain about Seattle Anna, the recluse who hid away in an apartment full of plants. That woman would have been harder to convince.

Uncomfortable with this self-examination, Anna continued reading.

As you know, many years ago our son left home and never returned. I have shared what transpired that night with very few. Those who know the story have kindly kept it to themselves. I share it with you, that it perhaps may be of some benefit as you examine the circumstances of your own life.

The night Gabe left began as one of celebration of our nation's independence. After the usual barbeques, fireworks were the order of the night, as is custom. Gabe had—without my permission—obtained some that were both illegal and dangerous. As so many young people do, he believed himself invincible. No harm could come to him, no matter how he flirted with it. No physical harm did come to him that night, but to his mother, who was blinded when one of the fireworks Gabe set off went awry.

Anna gasped. Mrs. Steiner's son caused her blindness? Anna couldn't imagine the anguish for all involved. She didn't want to imagine it, yet her eyes were again drawn to the page, to a story she wasn't certain she wanted to read.

It was as terrible a scene as you can imagine, and I do imagine it frequently, even these many years later. Gabe and some of his friends, quite a distance down the drive, away from the house, were lighting fireworks in every way imaginable. Though nearly past his teenage years, he hadn't quite left the desire to blow things up behind yet.

His mother and I and our guests lingered on the lawn, enjoying each other's company. Suddenly Gabe yelled—not his usual, excited shout that we heard each time he'd successfully launched one of the rockets—but a panicked cry of warning. The firework had tipped, spun on its side, and shot toward us. His yell coincided with the explosion, right in front of Delores' chair. Her scream of pain is also something I'll hear to my dying day.

We rushed her to the hospital—no small feat, given the distance and the traffic due to the celebrations. It was faster for us to drive and meet the ambulance partway, so we did, all the while praying she would be all right. Her hands were severely burned, as was her face. I cannot begin to imagine the agony she was in. She was taken into surgery. Gabe was beside himself, bawling like a child, and repeating how sorry he was over and over again. I was too furious to offer either comfort or consolation and at one point remember telling him to shut up before leaving the hospital to wait outside.

The next day, after we had learned Delores' sight had irrevocably been taken, I—instead of showing compassion for my son, who was already buried under a mountain of regret and sorrow—took out my anger and grief upon him, saying, among other damaging things, that I would never, ever forgive him for what he had done to his mother.

He fled the hospital, and I let him go, staying to tend to Delores. It was the last time I ever saw Gabe. The last conversation we ever had.

"Oh, Mr. Steiner." Anna clutched the letter tightly as a tear splashed onto it.

If I thought Delores' grief over losing her sight was great, it was nothing in comparison to her sorrow over losing her son. When a year had passed without word, I was humbled enough to realize I'd done wrong—that my haste and harshness were responsible for the breach between us. It took *some time, but I located Gabe and wrote him a letter of apology. It was returned unopened, as were all the other letters I sent.*

I decided to go see him in person. I was refused entry at both his place of business and his home. It seemed my son had followed my example well and would never, ever forgive me for what I had said to him in anger.

Anna paused reading to brush the moisture from her cheeks. She couldn't imagine not having her parents in her life, or feeling that kind of animosity toward either of them. She couldn't imagine how it must feel to have caused someone she loved so much harm—both as Mr. Steiner and his son had done. How had they each dealt with it for so many years? How did one recover from something like that?

Did Eli know this story? Had it been passed down in his family lore until Mr. Steiner was made out to be some kind of monster? Was that why Eli had never come to visit him during all those years they'd corresponded?

Anna shifted the papers, so the second page was on top.

I tell you this story now, not to change your memory of me, as I hope it will not—you knew me to be a stubborn, silly old man long before this confession—but to prompt you to act while you are young and have time. Both my son and I made terrible mistakes—the worst of it being that they hurt and deprived Delores. Gabe took her sight, but I took a piece of her heart when my words sent him away. Though I have long since forgiven him, it has taken a lifetime for me to forgive myself.

You have done no one a grave wrong, excepting yourself and family and friends by staying away from home so long. Your self-enforced exile came not because of a parent's harsh words but because of your friends' betrayal. I would propose to you that Carson and Bree, like my son Gabe, are good people who made a serious mistake. As Gabe's wrongdoing should not have been enough to banish him from his family and home, you should not allow your friends' wrongdoing to keep you from your family and home.

Anna, you are the one being hurt the most by staying away, as was Gabe—essentially cut off from his family for the rest of his life. Also like Gabe, you are hurting others. Delores and I missed out on the blessing of being grandparents and great-grandparents. What should have been a joyful legacy became a void. Your parents are hurting because you have gone. They miss you, Anna. As do your siblings and friends—even and including those who betrayed your trust.

It is my final wish that you will stay in or at least close to Holiday and all that was once dear to you here. I hope that you will find a way to forgive and find a happy path forward, filled with a family of your own and the exciting opportunities you once yearned for.

Don't make the mistake I made, Anna. It was pride that kept me so long from apologizing to our Gabe, and I've no doubt it was pride that kept him from me. The night his mother was blinded, I was most angry with myself, for my inability to protect her, to help her, to ease her suffering. And I took that anger out on my son.

You, too, have had cause to be angry, but don't let your pride—or the humiliation you suffered—be the cause of a lifetime of sorrow and regret as mine has been. Come home while there is still time. Mend fences—all of them. Find another to love.

Delores and I will be watching over you. I expect to hear the old record player soon and that you'll find a way to make our once-joyous home that way again.

Much love,
Gabriel

Eyes blurry, Anna drew her knees to her chest and pressed her face to them, sobbing. Not for herself this time, but for Mr. Steiner and his son. For Mrs. Steiner and the losses she'd suffered. Even for Eli, for the grandparents he'd never known and the family he'd never had.

Why did life have to be so hard? Why did the happiness that once came so easily to her seem so fleeting? Could she change that? Could she ever get it—and her old self—back?

I have to try. And I have to stay—for Mr. Steiner. She would honor his last wish.

Chapter 30

ELI CLOSED THE door to his office, strode quickly to the chair behind his desk, and swiveled to face the window. Instead of looking at the view he held his phone closer to his face, eyes glued to the screen showing Anna seated on the stairs inside Gabriel's house. She was hugging her knees to her chest—and crying.

Why? What had happened? Who'd upset her now? With every second she stayed on the stairs, his worry increased.

The notification on the alarm company's app had come through twenty minutes ago, but he'd been in the middle of a meeting. As soon as it was over, he'd opened the app on his phone and clicked on the camera that viewed the front of the house. The Excursion parked in the driveway alleviated any worry he might have had that someone had broken in, but he'd been curious to know what Anna was up to, so he'd switched to the camera that viewed the foyer. Now he almost wished he hadn't.

Out of sight, out of mind. If only.

Since his return, too many of his thoughts had been centered in Holiday and around one woman. Seeing her in distress wasn't going to help.

Eli checked the cameras and confirmed she was alone at the house. *Good.* Perhaps she'd just come there to cry, or something had happened at work that upset her. For a woman who'd once spent a summer swimming with sharks, she was pretty fragile these days.

What he'd come to think of as his protective instinct

toward Anna kicked in. He didn't want to coddle her, but he wanted to help her become strong again—the kind of woman who wasn't afraid of sharks or alligators—or men.

Why am I thinking about this, anyway? He wasn't going back until December—and only then if he absolutely had to—when she'd be leaving. He'd already decided he was done with Holiday and Anna Lawrence. They'd messed with his perspective, and his only goal now was to get back to where he'd been—content with his life. Concerned only about making more money. Because contentment and cash couldn't fail you. *Like parents do. Like people in general.* Look what had happened to Anna.

She'll be okay. She was okay. He watched as she rose from the stairs, wiped her eyes, and tucked a paper in the back pocket of jeans that looked way too good on her. She moved to the round entry table and began cleaning it, then placed a gorgeous arrangement of flowers in the center.

Ah. The weekly flower delivery. She'd probably just been sentimental about it. He expected her to leave, and when she walked out of view of the camera he switched to the front porch view again. A minute passed, and Anna didn't come outside. He went back to the foyer and found it empty.

He found her in the parlor, the console record player propped open. She appeared to be dusting the furniture, dancing and swaying about the room as she worked.

A smile grew on Eli's face as he reclined in his chair, thoroughly entertained. Whatever had upset Anna, she seemed to have recovered quickly.

That's my girl.

No. She's not. He closed the app and stared at the magnificent view from his window, hauling his thoughts back where they belonged. *Chicago.* This was his town, his place. *Big-city living. Cubs games, the symphony. Movie theaters. Normal grocery stores. Great, plentiful food. Showers with water pressure. No obligations.* No people nosing in his business. No complications. No connections. No real friends. No love.

Eli whirled the chair about and faced his desk and the work waiting for him. If he couldn't focus on being happy and content here, he could at least concentrate on all that needed to be completed. He'd barely caught up from his absence, and he didn't want to fall behind again.

His phone rang, jarring him from his thoughts. Anna's name, along with the picture he'd snapped of her the night they'd had dinner together, flashed on his screen. His heart practically did a jig.

Oh no. Not going there. If parents could let you down, just think what a woman could do. He could get seriously messed up.

Like Anna.

The phone continued to ring. His finger hovered over the screen, wanting desperately to answer and yet—afraid.

I'm no different than she is. No better or better off. Anna had done a pretty good job insulating herself from the world the past few years, not dating men and all. *And I'm doing the same, safe here in my comfort zone.*

The phone continued to ring, then went to voicemail. Eli ignored it for a good five minutes while he went over a transfer of title. But his mind wasn't where it should be. And his heart definitely wasn't in his work today—since he'd returned, really.

Was it because his paycheck no longer mattered quite as much, now that Gabriel had set him up so well? Or, was it because he'd had a glimpse of something better, of what might have been, the potential for what still could be?

His mind flashed to dinner at Anna's parents' house and then sitting close beside her at church. Such simple events, yet they had been meaningful to him.

Giving in, Eli opened his voicemail, closed his eyes, and leaned back in his chair, listening to Anna's voice and feeling an odd tightening in his chest.

"Hi, Eli. I have a question to ask you. Give me a call when you get a chance. I hope everything is going well back home. I went to Mr. Steiner's house today and started cleaning. I'll get some help to start on the yard next week. Bye."

Short, simple, to the point. She'd given Eli no hint at all that she might be interested in him—other than her feelings of betrayal when he'd told her about the will. Prior to that she thought he'd been spending time with her because he wanted to, not because he had an agenda.

Eli picked up a pen and drummed it on his desk. He'd had an agenda, a neat order of operations, which he'd mostly checked off. Meet Anna. Tell her about the will. Get her to agree to stay in Holiday. Return to Chicago and forget about the whole thing.

Items three and four hadn't gone so well. For that matter, two hadn't been smooth sailing either. But he'd succeeded in what he'd most wanted—meeting the woman from his great-grandfather's stories. And now that he'd met her . . .

Eli set the pen down, though he felt like chucking it across the room, along with everything else on his desk. Now that he'd met Anna his entire life was upended. He couldn't forget her or that quirky little town.

Maybe you'll be surprised, he'd told her on the plane, hinting that her visit might be more than she'd anticipated. His certainly had been. Who was the surprised one now? A begrudging smile slowly curved his lips upward. He picked up his phone and looked at Anna's picture—again. As he had every single day since his return home. His eyes narrowed in on her mouth, on lips that had only been kissed by one man, a very long time ago.

Eli closed his laptop and slipped it into its case. He was done here for the day—maybe for good.

It was time to find out what Anna's question was and answer some of his own.

Chapter 31

ELI HEARD ANNA coming before he saw her—the steady rhythm of her sneakers, a light, sure step, treading over the brittle leaves, interrupting the still quiet of the early morning. Apparently being back in Holiday had driven her to take up running again. *Good.* He ought to have come earlier and joined her. A half-hour jog in the morning did wonders to clear the mind and wake the body. His still felt stiff from yesterday's long drive.

It seemed darker than usual for this time of morning as he watched her approach from the end of the street—probably the storm that was forecast making an early appearance. When she was a couple of houses away, he confirmed the runner was, indeed, Anna, with her tall, willowy figure and the way her ponytail swished back and forth. The day he'd helped her shoot the old pistol, he'd realized how perfect her height was—in relation to his and being close—as well as everything else about her. Just like his great-grandfather had been telling him for years. A corner of Eli's mouth lifted. *You may have won, Gabriel.*

So that was it, then? He'd decided to go for it—for Anna. To drop his entire life in pursuit of the woman he'd dreamed about for years. The whole fourteen-hour drive down here he'd debated with himself.

This is madness. Turn around and go home.

Holiday feels like home—or like it could be one. More than any he'd known.

She doesn't trust men.

She's been hurt, and I can fix that.

I can't just leave my job. I have to make a living. I didn't go to law school for nothing.

I'll use my experience and degree to grow Gabriel's portfolio. Legal work doesn't have to be a nine-to-five gig anymore.

This is what the old man wanted.

It was that thought alone that had brought Eli here in the first place. He'd owed it to Gabriel to at least come see the place before he turned it all over to Anna. He owed it to him to meet Anna too.

The old man was sly. Eli would bet that his great-grandfather had known exactly what would happen when Eli laid eyes on Anna. He hadn't even been in Holiday yet when he'd felt that first jolt of attraction. He'd noticed her when he sat beside her on the plane, even with her headphones on, face glued to her phone.

Then, after they landed and he'd realized who she was, his heart had thumped in recognition. She hadn't told him her name, but somehow he'd known.

And later that night, when she was the one to show enough compassion to give him some food, he'd really known. And fought it all the way. *No way, no how.* Anna Lawrence was the last person on earth he could be interested in.

Yet, here he was. White flag raised. Hopefully she wouldn't fire at him.

He'd planned to catch her as she left for work, but this was even better. Eli pushed his foot against the floor of the Lawrences' porch, gently rocking the swing as he waited for Anna to turn up the drive and notice him.

A few seconds later she did, stopping cold in an impressive move from fluid motion to ramrod straight. They made eye contact, and he caught the changing emotions skitter across her face. Shock, fear, relief, anger. She began moving again, marching toward him, arms swinging, feet striding purposefully.

Uh oh.

"You startled me."

Given her expression, he'd expected something harsher and took her simple accusation as a good sign. "I didn't mean to. I'm sorry."

"For a second I thought you were someone else." She propped a foot on the bottom step and bent over, stretching.

So I can't see her face? Too late Eli remembered the dinner conversation and her brother's awkward reminiscing of Anna and Carson on the porch swing.

Eli practically jumped from the swing, wanting to separate himself from her sad memories as much as possible, and wondering if she'd been expecting Carson to come by, to visit her alone. Or if it really was just a memory that had jarred her.

After having dinner with Bree and Carson, Eli didn't think Carson would be stopping by anytime soon or ever—at least without his wife. And Eli really hoped Anna wasn't wishing for that.

He wandered closer and leaned forward over the rail. "I'm not an axe murderer or an ex-boyfriend. Just the guy who made you furious a couple of weeks ago."

"Not your fault. I probably overreacted."

"*Probably?*" He looked down at her.

She glanced up with an expression that told him not to push it. Eli decided that was wise, given that he wanted to be in her good graces again—for a start.

"So—you're back. Did you decide you want the entire inheritance after all?" Anna switched legs and continued stretching, bending over with her nose to her knee. This caused her t-shirt to rise, revealing a bare strip of her lower back. Eli felt his blood pressure elevate with it.

"Uh—not exactly." *Maybe. I'm not sure yet.* "You said you had a question for me."

"One that could have been answered during a phone conversation." Anna looked up at him, suspicion in her narrowed eyes and pursed lips.

"Okay." Eli held his hands up in surrender. "I came back to see you. I didn't like the way we left things last time, and I wanted to make it up to you."

"What did you have in mind?" Anna finished stretching and ran up the steps.

Here goes. "How would you like to go to the beach today?"

"I always like that, but I've got to be at the Mulberry in forty-five minutes." Anna raised an arm, wiping sweat from her brow. "And I've got to shower before."

"What if I took care of that for you?"

"Excuse me?" Anna's glare would have frightened off a lesser man.

Eli held a hand out, palm forward as he shook his head. "Not the shower. I meant what if you didn't have to go into work today?" *Or tomorrow.*

"No choice." Anna turned away and reached for the handle on the screen door. "The Holiday Hoedown is tomorrow. The Mulberry is a major sponsor. I've got a lot to do for it still, and I have to be there to run our booth."

Among other things. Hadn't the pumpkin delivery guy asked her to save him a dance?

"I'm sorry, but I really can't go," she said.

"You could have Carson cover for you," Eli suggested. "Benefits of being the boss. Make him slave away all day while you swim."

"The last weekend in October is a bit cool for that."

"Not in Florida." Eli waited, figurative fingers crossed that she'd take the bait.

Hand still on the screen door, Anna turned to him. "You want to take me to Florida? Seems a bit far for a day trip."

"True. So we'd probably want to make it a weekend kind of thing. You know—visit your parents, hit the beach for some sand and sun..."

Anna's breath hitched at the mention of her parents, and a tenderness softened her gaze. He could tell she was wavering. If the pull of the ocean wasn't strong enough, it seemed the lure of visiting her parents might be.

"What about the hoedown?"

He shrugged. "What about it? I'll convince Carson to cover that too. Then we'll hop in the car and be off." He inclined his head toward his BMW parked on the street.

"You'd do that for me? Talk to Carson and then drive me all the way to Florida?"

The earlier dismissiveness was gone from her voice. Eli refrained from pumping his arm in victory. He wasn't quite there yet. "Actually, I'm planning on doing it whether you want to go or not. You need to get out of dodge for a while. I'm hoping you'll come peaceably. If not, I'll be forced to kidnap you."

Anna's mouth twitched. "I see your ploy. If you kidnap me and go to jail for it, you won't be able to deal with the house. It'll all be on me."

"Yeah—no. I've seen the inside of prison during a stint as a DA intern. I won't be going there. If I have to kidnap you, I'll have to be thorough. Maybe brainwash you as well, so you believe you wanted to come."

"I do want to come."

Her smile was like the sun coming out.

Eli grinned. "It's working already."

Anna leaned against the plush leather seat of Eli's BMW. "Nice ride. I like it much better than the truck."

"Me too." Eli propped his elbow in the open window as he drove, then glanced in the rearview mirror. "Looks like we're getting out of town just in time. Check out that sky."

She'd seen it already. Rain was headed their way, and lots of it. "The town council already made the decision to move the hoedown inside to the community hall instead of having it at the pavilion at the park. No hayrides this year."

"Bummer," Eli said. "But at least you know you're not missing the best parts. Without hayrides or your mom's chili it's a wonder they don't cancel the whole thing."

"You're making fun of us Southern folk again, aren't you?"

"Me?" Eli clapped a hand to his chest, as if wounded. "Never. I've heard so much about that famous chili, I'm disappointed too." His quick wink confirmed his level of sincerity.

"Maybe my mom will take pity on you and make some while we're there." Anna wasn't sure whether it was the car or what, but Eli seemed a different guy from the one who'd been here a couple of weeks ago—more laid back, less of an agenda. Maybe the new attitude—and this trip—were all part of his plan. To win her over into taking on Mr. Steiner's estate so he wouldn't have to return in December.

She couldn't say the thought of accepting those terms hadn't tempted her the past week. The longer she was away from Seattle, the less she felt like returning. But she had to, right? She couldn't just live in Holiday and not have a job. And working at the Mulberry didn't count. Working with Carson wasn't acceptable. Though somehow she had managed to accept it, or deal with it—and him. They definitely weren't friends again, and certainly never would be like they had been, but she couldn't seem to find it in her to be as angry with him as she had been when she first came home.

Maybe it had been hearing Bree's story about the circumstances of their betrayal. Or the way he was helping to bring the market into the right century. That he was doing Anna a favor this weekend, representing the Mulberry at the hoedown and chili cookoff, helped a tiny bit as well.

While she'd showered and packed this morning Eli had gone over to the Mulberry and taken care of arrangements. According to him, Carson had been very willing to take over her weekend responsibilities. Anna supposed she'd see just how willing he had been when they worked together again next week.

Bree had made a point of calling or stopping by every single day since their forty-eight-hour applesauce fest. Anna suspected it was because Bree feared losing the tentative ground they'd regained in their friendship. Anna feared that too, so she'd eagerly accepted almost all of Bree's invites, even attending the literacy class she taught at the Mulberry last night. What she hadn't been able to do was to visit Bree at her house. She wasn't ready for that yet, to spend time in the place where Bree and Carson and their daughter lived, to witness firsthand the life they'd built together.

Still . . . Mom was right. The ache of the past became a little less each day.

Her brother had been right too. People seemed to have mostly forgotten the drama at the church nearly four years ago. Life moved on.

For everyone else, at least.

Anna still felt like she needed a jump start after having a dead battery for so long. The possibility of a job closer to home had her looking—and thinking. Not that Eli needed to know that yet. Even if she did come back to Holiday or somewhere nearby, she didn't think she could ever live all alone in Mr.

Steiner's gigantic house. Even if she eventually married and had a family, she didn't want or need all that space. Yet, she didn't want the estate going to a stranger.

What to do? Convince Eli to stay. By his own admission he'd never seen much of the South. They'd see at least a bit of the countryside this weekend. She'd do her best to get him hooked on warm winters and Southern hospitality.

"A little warmer down here than it is in Chicago right now?"

"A lot warmer. We had an early cold snap. Usually it's not that bitter until January."

"Was it the cold that made you decide to head South again?" Anna asked, still baffled as to what had really brought Eli back. They'd each been cordial enough the last time they spoke, so he needn't have felt bad about the way they'd left things. And considering the way she'd flipped out on him a few times previously, she'd given him no reason to want to spend time with her. Eli had offered her a mansion and enough money to set her up comfortably. Maybe he'd come back to renegotiate that offer, after realizing she must have some form of insanity to refuse it.

"The cold didn't really figure into my decision. It was more a feeling that I should come, that I shouldn't have left things the way we did. Plus, I was highly curious what question you wanted to ask." Eli glanced at her. "I was glad you called. I wasn't sure you'd ever really want to talk to me again—about anything. I shouldn't have tried to dump the whole living-on-the-estate thing on you. I'm sorry, Anna."

"And I'm sorry I freaked out," Anna said. He'd driven all the way back down here—to *apologize?* "I hadn't ever imagined Mr. Steiner would leave anything to me—let alone half of *everything*."

"I was as surprised as you—that he left anything to *me*," Eli added. "I certainly don't deserve it."

"Is that why you don't want it?" Anna asked. "Or is it just that to accept would be to disrupt your life—on some level at least."

"A bit of both, I think." Eli hit the button to roll up his window as they left the county roads and merged onto US 90 E. "Hey, we're in Florida already. That was a short drive."

"If only." Anna smiled. "Though compared to yesterday's drive, this one should seem short."

"It will be more pleasant, anyway," Eli said. "With your company."

"Thanks," Anna murmured, not sure what to do with that compliment. Was he flirting? Trying to sweeten her on him so . . . Maybe Eli *had* been completely honest when he'd said he intended to brainwash her. It *might* be working already.

"So, what'd you want to ask me?"

"Um—" *How to begin a potentially difficult and/or illuminating conversation about his relatives?* "What would you think if I painted the front porch columns at your great-grandfather's house?"

"*Paint?* That's what you sounded so serious about in your message?"

"It is serious," Anna said. "Color can make all the difference to curb appeal."

Eli snorted. "As long as you're not going with fuchsia or something like that, whatever you choose should be fine."

"Darn." Anna snapped her fingers in mock seriousness.

Eli glanced at her again. "You bought it already?"

"No." She shook her head. "But you did." Her grin turned to a smirk as she waited the second it took for him to get her joke.

"So that's the kind of mood we're in today?" Eli's head bobbed. "Okay. I'll take goofy, terrible-jokes Anna over ticked-off-at-me Anna. It's all good."

"It is," she agreed. "Except . . ."

"There really was something you wanted to ask me?"

"Yeah."

"Lost your nerve?"

"Kind of."

"Let me take the pressure off," Eli said. "Yes, Anna. I would love to go out with you. I'd be honored to be your first date in almost four years."

"What?" she spluttered. "You think I was calling you in *Chicago* to ask you out?"

"Either that or you missed the sound of my voice and wanted to hear it again."

"Wow. That whole I'm-an-attorney-and-drive-a-BMW thing has really gone to your head."

"Nah. I'm competitive is all. Point for me. The score is tied now."

"For now." He was definitely flirting, and this time she was enjoying it. Too bad she had to ruin their lightheartedness. "Actually, what I wanted to ask was if you knew about this." She leaned forward, pulling Mr. Steiner's note from her purse.

Eli's expression turned puzzled as he looked at it. "That's Gabriel's handwriting."

"I found this at the house. You didn't see it when you were there?"

He shook his head. "Where was it?"

"In the foyer, beneath the doily on the table. I noticed it when I brought flowers last Wednesday."

"That was nice of you. It seemed kind of an odd request of his in the will, but not so much to you, I'm guessing."

"It's odd only because no one is living there to enjoy them," Anna said. "But Mr. Steiner didn't want the house empty long. He wanted it filled with music and flowers and people again—like it used to be."

"When was that? Not in his time. The two of them rattling around in that old place couldn't have been much noise."

"Not then," Anna said. "But before. When your grandfather still lived at home." She paused, hoping that sharing the story with Eli was the right thing to do. Maybe he knew already. If Mr. Steiner had wanted Eli to know, wouldn't he have told him in his own letter? "Do you know why your grandfather left home and never returned?"

"An argument with his old man," Eli said. "There was never really much talk about it in my family—never much talk about anything," he added, a sour note to his voice.

"This letter explains." Anna withdrew the paper. "I thought you might want to read it."

"You're being serious again."

"It is serious, Eli. And sad. So sad."

"You mean it made you feel that way."

"It will make you feel the same."

"And I was in such a good mood." He pounded the steering wheel.

"It'll keep." Anna looked out the window at the passing scenery. "I know just the place to stop for a break. I'll share it with you then."

Chapter 32

Eli followed Anna's directions to the Maclay Gardens State Park in Tallahassee. They were a little over halfway through their trip, and taking a break would be nice. It wasn't that the six-hour drive was terribly long, but after a full day in the car yesterday, he was restless. He was also curious about the contents of her letter.

"My mother took me here years ago." Anna unbuckled her seatbelt as he parked. "They have the most gorgeous flowers and plants."

"I gather you're into that sort of thing—after all those years of bringing flowers to Gabriel."

"I do love growing things," Anna said. "I never realized how much until recently. I had to ask a neighbor to water my plants for me while I was gone, and she was shocked when she saw how many I had."

"How many do you have?" Eli asked, curious.

"Forty-seven." Anna ducked her head and gave him a sheepish expression. "I bought them one at a time, and they don't all need to be watered every day, so it never seemed like that much."

Eli laughed. "Do you expect they'll all be alive when you return to Seattle?"

"No." Anna shook her head. "I knew that when I left. Opportunity cost, I suppose."

"We'd better make sure the opportunities are good, then. Let's go." Eli locked the car as they got out. They headed toward the entrance. Anna led him through a garden first and proclaimed it nearly barren compared to the springtime when she'd visited with her mother.

"If this is barren, I can't imagine what it must look like in spring. You should see Chicago this time of the year. Once the trees lose their leaves, it's nothing but brown." Eli walked a step behind Anna, enjoying the way she was stopping to examine—and name—many of the plants.

"All the more reason to move to the South." Anna threw a flirtatious smile at him over her shoulder before continuing down the path.

"Oh, no," Eli said, shaking his head, though he was enjoying their banter and already contemplating such a move. "Who's supposed to be influencing who on this trip?" If only she realized how she'd affected his life already.

"We'll see." Anna's shoulders lifted in a carefree shrug.

They considered renting bikes but decided to walk instead, both in favor of taking a break from sitting. With a map in hand, they hiked the Big Pine Nature Trail through a wooded hillside.

"I can't believe it's nearly November," Eli said. "I feel like I've gone back in time to summer camp."

"These pines smell amazing, don't they?" Anna inhaled deeply. "Mom will be jealous we stopped here."

"She'll be happy you took a day off from the store," Eli predicted.

"I'll bet she needs a break," Anna said. "It's got to be hard seeing Dad so sick and being away from home at her favorite time of year."

"Let's give her a break, then." Eli stepped to the side to avoid a root coming out of the ground and nearly bumped into Anna. His arm brushed against hers, and she jumped.

Still skittish. How to fix that?

"Sorry," she mumbled.

"Me too," Eli said.

"What?" She turned to him, mouth turned down in confusion.

"I'm sorry I startled you." He paused, considering his next words "And I'm sorry that you've been touched so little for so long that it frightens you."

"I wasn't—I'm not—"

"You are. Afraid." *Of being hurt again.* "Nearly four years without a date is a long time. I think I could help you with that."

"I'm fine, Eli. I don't need any charity dates."

"I know. Half of Holiday wants to take you out—if not marry you."

She grimaced. "Don't remind me."

"Besides," he continued. "You invited me for a charity dinner. I figure I owe you something."

"Nothing." She turned away from him and started walking again as another couple, coming from the opposite direction, approached.

Eli walked beside her in silence until the couple had passed. But he wasn't ready to let this go. He'd brought up her problem—or part of it, at least—and he couldn't leave it at that. Telling Anna without doing anything to help would only hurt her worse.

"Anna." Instead of touching her arm to get her attention, he jumped in front of her on the path.

"Yes?" Curt Anna who'd greeted him this morning was back. Darned if he didn't like her in that mood too. No doubt she could manage the market and get things done as needed. He wondered if she didn't run the lab where she worked as well, and all the guys there were too intimidated by her to ask her out, to see if maybe she'd changed her mind about not dating. He was determined to change it. Even if it meant that she didn't care for him. He owed it to her—or to Gabriel. There was a cycle of owing somewhere in the odd complexity of their situation. Anna had cared for his grandfather. He in turn had cared enough for Eli to write to him and entrust his estate to him. *Now I need to care for Anna, to help her get over her broken heart once and for all.*

The first step, as Eli saw it, was for her to be comfortable around men again.

"May I try something that might help?"

She rolled her eyes. "I don't need help, Eli. If I did, I'd see a therapist. Not a real estate lawyer."

"Point taken. And you don't need a therapist. You need to get used to being around guys again."

"I work with a lab full of men." She folded her arms across her chest in a classic defensive stance.

"Who rarely interact with you—am I wrong?" Eli leaned closer so she had to meet his gaze.

"So?"

"So you admittedly don't date and rarely talk to or interact with men."

"Since returning to Holiday, I have."

Eli thought of the men at church—the farmer, the mama's boy, and Donald, the seeker of dessert—and those she saw at the market. The town Santa, the old guy who helped at the soda fountain, and Carson. "Those guys don't count. Especially Carson. He really doesn't count."

"Your point?" Anna muttered. One foot began an angry tap on the hard-packed dirt.

"I'm fairly normal." A corner of his mouth lifted in half a smile.

"Jury's still out on that one. You tried to give away your entire inheritance already, remember? Who needs help worse here?"

He grinned at her gumption. "We'll worry about fixing me later. This is about you." He extended his arm toward her, palm held out. "May I hold your hand, Anna?"

Her eyes flew to his, confusion and fear clearly evident in their brilliant blue. But she wasn't crying, wasn't running away.

"Why?"

"So you can get used to the feeling of touch again. I think you've been without it for so long that it unnerves you."

She said nothing but swallowed and looked down at his outstretched hand.

"I won't hurt you," Eli said quietly. "This has nothing to do with the inheritance. I value your friendship, Anna. Let me show you by being a good friend in return."

Seconds passed. Eternity, it felt like. He'd never before asked permission to hold a woman's hand. Those few he had held, he'd always just taken casually, during a movie or while walking. None had ever refused him or even made it seem like it was a big deal. This, however, seemed gargantuan. *To both of us.*

At last Anna's arms unfolded. Her hand moved slowly toward his, as if it was in a battle of wills with her mind.

Contact. Her hand landed in his, and with utmost care Eli closed his fingers around hers.

They stood still a minute, not moving, simply savoring. Or he was, at least. Anna's hand felt so right in his. He wasn't sure his would ever feel right again when hers had gone. So he had no intention of letting it, or her, go anytime soon.

"Thank you," Eli whispered, though there was no one around to overhear their conversation. The surrounding, sheltering trees made this place seem almost sacred. A tiny miracle had occurred here, in this hallowed grove. The silence lasted perhaps thirty seconds, before singing came from behind them. Eli looked down the path at an approaching Cub Scout troop. He moved beside Anna, and they began walking again, hand in hand, down the trail.

The overlook of Lake Hall off of the Big Pine Nature Trail was the perfect place for a picnic and lovers. Too bad she had neither.

Anna stood beside Eli, staring down at the expanse of blue beyond the trees. The shores were relatively empty at midday on a Friday in late October, but she guessed that on weekends, particularly during summer, the crowds would be significant.

Today she was grateful for the solitude, and almost sorry she hadn't brought a picnic, or at least a blanket to spread out on the ground so they could stay awhile. Once they left, the magic would be broken. The spell that had come over both of them at this place would evaporate, as if it had never been here at all. And that would hurt, a little at least. More, the longer she prolonged it.

She wasn't imagining this. Eli felt it too. He hadn't been able to hide his expression when their hands joined. For her part, it felt as if a wave of tender emotion had crashed into her and made its way to her heart.

He wanted to help her, he'd said. It had been the same at church, when he'd put his arm around her and pretended to be her beau. What if she wasn't capable of accepting that help without feeling? What if he wasn't able to give it without entangled feelings as well? What then?

Was he trying to soften her, or was he growing soft *for* her? If only she knew. Not that it would have made a lot of difference to her emotions. They seemed to have exploded out of some box that had been on a shelf these past years and were attaching themselves quite rapidly and firmly to Elijah Steiner.

The rebound phenomenon. She'd watched roommates go through the same at college after a break up. Her breakup with Carson wasn't exactly yesterday, but she hadn't had another relationship since, so this had to be the rebound, right?

I don't want it to be.

They'd been at the park over an hour already, but Anna couldn't summon the suggestion that they should go. Standing here, shoulder-to-shoulder with Eli, her hand snug in his, in this peaceful place, felt too good. She'd not only missed Carson, but she'd missed having a boyfriend in general—being cared for and tended to. He'd always been good at that. She'd been the one who'd been neglectful at times.

I'll be better next time. Next time? Where had that come from? Since leaving the church and Holiday that fateful morning, she'd never once considered a next time—another person, falling in love again.

Until now.

Don't go there, her conscience warned. Eli would be back in Chicago in a few days, and come December she'd be who knows where.

Eli gave her fingers a gentle squeeze as he looked over at her, a smile lighting a face that was already too handsome for anyone's good.

"See, this isn't so bad, is it?"

It's amazing. Anna shook her head, not trusting herself enough to speak.

"Ready to share your letter now? Or have you changed your mind?"

In answer, she used her free hand to pull the envelope from her back pocket. "Would you mind reading it? I'm not sure I can—aloud, anyway."

"Sure." Eli led them farther off the path, to a large pine with grass at its base.

With reluctance she freed her fingers from his and they sat, each with their back partially against the trunk.

Eli took the letter and began to read. "'Dearest Annabelle—'" He paused and looked over the paper at her, his brows raised. "Dearest?"

She nudged his foot with hers. "Don't be creepy. Mr. Steiner was like a grandpa to me."

"*I* was never called 'dearest,'" Eli grumbled, only half teasing, Anna guessed. She was starting to get the feeling that his lack of family did bother him.

Eli continued, not stopping again until he came to the line about their inheritance having conditions. He snorted. "I'll say they're stringent. He expected us both to *move*."

"Shhh." Anna nudged him again, closer to a kick this time. "Don't judge. Just read."

"All right." Eli retaliated by leaning into her shoulder. "'As you know, many years ago our son left home and never returned . . .'"

Eli's voice grew quieter, more subdued. *Reverent*, Anna might have said, as it became apparent he, too, was touched by the story.

"That was the last time they spoke." Eli stopped reading and looked over at her. "Wow. That's awful. So much worse than I thought."

Anna nodded. "It's so sad. I can't imagine how they each must have felt."

"I can't either, though likely for opposite reasons. My dad never yelled at me, hardly bothered talking to me. If we never spoke again . . ." Eli shrugged. "I'm not sure either of us would be missing much."

"That's just as sad." Anna reached out and briefly covered his hand with hers. "I'm so sorry, Eli. I can't help but wonder that if this thing with your grandparents hadn't happened—if your life might not have been very different."

"If my father had had a better relationship with his dad—because his dad hadn't had this falling out with his parents—

then it might have trickled down to my father having a better relationship with me. He might have known *how* to be a father."

"Yes."

"We'll never know." Eli shifted the papers and continued reading, nodding his agreement when he got to the line about Mr. Steiner being a stubborn, silly old man.

"He was a delightful, charming old man," Anna corrected.

"So delightful he schemed to make you move back home."

"A little meddlesome too," Anna agreed, but there was no censure in her voice.

Eli continued, a slight catch to his as he read his great-grandfather's words about missing out on the blessings of being a grandparent. "Void is a good way to describe it. Or *de*void. My family life has always been devoid of any kind of love or affection. It would have been nice having grandparents who cared."

"'It is my final wish that you will stay in or at least close to Holiday and all that was once dear to you here. I hope that you will find a way to forgive and find a happy path forward, filled with a family of your own and the exciting opportunities you once yearned for.' He's referring to sharks, I assume," Eli teased.

"That and monstrous trout." Anna was glad she'd shared the letter with him. It was easier to read this time, and it helped having someone equally, if not more, connected to talk with about it.

Eli finished. "'Mend fences—all of them. Find another to love.'"

Anna felt a blush creep up her face.

"Well." Eli folded the letter and handed it back to her. "You've got plenty to accomplish. There are a whole lot of fences in and around Holiday, a good number of them in need of repair."

She laughed—actually laughed. Her gratitude for Eli's sense of humor grew. "I probably won't get them all fixed by December."

"You never know." Eli stood and held a hand out to her.

Anna accepted it, more easily this time, and he pulled her to her feet, so they stood nearly toe to toe. He didn't release her.

"Thank you for sharing that with me. I wouldn't have ever known otherwise."

"You should know. It's your family history."

"Pretty sad history." Eli looked out toward the lake, but she didn't think he was taking in the view, but avoiding her gaze.

He had wounds of his own, possibly deeper and more lasting than hers. He'd not said much about his family before, but since his return she could see it weighing on him. Had something happened to cause that change? Or was he simply being more open with her now?

A raindrop hit their joined hands. Anna raised her face to the darkening sky, and another brushed her nose.

"We should head back," Eli said.

"Probably." She hoped he'd keep holding her hand.

He turned away from the lake, pulling her with him, no sign that he was about to let go.

Chapter 33

"ANNA! WHAT ARE you doing here?" Mom jumped up, the knitting in her lap spilling to the floor.

"I came to see you and Dad. I thought you might appreciate a visit." Anna stepped from the breezeway through the open doorway into the tiniest living room/kitchen combination she'd ever seen. She stooped to collect the ball of yarn before it could escape the apartment, then straightened to give her mom a hug.

"I do—he will." Mom pulled back, studying Anna. "But who's managing the hoedown and cook-off this weekend?"

"Your extremely capable manager over internet orders."

"Carson?"

"The one and only." *Your almost-son-in-law. The only man I've ever loved. The only one I've ever kissed.* Eli's face appeared in her mind. What would it be like to kiss him? Anna banished the thought and gave herself a mental scolding. This rebound thing could get out of control quickly if she wasn't careful.

"You look good—changed," Mom said. Her eyes roamed over Anna's face. "Better."

"I'm getting there." Anna pulled a jar from her purse. "Bree helped with the applesauce. I thought you and Dad might like some."

"Oh, Anna. I'm so proud of you." Mom scooped her into another hug. "I knew you could do it."

"Truthfully, it about killed me. I may never be able to eat another apple as long as I live."

"I'm not talking about the sauce." Mom pulled back and

gave Anna a little shake before releasing her. "I knew you could forgive Bree and the two of you could be friends again."

"That was hard too," Anna admitted. Avoiding her mother's searching gaze, she glanced around the tiny apartment. A love seat, television, card-sized table, and two chairs took up most of the space. A kitchenette along the back wall completed the room. A partially closed door had to lead to the bedroom and bathroom. It made her apartment in Seattle seem spacious.

"But you are friends?" Mother set her knitting on the loveseat and moved toward the kitchenette.

"We are. Not where we once were, but on our way."

Mom opened the narrow fridge and took out a pitcher of water. "And Carson?"

Anna suppressed a groan. Twice in two minutes his name had been brought up. A state away, and she couldn't escape him. "We can't exactly be friends the way we used to. But I'm not yelling at him or anything." *Except that first day.* "We're cordial enough with each other. But that's it. He's got a wife and a life." *I need a life.* Again Eli's face appeared unbidden.

"Hello, Mrs. Lawrence. Nice to see you again."

Anna started at the feel of his hand on her shoulder. Tilting her head, she looked up at Eli and tried to ignore the warmth of his palm through her shirt or the havoc his simple touch caused her senses. "I thought you were going to find us a hotel." *That didn't sound good.*

"I was," he said. "But then I thought I should make sure we're actually staying the night." He came forward and looked to her mom. "If it's an okay time to visit."

"It's a wonderful time to visit." Mom crossed the small space quickly, the water glass in her hand—the one Anna was pretty sure had been intended for her—held out to Eli instead. "Welcome." Mom wrapped her free arm around him. "How nice of you to come with Anna."

Mom has her own rebound issues. "It was Eli's idea. He suggested it. He drove."

Her mother beamed as she looked back and forth between the two of them. Eli took a long drink of water, then peered at Anna over the rim of his glass, seeming almost bashful. Anna clasped her hands in front of her, secretly daring him to make a graceful exit back to the friend zone now, given that—to her mom—a road trip practically signified engagement.

Anna wasn't prepared for the way Dad looked. Mom had warned her, but it hadn't been enough. Nothing could have prepared her for seeing the man she'd always looked up to—figuratively and literally—lying still, his skin pale, expression wan, hair gone, body weak. How could this be the same man who'd tossed her in the air in the swimming pool, raced her around the high school track, and just a few, short weeks ago, imparted more of his sage wisdom? Today he could hardly speak.

"Hey, kiddo." He mustered a fleeting smile. But even that seemed too much to hold onto long.

"Hey, yourself." Anna leaned over and kissed his forehead before reaching for his hand. "I'm not sure I like this new look on you, Dad."

"Don't need a haircut as often now."

Anna's eyes drifted to his now-bald head. Without hair he looked so much older. Or perhaps it was the combination of the baldness, the bags beneath his eyes, and the sickly pallor of his skin. "I'm glad there's some benefit. I suppose you'll save on shampoo as well."

"Won't make up for the cost of all this." He made a feeble attempt to wave his free arm, indicating the room.

"This place isn't so bad," Anna said, noting that there

were two, twin-sized beds instead of one, larger one to be shared. No doubt it was better for Dad that way, as he was in pain or felt ill after his treatments. Still, it made her sad to think of even that much separation between her parents. Mom had long proclaimed snuggling one of the best benefits of marriage. "It's better than being stuck in the hospital the whole three months."

"Been there too much already," he mumbled.

"So I heard." Anna frowned. "Truthfully, I didn't believe it. So I came up here to see what was really going on—if you and Mom were off having a second honeymoon while I slaved away at the store."

Dad gave another almost smile. "Lousy second honeymoon."

"Yeah." Anna's other hand joined her first, holding onto his that felt so very fragile. "What happened to crushing that walnut-sized thing inside of you? I'm keeping my end of the bargain, but you don't seem to be faring as well."

"It's a damn hard nut. Shell's almost impossible to crack. They're trying to kill me to get at it."

"Hmmm. Mom thinks you're being a bit of a baby. You know, about all the throwing up and everything. After all, she was nauseated a good nine months with each of us kids. And she didn't let that stop her."

"Did too," Dad said. "Who do you think did the laundry, changed diapers, and washed dishes during her pregnancies?"

"Her knight in shining armor." As the youngest, Anna had only heard the stories of how sick her mother had been while carrying each of them. And the way Daddy had held the family together during those difficult times. They'd wanted four children, but after Anna's pregnancy nearly killed Mom, they'd decided to enjoy the three they had.

"Held her hair out of the way more times than I can count

while she bent over the toilet," Dad grumbled. "Least I was considerate enough to lose my hair."

Anna barked out a laugh. "Oh, Daddy. There is some spark still in there, I see. That's good." She gave him a hard look. "Don't you dare lose it."

He gave her hand a firm squeeze. "I won't. This being sick is just for your mother's benefit. Turnabout is fair play and all that."

"I think you're even now. You can get well anytime." Anna felt tears building behind her eyes. Why had she waited so long to come home? Her reasons for staying away seemed stupid and silly. She'd missed out on precious time with the two people she loved the most. *No more.* She'd find a job closer to home—within driving distance for Sunday dinners at least a couple of times a month. "I've started running again. When you're better we're going to go out on the river trail."

"It's a date." Dad closed his eyes and breathed in deeply. "Until then, you're doing fine on your own. Your spark's returning. You're making better progress than me."

Chapter 34

ELI STARED DOWN the long expanse of shoreline that was Jacksonville Beach at sunset. "This looks like the picture from every spring break ad I've ever seen." A few groups of people still dotted the sand, but most had packed up and gone home for the day. They passed a lifeguard climbing down from his chair.

"It's a nice beach," Anna said with far less enthusiasm than he'd imagined. "I'm sorry it's too late to swim." She glanced at him. "And that I'm not in much of a mood to."

"Not a problem." Eli's hand brushed hers as it swung at her side. Taking a chance, he caught her pinky in his and held on. She didn't say anything, but neither did she stiffen or act startled. After a few, heart-pounding seconds passed he captured the rest of her hand as well. "I'm sorry about your dad."

She'd been visibly upset after her visit. Eli hadn't gone in with her, but he guessed from Anna's stricken expression that her dad was worse off than she'd imagined.

"Me too. But he's going to be okay. It's just hard seeing him like this."

I can't imagine. Eli wondered what he'd feel—if anything—if something life-threatening happened to one of his parents. Would they even bother to tell him?

"I'm sorry about *your* dad," Anna said, fixing him with a knowing expression, as if she'd been privy to his thoughts.

"My dad is fine," Eli said, a little too quickly.

Anna stopped and turned to face the ocean. "I keep

thinking about losing my dad, how frightening that is and how much it would hurt. But it's like you never really had one to lose. I think that's got to be worse."

"I don't know." Eli shrugged. He followed her lead, walking closer to the water. "Maybe it's one of those 'you don't know what you missed if you didn't have it to begin with' things."

"But you do know—or you guess at it," Anna said. "You must have had friends whose parents were different. You've seen that mine are."

"Your parents are great. I like them a lot. That hug today from your mom . . ." *So freely given.* She probably hadn't thought a thing about it, but he had. It felt good to be held by someone, to think that someone cared about him. He'd been worried about fixing Anna's issues with lack of affection, but it seemed he had some issues of his own.

The remnant of a wave rolled over their feet, making them both jump a little and keeping Anna from saying any more about it. He was glad. Guys didn't need affection. Or they didn't talk about needing it, anyway.

But she had been listening. "When is the last time your mother hugged you?"

"No idea."

Anna faced him, eyes glittering with more unshed tears.

Man, this woman could cry.

"What is a memory you have of her hugging you?"

"I don't have one. She wasn't a hugger." A lot of people weren't. No big deal.

"No memory. Not one?" Anna's mouth hung partway open. "She *never* hugged you—or held you?"

Eli shook his head. "My family isn't anything like yours."

Anna couldn't seem to accept that answer. "Maybe she did when you were little. You probably just don't remember. She would have held you a lot when you were a baby and picked you up often as a toddler. Even grade-schoolers are often held on their parents' laps."

"I had a full-time nanny until I went to elementary school. Then I had a sitter until around six every night. And no, my parents didn't do the tuck-in-bed, read-a-story, kiss-goodnight thing." The only reason he had any clue about that ritual was the evening he'd spent with Carson and Bree.

Anna didn't say anything to this but stepped in front of him, so they were facing one another. "May I try something that might help you?"

"Excuse me?" He wasn't the one with the problem. It was his parents who had missed out—on pretty much everything.

"May I try something that might help you?" Anna repeated. Her hand wiggled free of his and clasped the other in front of her, sandals dangling from her fingertips as she looked at him expectantly.

"I don't need help, Anna." This conversation was starting to feel familiar. "If I did, I'd see a therapist. Not a marine biologist."

She smiled. "Well, we are at the beach. And you don't need a therapist. You need to get used to physical affection."

"I'm not the one who's gone four years without a date. I work in an office full of attractive women. If I want affection, I can—"

"I'm not talking about that kind." Anna scowled. "You need to learn what it's like to be hugged frequently by a mom, or at least to have a friend's arms around you. You need to know you have worth and you're cared for and . . . cherished."

"Cherished," he repeated, liking the sound of the old-fashioned word. "I've definitely never felt that."

"Every child should feel cherished."

Carson and Bree's daughter came to mind. She certainly fit that description. "What are you proposing?" Eli asked. "I'm not a child, and your mom isn't readily available to hand out hugs."

"I could hug you," Anna said. "Not as a mom, of course, but as a friend."

Cool. Though he doubted he'd be having feelings of friendship being that close to Anna. "What prompted this?" he asked, trying to figure out the connection between her visit with her father and their present discussion. Maybe Anna wanted a hug, and this was her way of trying to let him know.

"Your reaction around my mom today. When she let you go, you had this odd expression on your face—almost shy, obviously surprised, and very pleased. And then . . . yearning."

"You read all that in my expression?" And he'd thought he'd hidden well behind his water glass.

"I did." Anna folded her arms in front of her, as if challenging him to deny it.

He wasn't going to, wasn't about to fight this. "Maybe you went into the wrong profession. It's not too late to go back to school to be a psychologist." *Or a psychic.*

"I get it from my dad." Anna's eyes teared up again. "And a little from Mom too. They were always so in tune with me. I think that's what happens when you . . . care about someone."

Eli's heart beat a little faster than normal, and a feeling of warmth unfurled inside of him. *She cares.*

"So . . ." Anna raised up on her toes a few times. "May I hug you—as a friend—"

"—who cares," Eli finished.

"Yes." She gave an emphatic nod. "I believe it will be good for you. Part of your therapy and the beginning of a life in which you are both comfortable being embraced and embracing others."

Eli didn't see that he was going to have any problem with either of those, at least as far as Anna was concerned. He opened his arms wide.

She dropped her sandals, took a hesitant step forward, then wrapped her arms around him. He reciprocated, going a step farther, bending his head and leaning close so they were nearly cheek to cheek. He closed his eyes, savoring everything about this moment, from the smell of her hair to the feeling of her body pressed close to his, to the sounds of the ocean—gulls overhead and waves rolling onto shore.

Seconds passed. He felt Anna relax and feared she'd step away, but instead she laid her head against his shoulder. He held her a little tighter. She was right. This was some kind of amazing therapy. The stresses and worries of the last week began slipping away, unimportant details of his life. What really mattered was right here, right now. *Anna. In my arms.*

As it had been when he'd held her hand, he didn't want to let her go. She appeared to be in no hurry to move either, and Eli hoped she was experiencing the same benefits, with her worries fading into the background as well.

The breeze picked up, and they swayed slightly with it. Anna's face nuzzled his shirt front, and new thoughts cropped up that had nothing to do with being comforted.

So close. All he had to do was to reach down and touch her chin, lift it slightly for her mouth to meet his. It was all he could think of, suddenly. He hadn't intended to move so fast, but she was the one who'd instigated the hug. And if he'd needed a hug, she needed to be kissed. He could be the first one to kiss her in so many years. *The only one,* his possessive nature declared.

Eli tilted his head slightly down, making what he hoped was a subtle first move. Before he could touch her chin, Anna tipped her face up to his. Their eyes locked. Hers were no longer sad, but hazy with another emotion. *Desire*—if he was as good at reading her feelings as she was at reading his.

Anticipation surged through him. He released her waist and inched a hand upward, wanting to touch her cheek when they kissed. Anna's lips parted slightly, her breathing as shallow as his felt.

It was as perfect a moment as they come, on a beach at sunset. But still, he felt honor bound to ask. "Anna, may I—"

She pitched forward onto him as a breaker crashed into her from behind, knocking her off balance and Eli backward onto the sand, where they fell in a sopping wet, sandy heap.

Anna scrambled off of him, alternately muttering apologies and curses. She brushed sand from her wet pants and hurried to retrieve her sandals before they could wash out with the tide.

Eli checked the pocket of his cargos and found his flip flops and phone still there. He took his time getting up, not at all minding the view as Anna hopped about.

"Not afraid of a little sand and water, are you?" He was disappointed they hadn't kissed, but maybe it was for the better. His clearer head was alerting him to danger if he continued on his present course. Anna wasn't just some woman he might casually date. And Lacee was right. He did have problems with commitment. In the past, at least. But he couldn't now. Not with Anna. He'd told Carson he wouldn't hurt her, and he meant that. Holding hands was one thing, but if he kissed her that crossed a definite line from friendship to—

"I'm not afraid at all." She scooped up a handful of wet sand and flung it at him.

"Hey!" Eli jumped up, brushing the wet clump from the front of his shorts. "I look like I wet my pants."

"Me too." She turned around, showing off her soaked backside. "Now we match."

"I don't think so." Eli shook his head slowly, holding back a grin until the exact second another breaker caught her unaware.

Anna shrieked and ran farther up on the shore.

"For a beach girl you're kind of a wimp," he teased.

"I'm not a beach girl. I'm an ocean girl. When I'm in a wetsuit it's different."

Eli's grin widened. "I'm sure." Anna in a wetsuit was enough to keep his imagination busy all night.

Chapter 35

ELI HELD THE chair out for Anna as she took a seat at Jax Beach Brunch Haus. "You sure you don't want to grab something to go and take it back to your parents' place?"

"We have the rest of the day with them," Anna said. "And it was really nice of you to stay with my dad while Mom and I went out last night. We had a good visit."

"I got a couple of hugs out of it, so I came out all right too." Eli took the chair across from Anna and nearest the window. They'd just come from a brisk walk/jog along the beach, and he felt more than ready to consume whatever calories they'd burned. When Anna had suggested walking along the beach this morning, he hadn't realized it would be more than a casual stroll.

"I'm sorry my dad was asleep by the time we got there last night. Maybe today the two of you can visit while Mom and I go pick up some groceries."

"That would be nice." A tad uncomfortable as well, perhaps, but Eli was looking forward to spending some time with Anna's dad. He'd been the least talkative of the bunch at the family dinner Eli had attended, but Anna seemed so close to her father. Eli was more than curious as to what that looked like and how that worked from both sides.

"What are you getting?" he asked, eying an omelet being delivered to a nearby table.

"Crepes," Anna declared. "Stuffed with berries and whipped cream."

"Mmm. Sounds good." Except that he needed some protein this morning. Some slices of bacon, a few eggs . . .

Anna's phone rang, interrupting his rumbling stomach. She pulled it from her jacket pocket and looked at the screen. "It's Bree."

Her easy smile would have surprised Eli, had Anna not shared the details of the renewed friendship with him yesterday.

She swiped her finger across the screen and answered. "Hi, Bree. What's up?"

Anna's tone changed quickly, her expression falling with it as Eli listened to a chorus of "No's" and "That's terrible's." Then finally, "We'll head home as soon as we can. Tell everyone we'll reschedule. I'm not sure when or where, but we'll think of something."

"What's wrong?" Eli asked as soon as she'd ended the call.

"The storm blew out a wall of windows and took a chunk of roof off the community center. A bit of a mini tornado, I guess. Bree said not much else in town was damaged—only a few trees down and the usual debris. Fortunately it happened last night and not tonight, when everyone would have been inside the community center. No one was hurt."

"But they can't have the harvest-and-chili thing there?"

Anna pursed her lips and nodded. "Bree said it's still raining pretty hard."

"That's unfortunate." Eli's eyes drifted to the menu once more, relieved that it wasn't such a tragedy after all. He'd never been inside Holiday's community center, but from the outside at least, it had looked like it had seen better days. Maybe it was a good thing it had been damaged and would need some repairs or even rebuilding. "Why reschedule? Can't the town skip the event until next year?"

"They could," Anna said. "But that means no Halloween for the children. Holiday is too rural and too small for traditional trick-or-treating, so the kids always get to play games and have treats at the hoedown. It's a pretty big deal for everyone—young and old. When you live in a small town, things like this are important."

"Okay, so we'll figure out a plan to reschedule in a couple of weeks. Why the rush to get back?" Personally, he was enjoying Florida—neutral ground for both of them, where they were free from restrictions or others' expectations. He wasn't worried about Twenty Questions from Rosie at breakfast this morning and hadn't worried people would start gossiping about their hug on the beach. "What can *you* do?"

"I don't know." Anna began drumming her fingers on the menu. "It's not only rescheduling this that we have to figure out, but what to do with all the food and everything prepared for tonight. Then there's the problem of where to hold the Christmas pageant. That's an even bigger deal."

"Maybe, but it isn't *your* problem."

She looked up, eyes narrowed. "What do you mean?"

Uh oh. Hostile-Anna alert. They'd been having such a pleasant morning, and their time together yesterday was still fresh in his mind. He'd been eager to see where today took them. "Exactly what I said. It's not your responsibility to find another place to have the hoedown or the pageant."

"Not all alone, it isn't," Anna said. "And maybe not directly, but if the able community members don't care enough to do something—and then actually do it—how do you think anything will happen? It will be cancelled. Children will be disappointed. The elderly will be lonely. Teenagers will have more time on their hands than they already do. Holiday may be tiny, but its citizens are strong. Our community is. Because we make it that way—all of us."

Eli wasn't entirely convinced about the "all of us" part—no doubt there were some slackers there. He'd met a few already during his short stay. But Anna did make a good point, and seeing her so impassioned about and invested in her home town could only bode well for the possibility of her staying past December.

"You're right." Eli closed his menu, pushed back his chair, and rose. "Let's order to go, stop by to see your parents a bit longer, then hit the road. We have a six hour drive to figure out a solution."

Eli's finger hovered over the screen of playlists. "What kind of music do you like?"

"Everything." Anna's voice was a bit unsteady as she waved a last goodbye to her mom through the passenger window. "Since I've been back home my bluegrass roots have taken over again. But I love pop and modern and country."

"And classics?" Eli asked.

"Classi*cal*, yes. Your grandfather made sure of that. But pop or rock classics . . . I like some, not others. I'll tolerate Elvis, but he's not my favorite." Just saying the name called up strains of "Hound Dog" running through her head. "My sister had every song he ever released and played them over and over and over."

"No Elvis here," Eli promised. "Just some good stuff from the 70's," he said as John Denver's "Country Roads" started.

"Really?" Anna stared at him, searching for a hint that he was teasing about her country roots. "A Chicago boy knows this?"

Eli shrugged. "My tastes are kind of eclectic too. John was a staple at camp. One of the counselors had a guitar, and we had sing-alongs. That sort of music seemed appropriate for today's drive."

"It is." Anna settled against the comfortable seat again and closed her eyes, trying to imagine a younger Eli at summer camp. The image warmed her heart and hurt at the same time. She'd gone camping a lot too—with her family.

How was it that for someone who hadn't had much of a family, he'd recognized her need to be with hers this weekend? She looked over at him. "Thank you, again, for taking me to see my parents."

"It was fun," he said.

"It was." Visiting her parents had been good, but it had also been stressful. Seeing Dad so ill was hard, though he'd rallied enough today to sit with them and visit. She was glad she'd gone but felt ready to be home.

Holiday? Was she truly thinking of it in those terms already? For most of her life it had been home and—thankfully—once again was a place she felt she could return to and find more than angst waiting. Four weeks into her stay, and she'd figured that out, at least. Could Seattle possibly be home as well? Maybe, but she would have to change her outlook. She'd have to embrace living there—the people, from her co-workers to her neighbors. She'd need to attend church, to find a community. To start thinking about someone besides herself.

Maybe the best thing was to start over elsewhere, somewhere that wasn't Holiday but also wasn't so far away.

"Country Roads" ended, and "Matthew" began. Eli hummed along. He didn't have a bad voice.

"I always envied the boy in this song." He sounded wistful. "Riding on his father's shoulders, working alongside him . . ."

Anna nearly reached out to touch him before she checked the impulse. Yesterday's hand-holding, hugging, and what she suspected was a near kiss seemed almost a figment of her imagination. Eli hadn't initiated anything between them today, keeping a respectful distance out in public, and making sure to seat himself in one of the kitchen chairs—instead of beside her on the loveseat—while at her parents' apartment.

"There must be some good things about your life growing up. Your family didn't lose their house or livelihood. You had enough to eat and a lot of opportunities. For as charming as life in the country is often made out to be, there are a lot of hardships with it." *Way to talk him into staying.*

"So I've seen," he said. "Driving around Holiday is evidence enough."

"Convince me of the merits of your big city, then." Anna angled her body toward the driver's side. "Tell me the great things about growing up in Chicago."

"Well..." Eli rubbed his chin. "On St. Patrick's Day they color the river green."

"I've heard about that," Anna said. "How long does it stay that way?"

"I'm not really certain," Eli admitted. "Maybe a couple of days. But it is pretty cool when they do it."

"What else?" Anna prompted.

"As a kid I got to go on a lot of field trips to the museums they have there. And Lake Michigan is pretty awesome. I spent a lot of time at the beach too."

"See, you did have family activities."

"Actually I went with my summer day camp group." Eli sighed. "Don't think my parents are awful. They're not. They simply weren't meant to be parents. I was never part of their plan. Now that I'm grown up, I see that."

Anna said nothing to this. Parents who didn't parent was as foreign a concept as they came. Hers had been all in. *How blessed I've been.* She couldn't wait to have them home again and didn't understand how she'd been able to stay away for so long.

No more, she vowed. Even if Holiday wasn't ever her home again, it could at least be a place she visited often.

"Ready to brainstorm solutions for the community center?" Eli asked, likely wishing to change subjects.

Though he'd opened up to her more this weekend than he had previously, Anna could still sense his discomfort with the topic of family.

"Sure. The need's not quite so immediate now. From Bree's latest text, it sounds like there's already an alternative for the hoedown. They're going to go ahead and hold it tonight, at Clarence Ward's barn. A bunch of people are over there right now, cleaning up the place."

"Two birds with one stone," Eli said. "I've driven by there, and—"

"—He's a single dad," Anna reminded him. "Keeping the old barn clean probably isn't high on the priority list."

"True," Eli said. "Still, I don't envy anyone that clean up. Since it looks like we're not needed after all do you want me to turn around and we can extend our visit until tomorrow?"

"No thanks," Anna said. "I should get back, and I've been worried about something else, actually. It's almost November, and to my knowledge no one has been doing anything about Sub for Santa. With your grandfather gone, I'm not sure who's going to head it up."

"Why do I get the feeling that's a loaded, leading question?" Eli's gaze shifted toward her suspiciously.

"Well . . . You are his heir and the manager of his estate. It only makes sense that you would take over that responsibility. Not all of it, of course," she added hastily, at Eli's horrified expression. "I found the paperwork in a file at the Mulberry, and I'd planned to bring it tonight—that's usually when we start to get families signing up. I can take care of everything on that end."

"Sounds like the easy part," he grumbled. "I know none of the people who will be receiving these gifts. I don't even live close enough to—"

"That's just it." Anna leaned toward him excitedly. "You

live in the land of stores. In Holiday I'll be limited to what Amazon can deliver."

"Which is just about everything these days," Eli pointed out.

"Yes, but it's not the same as actually shopping for an item—finding the perfect bike for a child or the exact doll a little girl wants." True, she'd found some cute dresses for Julia online, and Mr. Steiner had shifted most of the shopping to that venue the past several years, since his wife's passing, but Eli didn't need to know that.

"So you're suggesting that I take over for my grandfather, buy all this stuff, and ship it down to you?"

Anna shook her head. "No. I'll help you with the shopping. I could come up for a weekend, and we could go together. It would be fun. Then I can take it with me when I return."

"You're willing to spend twenty-eight hours in a car, a couple of days shopping, and who knows how many more wrapping because . . ."

"It's Christmas." She didn't have to ask what his Christmases had been like. She could guess well enough. Had his parents found some place to ship him off to every December, or had they simply ignored him the whole holiday break? "I think I need this, Eli. I need to get lost in something bigger than myself. And who knows? It might be good for you too."

"The estate is bigger than yourself—a lot bigger. You could lose yourself in that." He flashed her a hopeful smile.

Anna rolled her eyes. "I delivered flowers, dusted, and mowed the lawns last week. I promise I'll do my part."

"*You* didn't actually do the mowing, did you?"

"Of course. There's a ride-on mower. It's not that hard. Just takes a few hours."

Eli shook his head. "He left us money for that. There's

more than adequate funds for gardening, cleaning, and repairs."

"Great." Anna clapped her hands together. "What we save doing the work ourselves, we can put toward the Sub for Santa program."

"You're not going to give this up, are you?" Eli reached a hand up to rub the back of his neck, but Anna could tell he was wavering. She'd seen it in his expression when she'd mentioned coming up to Chicago.

"All right," he finally conceded, taking hands off the wheel for a second to hold them in the air. "I'll do it."

"Great!" Anna exclaimed, feeling the first stirrings of excitement for Christmas that she'd felt in a long time. "Just for that, I'll save you a dance tonight."

Chapter 36

YET ANOTHER SURREAL *experience*. Eli sipped from a bottle of sarsaparilla as he surveyed the activity in the barn. Fresh straw on the floor and the table full of chili and baked goods helped to mask any former, unpleasant aromas, and it was difficult to imagine this was the same place he'd driven by previously. Where had they hauled all the piles of junk off to?

The outside was still in need of paint, and the yard was mostly dirt, but he had to admit that the inside of the barn—with lights strung from the rafters and a stand for the musicians set up at the far end—had transformed nicely.

Of course it helped that front and center, in the middle of the dance floor, was the prettiest woman he'd ever had the fortune to lay eyes on. Considering some of the beautiful women he'd met through his profession, that was saying a lot. But Anna's beauty was different, more natural. She came by it without trying, and he doubted she realized it herself.

"Allemande left," Ernie Jensen hollered from the front of the room. Apparently Santa had a side gig as a square dance caller.

Anna whirled by Eli, blonde curls flying, blue gingham skirt whipping around her. The pumpkin delivery guy was her partner, and he looked to be having as fine a time as she was.

Eli wondered if it was appropriate to cut in on a square dance. Though if he did, he'd be expected to do-si-do and all the rest. Better to wait for a more appropriate song and claim his dance then. With that in mind, he wove his way through the crowd—had all seven-hundred-plus of Holiday's residents come out tonight?

"You're still here. You didn't head back to Chicago yet?"

Eli pulled his gaze from the dance floor to Carson, standing in front him, a similar bottle in his hand.

"Chicago seemed a bit—dull after all the excitement down here." Eli smiled at Anna as she whirled by again.

Carson followed his gaze. "I can imagine."

"Of course if the Cubs season hadn't been over, that might have been different."

"Keep trying to convince yourself," Carson encouraged. "But even baseball pales in comparison to Anna."

Eli whipped around to face him. "You still love her." Accusation rang in his words, and a sick feeling began in his gut.

"Of course I do. I always will." Carson's voice was nonchalant, as if it wasn't a big deal. "Anna and I learned to walk together. We learned to ride bikes together. Got our braces on the same day—I'm pretty sure that one was orchestrated by our mothers to postpone our first kiss. They were best friends, and we were too. I spent as much time with Anna growing up as I did with my brother. She's like a sister, and I love her as much as I love him."

Might have mentioned that last part first. Eli gave a tight-lipped nod. Some of the tension in the pit of his stomach released. "Who's she dancing with now?" Pumpkin delivery guy seemed awfully friendly with her.

"Charlie," Carson said, in that same matter-of-fact tone. "My brother. He's had a crush on her forever, though it's never been reciprocated."

"Ah." A little more of Eli's unease subsided.

"I'd probably encourage him if I thought it would do any good, but Anna needs someone stronger—more adventurous. She's always liked life on the edge. She's never been afraid to try new things or tackle just about anything."

"I'm starting to see that now." Eli met Carson's gaze. "But

that isn't how I'd describe the woman I met when I first arrived in Holiday. You and Bree certainly did a number on her."

"We did." Carson didn't look away. "And we'd like nothing more than to make it right with Anna—to see her as happy as she deserves to be."

"As happy as we are," Bree said, joining the conversation as she came up beside her husband. "We're glad you came back, Eli."

"Don't pin your hopes on me," he said, waiting for the familiar panic to set in—the one that always occurred when a woman, or someone close to her, started to hint that things might be about to get more serious. But instead of panic, he felt hope and a sense of elation he'd never experienced before. "I haven't quit my job yet."

"Yet," Bree said. "Meaning it's on your agenda? That's your intention?"

"Yeah. I think so." He thought so more and more each day. "But what about Anna's job? She hasn't said anything about leaving Seattle."

"*Yet.*" Carson raised his bottle in a toast. "Here's to your giving her a reason to."

Before Eli could respond he was waylaid by a fairy, pink wings and all.

"You came back!"

Eli peered down at the waif wrapping herself around his legs. "Hello to you too, Miss Anna."

She giggled. "I'm not a miss. And tonight I'm not Anna. I'm a fairy. See my wings." She turned so he could get a better look at what appeared to be a pair of glitter-encrusted tights stretched over coat hangers. Apparently Carson and Bree had no money for furniture *or* Halloween costumes. *Kudos to them for ingenuity.*

"Pretty fancy." Eli crouched down to her height. "Just don't go flying off with some boy tonight."

Anna leaned forward, cupped her hands over her mouth, and whispered in his ear. "I can't *really* fly."

"Ah." He caught her eye and gave a solemn nod. "Your secret is safe with me." He clasped a hand over his heart as evidence of his vow.

She smiled, took Bree's hand, then turned to go as Eli stood.

"I hope you come over to tuck me in again," Anna called over her shoulder. "You make the best horsey noises."

Eli nearly choked on his sarsaparilla. "Not likely, kid," he said too quiet for her to hear.

"What was that all about?"

He turned and found Anna—grown-up Anna—beside him. Her gaze left his and followed fairy Anna as she moved along the refreshment table with her parents and piled a napkin high with one of each of the several cookies on the trays.

"Horsey noises? Tuck-ins?" Anna asked.

"You're not dancing anymore?" Eli stared at the dance floor. How had he missed the end of the reel or whatever it was they'd been doing? "I—uh—went to Carson and Bree's house for dinner the last time I was in town. They invited me over."

"Oh." Anna pursed her lips and crossed her arms. "And while you were there did you throw something at Carson—as you'd suggested when *we* had dinner together?"

"No." Eli looked down at the empty bottle, wishing it was a beer. He suddenly had a feeling he might be in for a long night. "They shared some things about Gabriel. And then I tucked their kid in bed—because she asked me to—and I went home."

Anna nodded again but didn't say anything.

"Don't be upset." Eli stretched a hand out to touch her arm, but she shrugged out of his reach.

"It doesn't mean anything. There aren't sides here," he said. "And in spite of what they did, they aren't the enemy."

"I know." Anna sighed. "I've forgiven them—or Bree, at least. Carson is a little harder. A little more complicated."

Eli lowered his voice and stepped closer to her. "Do you still have feelings for him?"

"No!" Her widened eyes and horrified expression convinced Eli she spoke the truth.

"I don't want to be with him like that, but I do wish I could find a way to be his friend—that's appropriate. For as rotten as what Carson did was, I still miss his friendship. I wish I could go back to the days when he and Bree and I were all just friends. Nothing more."

Eli released the breath he'd been holding and reached for Anna again, keeping her hand in his this time when she would have pulled away. "That statement's a far cry from the woman who had an outburst at the Mulberry a month ago. I'd say that's quite a bit of progress."

"I suppose." Anna stared past him.

Following her namesake?

"It's still hard. And for some reason, one of the hardest things is their little girl. I know she's not theirs—biologically, I mean—but she belongs to Carson and Bree, and they belong to each other. And—"

I belong to no one. Eli read the thought as clearly as if Anna had spoken it out loud. The swell of protectiveness he'd felt toward her before surfaced again. But this time he didn't have any desire to punch Carson on her behalf. That wouldn't really help Anna at all. Instead Eli wanted to continue what they'd started yesterday. He wanted to heal her.

"Come on. Let's dance." Keeping her hand in his, he tugged her toward the packed floor, where some sort of couples swing was underway. They passed a crestfallen Clarence, who looked as if he might have been making his way toward them.

Sorry, buddy. She's taken. Eli led Anna all the way to the center of the room, lest someone try to snag her from him during the dance. He'd no sooner stopped and faced her than the song ended and everyone around them began clapping.

"Folks," Carson called from the stand. "We're going to let the band take a fifteen-minute break, so they can have some dessert before it's all gone. In the meantime, we'll keep the music going but slow things down a bit." He gave a nod to Eli as strains of Coldplay's "Something Like This" began.

Thanks. Eli pulled Anna close and wrapped one arm around her waist. "This is a good song to practice that hug thing you taught me."

She looped her arms around his neck and tilted her head, looking him in the eye, a slight smile curving her lips. "So it is."

Eli returned her smile, then bent his head slightly, so their faces were as close as they had been yesterday. As before, he felt Anna gradually relax. His other arm slid around her waist as he held her close. They swayed slowly, turning a tight circle in the center of the packed floor. He closed his eyes, oblivious to anything but Anna, the lyrics of the song, and the emotions crashing over him.

How much *did* he want to risk? A lot—but everything? His job, his career, life as he knew it? He didn't just want someone to kiss. He wanted Anna. A kiss wouldn't be nearly enough. He wanted . . . what Carson and Bree had. What Anna's parents had. A wife, children. A family. It *was* everything—everything he'd never had and would never have if he continued with his present life.

Eli hugged Anna tighter and pressed his cheek to hers. He wanted this woman in his arms. And if he had to move to the-middle-of-nowhere-Alabama and live in a drafty old house with ghosts and old plumbing to have her, then so be it.

The old man was sly, all right. A genius too.

Thank you, Grandpa.

Chapter 37

November

ELI PARKED ON the street in front of the church. "Stay there," he said as he opened the door and got out.

Anna unbuckled her seatbelt and watched as Eli ran around the front to her side and opened her door. "For a northern city boy, you're quite the gentleman." She accepted his hand and allowed him to help her out, only too aware of the other parishioners watching. Of all the places he might have parked, this was the most conspicuous, and it didn't bother her one bit.

As if anyone would question whether they were dating after last night. One dance together had led to another and another. When they weren't dancing Eli had held her hand or stayed by her side as they participated in the games. He'd even made a good attempt at the pie-eating contest, coming in third and looking adorable with his face covered with chocolate and whipped cream.

"Now I know what you'll look like as an old man," she had teased. "A scruffy beard interspersed with white."

"What's that smirk for?" Eli kept her hand as they made their way up the walk to church.

"Just remembering how ridiculous you looked with pudding all over your face last night."

"Hmph. You might have helped me clean up instead of pushing me away. Carson got his whipped cream kissed off by—" Eli shut his mouth abruptly, then turned to Anna, apology and regret in his expression. "I can't believe I said that. I'm sorry."

"It's okay. Really." Anna gave his hand a little squeeze to show she meant it. She *had* felt a little hiccup of pain at the mention of Carson and recalling his and Bree's public display of affection, though it had been rather exaggerated and joking. But, as with last night, Anna's pain was fleeting. What would have likely had her fighting off tears a month ago only pricked at her heart now. She was getting better, and it was largely because of Eli.

He's not a rebound, Anna reminded herself yet again. She and Eli were friends—good ones. They were also teetering on the edge of more, holding hands and dancing close as they had last night. She'd been in middle school the last time she'd wished a *friend* would kiss her. That had led to a relationship that had lasted years and one she had hoped would continue forever. *Why can't this be the same?*

He'd come back to Holiday, hadn't he? That had to mean something. But Eli also had a flight to catch later today. He was leaving his car here but had to be back at work tomorrow morning. She didn't want to think about that right now. This morning was theirs, and she intended to enjoy every minute.

"Good morning, Annabelle, Elijah." Reverend Armstrong greeted them at the door. "So good to see you both."

They dropped hands to shake his. Eli then placed his hand at the small of her back, sending a little thrill up her spine as he guided her toward her family's regular pew—blessedly empty today.

Anna scooted to the middle, and Eli followed, leaving little space between them. His arm extended over the back of the bench behind her, and he leaned close.

"Has anyone ever shortened your name from Annabelle to Belle?"

Anna turned to him. "No."

"They should." His eyes sought hers. "Maybe I will. Maybe from now on I'll refer to you as my southern Belle."

My. "What should you be, then? My Chicago gangster? The last half of your name sounds sort of ruffianish—Jah."

Eli's brows lifted. "If it's bad boys you like . . ."

Anna refrained from answering. Right now, at least. The benches around them filled in as Betty began pounding out some ghastly piece on the organ. Reverend Armstrong visibly winced as he strode up the aisle toward the pulpit. He was nearly there when Anna sensed someone standing in the aisle beside their bench. She braced herself as she turned to look, fearing it was Gladys gearing up for another attempt at bullying her into a date with her son.

Instead, Bree stood there, a hesitant smile on her face. "May we join you?" Her daughter stood behind her, sandwiched between Bree and Carson.

Another little jolt struck Anna's heart, but she willed it away, imagining herself plucking out an arrow before it could burrow deeper. "Of course." She wasn't certain if her smile looked forced or not, but her voice, at least, sounded genuine.

Eli gave her shoulder a squeeze and leaned close again. "That's my Belle."

Tears of gratitude sprang to Anna's eyes as she uttered a silent prayer of gratitude to God—and Mr. Steiner—for sending her someone to help her through this.

Betty struck a final, window-rattling note, and Reverend Armstrong's calm voice took over, inviting them to pray and then launching into his sermon. Usually they sang a hymn first, but perhaps today he'd had all of the organ he could take.

This morning he spoke of the storm that had destroyed the community center, comparing it to the storms of life. He drew a brilliant comparison, and Anna sat riveted, her mind and heart absorbing every word as Reverend Armstrong talked about starting over, moving on, and leaving the past behind.

"We all have memories of marvelous times and events in the community center—Christmas pageants, Miss Holiday competitions, scout activities, the summer of senior swing dances—" His eyes caught Anna's, and they exchanged a smile.

"We will ever be grateful to the Steiner family for providing us such a magnificent building so many years ago. And just as we will not let the memory of the storm that took our community center from us taint our other, happier memories there, we must not let the difficulties and negative, even painful, experiences of our lives ruin the good. We will all have times when we must rebuild, reboot, or move on. Change is our constant. Our challenge is to take what is good from the past, leave the rest behind, and move forward to something better. In the coming weeks as the community center is dismantled, and then eventually rebuilt, may you remember this metaphor in your own lives.

"The Savior was all about rebuilding, being reborn, and changing our inner selves to be better, to live the higher law of loving one another."

A higher law. A different kind of love. *Of course.* An infusion of relief swept through Anna, followed by a peacefulness that settled over her, as if a heavy, smothering blanket had lifted and been replaced with one that was lighter, fresh, clean.

I can still love Bree—and even Carson. She could love them as God loved—not for personal reasons, or to benefit herself, but because it was the right thing to do, and because they were good people and deserved such love.

And if they weren't good? her mind demanded, still trying to rally to its previous, defensive position, where it had been easier to hide behind the walls of hurt and humiliation.

Then I would love them, anyway. Or she would try her best to. Holding onto her feelings about what they'd done was only hurting herself. Letting that one incident—enormous though it had been—ruin years of friendship was only hurting her as well. For the past month both Bree and Carson had shown her that they were willing and wanted to move past that, to welcome her as a friend once more. They'd simply been waiting for her to accept.

After services ended, Anna lingered in her seat, almost afraid to move and shatter this newfound peace. After so long in what had been such a dark space, she wanted to bask in the light as long as possible.

"Be right back," Eli said, rising and sliding past Bree, Carson, and their daughter as they packed up the books and crayons they'd used to keep her busy during the sermon.

"Thanks for sharing your bench," Bree said after he had passed.

"It's not mine," Anna replied. "Not my parents' either. We've just sat here as long as I can remember." She watched Eli as he approached and began speaking with Reverend Armstrong.

"It's tradition," Bree said. "There's a lot of that in Holiday." Her little girl ducked through the space between Bree's bent arm and her lap, peeking at Anna.

"Are you still mad because I have your name?"

"No," Anna said, shocked to hear that the child thought that of her. *Why shouldn't she? After my performance that day.* "Not at all." She scooted closer, but little Anna pulled back, hiding behind Bree once more.

"I was never angry—with you," Anna added honestly. She had been furious with Carson. "I was surprised, and now I'm very flattered that your parents named you Anna. I think it suits you well."

"You have no idea." Bree slid a knowing gaze toward her

daughter. "Precocious, adventurous, no fear of anything . . . She's *just* like you were."

"That's marvelous." Anna leaned forward, peering around Bree to see her daughter. "I'll bet you have wonderful adventures. I used to."

"Mommy has told me some," little Anna ventured.

"Maybe someday I can tell you about her when she was a little girl," Anna said. "She was my best friend, you know."

Little Anna nodded. "Until she made you sad and you went away for a long time."

Anna's breath hitched. Her eyes flickered from Anna's to Bree's, which still held a mountain of regret. Suddenly Anna wished nothing more than to free her from it.

"I'm not sad anymore." She willed that to be true. "I came home," she said, speaking to little Anna. "And your mother is most definitely my best friend again. Your father is too."

Carson, who'd been busy putting crayons back into a box, looked up at this, eyes widening with surprise. They met Anna's briefly, and she felt another flicker of pain, followed quickly by hope and, once again, relief. She'd never stopped loving him, but she didn't *feel* love for him anymore. Anna released a breath and offered him a genuine smile.

"What about me? I thought I was your best friend." Eli stood in the aisle, hand braced on the back of the bench, brows raised as he looked down at her, his gaze far warmer than that of a simple friend.

"You are." Anna stood. "There are friends, and then there are *friends*."

Chapter 38

"Where are we going, and what were you talking to Reverend Armstrong about?" Anna asked as Eli headed the car the opposite direction of her house and Mr. Steiner's estate.

Instead of answering he whistled and rolled down the driver's window to let in the breeze. November weather in Holiday really was spectacular.

"Eli?" Anna leaned forward to stare at him, a hint of frustration in her eye.

"Full of questions today, aren't we?" He drove slowly down Main, to prolong their arrival at his destination. Unfortunately, he couldn't prolong it too much. He only had a couple of hours until he had to leave for the airport. "I think I quite like this—knowing something about your town that you don't."

"What do you know?" She grabbed his sleeve as if to wrest the secret from him.

"Sorry. No hand-holding while driving," Eli said. "Safety first." He gripped the steering wheel with exaggerated precision and stared straight ahead.

"Fine." Anna flopped back in her seat. "I can find out when you leave, you know."

"You can find out right now." Eli pulled the car into a parking spot in front of the community center. Before Anna could question what they were doing here, he was out of the car and around to her side to open the door. "Some of the men have already been inside to clean up and have braced the damaged wall, so it's safe to go in and look around."

"And we're doing that because . . ." Anna caught his hand.

Eli smiled to himself. *What a difference a weekend makes.* "I want to see what it looked like inside. It's part of my family's legacy, right?"

"Yes, but it looks like there's not much left to see." She leaned back to look at the caved-in roof and west wall.

Instead of going in the front doors, crisscrossed with caution tape, they made their way around to the damaged side and entered easily through the door-sized opening that the storm had torn away.

"Lathe and plaster?" Eli said, touching a piece of the crumbling walls. "Seriously? Wasn't this place built in the 60's or 70's?"

"The building itself was here long before that," Anna explained. "It was an old feed store, if I remember correctly. Your great-grandparents paid to have it cleaned up and refurbished, the stage added, a sound system . . . I doubt too much structural was changed."

"It should have been." Eli shook his head. "Considering the storms you get down here."

They paused inside, allowing their eyes a moment to adjust to the dimmer light. Rows of chairs had already been stacked against the far wall, the stage curtains taken down, and the wall visibly braced. The carpet had been torn up and was stacked near the front doors. The bare floor beneath had been swept, with the resulting pile of debris lying in the center of the large room, above which a shaft of sunlight shone through a gaping hole in the ceiling.

"It's such a shame." Anna wiggled her fingers free of Eli's and walked to the stage. Instead of going up the stairs, she used her hands to hoist herself up.

"So this is the place where you gained your Miss Holiday fame."

"The very." She smiled wistfully.

"I would have given a lot to see that." Eli joined her, sitting beside her on the stage. "If this had happened to a building in Chicago, there's no way this place wouldn't have been vandalized by now. That all the chairs and props and the podium are still in here is pretty amazing."

"That's small-town life for you. Every single person in Holiday has memories in this building and a literal investment in it. The Holiday Knitting Society sold scarves and hats and blankets to raise funds for the newer stage lights several years ago. Boy Scouts went on an outing to cut down the Christmas tree each year. Girl Scouts always made the decorations. The seniors played bingo here. The teenagers held dances."

"*With* the seniors sometimes," he recalled from Gabriel's letters.

"That too." Anna swung her legs in unison with Eli's.

Or maybe it was his swinging in time with hers. Either way, they felt united, sitting here reminiscing about a past only she had known but that his family had helped to create.

"What would you think about continuing the Steiner legacy to this town?"

"What do you mean?" Anna turned her head to look at him.

"What if we gave Holiday a new community center?" He paused. "And a library."

"I think that would be amazing." Anna looked around the room, as if imagining it rebuilt. "Why are you asking me? And what would my part of *we* entail?"

"I'm asking because you're practically a Steiner now."

Her head jerked up at that, and Eli hastened to add, "Half of the estate is yours, remember?"

"Yes, but—"

Was that a twinge of relief or disappointment? "You were trying to forget?"

"Something like that. I meant it when I told you I didn't want anything. Any money or—"

"That's good," Eli said. "Because what I'm proposing, is going to cost a lot of it. We'll have to sell some of Great-grandfather's shares in some of his other funds to make this happen. And certainly we won't see a whole lot of return for it—other than that warm, fuzzy feeling you've told me about." *Proof that this place, or more likely, this woman has brainwashed me.*

"Why do it, then?" Anna challenged. "Why would Mr. I-live-for-my-paycheck want to blow a bunch of money on a town full of hicks?"

"Ouch." Eli clapped a hand over his heart. "You're talking about my relatives here. My ancestry. And more importantly—yourself. You, Miss Annabelle Lawrence, belle of the South, are most certainly *not* a hick. And as for those who are, I think a library might do a lot to change that. Education is the ticket out of poverty, or so Gabriel and your parents believed."

"And just where do you propose to locate this library?" Anna asked. "Are you planning to add a second story on here? Or do you think the old library at the end of town could be refurbished too?"

"Considering that it hasn't been used since The Great Depression—if what I've heard is correct—then no." He shook his head. "This building is a no as well. The whole thing will have to come down. We'd have to start from scratch. But I have another idea . . ." Eli waited, wanting her to come to the same, brilliant conclusion he had.

Anna nudged him with her shoulder. "I was never any good at Twenty Questions. Just tell me already."

"Isn't it obvious?" Eli stared at her and gave his cheesiest smile, the one he'd felt burgeoning inside since church when the idea had struck him, almost like an epiphany from heaven or the proverbial lightning bolt.

"As clear as mud." Anna frowned.

"Fine." He gave an exaggerated sigh. "It came to me during the sermon, when Reverend Armstrong was talking about making something new and better. Holiday needs a new community center, and it could use a library. We—the two of us—have an old, empty building—a historic, *large*, old, empty building. Why not turn it into something useful? The main floor could be the community center and the upstairs the library."

Anna's mouth opened partway, but no words came for several seconds. "Mr. Steiner's house? Your family home?"

"Yes." He jumped off the stage and moved in front of her, taking her hands. "It's too big for anyone to live in. You know that as well as I. We're long past the age of families with a half dozen or more children, a houseful of servants, and elaborate dinner parties. Would either of us really *want* to live in that place?"

"I thought we had to," Anna said. "For five years, at least."

"We have to live on the estate, but the documents don't specify that it has to be in the house. We could build something smaller and in the meantime move a trailer onto the property or something."

"Or refurbish the apartment above the carriage house." Anna's face brightened. "I've always thought that building was charming. And that would work as a place for us to live—separately when we're taking our turns."

Her simple *us* would have sufficed, but one thing at a time. "Great idea." Eli nodded enthusiastically. "And I think the main house could be a really great gift to the town. We would be preserving a piece of history and doing something meaningful with it too."

Anna pursed her lips. "It would need a lot of changes—moving walls and updating electrical and plumbing, building a stage..."

"It would," he agreed. "But I think it could work. The square footage is there. That's why I came over here first. I wanted to see for myself the kind of space we were talking about. Want to go over to the house and take a look? Dream a little?"

Anna's hesitant expression morphed into a smile. "Okay."

Eli tugged her forward, released her before she jumped, and caught her at her waist. She landed lightly in front of him, but his hands lingered. They stood looking at each other, toe to toe.

"We don't have to do this," he said. "If you don't feel good about it or—"

She pressed a finger to his lips. "It's a great idea. I might even be a little jealous that you thought of it first."

He wished her lips were jealous of her finger and would move in to take over. *Not here. Not now.* The idea of kissing Anna had been in the forefront of his mind since their hug on the beach Friday night. That would have been a romantic location. This was not. But he had an idea about that too.

"Come on." She stepped from his embrace before he could be tempted further.

"One minute." Eli walked over to the glass cases mounted on the opposite wall. Somehow they'd survived the storm mostly intact. He stood in front of them, eyes scanning the photos and memorabilia crammed inside until he found what he was searching for—plus a few more, bonus pictures. He slid the case open and reached inside, removing a picture of Anna in a wetsuit, with a giant fish draped across her arms. He grabbed the accompanying newspaper article and then the photos of three consecutive years of Miss Holiday pageants.

"What do you want with those?" Anna grimaced. "That crown was so atrocious. The teeth always got caught in my hair."

"I think it becomes you." Eli held up one of the photos beside her. "Yep. We'd better see about getting you another tiara. You can be Miss Mulberry now."

"Nice." Anna turned her back on him and flounced toward the exit.

Eli held his prize carefully and followed.

"In order to keep the stairs we'll need to orient the theater this way. The stage will be in what is now the parlor, and seating will extend back through the foyer and into the dining room." Eli stretched his hands out as he walked the proposed outline.

"What about the walls and pocket doors?"

"They'll have to go and be replaced with beams. We'll have to open up the whole place. But we can salvage the doors and any other period pieces that have to come out. If we don't end up reusing them here, maybe we can in the carriage house apartment."

"Maybe." Anna wasn't entirely convinced yet. "Mr. Steiner's house won't be Mr. Steiner's house anymore if we tear it all up."

"It will be something even better—something the whole town can enjoy for generations to come. It really will be a community center—much more than Holiday has ever had. The knitters and the scouts can still meet here, and there will be a stage for the Miss Holiday and Christmas pageants, and a floor for dancing at the harvest social, but there will also be access to books, computers, music, and movies—knowledge."

"How do you propose purchasing all that—knowledge?"

Anna hated playing devil's advocate, especially when Eli was so clearly excited by this.

"We'll have to apply for some grants, or maybe start a nonprofit. I don't know the details yet. We'll have to figure all that out." He walked to the window and looked outside. "There's plenty of room for a park out there as well. One with new playground equipment and picnic tables, a pavilion— maybe even a baseball diamond."

"You're scaring me," Anna admitted. "I don't want to bankrupt Mr. Steiner's portfolio the first year."

"We won't. Don't worry." Eli turned from the window and came toward her. "Don't you think he would like this?"

Anna thought about it, about Mr. Steiner and his wife. She looked around the vast space, empty now. "We'd also be preserving the house, right? The outside wouldn't change, and we'd keep or replicate the molding and fixtures?"

"We can do whatever you deem best. You can be in charge of the interior. We have to get an architect, but I don't think we'd necessarily have to have a designer."

"I think we would," Anna countered. "My training as a marine biologist isn't going to go far with a project like this." But she had to admit the idea of transforming the house was growing on her. It *was* too big to live in. Too grand. But would Mr. Steiner—generous as he had been—truly approve?

"What did your great-grandfather expect us to do with all this?" she asked aloud, turning a circle and taking it all in. She paused before the stairs, waiting for Eli to join her so they could go up to the second floor to talk about logistics for a library.

After snatching a rose from the vase on the foyer table, he stopped in front of her. "I think . . . he wanted us to be happy here." Eli handed her the rose.

"How?" Anna twirled the stem in her fingers. "When he knew I had run away to Seattle and you never wanted to come here to begin with? What did he think would happen when he left this place to us?"

"I don't actually think he was all that concerned about the house," Eli mused as he paced out the width of the stairs.

"Of course he was," Anna argued. "Why else would he insist that at least one of us live here for the next five years?"

"Why indeed?" Eli recorded the width in his notes on his phone, slipped it back in his pocket, then came to stand in front of her. "What if this old house was just the vehicle for what Gabriel really wanted to have happen?" Eli took her free hand in his. "What if what he really hoped for was—this?" With a gentle tug he pulled Anna close.

"Eli?" Her heart raced as she read the unmistakable desire and intention in his gaze.

"I think he hoped *us* would happen."

Us.

Their gazes locked. Eli tilted his head and leaned in, brushing his lips across hers for the merest second before Anna pulled away.

"I can't—I don't do the casual-dating thing." *No rebound.* She was breathless, though what had happened could hardly be called a kiss.

"That's all I've ever done." He didn't release her with the confession. "I'd like to try something different. This *feels* different," he clarified.

"What if it's not? What if you go back to Chicago, and I go back to Seattle with a fresh heartbreak. I can't—"

"*Would* it break your heart if we parted ways?"

"Yes." She nodded. "I don't know how or why—it's all happened so fast—"

Eli's lips silenced hers. His strong arms wrapped more firmly around her this time, as if unwilling to let her go. Anna stood frozen beneath the warmth of his mouth, until the onslaught of heat and emotion quickly became too much.

Leap, her thundering heart ordered, and at last her brain and body complied.

Her hands, mashed against the front of his shirt, crept upward to his shoulders and around the back of his neck. The rose fell from her fingers as they clasped behind him, pulling him as closely as he held her.

"Anna," he managed a reverent whisper between kisses. Then they were lost in each other again, swept up in a passion that roared as loudly in her ears as the surf pounding against the shore.

Our souls *connected.* Bree's words echoed through Anna's mind.

I understand now. Her own soul took flight, soaring as free and happy as she'd ever felt, right here encircled in Eli's arms.

He pulled back slightly, ending their kiss, catching his breath as Anna was.

"You're crying." He reached up to brush moisture from her cheeks.

"I didn't mean to—I didn't realize."

"And *I* meant to ask you if I might kiss you before I did. Forgive me?" he asked, his voice concerned and his expression uncertain, vulnerable.

"There's nothing to forgive." One of her hands slid forward to cup his cheek. "These are happy tears."

A corner of his mouth lifted. "You mean you cry when you're happy too? I can't win."

"But you are winning," Anna insisted. "The tears are because you're making me feel things I haven't felt for a very long time—or ever."

"Good things?" he asked hesitantly.

"Very good."

The other side of his mouth lifted. "In that case, maybe I should make you feel some more."

Her grin matched his. "Please."

Eli leaned close again but then paused. His eyes darkened. "Do you know how long I've dreamed of this moment—of kissing Annabelle Lawrence?"

She shook her head. "A day? Maybe two?"

"Years." The breath of his whisper warmed her lips. "Half a lifetime. Great-grandpa knew it, too. That was why he called both of us home."

"So you could kiss me?" she asked, amused.

But Eli's look only intensified. "That, and much more."

Chapter 37

LOVE. NEITHER SHE nor Eli had voiced the word, yet it hovered nearby, ready in the wings when the time came. *So soon?* Impossible, wasn't it? Was that too big a leap without looking a lot longer first? In spite of this worry, Anna hummed as she practically floated around the kitchen, her spirits soaring as high as the heavenly aroma of the fresh-baked pumpkin pie cooling on the counter.

Collecting the salad bowl, dressing, and rolls, she sidled past Bree into the dining room, placing her offerings on the table set for two. Bree followed, a platter of fried chicken in one hand and a plate of corn on the cob in the other. Anna hurried to take it from her.

"Thank you so much for helping me." She flashed Bree an appreciative smile.

"You would have done fine on your own. Cooking is in your genes."

"Maybe," Anna murmured skeptically. "It took those genes long enough to make an appearance."

"You just needed someone to cook *for*," Bree insisted. "Be glad you weren't thirteen when that happened."

"I am." Anna turned from the table to her best friend. "Thank you, Bree. For everything. I wish—I wish I'd been a better friend during high school and after."

"What happened in the past doesn't matter now," Bree said, reiterating Anna's words. "We're both human." She gave Anna a quick hug, then stepped back and began untying the strings of her apron. "The guys should be here any minute."

"It was kind of Carson to pick Eli up from the airport." Anna followed Bree back into the kitchen.

"He was practically there already. It worked out well with his meeting schedule this week."

"Tell him I said thanks again, just the same." Anna had planned to drive Eli's car to Mobile to meet his flight, but staying here had allowed her to prepare a nice dinner, as well as extra time for her nerves to get worked up. "You're sure you don't want to stay? We've got plenty."

"And interrupt your romantic reunion?" Bree shook her head. "No way." She placed the apron on the hook behind the pantry door, then grabbed her purse from a stool. "I'm going to walk over to my dad's to pick up Anna. Carson's meeting me there. I don't want you to waste a minute of your time alone with Eli."

Anna wrung her hands. "Have I lost my mind with all this?" She brushed a hand across the front of her dress and inclined her head toward the pie.

"Not your mind, but your heart—quite possibly."

"We haven't even known each other that long," Anna protested. "What if I'm making the mistake of my life?"

"What if you're not?" Bree countered.

"I can't live through being hurt again." Anna's eyes clouded as she looked out the window. "And doing all—this—is only making it more likely I will be."

"Cooking a nice dinner, dressing up, taking care to look your best, and even the nervous, fluttery feeling you've got is all part of the ritual of falling in love. You have to put yourself out there, Anna. You have to give your heart if you hope to get one in return."

"It wasn't like that before." Anna hadn't realized she'd spoken the thought aloud until she saw Bree's slow, careful nod. Anna brought a hand to her mouth.

Bree placed her hand on Anna's arm. "Familiarity was

the likely culprit. Carson was as much like a brother to you as he was a boyfriend. You'd grown up together. He'd always been there, and you thought he always would be."

"I took him for granted," Anna said, hearing the astonishment in her voice. How had she not seen this before? For so long she'd been hurt and angry, blaming him—them. But she was at fault too. "I did love him." She looked to Bree for understanding.

"You did," Bree concurred. "But not like I did—like I do. And not in the way you and Eli may love each other. You'll only know if you give it—him—a chance."

Not two minutes after Bree left, Eli arrived. Anna watched from the kitchen window as Carson's car pulled away from the curb and Eli came up the walk, a small duffel slung over his shoulder.

Not staying long, then. She knew this already. They'd talked and texted every day of the past two weeks, since he'd returned to Chicago to give his employer notice and start wrapping up his life there. Eli had explained that he couldn't simply leave after the two weeks were up. There were clients and cases that would still require his attention—a few even after he moved here. Notwithstanding, he had committed. Regardless of what Anna did or whether or not she returned to Seattle, come mid-December, Eli would be Holiday, Alabama's newest resident.

She left the window to wait at the front door, standing hesitantly on the opposite side of the screen as he approached. Considering the hours they'd spent talking over the past several days, she felt inexplicably shy. Her hands twisted in the front of her apron, and belatedly she realized she'd neither removed it as planned nor taken her hair down from the messy bun topping her head.

Eli ran up the steps, taking them two at a time. Anna smiled as she touched the screen to push it open, but he was already pulling it toward him. His duffel dropped on the floor beside her, and she found herself enfolded in his arms in a hug that felt spectacular.

"Man, these are addicting."

"Just mine are, I hope. Or have you been hugging everyone at the office too?" Anna burrowed further into his embrace, appreciating the strength of his arms around her and the now-familiar scent of his cologne.

"Just yours. And I missed these too." He released her and stepped back as his thumb brushed her lips. Unmistakable desire flared in his eyes a second before he dipped his head and began kissing her thoroughly.

Anna clung to him, her fingers pressing through the sleeves of his shirt, as if seeking direct contact with his skin. "Eli," she murmured after several long, drugging seconds when he made no move to stop and would not release her. "What will the neighbors think?" she whispered against his lips.

"That I'm smarter than they first gave me credit for, since I came back." With a grin that promised more later, he nudged his duffel farther inside with his foot, then pushed the front door closed.

Anna stood awkwardly, heart thundering loud enough for him to hear, her breathing shallow. She clasped her hands in front of her. "Dinner's ready."

"It smells delicious." Eli caught her hand in his as they walked to the dining room. He held her chair out, and Anna slid into her father's seat at the head of the table. Eli took her mother's.

She said a brief blessing, and they began filling their plates, twice bumping hands in the process. Anna wished she'd left the windows open. It was so hot in here. No doubt her face and neck were red.

The third time their hands accidentally touched Eli grabbed hers and held on. "What's wrong, Anna?"

She shrugged. "I'm not sure."

His brow arched. "Not sure or not sure you want to tell me?"

Anna sighed, and her shoulders drooped. "This is new territory for me," she admitted. "I never did things like making dinner for Carson—I was too busy with school. I think I'm just realizing I don't know how to be a very good girlfriend."

Eli smiled. "Is that what you are? My girlfriend?"

Anna tried tugging her hand away. "I don't—didn't mean—"

"I like the sound of that." He moved his chair closer. "This is new for me too." His voice and gaze softened. "I haven't ever shared an inheritance and a house with anyone before. I've never wanted a hug so badly as I have the past two weeks. I've never looked forward to being with someone the way I look forward to being with you."

Anna stared at their joined hands. "What happens when we're not together anymore?"

"You mean while I'm wrapping things up in Chicago—or when you go back to Seattle?"

"Seattle." Anna swallowed and looked up at him. "I have to go back for a while, at least."

He nodded. "I get that. I'm in the same boat."

"How can you just leave your life there?" Anna asked. "With how much you love the Cubs and your paycheck—your condo and takeout."

"Southern cooking is a whole lot better than takeout." Eli released her hand and dug into his chicken as evidence. "Plus," he said around bites, "I'm keeping my season tickets.

We won't be able to go to all the games, but I'll sell the tickets we won't be using, and that can offset the price of travel for those we fly."

We. "You're giving up so much," Anna said, panic welling with each word. "Is Holiday worth it? I know you're excited about redoing the house, but what about when that's done? What will you do then?"

Eli started on his potatoes. "I've been thinking about starting my own practice. Not in Holiday, but nearby. Fairhope, maybe. I wouldn't have to be at the office every day."

"But what if—" Instead of finishing her thought, she picked up her fork and started on her salad.

"What if things between us don't work out?" Eli stopped eating and met her gaze.

Anna forced a piece of lettuce down her throat and reached for her water. "Yes," she rasped a few seconds later. "There's no guarantee that they will. And if they don't, and you've picked up your entire life and moved it here..."

Eli leaned back in his chair, a thoughtful, but unconcerned expression reflecting in his eyes. "I hope they do *work out.* Which is extremely uncharacteristic of me. I've never said that, never wanted any kind of long-term relationship with a woman. But—" He leaned close, taking Anna's hand once more. "There's something magical going on down here, something special about this town. And more importantly, about you. It feels like my whole life—or at least since Gabriel sent me that first letter—has been pointing me in this direction."

"That's a whole lot of expectation for me to live up to."

"I wish you'd realize you're doing it without even trying—just by being yourself. Whereas, I *don't* have much of a reputation to live up to. Gabriel's track record is far better than mine. About the best I can offer you is a promise that from here on out, I'm aspiring to be the man he was—

generous and selfless. A lot like you." Eli brought her hand to his lips and kissed it. "I can tell this is putting pressure on you—to stay here in Holiday, to quit your job and uproot your life." He let out a slow breath. "And just because I'm ready for that doesn't mean you are. Take your time, Anna, and I'm convinced time will sort this all out."

His words eased a knot of tension she hadn't even realized was there. "Thank you." Anna smiled—without the nerves this time. "I'm better here now, but I'm still not sure if it's where I should stay."

"I understand."

Anna sensed the tremor of hurt beneath his words and wanted to reassure him, but she couldn't. Not yet. It had all happened so fast. It was only a little over six weeks ago that they'd met. Was it possible to fall in love with someone so quickly? Eli might feel like he had known her longer, but she hadn't had the advantage of Mr. Steiner's letters.

Six weeks. Half of my time in Holiday passed already.

This brought its own little wave of panic. There was so much to be done still, so many things she wanted to do for her parents before they came home. So little time to spend with Bree, so much more to learn about Eli. And now they had this enormous project ahead of them as well.

The air in the dining room felt heavy, as if weighed down by all her serious thoughts and their discussion.

"If things don't work out there's always Betty," Anna said, in a lame attempt at levity.

Eli barked out a laugh. "She does make a good pie."

"So do I." Anna rose from her chair and went into the kitchen to retrieve their dessert. When she turned with the pie in her hand, Eli was right behind her. He caught the plate before it could fall and placed it back on the counter.

"Dessert later." He took her in his arms once more. "And you can bet I'll want seconds."

Chapter 40

SATURDAY MORNING'S SPECIAL session of the town council met around Reverend Armstrong's kitchen table instead of at the disabled community center. Since the council was made up of volunteers and never decided on matters of government beyond items such as whether to plant petunias or cosmos on Main Street; whether or not potato salad should be banned from the Fourth of July picnic—several residents had come down with food poisoning a few years earlier, and Katherine Marner's German potato salad had been blamed; and when the town Christmas tree should go up and come down, there were no council chambers or even a city center.

The wider county government took care of larger matters, which mostly left Holiday's seven hundred citizens to manage themselves. Holiday had never had a mayor or an election, that Anna was aware of. Instead, with good people like Reverend Armstrong and her parents and Mr. Steiner at the helm, the town ran smoothly. Excepting the occasional problem—like Everett Jacobs' speeding.

And I took care of that.

The memory brought a smile to Anna's face, as did Eli's hand in hers, swinging jauntily as they strode up the Armstrong's walk. Six weeks ago she would have dreaded any errand that might have brought her to this very familiar door—one she'd walked through without even knocking on hundreds of times over the years. But today, with Eli at her side and her old confidence steadily returning in increments, she felt only flurries of excitement.

Last night they'd spent the evening with papers spread

out across the dining room table, as Eli gave her essentially the same presentation he would give the council this morning. She wondered if he'd gotten any work done at all the past two weeks, as what he'd prepared had to have taken him a considerable amount of time.

The county would need to sign off on the building permit, after plans from the architect and engineer had been submitted and reviewed, but first, this morning, the council had to approve of Eli's vision. It had grown exponentially, and Anna felt eager for everyone to hear it. What he was proposing was huge—not just in the scope of the project, but in its potential to help Holiday's residents.

Instead of Reverend Armstrong, Charlie stood at the door greeting everyone as they arrived. His face brightened as he spotted Anna and reached to shake her hand. His smile fell when he saw it already nestled in Eli's.

"So it's true, then?" he asked, looking back and forth between them.

"What is?" Anna asked, curious about the latest gossip.

"Hotshot lawyer here is sweeping you off your feet by throwing around a bunch of money for a new community center."

"Hmm." Anna leaned into Eli. "Not quite accurate. I actually liked him better before I knew about all the money."

"That's because half of it is hers." Eli turned to Anna and planted a kiss on the side of her head. "This Southern belle totally shirks responsibility. She tried to foist it all on me, if you can imagine."

"I do not shirk. Who's been raking leaves in that gargantuan yard the past few weeks?" With a parting smile to Charlie, Anna tugged Eli behind her into the house that had once felt almost as much like home as her own. As with the first time she'd entered the church again, Eli made this visit less painful than she would have supposed it to be.

"You should take care with his feelings," Eli whispered. "Charlie has a crush on you."

"He does not." Anna glanced back toward the door.

Eli nodded. "You don't see it, but I do. And Carson confirmed it the night of the hoedown."

"Charlie has always been like a little brother to me," she said, keeping her voice to a whisper as well.

"Not in his mind."

Reverend Armstrong ended their debate. "Welcome, Annabelle, Elijah." He beckoned them into the crowded kitchen.

"Thank you, Reverend." Anna took a seat at the table, marveling at the lack of angst she felt at being here. Eli set his laptop case beside her as his eyes traveled over the assembled group. Anna wondered what he thought of Holiday's esteemed council. Her father was absent and would have been the youngest here. Most of the other council members looked far too old to be in any sort of position to make decisions aside from what level their hearing aids should be set at.

"Welcome, everyone," Reverend Armstrong began. "Thank you for meeting on a Saturday. Gabriel's great-grandson has flown in from Chicago to present his ideas for a new community center."

"Looks like he flew in for other reasons too." Ernie winked at Anna.

She felt herself blush but reached up to her shoulder to cover Eli's hand, resting there.

Reverend Armstrong's smile only grew. "Let's welcome him and give him our attention." He stepped aside, and Eli moved into the space he'd vacated at the head of the oval table.

"Good morning."

Ladies and gentleman of the jury, Anna added silently and wondered if the thought had crossed his mind as well.

"Thank you for your willingness to meet today. Before I

present my ideas for a new community center, I'd like to share my reasons for this proposal."

"Proposal?" Lilly Ann Sturges' knitting needles stilled as she looked at Anna expectantly. "Is someone getting married?"

"Not today, Lilly." Reverend Armstrong said, but not before Anna felt the heat creeping up her face. Eli, however, appeared not to have even heard the comment.

"When I was in high school, my great-grandfather began sending me letters once a month. Though I didn't know it, or her, at the time, Anna had encouraged him to write letters to his family, to help ease his loneliness, after his wife passed away."

Ralph Prior, who'd lost his own wife five years earlier, nodded sagely.

Eli continued. "I was the fortunate recipient of those letters, and they continued for years."

"He was a good'un," Ernie said, and the others nodded their agreement.

"After his passing, I was named executor of my great-grandfather's estate and, along with one other person, am the recipient of most of it, the house and grounds included."

"Bah. What's a city boy going to do with all that?" Stewart McKay—self-appointed town grump and ever the naysayer on the council—demanded.

"That's what he's here to tell us," Reverend Armstrong said, shutting Stewart down before he could continue the negative string of thoughts no doubt crowding his mind.

Eli exchanged a look with Anna, as if to say, *tough jury.*

"To be honest, I didn't want anything to do with the estate, but I decided to come down here to see it, and the town Gabriel had told me so much about. His stories about Holiday, and one particular resident—" Eli's gaze slid to Anna— "intrigued me. Could it possibly be true that a teenage girl once bet a state-champion fisherman that she could out fish him—and then did?

"Saved Betty's organ," Lilly recalled, needles clicking away.

"Lord help us all," Stewart grumbled.

"I believe he has," Eli said enthusiastically. "I came here to see if there was really a place where bicycle parades are still held on Main Street, and senior citizens and seniors in high school spend Friday nights dancing together. A place where leftovers from the market and diner are delivered faithfully to those in need, each and every week. A place where neighbors are friends and genuinely care about one another."

"What was your conclusion?" Reverend Armstrong asked.

"Yes, to all of that and more," Eli said. "I admit I didn't care for what I considered nosiness at first, until I came to see it for what it is—concern for one another, for our fellow beings you would say."

"God's instructions," Reverend Armstrong said. "I'm a mere follower."

"You all are," Eli said. "So much so that when I returned to Chicago, the differences were clear, and I found I no longer wanted to live in the world as I've known it and as most do."

"So you're back here to rebuild the new community center. Yee haw," Stewart said sarcastically. "Don't worry. We'll put your name all over it, just like Gabriel's is plastered everywhere."

"I don't propose that we rebuild," Eli said. "The building on Main is old, and the entire structure would need to come down."

"So you're cheaper than the old man." Stewart glared at Eli, challenging him.

Eli ignored the barb. Anna wondered if members of the court were kept in better check than Mr. McKay.

"I have a different solution in mind." Eli glanced at Anna, and she slid the folder from his bag toward him. He opened it and passed copies around to everyone at the table.

"As I stated earlier, I am the executor and beneficiary of Gabriel Steiner's property, including his house and grounds. As a requirement of this responsibility, I will be residing on the property for at least the next five years. What I won't be doing is living in a house that could be better put to use—for the benefit of the entire town. I propose that it be remodeled to accommodate a new community center, a library, and a small charter school. The grounds outside would also be altered to include a new city park, complete with a pavilion and playground."

Murmurs of astonishment rippled around the table. Even Stewart was speechless for a minute before rasping out, "Why a school? We don't want a bunch of urchins invading our town."

"This school would be specifically for residents of Holiday and the surrounding back country. It wouldn't pull from other communities." Eli placed his hands on the table and leaned forward, looking in turn at each person seated there. "Poverty continues to be a significant problem here. I believe the way out of poverty is literacy. Having a local school would allow more children growing up here to receive an education. And that could lead to upcoming generations finally breaking the cycle of poverty."

Lilly Ann Sturges set her knitting aside and began clapping loudly. After a second's hesitation the others followed.

"I like it," Ernie declared, slapping the table. "And Gabriel would have too."

"What about the other person you mentioned?"

Anna looked up to see Charlie standing in the kitchen doorway. Eli turned to face him.

"You're not the only person who inherited, are you?

Didn't you say you were sharing the estate with someone else?"

Anna winced inwardly at the accusation and jealousy she heard in Charlie's voice. It seemed he wasn't in favor of the project. *Because he doesn't want Eli to stay? Because of me?*

"Charlie, this is a council matter," Reverend Armstrong said gently.

"It's a fair question," Eli said. "And you're right, Charlie, there is another person to consider in all this." He held his hand out to Anna. She took it and stood beside him.

"What do you say, Miss Lawrence?"

Anna smiled at Eli before facing the astonished expressions of the council. Only Reverend Armstrong did not appear surprised. She wondered if perhaps he had known of Mr. Steiner's intentions before he died.

"I wholeheartedly agree with this plan and am happy to see our joint inheritance being used for the good of the whole town."

Chapter 41

THE FRONT DOOR of Mr. Steiner's house opened, and Eli strolled outside, barefoot and wearing torn jeans and a Cubs t-shirt. He held a mug in his hand, which he raised toward Anna in greeting as a smile lit his face.

After parking the Excursion she climbed out and started toward him.

"Good morning, beautiful," he said as she crossed the driveway. "Missed me already, did you? It's been, what—all of seven hours?" Eli glanced at his watch.

Six hours, forty-five minutes since they'd shared a lingering kiss on her porch late last night, but she wasn't about to let him know she was keeping track that closely. Instead Anna rolled her eyes. "Are all attorneys this full of themselves?" She started up the porch steps.

"Only the good ones." He grinned before taking another sip from his mug. "Man, I love this weather. Look at this—" He wiggled his toes. "Bare feet in November. It's amazing."

He was amazing. That he was real and moving to Holiday was incredible. And when he'd kissed her last night it had been spectacular.

Eli set his mug on the railing and snagged Anna with one arm as she tried to move past him. "Not so fast." His other arm twined around her, followed quickly by his mouth on hers.

"I thought—"

His lips smothered her attempted protest.

"The architect—will—be—here any minute," Anna finished in a rush. With her hands firmly on Eli's shoulders she pushed him away.

"He's not coming until nine o'clock," Eli said casually and leaned in for another kiss.

"But you said—"

"My mistake." His mischievous grin said he'd misled her on purpose. "Can't blame a guy for wanting to spend a little more time with his girl, can you?"

His girl. In answer Anna switched from pushing Eli away to pulling him close, kissing him first for a change. After a weekend spent together, her shyness and uncertainty had fled, and she felt as exuberant and alive as she had when dancing in Eli's arms the night of the hoedown.

"Someone is hungry this morning," he said, breaking off their kiss after several long seconds.

"Starving," Anna said.

"Let's go to breakfast. My treat."

"With *our* money?" she teased.

Eli shook his head. "Mine." He released her and bent to retrieve his shoes beside the door. "I'll drive."

They headed into town and parked in front of Rosie's diner—right next to Carson and Bree's car. Bree got out and waved at Anna. She waved back, uncertain.

What are they doing here?

Eli's guilty look answered her unspoken question. "Double date?" he suggested.

"I thought you didn't like Carson."

"I didn't—at first. Guy rubbed me wrong until I realized that he and Bree are solid, and they would genuinely like to see you happy."

"I am happy—see." Anna forced a grin, then folded her arms and watched Carson and Bree's backs as they entered the diner. "I don't suppose we can go somewhere else now."

"Sure we can," Eli said. "Bit of a drive, but if that's what you'd prefer . . ."

They wouldn't make it back in time to meet the architect

if they went somewhere else. Plus, Bree might have her feelings hurt.

"I wasn't ready for this," Anna protested.

"Maybe not, but you're running out of time here. Over half of your trip has passed already. You and Bree have made your peace, and it seemed like you and Carson had as well, a couple of weeks ago at church."

"Forgiving them is one thing. Hanging out with them is another."

"I realize that." Eli paused and swallowed, as if carefully considering his next words.

As he should. Anna's eyes narrowed. "Whose idea was this?"

"Mine," he admitted. "But Bree and Carson readily agreed. They're on board."

"Would have been nice to know a boat ride was in the works," Anna muttered. At the very least, breakfast promised to be awkward. At worst—something might be said that would dredge up the past hurt she'd been trying so hard to put behind her. "Why would you do this?"

Eli took her hand. "You told me once that this town is too small for you and Carson and Bree. I guess I'm hoping you'll see that isn't true anymore, that it's still your place too. Because I'm staying in Holiday, and I'd really like you to be here with me."

"So this is all about you?" Anna huffed, with feigned anger. Eli's admission had only softened her heart. *He wants me—with him.*

"Absolutely." His lopsided grin appeared. "You know us big-city folk, always looking out for number one."

"I ought to make you number one it in there by yourself." Anna reached for the door handle.

Eli gave the hand he still held a squeeze. "But you won't?"

She returned his half smile. "Not today."

"I'm glad you took my recommendation and decided to go with Gage." Carson paused to take a bite from his stack of pancakes.

"*You* found the architect Eli's been telling me about?" Anna looked from Carson to Eli for confirmation.

Carson nodded and took a drink of juice before answering. "I did the web design for the business Gage and his wife started and got to know them both. They have an adopted daughter as well. He'll do a great job, and more than that—he's a great person."

"Is his wife an architect too?" Anna asked, wondering why they weren't having her draw up the plans if that was the case.

"Hailey's an interior designer," Bree said. "Together they started a nonprofit a couple years back. They design and decorate spaces for at-risk children—day-care centers, low-income schools, hospitals, and even apartment complexes. I don't know if you've thought about using a designer too, but she'd be perfect for the job."

"Sounds like we need to look at their website," Anna said. They'd definitely need a designer. "Are they both coming today?" she asked Eli.

He shook his head. "No. Anyone would have had to travel out here, so I figured a few extra bucks to fly Gage in from New York was worth it, but I didn't offer to purchase a ticket for his wife. We need to get plans drawn up before we think a whole lot about details on the inside." Eli paused his explanation to take a bite of his omelet.

"Realistically you're looking at, what, starting in February or March?" Carson asked.

"That may be optimistic," Eli said. "A lot depends on how

quickly the county turns things around, and if we end up needing a zoning change or a special permit."

"Which leaves us with the problem of where to host the Christmas pageant this year," Anna said. "Sure, we could fit everyone in Mr. Steiner's—" at Eli's look she stopped abruptly "—in our house as it is now, but not in the same room or in such a way that any sort of performance could take place." She glanced around the table. "This is where you all chime in with suggestions."

"Cancel it this year?" Eli suggested.

"No!" Anna, Bree, and Carson all answered at once.

"It's tradition," Anna explained.

"It's more than that," Bree added. "For some families—some children—it's the only bit of Christmas spirit or cheer they have to look forward to."

Anna wondered if Bree had fallen into that category in the years after her mother died. In spite of Bree's best efforts to make her house festive and the holiday happy for her brothers, it hadn't ever really felt that way at the Wagner home.

"Bree's right," Anna said. "And the Sub-for-Santa program is equally important for the same reason. We have to figure out a way for that to happen this year as well."

"Not a problem." Bree propped an elbow on the table and smiled.

"What do you know that I don't?" Carson leaned sideways and nudged her.

"A lot of things," she teased, the two of them exchanging a look that made Anna feel she was eavesdropping on an intimate moment.

Before she could steel her heart against the inevitable stab of pain, Eli's arm was around her, his hand giving her shoulder a reassuring squeeze. She glanced at him, and he winked, as if to say, *you've got this.*

I do. She took a deep breath and smiled. Each day being here got a little easier. Bree and Carson became more the friends she'd had forever and less the two people who'd broken her heart. *Because it isn't broken anymore?* The thought worried Anna. She was grateful to Eli for his support, and she couldn't deny her growing feelings for him. But if their relationship didn't work out would she be right back to where she'd started—or worse?

"Don't look so worried, Anna," Bree said. "Mr. Steiner made sure that Holiday will have a Sub-for-Santa program for years to come."

"Are you sure?" Eli turned to Bree, a frown on his face. "I'm sorry, but I haven't seen anything about that charity in any of his estate documents or his will. And I've looked a few times, since Anna's mentioned this more than once."

"You won't find anything there," Bree said. "He set up a money market account in my name and Anna's two years ago. It has ample funds to allow us to continue the Sub-for-Santa program for at least another five years."

"That would be about $15,000," Anna said, remembering that they'd typically spent about $3,000 on gifts each year.

"Twenty-five was the original deposit," Bree said. "It's down to $18,000 now. It grows a little interest each year, but not nearly enough to make up what we've spent."

"Sounds like we need to come up with a way to make it a perpetual fund," Eli said. "Some sort of fundraiser or income source that will allow it to continue to grow and will ensure the program continues."

"The Miss Holiday pageant would be a good start," Anna said. "A percentage of the tickets and entry fees could be used for that, while the rest still goes to the general town fund. It wouldn't be a lot, but it's something."

"Two years ago—" Carson, who'd been uncharacteristically quiet, looked at Bree in disbelief. "I can't believe you never mentioned before that your name is on a joint account worth thousands."

Bree shrugged. "Mr. Steiner asked me not to tell anyone as long as he was alive. And after that I forgot. I've had a few other things on my mind."

"Like perfecting your award-winning chili recipe," Eli said, grinning before he shoveled another bite of eggs in his mouth.

Anna picked up her own fork again. They would have to leave soon to meet the architect.

"That blue ribbon did take a lot of work," Bree agreed.

The three of them looked at Carson, Anna trying to gauge whether or not he was upset at having been left out of a rather significant transaction.

"Mr. Steiner trusted you with that amount of money, even knowing how much we could have used it—could still use it," Carson added.

"Of course." Bree sounded affronted. "It's for Christmas, for people who have a lot less than we do. You wouldn't have touched it, so why do you think I would have?"

"I don't," Carson said. "I know you wouldn't. I just didn't realize Mr. Steiner felt the same."

"I doubt he was thinking much about the money," Anna said.

"I'm pretty sure Gabriel was always thinking about money on some level." Eli snagged the bill from Rosie before anyone else could. "He had to be, based on his finances and the many pies he had his fingers in—even at his age."

"Maybe," Anna conceded. "But when he put Bree's name and mine on that account, he knew it was something that would bring us together—not the money, but the responsibility for it and for Holiday's Sub-for-Santa program."

"You're right." Bree's smile was wistful. "Mr. Steiner and your mom and I headed it up the past couple of years, but he always told me there would come a time when he, and even your mom, wouldn't be able to do it anymore. He said it would be up to the two of us then, you and me."

"Sly, if not subtle," Eli said thoughtfully.

"Not subtle at all," Anna said, giving him a pointed look. Carson's presence at the Mulberry—also orchestrated by Mr. Steiner, according to Eli—ensured she'd had to interact with him. And if she and Bree hadn't reconciled already, over a few hundred quarts of applesauce, it would have happened as they worked together supplying Holiday's less fortunate children with a Christmas.

And Eli . . . Anna's gaze softened. *Mr. Steiner's last gift.* He hadn't been here to help her mend her broken heart, so he'd sent his great-grandson instead. *And hoped I would love him in return.*

Perhaps she should have felt angry, or at least annoyed with such meddling in her life. But with Holiday's sun spilling through the diner window, her friends seated across from her, and Eli beside her, Anna felt only warmth and gratitude. And not at all lonely, for the first time in a very long time. Small-town folk often meddled in other people's business. Mr. Steiner had been no exception, but he'd acted out of love.

Such a simple concept, but one that had eluded her the past few years when she'd been acting out of fear instead. But this morning she vowed love would be her new and everlasting approach to life.

Chapter 42

"It's been an amazing four days." Anna leaned her head against Eli's shoulder as they gently rocked back and forth on the porch swing. He'd been hesitant when she'd suggested they wait on the porch for the shuttle that was coming to drive him to the airport. The swing held a lot of memories, after all. Now the most recent, with him, would be there to warm her heart when he wasn't.

"If only the next four weeks would go by as quickly." Eli held her hand in his, resting on top of his thigh.

"I still say we should squeeze a Christmas shopping weekend in there somewhere," Anna said, not at all looking forward to the separation they were facing. If not for the many upcoming responsibilities at the store and with the Sub-for-Santa program, she would have felt even more dread. But she had as much work to do here as Eli did in Chicago. Plus, she had to figure out what came next. That seemed an easy decision when he was around, but they'd both agreed she needed some space and time to make the right choice when it came to her career and future. The last few weeks had felt a bit like a fairytale, and now it was time to face reality. No matter how much she had ended up enjoying her time in Holiday, Seattle was still waiting—with everything, from her job, to her apartment and houseplants. Even if she decided she wanted to move, she couldn't simply walk away.

"Neither of us have time for shopping like that," Eli said. "My weekends are going to be busy packing and getting my condo ready to sell. And if you have any free time, you should go out to see your parents again."

"Speaking of which . . . When are you going to tell your parents that you're moving?"

"Never—or at least, not until they call me. Which may be never."

Anna sat up straight and looked at him. "You can't mean that, Eli."

"I do," he insisted. "The last time I called I realized that they really don't want to talk to me. They certainly don't need me, and they aren't interested in any kind of familial relationship. I'm always the one to reach out to them, and I'm done."

"But shouldn't they at least know you've moved?" She couldn't understand parents who behaved like his. Even after she'd fled Holiday her parents had still tried to be a part of her life.

"Why?" He shrugged. "They don't bother to let me know where they are or when, if ever, they'll be home. If I died tomorrow I doubt they'd come for the funeral."

Anna gasped. "Don't say that—especially the part about you dying."

"I don't intend to anytime soon." He leaned toward Anna, and she tipped her face up to meet his. He kissed her again, as he had so many times over the long weekend, but this time there was a sad note of farewell included.

A van pulled up in front of the house before their lips parted.

"Time to go." Eli held her chin a moment, then kissed her once more quickly.

"The time will go fast," Anna said. "We can talk and text every day." They both rose from the swing, and Eli picked up his duffel. She followed him down the steps.

"Don't go falling for someone else while I'm gone, like Donald or Clarence—or Charlie." Eli's eyes darkened with concern as he spoke the latter.

"Don't you go falling for some big-city girl. Remember me, or at least remember I'm holding your car hostage." She inclined her head toward his BMW parked in the driveway.

"Not only that, but I think I left my favorite jeans at the estate."

"You mean the ones with all the holes?"

He nodded. "I got muddy walking around the property, so I washed them. On my way over this morning I remembered I'd left them in the dryer."

Anna clasped a hand over her heart. "You chose time with me over going back to get your favorite jeans. I'm touched, Eli."

"You should be." He reached the van.

"Maybe it's for the best," Anna said. "Maybe the jeans fairy will replace them for you while you're gone."

"Don't you dare," Eli called over his shoulder. "It took me years to get those that soft."

Anna laughed. "Haven't you ever heard of sweats?"

He opened the door, stepped inside the van, and took a seat before frowning her direction. "I can't wear sweats to a Cubs game. Take care of my pants while I'm gone."

"All right." She raised her hand in farewell as he slid the door shut and the van backed out of the driveway. She stood on the lawn, watching until it reached the end of the street, turned the corner, and disappeared from sight.

Four weeks in Holiday without him. She shook off the melancholy that was threatening and turned and ran up the steps. It was time to make some lists of things she had to get done. For the market—complete the quarterly inventory, continue training Ella on the register, and order pies and turkeys, cranberries, and extra bread and rolls.

At Mr. Steiner's house—start packing up everything from records to the artwork, to the dishes, rent storage pods and have them delivered to the property, then move the furniture into them. Check out the carriage house apartment to see what needed to be done to make it livable for Eli. Anna had visions of surprising him with a new, modern bathroom before he returned, but realistically the best she'd probably be able to do in four weeks would be to give the apartment a good cleaning and replace the shower curtain and bathmat.

And at home—a good cleaning here would be helpful too. Anna looked ruefully at the leaves that had blown into the corners of the porch. She wanted the house to be sparkling for her parents when they came home. That task alone could keep her busy for a solid week. As would filling the freezer with meals for their return, and setting up the Christmas tree and hanging the lights. *So much to do . . .*

And somehow, in between all that work, she had to figure out what to do about Seattle.

"Anna, you've done such a marvelous job. I don't know what we would have done without you." Mom's emotion-filled voice wavered, making Anna long for a hug even more than she had before calling.

"Right back at you, Mom," Anna said, trying—for both their sakes—to keep the tone light. "You and Dad did a pretty great job yourself, raising us kids, all those years."

"We did. Which is exactly why I'm going to call your brother and sister and get them over there to help you. Don't even think about getting on the ladder to hang the lights."

Too late. Anna glanced out the front window at the ladder still propped against the house. She'd hung the lights first thing this morning, while the weather was nice. The forecast called for a week of storms, and she hadn't wanted to be up on the ladder in the rain.

"What I really need help with is the ordering." Anna moved from the kitchen to the dining room, where she had forms spread out all over the table. "I don't have a feel anymore of how many birds and pies we need for Thanksgiving."

"More than you'd believe." Mom laughed lightly, and the sound eased the grip on Anna's heart a little. Their conversations had been somber the last few times they'd talked. Dad still wasn't reacting great to the chemo, and they wouldn't even know if the aggressive treatments were working until they were all over.

"It's not just making sure to order enough for Thanksgiving," Mom continued. "People tend to *keep* eating in excess after that, all the way through Christmas. You'll be hard pressed to keep enough pies in the market, and rolls and other baked goods are nearly as popular too. It's all the family gatherings and the cool weather, I think," she added.

"Cool." Anna rolled her eyes. As if sixty- and seventy-degree temperatures were practically cause for frostbite.

They talked another half hour, Mom walking Anna through each order and reminding her to rent a refrigerated truck to park in back of the market as well. They'd need the extra cooler space for the next month, she insisted. By the time they ended the call Anna felt satisfied she'd had all her questions about the Mulberry answered. Unfortunately, she hadn't asked about the things really concerning her.

To move or not to move. Should she throw away the last few years and try her luck getting another job in marine biology elsewhere, closer to home? Should she change careers altogether or not even worry about working for a while since, thanks to Mr. Steiner, she no longer had any kind of immediate financial needs? Should she take a chance on Holiday, and specifically Eli? Was she ready to leap again?

Her heart certainly leapt each and every time he sent a text or called her. He made her laugh and had mostly cured her from crying. His kisses and touch thrilled her. Walking and talking with him seemed like pure joy. He was a companion as she'd never had before—their relationship at a level hers with Carson had never quite reached. She wanted to know everything about Eli and cared about the things he was passionate about—even baseball, which had never been of particular interest to her before. And it seemed Eli felt the same about her. He wanted to know everything about her job, her dreams, her opinions. It didn't matter who did more of the talking during their phone calls. It was always a satisfying conversation.

 She and Eli had plenty of separate interests, but their commonality—Mr. Steiner and caring for his estate—had somehow merged them. Eli wanted Holiday to have a library. Anna had the idea to paint one of the walls like an ocean scene and fill that room with books about sea life. Eli liked the idea so much that he suggested they have each room of the library revolve around a separate theme. A mini aquarium could accompany the sea life section, a rocket simulation could be part of the space room, along with a mural of the solar system on the ceiling. Of course there needed to be a section on farming and others on history. Before they'd realized, it had been two in the morning and they'd run out of rooms in the upstairs of the grand house. Before, Anna had both wondered how they would fill it with books and how they would attract people to come visit. Eli's vision solved both problems. Their library would be so much more. He said he couldn't wait to get back and get started on it.

 Anna shared his enthusiasm, but eventually—a couple of years from now—even that project would be complete. What then? She wasn't a librarian, and didn't see herself in that role. Eli planned to open his own law practice, so it wasn't as if he would be left without anything to do once the transformation of Mr. Steiner's estate was complete.

 The estate... Mr. Steiner's will, his house, the stipulation that at least one of them live on the premises for the next five years—all of that was only the vehicle for something much, much larger. Something that, seven weeks ago, Anna couldn't have imagined in her wildest dreams.

And now—she couldn't imagine her life without it. Without love. Without Eli.

"So that's it, then?" she questioned out loud as she gathered up the order forms still scattered about the table. She tapped the end of the stack on the table with a note of finality that she wished she felt. Eli had committed to be all in; so why couldn't she?

Chapter 43

ANNA SLIPPED ON her Mulberry apron and walked from the back of the market to the front. Inventory was at the top of her list. But a quick glance around the large room showed things already out of balance. The bread shelves were crammed with twice the usual amount of loaves, buns, and pastries. Ice chests—the kind used for camping—were lined up in front of the cooler, and multiple egg cartons stacked in front of the already-full shelves where they were usually housed.

"Where did all these eggs come from?" she asked Mettie, the room's only other occupant. "And everything else? The bread, the—whatever's in the coolers?"

"This morning's orders," Mettie replied calmly, her words coming in time with her rocking chair. "Delivered early to beat the storm. Milk's in the coolers. I rounded them up from neighbors and brought them in. You're welcome." She looked at Anna as if expecting praise.

Instead, Anna clapped a hand to her head. "This is a disaster. Thanksgiving's over a week away. People around here don't shop this early. We'll never use all of this." Had she made a mistake and somehow mixed up the dates of the larger orders?

"They do if there's a serious storm comin'," Mettie said. "You haven't got the makings of a disaster here; you've just avoided one—thanks to me." She grinned, her dentures clicking.

"What do you mean?" Anna worked to keep her voice from rising, though her panic level definitely was. The Mulberry had been in the black since the first of October.

Somehow she'd managed to scrape out a profit—albeit a narrow one—each of the weeks she'd been here. There was no way that would happen this week, no way they wouldn't end up giving away all this extra food and eating the cost themselves.

"Late Saturday night, when the bursitis in my left knee flared, I realized a big one was coming," Mettie said. "So I hightailed it over to Ernie's and used his phone to call our suppliers and doubled as many orders as I could."

"*Doubled*?" Anna reached for the counter and sank onto the nearest stool. Her parents couldn't afford this. "Mettie, why would you—I don't—"

"You can thank me later," Mettie interrupted with a wave of her hand. "You couldn't have known, but I did. The knee never lies." She patted it affectionately and continued rolling her current ball of yarn, as if she hadn't a care in the world. "Best open those doors and let folks in. People want to be safe at home before the storm hits."

Feeling numb, Anna rose from the stool and went to the front window. As she flipped the sign to open, she caught a glimpse of the waiting crowd. She'd barely unlocked the door when they surged inside.

"Mornin', Anna." Clarence grabbed a basket and headed straight for the bread.

Betty Oxford followed, with what seemed like every member of the choir trailing behind. In a matter of minutes the market was crowded with friendly, chattering voices and more bodies than Anna could remember seeing here at once for a long while. Even folks who usually went to the Piggly Wiggly were here this morning.

Anna made her way to the cash register and began ringing up customers, one after the other as milk and eggs and bread, meat, produce, and dried goods began disappearing from shelves.

The store was abuzz with talk of the storm, and many stopped to consult with Mettie before making their way to the register. Ernie strolled in, and Anna took a quick break from the register to grab his usual cocoa.

"Folks are getting ready to batten down, I see." He took the whipped cream from Anna and added his own generous dollop when she slid the cup toward him.

"I'll say." She glanced up at the not-quite-frenzied shoppers. "I don't remember it ever being this crazy before a storm. I thought Mettie'd lost her mind when she told me she doubled our orders, but I don't think so now. People are even buying eggs—people who own chickens," she added, noting Clarence's full basket.

"Chickens get scared of the storms and often won't lay for a bit after," Ernie explained.

"Ah." Anna nodded, wondering how she hadn't known that, considering all the people she knew who had coops in their yards.

"Ever since the hurricane a few years back, folks here get a bit more panicked." Ernie brought the cup to his mouth and drank, leaving a line of white foam on his lip. "Power was out, bridge was washed out for a bit, whole houses smashed to smithereens, people missing—scared everyone good. Now whenever there's a tornado or hurricane warning—even just a tropical storm sometimes—people prepare to hunker down in case of the worst."

"I see." Anna gripped the counter as the first clap of thunder shook the building. The lights flickered overhead and came back on. *No inventory today.* Not if Holiday's citizens continued coming through the door.

"I'd better go," she said regretfully. She really did look forward to her visits with Ernie. Her to-do list switched gears quickly, to helping customers check out and making sure the generator in the shed out back had gas.

She passed Mettie on her way to the register. It seemed that *later* had arrived already.

"Thank you," Anna said, stopping long enough to place a hand on Mettie's shoulder.

Mettie reached up and covered Anna's hand with her thin, soft one. "Not a problem. I haven't missed a day of work in thirty years, and I didn't intend to start today. I'm here if you need me."

"Thanks," Anna said, feeling oddly comforted by her presence. "It's nice not to be alone."

But by midday she was alone, having sent Mettie home early, when it became apparent the storm was as serious as she'd predicted. By one the Mulberry was empty, as was Main Street outside. What leaves had still been clinging to the trees were being blown prematurely away, in the gusts of wind sweeping the street clean.

After putting the closed sign out and locking the doors, Anna used the time by herself to get started on the inventory. The back room, at least, still appeared fairly normal. The front of the store looked like it hadn't been restocked in weeks. The surplus of groceries that had seemed to spell certain disaster this morning had, in fact, boosted their sales. Maybe Mettie's trusty bursitis was why her parents had kept her on all these years. That, and because it gave an otherwise lonely woman a reason to get up each day.

While Anna was knee deep in stacks of quilting squares—one of their more popular items on the website—the power went out. Not surprising, the way the wind had been raging, and with Holiday's old utility poles all being above ground. It was doubtful they'd ever be replaced with the new, buried lines—not with the slim population in these parts. Anna braved the sleeting rain outside to start the generator that Ernie had delivered gas for this morning. Now she was really stuck here. She couldn't go home and leave it running, and she didn't dare turn it off until the power came back on. The coolers were considerably less full than they had been this morning, but they weren't empty, and she couldn't afford to risk losing the food left in them.

But with the store closed she was making good progress and would be grateful to get the inventory done—even if that meant pulling an all-nighter. It would be worth the missed sleep to have one thing crossed off of her to-do list. Besides, Carson would be working tomorrow, and he could cover for her so she could catch a nap if need be.

The minutes, then hours on the clock ticked by swiftly, Anna immersed in her task and in her continued mental calculations of how her parents managed to make a living running the market. Profit margins were slim to nonexistent on most products, and it didn't take a genius to see that Carson's online sales were what was really keeping them afloat. They might have made him the initial loan, but in the end they were getting much more from the deal.

By seven thirty in the evening the power still hadn't come back on, and Anna's stomach demanded something to eat. She grabbed an apple and a bagel from the front of the store. A burger and fries would have been far better, but a peek through the front blinds showed the street dark and empty and the diner closed. Everyone had gone home to be with their families.

Feeling suddenly lonely, she decided to call Eli. She was surprised she hadn't heard from him today. He usually called her on his way home from work, and they would talk a good hour while they were each getting things done. Anna returned to the back room, picked up her phone from the counter, and discovered why she hadn't heard from him this evening—her phone was dead.

Stupid. She'd been using it to track the storm all day and should have realized the battery wouldn't last.

Hands on hips, she gave a weary sigh as she looked around the room at the stacks of products and the notes taped to them. Her charger was at home. There would be no talking to Eli tonight if she stayed to finish what she'd begun. But she didn't have much of a choice now with the main power still out and the mess she'd made. Some semblance of order needed to be in place before the store opened tomorrow morning.

Anna finished her apple and cranked the radio louder. Alabama's *Mountain Music* blared from the speakers. Toe tapping, Anna dug into the stash of garden tools and began counting again.

Chapter 44

ELI STOWED HIS carry-on in an overhead bin, then made his way to the cramped middle seat of row thirty-two. Once wedged between two fellow passengers, he pulled out his phone, hoping a message had come from Anna during the minutes he'd been rushing through security and running to his gate. *No such luck.* He buckled his seatbelt as the plane started rolling away from the terminal—he'd been lucky to make it in time and get a seat at all. Eli set his phone on airplane mode and looked up at the flight attendant giving safety instructions in the event of a water landing. He tried to pay attention, though his thoughts were elsewhere.

It promised to be a long, uncomfortable flight, but probably nothing compared to what awaited him on the other side of the Atlantic.

Thirteen hours later he stepped from the Milan Malensa Airport to the brisk, overcast day outside. He paused a second to zip his jacket, then hailed a taxi.

"Ospedale Maggiore di Milano," he said in what was probably the worst accent the driver had ever heard. A few years of high school Spanish over a decade ago was all Eli had to help him muddle through Italian basics. How had his parents navigated the language barrier? How was his mom managing it alone now? And at a hospital, no less?

Eli climbed in back, and the driver sped through the city. The sights flashed by, Eli too exhausted to show much interest.

He hadn't slept at all on the flight. He checked his phone for messages—none. *Odd.* Surely Anna would have read his hours ago. But maybe she thought he was still flying. He hit the call button, wanting to hear her voice before he faced his parents—his father for what might be the last time. Pressing the ringing phone to his ear, Eli imagined Anna outside on her porch, the Alabama sunshine lighting her hair, and wished more than anything that he was there with her.

More than I wish my Dad could be okay?

The thought stopped him, and when he received the message that his call could not be completed as dialed, Eli hung up in frustration. He probably needed some international calling plan, but there hadn't been time to set anything like that up before he'd left. Twenty-four hours ago he hadn't known he'd be in Italy this morning. He'd planned for another busy day at the office, working on wrapping things up there, followed by another busy evening packing and getting his condo ready to list. His mom's call couldn't have come at a worse time.

A lot worse for Dad than me. Eli mentally chastised himself for worrying about work and packing when his father lay in a hospital dying. What if he was dead already, and they never had a chance to end things better?

Can *we end things better?* He wasn't sure. Perhaps his father would never even know he'd come. *But I am coming.* In spite of it all—the fact that the two people he'd most wanted love from had not wanted much to do with him his entire life—he was coming because suddenly they needed him.

It was what Gabriel would have done. And exactly what Anna would do. It was time to put his own words to the test— to forgive and move on. He prayed he could do it as gracefully as she had.

Chapter 45

"Anna? Are you all right?"

Lights flickered on overhead, flooding the room. Anna squinted as she lifted her head from her mother's work table. "Carson?"

He was staring at her like she was a zombie or something. She probably looked the part this morning. She ran her fingers through her tangled hair and attempted a smile. "Good morning?"

"Did you sleep here?" He sounded appalled.

She nodded. "The generator! Is it still running?"

Carson shook his head. "I turned it off a minute ago."

"Thanks. At two this morning the power was still out, and I didn't want to risk losing the coolers—so I stayed."

"Well, go home now," he ordered with one of his smiles that used to make her heart skip.

She felt relieved it no longer had the same effect. Still, she felt that old, familiar melancholy trying to worm its way into her heart.

"Mettie and I can handle things today. Besides, from what I hear, the entire town did their grocery shopping before noon yesterday."

"They did." Anna pushed up off the stool and waited a second for her vision to clear. Low blood sugar was likely messing with her. It had been hours since she'd had the apple and bagel, and that had constituted both lunch and dinner—and now breakfast.

"How bad was the storm?" On wobbly legs she made her way toward the storeroom.

"Category-three tornado. Took out four houses in the back country. Ripped shingles from a bunch of others, and generally made a mess all over town. The front windows of the gas station are out, and it finished off the community center—good thing everything had been moved out already."

"Was anyone hurt?" Ella's family lived in the back country. "Which families?"

"Johansens, Emery, White, and Millet. None of them were home. My dad had rounded them all up before the tornado hit, to shelter in the church basement with the promise of free food—and drink," Carson added with a wry expression.

"The Lord works in mysterious ways," Anna quipped. She'd only heard his dad say that hundreds of times over the years.

"So he does." Carson stepped aside so she could grab her purse from the shelf. "Speaking of which—you and Eli . . ."

"Yes?" Anna turned to him, uncertain what he was getting at.

"I think it's pretty awesome," Carson said, grinning. "I'm happy for you. Both of you, but especially you, Anna."

"Thanks." She clutched her purse to her chest and stared at him. Was this where she was supposed to say she was happy for him and Bree? She was, but it was still tough to talk about—especially with Carson.

"You never let me say it out loud when you first came home," he said. "But I'm sorry for what I did to you. I'm sorry for lying, for cheating on you. I'm sorry you went to the church and I wasn't there."

"But you aren't sorry about Bree?" Anna asked, heart pounding in her throat.

Carson shook his head. "No. I'm happy I'm married to her. I love her."

Relief dislodged the lump that had been swelling, constricting Anna's breathing. "Good. I'm glad you're happy together. Truly, I am."

"I know," Carson said. "You're good like that. Better than I ever was."

Anna held up a hand. "Don't go there."

He smiled. "All right. I won't. But it's good to have you back, and for what it's worth, I think you and Eli are a great couple. I wasn't sure he deserved you at first, but I think he's going to turn out to be even more awesome than Mr. Steiner."

"Me too." Anna gave Carson a last smile as she hurried toward the door, eager to get home so she could plug her phone in and call Eli.

"Italy?" Anna frowned at her phone and replayed Eli's choppy message. She could tell he'd been driving when he'd called—the sounds of a turn signal and traffic figured heavily into the background.

Best she could tell, he had gone to Italy to see his parents. Which made absolutely no sense at all. Not unless the situation between them had changed drastically in the past week.

She tried calling his number again, and once more her call went straight to voicemail. She'd already left a message, so she disconnected the call, discouraged that they couldn't talk right now and feeling a little bereft at the thought of him on the other side of the world. Chicago had been far enough.

Everything is fine. But the niggling worry that had started at the back of her mind wouldn't be quieted—not until she'd talked with him and heard for herself that all was well.

Chapter 46

ELI STEPPED INTO the semi-dark room, his eyes riveting on the still figure in the bed and the reassuring bleep of the monitor beside him.

"You're here." His mother rose from the lone chair in the room to greet him with a brief, awkward hug.

"Hello, Mother." Eli stepped from her limp embrace, thinking how different it felt from Anna's mother's almost-fierce, lingering hugs. Eli turned toward the bed. "How is he?"

"*He*—is—fine," his dad said, his voice low and gravelly.

"Good to see you too, Dad," Eli said, meaning it. Until a minute ago he wasn't certain he'd have that opportunity again.

"Why—he—here?" Even in his weakened state, his Dad sounded annoyed and didn't address him directly.

Eli fought the urge to turn around and walk out the door. His entire life he'd yearned for attention and approval from this man, but it didn't seem the heart attack had softened his heart any. Eli stuffed his hands in his pockets to keep them from acting of their own accord and attempting any physical contact with his father. "I came to see you, Dad. I was worried." *Not anymore.* The scowl on his father's pale face took care of that.

"He's only started talking in the past hour," Mom said. "It's a good sign, and they think he'll be out of the ICU as soon as tomorrow."

"That's great." Eli stared at his father, eyes still closed. They hadn't opened to acknowledge Eli, but that didn't surprise him. "Then what?"

His mother's thin shoulders lifted in a shrug. She lowered her voice. "I don't know—how long he will be here or when we'll be able to go home, to Chicago. I think we probably should, but I don't know how soon he'll be able to travel. And when he can there's so much to take care of first. We can't simply leave. Our lease here goes another four months, and we have a car as well. I'm not sure what we would do about that if we went home now. Plus our mail will have to be forwarded, and we've got some additional travel plans with friends . . ."

Friends. That hurt, though Eli supposed he shouldn't be surprised. His parents hadn't ever been loners, they'd just preferred people their own age to their son.

His mom looked at him expectantly, her head tilted slightly to the side as it used to on those rare occasions they'd actually had a conversation—usually about his grades or some activity he didn't want to participate in. He held in a groan as he quickly sized up the situation. He hadn't been summoned to his dying father's bedside. He'd been roped into coming so he could deal with a bunch of things his mother didn't want to do and his father wouldn't be capable of for a while.

What Eli had believed might be a few days or maybe a week here stretched before him indefinitely. He didn't want to think about his parents' to-do list. He had an employer and clients to wrap things up with and satisfy in the next few weeks and his own move to orchestrate as well.

But he was here now . . .

No time like the present. He pulled out his phone to start a list of things that needed to be done and saw that the battery was dangerously low. He reached for his charger in the pocket of his bag and realized it wouldn't do him any good with the outlets here. There hadn't been time to think of that or to purchase an international charger.

"Give me your address, and I'll talk to your landlord and

see what can be done." *Good luck navigating that conversation with Google translate.* "And can I catch a shower and a nap at your place as well? I've been up all night."

"Of course," his mother said, her nostrils flaring slightly at his brusque tone.

"While I'm gone come up with a list of every single thing that will need to be taken care of for you and Dad to leave Milan."

"How can I possibly—" His mother gestured to the bed. "Who knew this would happen? I haven't any idea what his recovery is going to be like."

"I meant your car and lease—utilities—things like that," Eli clarified. "Give me a list so I can start on it. Maybe, with a bit of luck, we can have you home by Christmas."

She looked up, eyes widening at the mention of the holiday. "Don't tell me you've got another idea about having family over? With your father's condition it wouldn't be advisable."

"Who would I invite?" Eli asked, giving her a sharp look. "Great-grandpa's dead—remember?" After Eli had started receiving the letters, he'd asked repeatedly for his father to invite his estranged grandfather for Christmas. Every year his parents had come up with a slew of reasons why a guest—any guest—would be inconvenient. Eli hadn't asked for a long time. Neither had he spent the holiday with anyone but himself. This year he wanted it to be different.

"*I* do have plans for Christmas, and I need to be back well before then. I'm in the middle of a move myself—to Alabama."

His mother gasped, then wrinkled her nose, as if a foul smell permeated the room. "You can't be serious."

Eli nodded. He didn't want to tell her more. Sharing those close to his heart would be to further risk her criticism, and he wouldn't stand for any slander against Anna or her family. Or Holiday itself, for that matter.

"Why, Eli? Why would you do such a thing?"

He turned toward the door before giving her a partial answer. "Because it's the right thing, and I should have done it long ago."

Anna turned the business card over in her hand, considering carefully before she made the call. Twenty-four hours had passed since Eli's cryptic message. She hadn't heard from him again, and she was worried. The only other number she had for him, the only way she could think of to possibly contact him, was to call his office—the second number listed on the card that had come in the envelope with the documents about Mr. Steiner's estate.

She didn't want to seem needy or like she was keeping tabs on him, but it worried her that Eli hadn't called. Since their trip to Florida they had spoken every day, often multiple times each day. This wasn't like him—something had to be wrong.

Going with her instinct, Anna punched the number into her phone and waited.

"Tanner and Barry Law, how may I direct your call?" a woman's voice asked after the third ring.

"Eli Steiner's office, please," Anna said, her fingers crossed.

"One moment." Soothing music followed, though it did little to ease Anna's concern. She stood and began pacing the length of her parents' family room. *Please be okay. Please—*

"Mr. Steiner's office, how may I help you?" a different woman's voice asked.

"May I speak with Mr. Steiner, please?"

"He's not in the office today. Would you care to leave a message?"

"Do you know when he'll return?" Anna's pacing picked up speed.

"I don't. I'm sorry," the woman said, not sounding as if she actually was. "May I tell him who called? Or perhaps I can assist you."

Anna considered her options. It wouldn't hurt to leave a message, but it didn't sound like she was going to get any information about Eli or his whereabouts. Surely if something terrible had happened—a car accident or other tragedy—his office would have known about it by now. *Would they share that information?* She'd never know unless she asked.

"Miss?"

"Yes. I'll leave a message," Anna replied. "Mr. Steiner and I are the joint beneficiaries of his late great-grandfather's estate. Eli—Mr. Steiner—left a message on my phone yesterday that I didn't understand, and I haven't heard from him since. We speak every day—about the estate," she added, hoping that lent some credibility to her explanation. "I'm concerned that something has happened, as he hasn't been in contact with me."

A long silence followed.

"Hello. Are you still there?" Anna ventured after what should have been plenty of time for the woman to formulate a response.

"Yes." The woman cleared her throat. "Miss—"

"Lawrence. Anna Lawrence."

"Miss Lawrence, it probably isn't my place to tell you this—"

"Yes?" Anna stopped pacing and pressed the phone closer to her ear.

"Mr. Steiner—Eli—is a player."

"Excuse me?" She couldn't mean— "As in a member of some team?" Anna rubbed her temple.

"Yeah," the woman said sarcastically. "Team heartbreak. He excels at stringing women along, making them think they are in a relationship that has the potential to be serious—and then—"

"—You're right," Anna interrupted. "I don't think you should be telling me this. I merely called to make sure he was safe. It really isn't like him not to call."

"It's exactly like him," the woman said. "I know, because I've been where you are right now. My name is Lacee, and I'm not the first woman he's done this to. I personally know two others, and I wish I'd listened to their warnings, which is why I'm telling you this now. I can hear in your voice that you care for him—Eli's good at gaining women's affections. Then, when things start to get real—all of a sudden he's out of there. One day you're this happy couple, and the next it's like the two of you don't even know each other. He's not good at ending things, so he just takes off. When he and I were dating he headed out of town when things started looking promising. I'm guessing that's what's happening again now—only to you. How long have you been dating? About two months?"

It was Anna's turn to be silent a long minute as she leaned against the back of the sofa, feeling shaken. "Thank you for your concern—and the information," she finally managed, evading Lacee's question, though that was probably an answer in itself. It would do no good to tell Lacee she was wrong, that Eli was different now. He'd told Anna as much before, and that he *used to be* afraid of commitment, but that she'd changed him. Anna wanted to believe that. She *did* believe it—mostly.

Chapter 47

THE BEDSIDE CLOCK read 1:33 a.m. when Anna pulled her vibrating phone from the charger and held it to her ear. "Mom, what is it? What's wrong?" Anna pushed back the covers and swung her legs over the side, her feet already searching for her slippers.

"It's me, Eli."

Fear for her father and the accompanying adrenalin rush fled Anna's body as quickly as they'd come, and she flopped back on the pillows. "You scared me."

"I'm sorry," Eli said. "I should have realized you might think the worst. I should have waited to call, but I really needed to hear your voice."

The sincerity of his words carried across the miles separating them. "I'm here," Anna said softly. "Where are you?"

"Italy. Didn't you get my message?"

"It was muffled," Anna said. "Lots of background noise like you were driving and talking from very far away. I thought it said you were going to visit your parents, but that didn't sound right. But then you didn't call again . . ."

"My phone died, and I hadn't had a chance to get a converter so I could plug it in here." Eli sounded tired. "It was a very last-second trip. My dad had a heart attack."

Anna sat up again. "Oh, Eli. I'm so sorry."

"Me too. Though probably not for reasons you think."

Anna froze, but her groggy brain started spinning. *What does he mean?* Was this it, then? Was he going to tell her now that whatever it was between them was over? But he'd just said he *needed* to hear her voice. Not the sort of thing a man about to break off a relationship would say.

"My dad doesn't really want me here, and my mom just wants me to run around taking care of things for her, for them. She expects me to handle of all the logistics so they can go back to the States. It hasn't been simple. I can't speak a word of Italian, and I'm trying to cancel leases and travel vouchers and sell their vehicle. Not to mention decipher what all the doctors are telling us." Eli proceeded to share his first forty-eight hours in Italy with Anna, and by the end of his explanation she wanted to cry—for him.

"I'm so, so sorry," she said. "Would you like me to come over there for a few days? I've got money in savings. A plane ticket wouldn't be a big deal."

"I'd like that more than anything."

She heard the smile in his voice.

"But you can't. You need to be with your parents next week for Thanksgiving—with your dad. You and I will have plenty of time together, but . . ."

Anna nodded at the phone, her throat temporarily restricted. "Yeah," she finally managed. "You're right. I need to see them." She wanted to as well, to hopefully see her father in a better place than he'd been in last time and to show him she was doing pretty well at eradicating her own cancer.

"Anna, there's something else."

Her breath caught, her emotions wavering somewhere between hopeful anticipation and dread. "Yes?"

"I'm not sure how long I'll be here. I'm hoping another week tops, but that may not be realistic."

"It's okay, Eli. They're your parents. I'd do the same for mine."

"I'd do the same for yours too." He laughed. "I'd rather be helping them." His tone turned wistful. "The thing is, being here with my parents, or the people who gave me life, anyway—they never really filled that parent role too well—has made me realize even more how much I don't want what they had. I don't want to be what they are. I want what my great-grandfather had, and so much more. I want you, Anna, and I love you."

"Eli—" Her response was cut short by the sob escaping from her throat and the tears that started sliding down her cheeks. *Love.*

"Are you crying?" Worry carried across the miles.

"S—sorry." Anna sniffled loudly. "Good tears." Hopefully he would believe her.

"A guy can't win with you. No matter what I say it brings on the waterworks."

"I wish I was there to give you a hug." She'd be much better at showing him how she felt than saying those three words, which felt frightening. It was perhaps the last piece of her reserve she still clung to. Once said, she would be completely vulnerable, her heart at risk. It was stronger now than it had been two months ago, but she didn't know if it was strong enough yet.

"I know it's soon to say something like that," Eli said, almost apologetically. "Especially to a girl who's only just started dating men again, after a four-year hiatus."

Anna choked out a laugh.

"So don't feel like you have to say it back," Eli said, his words sincere, soft. "I just wanted you to know where I'm at, and that I miss being with you, Anna."

"I miss you too," she said, pressing her lips together as if to kiss him. "And I can't wait for you to come home."

Anna tucked a blanket around her father. "I'll go grab a couple of pillows so you'll be more comfortable."

"We're in Florida." He tossed the blanket aside. "And I'm

not an old man. I can sit up by myself just fine." He winced even as he spoke the words of denial.

"Suit yourself," Anna said, worried about her dad's uncharacteristic grumpiness. "I'll get pillows for Mom and me. Those chairs aren't exactly comfortable." She inclined her head toward the plastic chairs that accompanied the cheap patio table they'd be eating Thanksgiving dinner on. The patio itself was nice, at least, with lots of surrounding greenery.

Mom stepped outside, carrying a small bowl of grits in one hand and an equally small platter of fried chicken in the other.

"It smells just like home." Anna inhaled the sweet scent of her mother's famous pecan bars as she went inside to get the pillows. She wished they *were* home, with Dad well and all her siblings and their kids there also. But until Dad's blood cell counts were up, his contact with others had to be limited.

"Home is anywhere your mother is," he said.

Anna returned to the patio to see her parents clasping hands and exchanging a loving look.

"That's more like it," she said. "For a few minutes I was worried we had Oscar the Grouch at our table."

"Sorry, Banana," Dad said.

Anna smiled at his teasing. As a child she'd found it impossible to escape the inevitable Anna Banana nickname. While complaining to her father about it one day, he'd come up with a solution.

"You don't like being called that?"

"No, Daddy." She'd stomped her foot and put her hands on her hips like Mom did when she meant business.

"No problem. We'll shorten it. From now on I'll just call you Banana."

It had fit, he'd insisted, as she was tall and slender with golden hair. He'd always teased that he'd bet she'd taste sweet too.

"Maybe we'll start calling you Oscar now." Mom leaned in and gave Dad a kiss on the top of his bald head before heading back to the tiny kitchen for the rest of their meal.

"No less than I deserve." Dad waved Anna over. "I'll actually take a couple of those." He leaned forward so she could place the pillows behind him. "I'm afraid I don't do pain very well."

"Neither do I." Anna fluffed the pillows, then dropped into the chair beside him. "You hide behind grumpiness. I hid in Seattle. Same tactic. Both have poor results."

"When did you get so wise?" His mouth lifted in the smile of a pleased parent.

Anna shrugged. "Hanging out with a couple of pretty smart people most of my life. It was bound to rub off sometime."

Mom returned, and they thanked the Lord for their food and health. Anna felt desperate to know more about the state of her father's, but it would be late December, at the earliest, before any of them really knew much.

"How is Holiday?" Mom asked when everyone had filled their plates with the simple, yet delicious offerings.

"Great." Anna smiled at her parents. "I'm so grateful for this time I've had there. I'm sorry it took this to get me to come home."

Dad waved away her apology. "Well worth it to see my *Anna* shining through again."

"You do look a little shiny." Mom's eyes narrowed a bit as she studied Anna's face. "Glowing, almost."

"Isn't that what Dad used to say to you when you were pregnant?" Anna passed the butter to her dad, careful to keep everything within his reach so he didn't have to move as much. "I promise I'm definitely not."

"It's also what happens when a person is in love." Mom exchanged a knowing look with Dad.

"Well," Anna said, working hard to disguise a smirk. "Donald has asked me out a few times."

"*What?*" Dad spluttered, the drink in his hand quivering.

"I'm kidding," Anna hurriedly reassured him. "Though he did ask me out."

"I imagine half the town did," Mom said with an eyeroll.

Anna nodded. "It might have become a problem, but Eli took care of that." She had both her parents' full attention now. She looked from one to the other, unable to keep the smile off her face. "He's wonderful," she blurted. "And he's moving to Holiday."

"To turn his grandfather's home into the community center and a library," Mom said. "We'd heard."

Anna guessed her mother had heard more than that. "Yes. He's going to live on the property at least five years. It was a stipulation of his grandfather's will."

"O-oh." Mom's brows rose in interest. "And what does that all mean for you?"

"I'm not entirely sure yet," Anna said. "Except for the part where I have to sign all the documents and checks and have a say in all the decisions."

Mom frowned. "What—why? Did you *marry* him? Is your last name Steiner now?"

"No!" Anna shot her mother an incredulous look. "Why would you think—never mind."

"I'm sorry," Mom said. "I know you've been spending a lot of time with him, and because of what happened before—at the church—I thought maybe you'd just decided to elope."

Anna stabbed her chicken with her fork. "I wouldn't do that to you and Dad." She glanced at her father, noted his strained expression and felt terrible for her part in making the meal uncomfortable. "I have to sign all the checks and have a say in all the decisions because Mr. Steiner left half of his estate to Eli—and half to me."

Chapter 48

December

ELI WALKED PAST the Christmas tree in the visitors' lounge down the hall from his father's room. "This place is a bit more cheery than the last." The rehabilitation floor felt more hopeful too. People here were on their way to getting better and going home.

"Somewhat," his mother agreed. "But it's still a medical facility."

Better than your apartment right now. Eli felt no love for hospitals—especially those where everyone spoke a different language—but he preferred this one over the boxes and mess he'd been dealing with, mostly alone. The numerous items his parents had collected on their travels had to be shipped home, and he was the unfortunate one packing them up and sending them off.

They reached his father's room, and Eli knocked, giving his dad a minute to compose himself for his next insult. He'd been anything but cordial to Eli the past several days, and if not for his mom's plea that he stay, Eli would have been out of here already. But, according to Anna, even her dad tended a bit toward grumpiness right now.

"It's the constant pain," she'd said. "We have to cut him some slack."

Eli had fed an entire spool of slack his dad's way and had come close to cutting the line several times. As he held the door to the room open for his mom, he braced for the next onslaught of unpleasantness. He didn't plan on staying long today, wouldn't have come at all, but his mom had asked if he would drive.

Now that his dad was stable, they didn't need to be at the hospital as frequently, but it was good to be there for the daily update from the cardiac rehabilitation physicians.

"Buongiorno." Eli greeted the doctor already standing at his father's bedside.

"You're late," his father barked.

We were sightseeing. Eli held back the retort as well as the truth that they'd been waiting around for a person who'd called about buying the car. Though Eli had shown it half a dozen times, so far they had no takers. He suspected it was because people were waiting for him to come down on the price—given it was fairly obvious they were leaving the country soon and needed to get rid of the vehicle quickly.

"Com'è andata oggi?" his mother asked the doctor.

How did it go today? One of the few phrases Eli didn't need translated anymore.

In broken Italian and English the four managed a conversation that somehow conveyed what Eli surmised to be a good day for his father. His heart was healing nicely after the quadruple bypass. His color was better. He was getting stronger each day. He would be discharged soon, likely in another day or two, but it would be a long while before he might be cleared for travel to the U.S.

"Docici settimane."

Twelve weeks. Another phrase Eli understood. That was the recovery period doctors had been prescribing from the beginning. But Eli didn't have twelve weeks to hang out in Italy. He didn't have two, yet he'd been here almost that long already. It was fortunate he'd given his notice before this all happened. Still, he'd committed to being in Chicago until close to the end of the year so he could leave things good there.

He'd hoped to surprise Anna by returning to Holiday early, a week or so before her parents came home and she returned to Seattle.

Not much chance of that now. An absurd combination of hope and obligation held him here. Once Anna had asked if he'd ever traveled with his parents. He hadn't—not to Disneyworld or D.C., or even on a camping trip. They'd never even taken him to the zoo, though he'd been there plenty of times with his summer camp group.

He'd always felt he'd missed out on something, never having a family vacation, but this experience had shown him that clearly wasn't the case. Even if his dad hadn't been ill, even if his parents had invited him, it would likely not have gone well. They had nothing in common with him, and it seemed they didn't want to.

Yet, for some reason, a part of him continued to hope that would change. And so he stayed another day and kept trying.

"Would you like to go for a walk, Dad?"

His father winced.

At the idea of a walk, or spending time with me?

"The doctors said the more you're up and about, the better."

"Don't tell me what's good for me."

"Fine." Eli held his hands up. "Just a suggestion." *Sit and sulk.* He looked around the room. Just one chair. And that would be for his mom. If the room had another chair, no doubt his father would have asked for it to be removed so he wouldn't have to look at his son for prolonged periods of time.

"I've got some work to do. I'll be in the lounge." Without waiting for either of his parents to respond, Eli left the room and headed for the sofa nearest the Christmas tree, desperate for a little cheer. The holidays were usually a bleak time, but this year was shaping up to be the worst ever.

Trying not to think about that, he checked and responded to office emails for a half hour, then gave into the need to hear Anna's voice. She'd been good to answer his calls no matter what time of day or night, even if she hadn't reciprocated his *I love you*—yet. She answered on the first ring, her voice a balm to his soul. Eli leaned back, smiling into the phone as he closed his eyes and listened to her tales of the latest Holiday goings on.

Christmas pageant rehearsals were well under way. There would be two performances this year, so everyone would have the opportunity to attend, as the church couldn't hold as many people as the old community center had.

Next year. If they were lucky. Maybe the Christmas pageant would be the opening event for the new community center.

Sub-for-Santa was in full swing as well, with his great-grandfather's house turned into holiday central. Anna and Bree and little Anna had been enjoying the record collection while they wrapped and organized presents.

"I wish I was there with you." Eli said when Anna had finished sharing all the news.

"I wish you were too," Anna said. "I miss you, Eli." Her tone changed from upbeat to a bit of melancholy.

"Good to know." He laughed. "I was a bit worried with the way you were going on about Ernie."

"Santa and I do go way back," she teased.

"Just so long as you and I are going forward."

Anna's breath caught. "I would like that."

"Eli." His mother's sharp tone cut in, severing the tenuous connection he'd felt to Holiday and the stronger one he'd been striving toward with Anna.

"I have to go," he said apologetically.

"Call later?" Anna said hopefully.

"Always. Bye." He hung up without telling her he loved

her again. It wasn't something he wanted his mom to hear. Anna was his secret to guard, to protect.

"Let's go get some lunch," his mom said, surprising him.

"All right." Eli stood and followed her.

Eli drove to a café downtown. They sat at a table by the window. After ordering, he took a minute to appreciate the view and think what a great trip this might have been under different circumstances.

"I need to tell you something," his mother said abruptly.

Eli pulled his gaze from the scene outside to her. "About Dad?"

She nodded. "Yes. And about me and you."

"Okay." Eli pushed his drink aside and leaned forward, arms on the table, giving her his full attention.

"I've debated whether or not to tell you for a long time," she continued. "I'd decided I never would, but since this fascination you have with Alabama has only grown, I feel I have to."

His curiosity piqued. "If you're going to tell me about the fallout between great-grandpa and Dad's father, I know all about it."

She shook her head. "I'm going to tell you about the fallout between you and *your* father."

"Fallout implies that there was something between two people to begin with," Eli said sarcastically. "That's hardly the case with Dad and me."

"You're right. And—there's a reason." Her voice strained, as if it was a fight to get the words out.

"I'd love to know it," Eli said. His whole life he'd been wondering what he'd done wrong, what flaw there was in his personality that made him unlovable. Not until he'd met Anna and her family had he realized the problem wasn't with him at all.

"Your father never wanted children. He was twenty-five when he took the steps to ensure he never had them."

"You mean he had—"

"—A vasectomy." His mother nodded.

"Seriously?" Eli frowned. "What kind of man makes that decision at twenty-five?"

"One whose own father wasn't much of a father—because of what had happened between him and his father. He didn't want to repeat history and felt it best to end the tragic pattern of Steiner father/son relationships."

"That's messed up," Eli said. "And no excuse for not loving a kid that came anyw—wait. Was it before or after that I—" He didn't finish the question. The answer was clear in his mother's strained expression.

"Two years after his vasectomy. Gabriel is not your father."

Eli pushed back from the table and slammed into the hard back of the chair. "Who is?"

"It doesn't matter. It was a long time ago—"

"*Doesn't matter?*" Eli gripped the table edge. "You don't think it might to me—to him. Whoever he is."

"He never knew. It was a mistake."

There it was. The phrase he'd been expecting all his life. He was a mistake. Not meant to be. Not welcomed into the home he'd come into.

"He was a colleague, and he married someone else about the same time you were born. What happened between us was a lone incident."

Even better. He was the result of a one-night stand.

"I loved your father—Gabriel," she clarified. "But our marriage had been struggling, and we'd been spending some time apart." Her mouth twisted in a wry smile. "There really is something to that seven-year-itch phenomenon."

The waitress arrived with their lunches. Eli pasted a smile

on his face and thanked her in his limited Italian, then pushed his plate aside the moment she left, his appetite long gone.

"So you had an affair but stayed married."

His mother pursed her lips. "Affair is a bit harsh. I made a mistake. One I've paid for dearly."

"How?" Eli demanded, folding his arms. From his view, he was the one who'd paid. For a lot of years.

"I couldn't end the pregnancy. I'd never really agreed with Gabriel's decision to not have children, so you felt like— a gift. I wanted to keep you—and keep my husband too."

If her admission was intended to mollify Eli's injured feelings, it seemed too little, too late.

"I waited as long as I could before telling Gabriel. I worked hard at our marriage during that time and was careful about my weight and how I dressed so the pregnancy wasn't obvious. By the time I confessed I was five months along. Gabriel was furious and very hurt, but he agreed to raise you as his. I had to promise him that you wouldn't impact our lives—that nothing would change, that we would spend more time together and mend our marriage. That I'd never stray again." Her voice rose with each word. "I had to convince him of my regret and sincerity, and the only way to do that was to put him first. Always."

"I would have been happy with second place," Eli muttered. "But I wasn't even in the race."

The lines creasing his mother's forehead deepened. "I worked extra hard, took every chance at promotion, accepted any assignment given me—all for you. You had the best nanny and schools, every opportunity and experience. None of that came from Gabriel. He gave you his name, but everything else was all on me. Every second of my life has been spent making sure he was happy and that you wanted for nothing." Her voice was rising again, so that a couple at another table nearby looked over.

"Nothing except what really mattered," Eli said. His words hit their mark. His mother flinched and looked down at her plate, but not before Eli caught the flash of pain in her eyes. He closed his own and took a deep breath, curbing his anger. Because what good would that do now?

He sipped his drink, then pushed the food around on his plate as he went over her words, her story again. *I couldn't end the pregnancy. I worked extra hard.* He'd always thought his mother cared about her career far more than him. He'd never imagined it as a vehicle to provide *for* him—all those things he hadn't wanted to do, the camps he hadn't wanted to attend. *So I wouldn't be around as a reminder of her unfaithfulness.* That she'd had to work so hard to pay for all those things infuriated him, made him loathe the man they'd just left at the hospital. *Not my father.*

It was still too shocking to be believed.

"I'm sorry," his mother said when several tense minutes of silence had passed between them. "I did what I thought was best, but I see now—it wasn't."

He didn't deny her conclusion. The slight empathy he felt for her situation didn't come close to matching years of neglect and loneliness.

"I'm trying to do the right thing now." She looked up at him, the plea in her eyes matching that of her voice. "You have no obligation to the Steiner family. Gabriel Steiner was not your great-grandfather, not really. You bear his name, but there is no blood between you. Don't go throwing your life away, moving to Alabama and fulfilling his last wishes. Be your own man, Eli. Don't tie your future to a man who, believing he was your grandfather, wrote you a few letters. Your life is worth more than that."

Chapter 49

ANNA HELPED HER father through the front door and into the family room and his favorite recliner. "Do you want anything to drink?"

"Sprite. And a bowl. The sickness will hit sooner or later."

"Sure thing, Dad." She'd been surprised by her mother's call yesterday morning. Her parents were coming home a week early, right after her dad's last chemo session.

"I can be sick at home as well as sick in Florida," he'd explained. "And the follow-up tests can be done at one of the local hospitals. No need to wait around for those."

After making sure Dad was as comfortable as possible, Anna joined her mother in the kitchen.

"Oh, Anna." Mom enveloped her in a hug. "It's so good to be home. I never want to leave again."

"I hope you don't have to." Anna lingered in her mother's embrace, enjoying the comfort it offered.

"Thank you for taking care of everything for us. The house looks beautiful, and I can't believe the freezer is full of meals."

Anna stepped from her mother's embrace. "I needed to learn how to cook. You needed some dinners for when you got home. It worked out well."

"I hope you shared some of your newfound skills with Eli." Mom arched a brow questioningly.

"I did—once or twice." What seemed like forever ago. Anna had also stocked Eli's freezer in the apartment above the carriage house. It was clean and comfortable and awaiting his return—or Anna's if he didn't end up coming back, as she was starting to fear. He'd gone from saying I love you the first couple of weeks he was gone to being withdrawn and distant the last two. She'd stopped asking about his father after getting a curt, angry response from him. She'd stopped asking when he'd be back in Chicago when he'd repeatedly said he didn't know. She'd almost given up hoping he would come back to her and Holiday when the last time they'd spoken—five days earlier—he'd said he might not be coming after all.

It was exactly what Lacee had said would happen. Anna had dismissed her words of caution almost immediately and then altogether after Eli's declaration of love. But now that warning rang in her mind and heart constantly. Anna was grateful for it and grateful that at least her heartbreak wouldn't be public this time.

"What's wrong, Anna?" Mother gave her a searching look. "Nothing. And everything. I thought Eli loved me. I believed he was going to move here and we were both going to get our happily ever after. But something's happened, something has changed, and he won't even let me in to talk about it."

"Oh, my darling girl." Mother scooped her into another hug.

Anna savored the contact and used the strength it gave her to keep her tears at bay. "I need to go back to Seattle," she said. "Sooner, now that you're home. If Eli isn't going to keep his end of the bargain, I'm going to have to be back here by the new year to take care of Mr. Steiner's home. I'm going to see the community center and library project through and make sure Mr. Steiner's legacy is preserved."

"And if Eli does come back?" Mother asked, holding Anna at arm's length.

"I don't know," Anna said honestly. "If he's here it might be better for me if I stay out west."

Chapter 50

ELI SHOULDERED HIS backpack as he made his way through the Birmingham International Airport and headed toward customs. It had cost him more to fly here than to Chicago, and he only had a day to spare before he had to be at the office, but seeing Anna was worth both the extra cost of the ticket and the red-eye flight he'd take tomorrow night.

But first he had to catch his connecting flight to Mobile in the next—he glanced at his watch—forty minutes. Picking up his pace, Eli made it to the customs line in under five of those minutes. Lines were short, thankfully, and he had only one item to declare. He'd done very little shopping in Italy but had come home with a lot of emotional baggage. Now to figure out how to share it with Anna without dumping the weight of it all over her. It had nearly buried him for the past twelve days until the morning before last when he'd awoken with a simple revelation that had changed his perspective.

I'm not a Steiner. Not only was he not related to his great-grandfather—what had felt like a crushing blow—but he wasn't related to the man he'd grown up believing was his father. And that thought was freeing. He didn't have to be anything like him. *There is nothing in me that is from him.*

But there was some of his great-grandfather in him, relative or not. Gabriel Steiner had believed Eli was his family and had treated him as such, reaching out to him, showing more love through his letters than either of his parents ever had.

This same man had loved Anna too—even knowing she

wasn't his blood. So why should it change things now? If the old man were alive, Eli felt certain that his mother's revelations wouldn't have changed anything. *He still would have left the estate to Anna and me.* So why should Eli let the truth change his life, the direction he was headed?

I shouldn't. A name is just a name. It doesn't make the man.

The thought had been like an epiphany when it came. But since then, doubts had tried to creep back in. He wasn't always successful at keeping them at bay. But he was pretty certain he knew who could understand. Who would listen. Who would help him heal. Whom he loved.

Ironic. When he'd set out to help her just weeks ago. Now he was going to ask for her understanding and acceptance of something even worse than being left at the altar. He'd been left at the cradle. Emotionally abandoned by the parents who'd raised him.

But it wasn't my fault.

Anna would see that. She would reassure him. And if he were very, extremely lucky, she would agree to keep reassuring him for many years to come.

Anna hurried through the airport, tears blurring her eyes, as the feeling of Bree's arms around her faded with each passing step. How long would it be before someone hugged her again? Would she spend Christmas alone again? How was she going to stand to be at work, in her little cubicle or even the lab—all day without hardly saying a word to anyone? She was flying west, straight into loneliness.

Anna took her boots off and placed her personal belongings in the trays at security. After going through the scanner, she retrieved her belongings and settled on a nearby bench to reassemble everything. She zipped one boot, then reached for the other when a man passing in the other direction caught her eye. Anna jumped up and craned her neck to better see, but he'd disappeared already, caught in the sea of passengers heading toward baggage claim.

Eli? She hadn't seen his profile. And a lot of guys were tall and fit like he was. But there had been something about the way he walked— She glanced at her watch, considering the time. Not enough to go back through security to try to find him.

If it had been Eli. Which wasn't likely. *His hair is shorter.* And he wouldn't come here, but to Chicago to catch up on the work he was grossly behind on now.

Anna sank onto the bench again and slipped on her other boot while fighting the urge to go back and satisfy her curiosity.

He would have called me if he'd changed his mind about coming back. He wasn't even in the country yet. This situation with his parents wasn't resolved. Doctors had said it would be twelve weeks before Eli's father could travel.

At last convinced that she'd been hallucinating, Anna collected her things and headed toward her gate. It was time to stop thinking about Eli and figure out what she needed to do.

Chapter 51

HOLDING A CUP of steaming cocoa between her mittened hands, Anna turned sideways to push open the glass door that led to her cubicle. Some days—as many as possible—she never even made it to her desk but went straight to the lab. But after so many weeks away she had no idea what project she was assigned to and what her responsibilities within said project might be. Bottom line, she was going to have to check her email and invest some time at her desk today.

Resolving to be as cheerful as possible about it and her position here, Anna started right in with greetings—something she'd rarely, if ever, done before.

"Good morning, Charles." She smiled at her balding, middle-aged co-worker in the first cubicle. "Hello, Karen. Good morning, Wes."

It became easier after the first few, and the smile on her face started to feel less fake and more genuine. She didn't know any of these people well, but that didn't mean that they weren't worth knowing. Maybe there was even a good friend among them, who'd just been waiting for her to show some semblance of humanity these past years.

"Hello, Mark. Good morning, Rick, Eddie." The latter was the man who'd asked her out when she first started here. At her unexpected greeting, he glanced up in surprise.

"Anna. Good morning—nice to have you back."

"Thanks," Anna said, keeping her smile, though she really didn't feel it was nice to be back. She felt homesick. More so than she'd felt when she'd first moved here and started this job, more homesick than she'd ever felt before.

Doing her best to ignore those unwelcome feelings, Anna continued her greetings as she turned the corner and approached her cubicle. "Good morn—" She stopped short at seeing someone seated at her desk, his back to her. She blinked once, twice, trying to clear her vision. It was like at the airport—she was seeing things, or rather people. One person.

"It is a good morning." The chair spun around. Eli looked up at her. "Now that you're here and I see I'm not in the wrong office."

"Eli." She nearly dropped her cocoa, fumbling the cup for a precarious second.

"Nice place." If he'd noticed her shock, he was ignoring it. Eli motioned to the half-dozen plants, a couple of them dead, crammed on her desk. He reached for the family photo. "Your dad looks really good here. We've got to get him back to this picture of health. Maybe we should start with some short walks and work up to a light jog by late spring or early summer."

We? "You're planning to hang out with my dad? You're going back to Holiday?"

"I hope to. I was there a couple of days ago—looking for you." Eli rose from her chair and stepped closer, a bulky manila envelope in his hands. "Your dad seems like a great guy, and I think it'd be in my best interest to get to know him better—considering his daughter and I share an estate now."

They shared more than the estate—friendship, and the memory of some life-altering kisses. Anna really hoped Eli wouldn't tell her parents about the latter, because nothing more had come of it. Nothing permanent.

She stared at the envelope. Documents Eli had forgotten to give her, maybe? Or paperwork because he wanted out? But he'd just said he hoped to go to Holiday. Whatever it was, why fly all the way here to deliver them? Big-city boy had to have used a fax machine before. Anna stared at him, still dumbfounded at seeing him *here,* in Seattle, at the university, in her cubicle. She'd planned to check her office email first thing this morning but now reached for her lab coat instead. She'd head over and find something to do. Because she wouldn't be able to get anything done here, with Eli around to distract her. Even if he left this very minute, just the memory of him in this space was going to mess up her concentration for at least the rest of the day.

"Aren't you going to ask what's in the envelope?" Eli tucked it under one arm as he helped her shrug her into the coat.

It felt bulky over her sweater, but Anna felt too cold to take the sweater off. She couldn't believe how cold she'd felt this morning. The fog had seemed to wrap itself around her, seeping right through her multiple layers. Too quickly she'd readjusted to Holiday's warmer climate, and now she'd spend several weeks paying for it.

"I'm a little afraid to ask what you've brought, after the last documents you showed me."

"These aren't from Gabriel, but a few things I realized I'd like to share with you as well." He took another step closer, pressed the packet into her hands and whispered, "There's also information on other positions you might consider. Jobs closer to Holiday and that might be a better fit for you."

"For me—or you? We've hardly talked in weeks, and you bring me this list." Her fingers tightened around the envelope. "What am I supposed to think, Eli?" He was standing right in front of her, but she couldn't shake the doubt his absence— both physical and emotional—had caused. He seemed like himself now, but just last week— *He's going to bail. Maybe he never really planned to stay in Holiday.* Her fairytale romance *had* been too good to be true.

Eli met her gaze without flinching. "I'm sorry I haven't been a good friend—or anything else—these past weeks. I'm not backing out of my promise. At least look at these," he pled, glancing at the envelope. "There's an opening at Dauphin Island Sea Lab Estuarium. Didn't you tell me once that would be your dream job?"

Dauphin. The word alone conjured a flood of happy memories. Anna clutched the bulky packet to her chest. "All right. I'll look at them." Beneath her lab coat and sweater her heart began to pound, from either the possibility of working at the estuarium or Eli's nearness. Maybe both.

"Do you promise?" Eli asked, his expression solemn, from his creased brow to the line of his mouth. "There's some very valuable stuff in there. It took me a while to find it. Promise you won't just throw it away without reading everything first?"

"I won't," Anna said. "That was kind of you to go to all that work—for me. Thank you. I'll look through all of it."

"Good." He sighed, his stance relaxing.

This surprised her, as Eli seemed so rarely nervous or stressed about anything.

"You don't have to come back unless you want to." He paused studying her. "But I hope you will. I understand if you're reluctant to—pick up where we were," he finished awkwardly. "I've been in a bad place, and I know I've taken some of that out on you."

"I've been known to react to stress poorly myself." She gave him a slight smile. "You've witnessed that a time or two."

"I don't recall anything like that." Eli's lopsided grin matched hers.

Anna glanced at the envelope in her arms, cherishing his gift of time, both in preparing it for her and bringing it all the way out here. *His apology?* Or a request for a second chance? She wanted to ask more, to know what had happened with his father, but recent experience had taught her to be wary.

"Well then, I guess I should be going. I have a flight to catch in a couple of hours."

"Today?" Anna asked, unable to mask her disappointment. It would have been nice to see him after work. Had he really come all this way just to give her some papers? By his own admission, Eli liked delivering things in person. Yet flying across the country to show her some job offers seemed extreme—even for him.

"Yeah. I'm incredibly behind. If I hadn't given my resignation already, I'd probably be fired."

"Right." Anna nodded. He was going back to Chicago. She'd be here in Seattle. Her eyes began to sting, the weight of loneliness bearing upon her. She focused on her chair and moved toward it, only to have Eli stop her.

He gripped her arm, pulling her to him. His other went around her. Then his lips were on hers, kissing her, not as he had—soft and slow, that first time beneath the chandelier in Mr. Steiner's house—but passionately, fervently, desperately, as if he feared it was the last time he'd ever have the opportunity, stolen as it was.

Anna's initial reaction to push him away melted quickly beneath her own desire and desperation to hold onto him, somehow. Against impossible odds. Eli had been her own, personal Holiday miracle—or nearly so. And now she was losing him.

Losing him . . . He pulled back, giving her a look so filled with tenderness that the tears she'd been fighting spilled over.

"Merry Christmas, Anna."

Around them her coworkers burst into surprised applause, many rising to their feet, the shock on their expressions enough to bring a smile to her face.

"This is Anna Lawrence, everyone," Eli said loudly, sweeping a hand toward her. "She's a brave, gutsy woman, former Miss Holiday, Alabama, who once spent a summer swimming with sharks. She holds the town record for the largest trout pulled from the river, plays a fair tune on the banjo, and has the kindest heart you'll ever know." Eli's expression grew tender as he looked at her. "She's been a little shy and quiet these past years, but no more. Oh, and she definitely dates men."

As if for additional proof, he leaned in for another quick kiss, leaving Anna's head spinning even more than it already was. "Look at *everything* in that envelope," he reiterated as he pulled away. "I really hope you like what you find. But, in case you don't, these guys needed to know the real you."

He turned away, waving as he headed down the row of cubicles. "Merry Christmas, everyone!"

"Merry Christmas," the office chorused back, the atmosphere more charged and excited than Anna had ever felt it.

She watched his back until he left, wanting to run after him, but still unsure. After the door closed she sank onto her chair and faced her computer, wondering how she was supposed to work today, and how she'd manage to leave that envelope alone until tonight.

Chapter 52

ANNA CROSSED THE bridge and drove past the road that led to her best friends' house. Slowing her speed to twenty-five, she drove down Main Street, a smile practically bursting from her as she drank in the sights. At dusk, the strings of Christmas lights that crisscrossed Main were just starting to glow. Wreaths hung from the lampposts—her mother's doing, along with the holly painted across the front of the Mulberry's windows. Christmas music piped from the diner's outdoor speaker, and at the end of the long street, the church steeple beckoned.

Anna glanced at the dashboard clock—6:50. The second showing of the Christmas pageant would be starting in ten minutes, and her mother had promised to save her a seat. Anna parked her rental car down the street from the church—the parking lot and street in front of it were already packed—got out, and hurried toward the building.

Though it wasn't that cold out, Anna kept her coat on and tucked her hands in the pockets, wanting to keep them there until the right moment. No telling what her mother would do when she caught sight of the antique ring on the third finger of Anna's left hand. And there was no way she could miss the cluster of diamonds that formed a dainty flower over a narrow ring of smaller diamonds that circled Anna's finger.

An eternity band. A symbol of a love that never ends. During a phone call in which Anna had cried more than she'd spoken, Eli had told her all about the perfect ring and his search for it at several Italian jewelers.

"Your love and appreciation for the older generation made me think of finding you an antique engagement ring. But I couldn't find one I liked and had almost given up when I saw that ring—the way the diamonds formed a flower. I knew it was meant for you."

Anna had considered removing it until Eli's arrival tomorrow, when he could slide it on her finger himself, but in the end she'd decided not to wait. Once she'd tried it on—after reading and sobbing through the pages of his story—she never wanted to take it off. It wasn't exactly a marriage proposal by mail, but pretty close. They'd spoken on the phone in the days since, Eli reaffirming his love and Anna finally brave enough to give hers.

He was somewhere between Chicago and Holiday right now, driving a moving truck with his belongings, and tomorrow they would celebrate Christmas together at home with her family.

Anna couldn't ever remember feeling happier.

She ran up the steps to the church, stepped inside, then froze, staring not at the angel choir and the pretend shepherds and wise men she'd expected to see up front, but at the back of a head too familiar to deny—even if his hair was a bit shorter than when she'd first met him.

Slightly in front of Eli, but facing her, Reverend Armstrong stood at the head of the long, center aisle. When he lifted a hand in recognition, Eli turned toward her as well, looking even more handsome in a tux than he had in his Sunday suit. His face broke into a smile, and murmurs of approval rippled among the congregation packed on the crowded benches.

Anna looked toward her family's usual spot and saw only her brother and brother-in-law and their families.

A hand touched her arm, and Anna turned away from the strange sights in the chapel to find her mother and sister and Bree standing beside her, the latter with something long and white draped over her arms.

"Anna." Her mother gently pulled Anna's hand from her pocket and bent closer to examine the ring. "It's beautiful."

"Mom? Chels?" Anna eyed the familiar gown in Bree's arms.

"Eli told us that searching for the perfect ring for you was the only thing that kept him sane those last couple of weeks in Italy. You were his rock." Mom looked up with tears in her eyes.

"So he bought you a rock." Bree giggled.

"What's going on?" Anna looked from Bree to Chelsea to Mom.

"Isn't it obvious?" Chelsea said. "You're getting married."

"Eli planned the whole thing," Mom said.

"He thought that this way—" Bree hesitated, biting her lip. "You wouldn't have the fear of being left at the altar again. He put that on himself. He's been standing there waiting for twenty minutes."

Anna clapped a hand to her mouth and turned her head toward him. "My plane was late."

"He knows," Mother assured her. "But are you going to make him wait any longer?"

Married. Tonight. Right now. They'd talked about a future together. And she was wearing his ring.

Leap.

"Yes," Anna whispered. "I mean, no. I'm not going to make him wait." A shiver of anticipation made its way down her spine.

Bree grabbed one of her hands, and Chelsea took the other as they led her from the vestibule through the side doors into one of the Sunday school rooms. A full-length mirror had been set up there, along with a table full of makeup and hair-styling tools.

Anna shrugged out of her coat and clothing as fast as she could, tossing them aside, not caring about anything except getting inside the chapel as fast as she could. She knew what it was to wait for someone there and didn't want Eli enduring one minute more than necessary.

She stepped into her wedding gown and felt a moment of angst, as the weight settled on her shoulders and she remembered the sorrows of the last time she'd worn it. She closed her eyes, banishing the bitter memory forever. When she opened them again Bree was looking at her with concern.

"I'm good." Anna squeezed her best friend's hand. "You're here now. And so is Eli." Until this very minute, she hadn't realized that the hurt of not having Bree there the morning she was supposed to marry Carson had been almost as deep as the pain he had caused.

With what felt like agonizing slowness Mom fastened the pearl buttons running up the back of Anna's gown.

"Would you like me to pin up your hair?" Bree asked, a container of bobby pins in one hand. Chelsea stood beside her, Anna's veil in her hand.

"No updo," Anna said. "There isn't time."

"Eli said to take all the time you need," Mom assured her.

Anna shook her head. "No. Not while he's standing there waiting in front of everyone. Just give me a minute."

Bree handed her a brush, and Anna moved to stand in front of the full-length mirror. She brushed her curls out to loose waves, then took the veil from Chelsea and placed it on her head.

"Oh, Anna." Mom was full-on crying now. "My baby is getting married."

"At last," Chelsea muttered.

Anna grinned at her in the mirror. "And look what a catch I made."

"Biggest fish in the river," Bree said.

Anna laughed and caught her carefree, happy reflection in the mirror. Fifteen minutes ago she thought she'd never been happier in her life, but now she was even more so. Fifteen minutes from now she guessed she'd feel even more joy.

"Let's go." She gathered the heavy layers of dress and turned toward the doors as Mom snapped a quick picture.

Chelsea and Bree carried her train.

When they returned to the vestibule the doors to the chapel were closed, and her father was waiting for her, still looking thin and weak, but better than when she'd last seen him a week and a half ago.

"You ready for this?" he asked.

"Are you?" Anna returned, only half kidding.

Dad nodded. "I've grilled your young man, and he's a good one. Maybe even worthy of Anna Lawrence."

"Oh, Daddy." Anna threw her arms around her father, careful not to hug him too tightly. He returned her embrace, his arms comforting and reassuring in spite of their weakened state.

"All right then," he said. "You ready to walk me up that aisle? 'Cause there's no way I can make it that far on my own right now."

Anna laughed and held out her arm. "Let's go."

Bree and Chelsea pulled the doors open and walked with Mom to their seats.

Betty raised both hands and hurled them toward the organ. A thundering chord ricocheted through the chapel, beginning a wedding march that sounded more appropriate for the *Bride of Frankenstein*. Anna didn't care. In fact, she loved it, loved everything about this moment and the man at her side and the one waiting for her at the front of the church.

Her nieces tumbled out of the family pew a few steps ahead of her and tossed rose petals onto the floor. Anna paused, turned to her dad, and gave him a kiss on the cheek.

"I love you, Daddy." She held onto him until he was safely seated, then turned to finish the walk on her own.

"Do you mind if I escort you the rest of the way?"

Anna looked over at Carson, half risen from his seat.

"It's what a best friend would do," he offered.

She nodded, her eyes filling with tears. "I'd like that."

Carson stood and held out his arm. Anna placed her hand on it, and they walked the short distance to the front, where Carson took her hand and placed it in Eli's. "Take good care of her. She's pretty special."

"I know, and I will."

Anna looked up at Eli, her happy tears spilling over.

"Already?" With his free hand he pulled a handkerchief, with initials EGS embroidered on it, from his pocket. "Guess I'd better get used to carrying these. I hear my great-grandfather did, and they will probably come in handy with my Southern Belle."

The shepherds, wise men, angel, Joseph, Mary, and baby Jesus all made their appearance shortly after the wedding ceremony. Still dressed in their finery, Anna and Eli crowded onto her family bench to watch Holiday's traditional Christmas pageant. Eli's arm was around Anna again, as it had first been all those weeks ago at church, his thumb stroking shivers of delight along her shoulder.

The church bells rang out after the conclusion of both wedding and pageant, and Anna and Eli rushed down the steps between well-wishers and beneath a hail of rice to his waiting car, not-so-mysteriously decorated by her brother and nephews during the pageant. Amid the cacophony of car horns sounding along the way they headed toward their estate, Anna anticipating an evening alone in front of the fireplace in the carriage house.

Instead a blaze of lights awaited them, the driveway lined with cars and the veranda decorated with lanterns, flowers, and ribbon.

Eli opened Anna's door for her and swept her in his arms to carry her up the steps to the main house. The front doors were flung open before they reached them, and Ernie's "Ho, ho, ho," bellowed a greeting.

"About time you got here. I can only hold the masses off from the cookies so long." He attempted to hide his own, cookie-laden hand behind him.

Anna laughed then threw her arms around Ernie in a quick hug once Eli had set her down.

"How'd I do this year?" Ernie asked, a twinkle in his eye when she pulled back. "Does returning your man top returning your dog? Had to go all the way to Chicago for this one." He bent his arm, the crushed velvet of his Santa suit nudging Eli.

"You did?" Anna's mouth fell open as she glanced from Ernie to Eli, who confirmed the story with a nod of his head.

"*Santa* drove back with me yesterday. We had a good, long chat about Holiday and one of its most famous citizens."

Anna leaned forward and gave Ernie a kiss on his cheek. "You did *very* well. Thank you, Santa."

Eli clasped Anna's hand in his and pulled her close to his side so they could greet their other guests.

It seemed the other half of Holiday—those who'd caught the earlier showing of the pageant—were already celebrating. The front hall, dining room, and parlor were packed with people, and the old console had been returned to its spot in the parlor and was dropping records, piping music through the house.

"You planned all of this?" Anna turned to Eli, the same expression of surprise on her face that she'd worn all evening.

"I had a little help." He wrapped an arm around her and

steered her toward the middle of the foyer, where the round table usually stood. Along with the other furniture it had been pushed aside to make room for a dance floor. "Folks in Holiday are like that, you know. Helpful."

"Don't you mean nosy?" Anna teased.

"The nosiest. Like the man who used to live here. The audacity of him, orchestrating something like this. Believing that he could bring the two of us together." Eli pulled her into his arms. "Dance with me, Mrs. Steiner?"

Anna smiled at the name. That was going to take some getting used to. "Every day," she promised. "For the rest of my life."

He twirled her around the floor with moves worthy of any Southern gentleman of old. When he tipped her back at the end of the dance she looked up toward the high ceiling and hoped the old Mr. and Mrs. Steiner were somehow looking down on them.

"Thank you," she whispered to the ghosts of yesterday. Because of them she was where she belonged, in Eli's arms and here in home sweet Holiday.

Michele Paige Holmes spent her childhood and youth in Arizona and northern California, often curled up with a good book instead of out enjoying the sunshine. She graduated from Brigham Young University with a degree in elementary education and found it an excellent major with which to indulge her love of children's literature.

Her first novel, *Counting Stars*, won the 2007 Whitney Award for Best Romance. Its companion novel, a romantic suspense titled *All the Stars in Heaven*, was a Whitney Award finalist, as was her first historical romance, *Captive Heart*. *My Lucky Stars* completed the Stars series.

In 2014 Michele launched the Hearthfire Historical Romance line, with the debut title, *Saving Grace*. *Loving Helen* is the companion novel, with a third, *Marrying Christopher*, followed by the companion novella *Twelve Days in December*. The Hearthfire Scottish Historical Romances include *Yesterday's Promise, A Promise for Tomorrow*, and *The Promise of Home*.

When not reading or writing romance, Michele is busy with her full-time job as a wife and mother. She and her husband live in Utah with their five high-maintenance children, and a Shih Tzu that resembles a teddy bear, in a house with a wonderful view of the mountains.

You can find Michele on the web: MichelePaigeHolmes.com
Facebook: Michele Holmes
Twitter: @MichelePHolmes

www.ingramcontent.com/pod-product-compliance
Lightning Source LLC
LaVergne TN
LVHW021754060526
838201LV00058B/3090